# "Frances, wait."

"Need to leave," she said between clenched teeth, taking another halting step away from Braxton.

He slid his arm around her back, bracing her against him. "Lean on me."

She ducked her head, wondering when she'd slipped her arm around him. Her fingertips grazed the silky weave of his shirt, sensing his taut muscles underneath.

They were in the hallway now, and she released a sigh as the cooler air soothed her heated skin. She started to pull away, but he tightened his hold.

Her world rocked in place as they accidentally cuddled. She couldn't breathe, couldn't think, only feel. The strength of his body against hers, his masculine scent rode the woody, jasmine aroma of his aftershave and shot to some primal part of her brain, triggering a warmth she hadn't felt in a long, long time....

Dear Reader,

*Hearts in Vegas* is my third "private eyes in Las Vegas" Harlequin Superromance (the first being *The Next Right Thing,* March 2013, and the second *Sleepless in Las Vegas,* December 2013).

This third book picks up with the story of P.I./security consultant Braxton Morgan, the twin brother of Drake Morgan, the hero in *Sleepless in Las Vegas*. On the surface, Braxton looks like the kind of guy for whom life is easy—he has rock-star Adam Levine looks, cool designer threads, a wry Hugh Grant sense of humor. But Braxton is a man who's made his share of mistakes in life, resulting in a lot of losses, from his former home and big-money career to his family's support. He's fighting hard to rebuild a new life, piece by piece.

And then he meets Frances Jefferies, who walks into his life the way sultry Lauren Bacall first walked into Humphrey Bogart's in *The Big Sleep*. And just like Bacall, Frances is mysterious, smoky, elusive...and Braxton says goodbye forever to his former playboy ways.

I really enjoyed writing the character of Frances, a magician's daughter who's skilled at sleight of hand. To learn more about this technique, I read several dozen articles by magicians and watched numerous videos of their performances. In my research, I fell in like with Teller, the quiet half of the duo-magician act Penn & Teller—in fact, I went to several of their shows in Las Vegas, and afterward met Teller, who is as charming and smart as you might imagine.

Braxton and Frances's story is about two people who once failed the ones they love, and whose priorities include earning back their families' respect, and maybe, finally, letting their hearts open again to love.

I enjoy hearing from readers, so I invite you to drop by my website, colleencollinsbooks.com, and let me know how you liked *Hearts in Vegas!*

Best wishes,

Colleen Collins

# COLLEEN COLLINS

―

## Hearts in Vegas

**HARLEQUIN® SUPER ROMANCE®**

If you purchased this book without a cover you should be aware that this book is stolen property. It was reported as "unsold and destroyed" to the publisher, and neither the author nor the publisher has received any payment for this "stripped book."

Recycling programs for this product may not exist in your area.

ISBN-13: 978-0-373-60858-4

HEARTS IN VEGAS

Copyright © 2014 by Colleen Collins

All rights reserved. Except for use in any review, the reproduction or utilization of this work in whole or in part in any form by any electronic, mechanical or other means, now known or hereinafter invented, including xerography, photocopying and recording, or in any information storage or retrieval system, is forbidden without the written permission of the publisher, Harlequin Enterprises Limited, 225 Duncan Mill Road, Don Mills, Ontario, Canada M3B 3K9.

This is a work of fiction. Names, characters, places and incidents are either the product of the author's imagination or are used fictitiously, and any resemblance to actual persons, living or dead, business establishments, events or locales is entirely coincidental.

This edition published by arrangement with Harlequin Books S.A.

For questions and comments about the quality of this book, please contact us at CustomerService@Harlequin.com.

® and TM are trademarks of Harlequin Enterprises Limited or its corporate affiliates. Trademarks indicated with ® are registered in the United States Patent and Trademark Office, the Canadian Intellectual Property Office and in other countries.

**HARLEQUIN®**
www.Harlequin.com

Printed in U.S.A.

## ABOUT THE AUTHOR

Colleen Collins is a member of the Romance Writers of America, Mystery Writers of America and Private Eye Writers of America, and has written several dozen novels in the romance and mystery genres, as well as three nonfiction books on private investigations. Similar to Frances in *Hearts in Vegas,* Colleen's favorite magician is Teller, the silent half of the comedy magic duo Penn & Teller.

### Books by Colleen Collins

#### HARLEQUIN SUPERROMANCE

1840—THE NEXT RIGHT THING
1893—SLEEPLESS IN LAS VEGAS

Other titles by this author available in ebook format.

To Marilyn Doyle

# *CHAPTER ONE*

IF TWENTY-NINE-YEAR-OLD Frances Jefferies had learned anything from her years as a pickpocket, it was the importance of blending in to one's surroundings.

Today, February 5, her task was to steal a valuable brooch from Fortier's, a high-end jewelry store in Las Vegas. To blend in with the Wednesday bling-shopping crowd, she'd put on a red-and-leopard-print top underneath a loose-fitting Yves Saint Laurent white silk pantsuit, and a pair of killer Dolce & Gabbana stilettos.

Time for one last practice run.

She retrieved two similar-size brooches from a dresser drawer. One, a rhinestone flower-petaled pin, was an exact replica of the diamond-encrusted Lady Melbourne brooch stolen ten years ago from a museum in Amsterdam. Its whereabouts had been unknown until it suddenly, and mysteriously, surfaced at Fortier's a few days ago. She slipped the replica into an inside pocket of her jacket and set the other pin on her dresser.

Watching her reflection in the dresser mirror, she practiced the sleight-of-hand trick, deftly plucking the brooch from the pocket and swiftly replacing it with the other pin, three times in succession. Each switch went smoothly.

Now for the finishing touch. She selected a pair of antique garnet earrings from her jewelry box and put them on.

Leaning closer to the mirror, she swept a strand of her ash-blond hair off her face, tucking it lightly into her chignon. Her gaze slipped to her lower cheek. This close, she could see the faint outline of silicon gel underneath her meticulously applied makeup. For anyone else to see it, they would have to be inches away, and she never let anyone get that close.

A few moments later, she walked into the living room, where her dad sat in his favorite chair, shuffling a deck of cards. A basketball game was on TV, the crowd yelling as a player dunked the ball.

"Still working on The Trick That Fooled Houdini?" she asked.

He grinned and set the cards on a side table. "Like Houdini, I can't figure out how Vernon did it, either."

Dai Vernon, Houdini's contemporary, had devised a card routine where a spectator's chosen card always appeared at the top of the deck. Houdini, who bragged that he could figure out any magician's trick, never solved this one.

Her dad, who'd worked as a magician his entire life, had never solved it, either. Sometimes he jokingly referred to it as The Trick That Fooled Houdini *and* Jonathan Jefferies.

"Going to work?" he asked.

His thinning dark hair was neatly parted on the side, and a pair of reading glasses hung on a chain around his neck. He had a slight paunch, but otherwise stayed in shape from daily walks and a fairly healthy diet, if one overlooked his love of peanut-butter-and-jelly sandwiches.

She looked at his faded Hawaiian-print shorts and Miami Heat T-shirt with its ripped sleeve, wishing he'd let her buy him some new clothes. But he liked to stick with what was "tried-and-true," from his haircut to clothes.

"Yes, off to work. If I leave in a few minutes, I should be there by three. The owner got back from a late lunch an hour ago. He and the security guard will be the only employees in the jewelry store the rest of the afternoon."

"Good girl, you did your homework." He paused, noticing her earrings. "Oh," he said, his eyes going soft, "you're wearing your mother's jewelry."

Frances's mother, Sarah, had been her father's tried-and-true soul mate. When she eloped at nineteen with a little-known Vegas magician, her wealthy family disinherited her. *If my upbringing had been happy,* she'd told her daughter, *disowning me might have mattered. Instead, it released me to a better life.*

The only items Sarah Jefferies had of her family's were a small jewelry collection, gifted to her by her late grandmother.

"Mom's earrings will be my calling card today," Frances said, touching one of them. She loved antique jewelry, especially early-nineteenth-century Georgian, the era of these earrings and the Lady Melbourne brooch.

"She's happy to know she's helping. We're proud of you, Francie."

He often spoke of his wife in the present tense, which used to bother Frances, but she accepted it more these days. Sometimes she even envied her dad's sense of immediacy about his late wife. Frances was painfully aware it had been four years this past summer— July 15, 1:28 in the afternoon—when they'd lost her, and shamefully aware of the pain she'd brought her parents in the months leading up to her mother's death.

Nearly five years ago, Frances had been arrested on a jewelry theft. It had been humiliating to be caught, but agonizing to see the hurt on her parents' faces. Especially after she admitted to them the theft hadn't been a onetime deal. After learning sleight-of-hand tricks from her dad as a kid, she'd segued into picking pockets in her teens, then small jewelry thefts by the time she was twenty. At the time, she selfishly viewed her thefts as once-a-year indulgences, but it didn't matter if she'd stolen once or dozens of times—what'd she done had been wrong.

Jonathan Jefferies blamed himself for his daughter's criminal activities, believing she had resorted to theft because he'd been unable to adequately support his family as a magician. When Frances was growing up, the family had sometimes relied on friends for food, or went without electricity, or suffered through eviction because there hadn't been enough money to pay the rent.

The judge, moved by Frances's difficult upbringing and her mother's failing health, had offered her a second chance. Instead of giving her a ten-year prison sentence, he'd suspended her sentence as long as she met certain conditions, a common solution for people with a high potential for rehabilitation.

For Frances, her conditions were threefold. One, either attend college or obtain full-time legitimate employment, including any position where she applied her skills for a positive end. Two, pay restitution to the victim. Three, do not break any local, state or federal laws.

The judge had added an ominous warning to the last one. *Miss Jefferies, that means you don't even pick up a dime off the street if it isn't yours. As much as your suspended sentence is a gift, it is also your burden. For the duration of your suspension, if you appear before the bench for any infraction, no matter how minor, the court will evaluate your case with a more critical, censorious eye. And that's mild compared to what a prosecutor will do.*

As if she had a yen to ever break a law again.

As far as college or a job, her probation officer matched her "skills" to Vanderbilt Insurance, a company that was looking for an investigator to track stolen jewels and antiquities.

Sometimes these investigations, such as the one today, required her pickpocket skills. She would be taking back the Lady Melbourne brooch, which was the legal property of Vanderbilt Insurance, since they had already paid the fifty-thousand-dollar insurance claim from the museum.

"Remember to feed Teller around six," Frances said. "Any later, he gets cranky." She'd named her cat after her favorite magician.

"He gets *cranky?*" Her dad shot a look at the fat golden-haired Persian cat lying sprawled across the back of the couch. "That cat is so laid-back, sometimes I put a mirror under his nose to make sure he's still breathing."

"I know you think he has no personality."

"I never said that. I merely *suggested* he might be suffering from narcolepsy." Yells from the crowd drew his attention back to the TV. "Idiot refs," he muttered, "calling fouls against Miami *again*. Might as well take off those black-and-white shirts and wear Celtics jerseys."

With a smile, she touched her dad's shoulder. He grumped a lot at these sports games, but she'd take that any day over those lengthy silences after he first moved in.

It hadn't been easy convincing him to move out of the apartment he'd shared with her mom. It wasn't long after her mother's death, and when her dad wasn't frozen with grief, he was going through old photo albums, cleaning or filling ink into one of her favorite fountain pens, watching movies they'd seen together, even the "chick flick" ones he swore he'd never see again.

He didn't want to be a burden, and Frances hadn't wanted to suggest he needed help.

"Still auditioning as an opener for that lounge act?" she asked.

He flexed his fingers. "Don't think so. Need the ol' hands to stop giving me a bad time."

His arthritis flare-ups were making it increasingly difficult for him to perform magic tricks. Moving his fingers as he practiced the card trick helped keep his joints somewhat mobile and stymied the arthritis.

"Gotta take off now, Dad."

"Meeting Charlie afterward?"

"Yes."

She typically met with Charlie Eden, her boss and mentor at Vanderbilt Insurance, right after an assignment to discuss the case. Although it was more common for Vanderbilt investigators to only provide written reports to their bosses, her situation was unique, as Charlie submitted monthly accounts to the court on her progress at Vanderbilt.

Today, if all went well, she hoped to also hand him the Lady Melbourne brooch.

But there was more to the case.

Vanderbilt believed the thief who stole the pin had also stolen four fifth-century-BC Greek silver tetradrachm coins worth several million dollars from a New York numismatic event two years ago. Both thefts had similar crime signatures, including state-of-the-art technology to circumvent surveillance systems and cutting torches to access vaults.

"That Charlie, he's a good man. Husband material, if you ask me."

"Dad, I've told you before, I don't feel that way about him."

"But he's gobsmacked over you."

"*Gobsmacked?* What does that mean?"

"Astonished. Over the moon. Heard a sports announcer use it the other day."

"Did he say he was over the moon about me?"

"No." He picked up his cards and started flipping through them. "Don't need to be a mentalist to read that man's brain. He'd like to make you his Zig Zag Girl."

Zig Zag was the name of a magic trick Jonathan Jefferies used to perform with his wife, where he appeared to cut her into thirds, yet she'd emerge completely unharmed. The secret was that the true magician was her mom, who knew when to zig and zag to make the illusion look real. Jonathan, who credited his wife with the magic that made their marriage work, liked to call her his Zig Zag Girl.

He flipped the top card over and frowned. "Plus, he's a lawyer."

Charlie, nearly fifteen years older than Frances, was a very successful lawyer. Women in the office swore he looked like Michael Douglas in his salad days, which was probably why Frances thought of the villain Gordon Gekko every time she saw him. Charlie had the distinguished career, dapper clothes, perennially tanned, handsome looks, but...something about him turned her off. Couldn't quite put her finger on it.

"God help me if he were a neurosurgeon." She leaned over and planted a light kiss on her dad's forehead.

This close, she caught a whiff of peanut butter. The man was incorrigible, and she was ready to say as much when she caught the pain in his eyes as he glanced at her cheek.

She quickly straightened, looked around for her clutch bag. "There's some leftover Chinese in the fridge. Maybe enough lettuce for a salad. Lay off the peanut butter, okay? I know," she said, anticipating his argument, "it's full of nutrients, and saturated fats are a good thing, but the doctor said *one* serving a day, which I believe you've already had."

"Bought some Spam the other day," he said, ignoring her instruction. "I'll probably make a sandwich with it."

"We're pathetic. One of us needs to learn how to cook."

"Yeah, your mom spoiled us. She'd never opened a can of soup when I met her, but after we got married, that girl..." He gave his head a wistful shake. "Studied cookbooks the way she did her old college books. By the time you were born, she made the best cheeseburger this side of Milwaukee. Some fancy French foods, too, when we had the money. What was that one with chicken and wine?"

"Coq au vin."

"Yeah, that's it. We should learn how to make that one of these days."

But they wouldn't. Sometimes Frances wondered if the two of them used their lack of cooking skills as a way of holding on to her mother. If neither of them replaced Sarah Jefferies's role as family chef, then that spot would always be hers.

"Wonder where I left my bag," she muttered, looking around.

"On the dining-room table we never eat at. Hey, baby girl, call me when you're done? I'll keep my cell phone next to me. I worry about you on these cases."

"You know me, Miss Cautious. I'll be fine. But I promise to call when I'm done."

Her dad had never owned a cell phone before she bought him one after he moved in. He thought they were frivolous—said phones were things to get away from, not have strapped to your body at all times. But after she explained she wanted to stay in touch, especially when she was out working a case, he gave in.

Walking briskly to the dining room, Frances called out, "I should be home around eight."

"So it's dinner with Charlie, eh?"

"*Business* dinner," she corrected, grabbing her bag. She opened it to double check that she had the key fob for her rental car.

"Valentine's Day is next week, you know," he yelled. "Maybe you two could—"

"No, we couldn't," she yelled back. "Love you. Bye!"

As she shut the front door behind her, Frances wished her dad would get off this Charlie matchmaking kick. She made good money, could comfortably support the two of them, so unless Ryan Gosling wandered into her life with a "Frances Forever" tattoo over his heart, she was fine without a boyfriend or husband.

Frances glanced at the distant dark clouds and hoped they weren't an omen. Despite her analytical side, she had a superstitious streak. Even after days of preparation, she'd still get "preshow" jitters.

Part of her suspended sentence had been to see a therapist, a lovely older woman named Barbara. She'd suggested that whenever Frances got the jitters, to remind herself she could only control what was in her power and let everything else take its course.

Only problem with that thinking was that Frances liked to control every aspect of her cases. Liked to know every nuance of an investigation, every possible fact she could dredge up. It gave her confidence. Some people felt she had *too much* confidence, but that was their perception. Or, she liked to think, an acknowledgment of her well-crafted illusion.

But letting everything else take its course?

That would take magical thinking on her part, something even a magician's daughter couldn't conjure up.

SITTING AT THE DESK in the reception area at Morgan-LeRoy Investigations, Braxton Morgan read the text message from his grandmother Glenda a third time, mostly because he couldn't believe it the first two.

I entered you in the Magic Dream Date Auction at Sensuelle on Valentine's Day. Raise $$ for Keep 'Em Rolling & the guy who brings in the highest bid wins a car!

It wasn't that Braxton was against raising money for Grams's favorite charity, Keep 'Em Rolling, which provided wheelchairs for those in need. The cause was close to her heart, as she was a wheelchair user herself. And he'd love nothing more than to ditch his clunker and drive a new car. Until recently he'd avoided any activity that put him in the public eye, but he was ready to get out and about again, test the Vegas waters.

Not so long ago, as the manager of the high-end strip club Topaz, he'd lived *la vida loca en Las Vegas*—plush penthouse, Italian designer suits, kick-ass Porsche. At first he pretended not to notice when his boss, a Russian named Yuri Glazkov, muscled people for money or forged documents. After a while he had to admit Yuri was a thug, but Brax figured that as long as he kept *his* nose clean, no problem.

But like that old saying "You are what you eat," you're also who you hang out with.

After a few years working with Yuri, Braxton had been willing to break a law here and there for his boss, justifying it by telling himself he never indulged in violence or threats, just fudging a few numbers. Hell, everybody cheated on their taxes, right? But after Yuri got arrested for tax fraud, Brax couldn't pretend he wasn't on his way to being a thug, too.

But, when he tried to leave his job at Topaz, Yuri threatened to go to the authorities with evidence and witnesses to a crime Braxton had supposedly committed. All mocked-up evidence, given by "witnesses" who were Yuri's buddies, but Braxton didn't want to be railroaded into prison, so he stayed, waiting for the day he could make a clean break.

Which he finally got last August when he and his brother, Drake, along with a handful of Vegas police officers and a sharp arson investigator named Tony Cordova, headed up a sting at the Mandalay Bay Hotel and Casino that resulted in Yuri's arrest on a slew of nasty felony charges, including attempted murder and extortion. After Yuri's defense attorney got him released on a half-mil bond, the Russian thug had been keeping a low profile. Which was fine with Braxton. No Yuri meant a happy, peaceful life, even if he had been forced to rebuild his from scratch.

At least he still had his designer clothes, but he was back living with his mom and grandmother, and drove a banged-up turquoise Volvo with two balding tires. He hated turquoise.

He looked at his grandmother's text message again.

He'd done his best to man up, never complain about his shift from big spender to budget shopper, but no way was he parading like a slab of beef in front of hordes of women fueled by hormones and free booze.

He glanced at the grandfather clock. Quarter after three. His mother would still be at her Wednesday bowling league, but Grams was either at home or her boyfriend's down the street. Since she'd just texted this message, she was probably available to read *his* response right now.

He began tapping the keypad on his smartphone.

Grams, I'm not a slab of...

The desk phone jangled. Why Val LeRoy, his brother's wife and P.I. partner, insisted on keeping this dinosaur landline service was beyond his understanding.

"Brax," yelled Drake from the back office, "get that? I'm on another call."

Braxton lifted the handset, mentally cursing the tangled phone cord that tied him like a leash to the phone.

"Morgan-LeRoy Investigations," he answered, staring at his unfinished text message to his grandmother. Sounded hostile. Not good. He punched the back arrow to erase letters.

Grams, I'm...

"My apologies," a man said, "I thought I dialed Diamond Investigations."

The caller had a strong Russian accent, which brought back bad memories. Although he detected a faint, almost imperceptible British lilt, which he'd never heard in any of Yuri's crowd.

"The agency name changed to Morgan-LeRoy Investigations last October," Brax explained, waiting in case the man had questions about the former owner, Jayne Diamond. Sometimes callers didn't know Jayne had died last October after a brief illness or that she'd bequeathed the agency to her protégé, Val LeRoy, and Val's husband, Drake Morgan, Braxton's identical twin brother.

"Ah, I see. I would like to speak to Mr. Morgan, please."

Probably meant his brother, as Braxton had only come on board recently as a security consultant. "Drake is on another call. I can transfer you to his voice mail."

Adjusting the sleeve of his blue-striped Armani shirt, he frowned at the phone, wondering if he knew how to do that. He tapped a button on the phone console that apparently turned on the speakerphone, because when the caller spoke again, his voice echoed through the outer office.

"*Braxton* Morgan," the man clarified. "I wish to speak to Braxton Morgan."

Brax hesitated. The Russian thing... Nah, he'd let the paranoia pass. Couldn't afford to turn down an inquiry for his consulting services. He set the handset on the desk and leaned back in the swivel chair. "Speaking."

"Excellent! My name is Dmitri Romanov, but my friends call me Dima. I am calling on behalf of my community. We would like to retain your services to help us."

"Which community?"

"The Russian community."

Which was a large one in Las Vegas, at least three thousand people. Didn't mean this call had anything to do with Yuri. "The problem?"

"We are concerned about our image and our ability to run legitimate businesses because of recent negative publicity regarding one individual. We want to know where he spends his time in Las Vegas and if he is still conducting criminal activities. His name is Yuri Glaz—"

"You called the wrong guy," Braxton snapped, wishing he'd listened to his instincts and canned this call. "Got problems with Yuri? Call the cops. Better yet, call the D.A., who I hope skewers that bastard to the wall at his trial next month."

Drake strode into the room. To the caller, he said, "Give us a minute."

He tapped the mute button so he could talk to Brax privately. Dressed in dark trousers, a dress shirt and their dad's tailored gray jacket, Drake rubbed his palm across his forehead. He wore his hair in a buzz cut, which only men with great-looking skulls could get by with, something Braxton learned when he was forced to buzz his hair, too, last August when he and Drake switched places. These days, Braxton's dark brown hair had grown back and bad in a short faux-hawk cut, which in his humble opinion made him look like Adam Levine.

"Maybe we should hear this guy out," Drake said.

"Over my dead body."

"Information is power."

Brax got the message. By hearing what this Dmitri guy had to say, they'd learn whatever dirt he might have on Yuri. If it was muddy enough, they could pass it on to the D.A. who could sling it at the upcoming trial.

He pressed the speaker button.

"Sorry, Dmitri, for my reaction," he said, adopting a more professional tone, "although you probably understand why."

"Certainly, Braxton. I, too, am upset with Yuri's unscrupulous ways. I am a respected businessman, ready to fund a significant venture, and I do not wish Yuri's reputation or his current activities to stand in my way. I am prepared to pay you well for your investigative efforts."

Braxton looked at the north-facing window and the steady stream of cars traveling along Graces Avenue, their hum like white noise. Sometimes there was only one way out of a problem, and that was to go straight through the messy dead center of it.

"I'm interested in the case," he said, giving his brother a here-we-go look. "Fill me in on the details."

"As you undoubtedly know all too well, Yuri is currently awaiting trial and under house arrest. An interesting phrase, *house arrest,* because with a little creativity and a GPS jammer, those ankle bracelets can slip on and off like a cheap bangle. Rumors are Yuri continues to loan-shark through a check-cashing store and fence goods hijacked from trucking companies." He exhaled heavily as though blowing out smoke from a cigarette. "We want you to investigate these rumors. If true, the community needs to distance themselves from these enterprises and advise the authorities that none of us are involved. If they are false, we can proceed with a clear frame of mind."

Braxton leaned back in his chair, wondering why the court had thought a bracelet could stop a guy like Yuri. "This will require two investigators, my brother and myself, each at one-hundred-seventy-five an hour, plus expenses."

Drake cocked a questioning eyebrow. At Morgan-LeRoy, the hourly rate varied depending on the case, but it had never topped $125.

After a beat, Dmitri said, "That is acceptable. Is one-fifty per diem sufficient for expenses?"

"This is Vegas, Dima, not Boise."

Dmitri chuckled. "Boise, my friend, is poised for a new era of entrepreneurship. Did you know China is establishing a state-of-the-art technology zone south of Boise?"

No, Brax didn't know. But he was catching on that this Dmitri fellow was knowledgeable, educated and loaded. As in money. Lots of it.

"Three hundred a day for expenses," Braxton said, making a rolling-dice gesture to his brother, "plus an additional two hundred each for vehicle rentals."

For the next few moments, he listened to the faint tapping sounds over the speaker, which he guessed was Dmitri adding up numbers on a calculator. Drake leaned against the far wall, his arms crossed, a look somewhere between amusement and incredulity on his face.

*Hot dog,* he mouthed.

Although the brothers' relationship had been frosty during the six years Brax had worked for Yuri, these days they shared their old camaraderie. Often they picked up on the other's thoughts, sometimes even finishing each other's sentences.

Brax grinned. When he'd accepted his brother and Val's offer to work as a security consultant at Morgan-LeRoy Investigations, he'd told them his number one goal was to bring in the bucks, so he was always pushing for higher retainers, bigger cases. "I want to be the agency hot dog," he'd told them.

Like him, Drake and Val were rebuilding their lives. Drake's home had been destroyed in a fire last summer, and Val, after losing everything in Hurricane Katrina, had started over in Las Vegas a few years ago.

Dmitri finally broke the silence. "On days when there are two investigators, we're talking one thousand for expenses, plus a three-fifty hourly fee. You are expensive, Mr. Morgan."

For a moment, Brax thought about explaining how chasing Yuri could get complicated and costly, fast. Plus, if he pulled up to a five-star restaurant or a high-end casino in his turquoise Volvo, he might as well spray-paint on it Gumshoe Tailing Somebody.

Instead, he said politely, "You're welcome to hire

another P.I., Dima, but gotta tell ya...*no one* in town knows Yuri the way I do."

Val, wearing a simple black dress, entered the room from the hallway that connected the agency to her and Drake's living quarters in the back. The overhead lights caught streaks of violet in her bobbed brown hair.

When she heard the name *Yuri,* her brown eyes grew wide. She sat in one of the guest chairs, her hand on her bulging tummy.

"I accept your terms," Dmitri said over the speaker, "with the understanding that we review your progress at the twelve-thousand-dollar mark. That is the amount of the retainer check my associate will drop off at your agency tomorrow morning at nine."

Val mouthed *Twelve thousand?* to her husband, who gave her an acknowledging nod.

"Braxton," Dmitri said, "I have an urgent appointment, so I must end this call, but I have something else I would like to discuss with you. May I speak with you later?"

After giving Dmitri his cell number, Brax ended the call and looked at his sister-in-law and brother, cupping a hand to his ear in a let's-hear-it gesture.

"You are the hot dog," Val said approvingly.

"*Agency* hot dog," Drake corrected.

Brax flashed them an I'd-try-to-be-humble-but-it's-so-true smile.

"As much as I would *so* love to be part of this

case," Val said, "My feet are starting to swell somethin' fierce—no way I could keep up on a foot surveillance." With a sigh, she looked at her left hand. "Fingers are swelling, too. Dropped off the family heirloom ring with Grams this morning so she can wear it for a while." She looked back at the brothers. "Since I'm out, you two split the retainer."

"You're the lead investigator," Drake said to Braxton, "plus you'll be working more of the case, so... sixty-forty?"

Brax racked up the numbers in his mind. "Seven thousand, two hundred...sounds like enough to get my own place."

Finally. His own bachelor pad. Not as posh as before, of course, but a place where he could play his music loud, toss a shiny new black satin cover on a king-size bed, invite a special lady over for his renowned spaghetti *alla puttanesca,* a bottle of Chianti and a homemade tiramisu dessert that would make an Italian mama weep.

Ah, a pared-down version of the life he left behind was almost his again....

He looked down at his cell phone.

Grams, I'm...

He didn't mind, much, paring down when it came to his new life, but forget *stripping* down, as in going shirtless, which was what he'd heard guys did in these date auctions.

But it wasn't an issue to be discussed in text messages. He needed to talk to Grams in person, offer a compromise, like his donating some money from his hefty retainer instead. Yeah, that might fix this problem.

He looked back up at Val and Drake. "Guys, mind if I take off early?"

Val did a double take. "You finally have a date, Brax?"

"Sorta." More like a sit-down negotiation with one of the grandest old ladies who ever graced this planet.

"That didn't come out right," Val continued. "Sounded as if you can't get a date when that's *so* far from the truth. Why, with your stud looks, you could be courtin' a different girl every night, so it's just odd you've been livin' like a monk for months now."

"Honey," Drake murmured, "you might be stepping over a line."

She looked at her husband, all innocence. "Because I mentioned an obvious fact? Why, even Grams is worried about him! That's why you—" She pursed her lips.

Braxton leaned back in his chair and checked out his brother, who was scratching his eyebrow. Which he always did when he was uncomfortable. Or guilty. "What'd you do, bro?"

"I, uh, paid the entry fee."

"Entry fee," he repeated, not liking where this was going. "To this brawn fest."

"Magic Dream Date Auction, yes."

Brax rocked forward on his chair, the front legs hitting the floor with a thud. "*You* think I can't get a date?"

"Hey, Brax," Val cut in, making a placating gesture, "it's not like that, really. It's just that ever since you moved in with Mama D and Grams, you stay home every night, get to bed by ten, never answer your former girlfriends' calls. You seem, well, defeated, flat… nothin' like my former bro-in-law."

"I don't stay home *every* night," he muttered, wondering if it were Mom or Grams who'd snitched about his not returning those calls. Probably both.

"Right," Drake said, "one evening you drove to a convenience store and bought a quart of milk."

Brax blew out an exasperated breath. "I can't believe this! I spend *years* being estranged from my family for hanging out with thugs, dating questionable women and skirting the Nevada criminal justice system, during which time Mom *banned* me from our childhood home. But now that I'm law-abiding, and yeah, okay, so I haven't been involved with a woman for a while, but that's *my* choice, by the way…" He gave both of them an and-you-better-believe-it look. "Where was I?"

"A law-abidin' citizen," prompted Val.

"Right. Now that I'm an upstanding citizen, my family can't hear enough about my uneventful, boring life? I suppose Mom's spilled that I still watch cartoons sometimes, too." He jabbed an accusing finger at Val, then Drake. "Maybe it's *you* people who need to get a life!"

"Brax," Drake said, "don't take it the wrong way."

"What's the right way? To joke about my do-nothing, go-nowhere, get-nothing life?"

"It's all right, dawlin'," Val said, drawing out the word *dawlin'* like a slow pour of molasses. "It must be awful bein' a former playboy. Like bein' an ol' James Bond sent out to pasture."

As if he needed that mental picture. An old Bond bull with a bunch of over-the-hill Miss Moneypennies.

"Look," he said, "I know you two mean well, but let's put the brakes on the matchmaking, 'kay? That includes any blind dates, Craigslist ads, surprise walk-ins, you get the picture."

Val frowned. "Surprise walk-ins?"

"Some hot blonde walks into the detective agency, needs to talk to a P.I. He falls for her story and her, and that's when his real troubles start. It's in every clichéd private-eye film."

"F'true," Val said, her eyes lighting up, "I recently saw *Chinatown,* and just like you said, the trouble started when a blonde walks into private eye Jake Gittes's office."

"I dunno," Drake said. "You've been a monk so long, maybe you need a little blonde trouble."

"Monk." Braxton snorted. "Now *you're* stepping over the line, bro."

"Yeah?" Drake countered. "Well, since I'm already there, gotta ask…still watching Donald Duck cartoons?"

"I don't need this." Brax picked up his phone and

stood. "I'm heading home to tell Grams that as much as I appreciate her—and your—concern to find me a date, I'd prefer not being auctioned off to the highest bidder."

He started walking to the door.

"Good luck saying no to Grams, bro."

"I never claimed to be a wise man," he said over his shoulder. "Just a savvy, determined monk."

## *CHAPTER TWO*

CLOSE TO THREE, Frances cruised her rented Mercedes sports car past the Passage-of-Love drive-through wedding chapel, its tunnel bright with gaudy lights and gold-painted cherubs. In the lot next to it was a rundown duplex, where a scrawny girl in cutoff shorts and a T-shirt sat hunched on the porch steps, solemnly watching a couple ride a motorcycle into the chapel. To Frances, those two buildings summed up downtown Las Vegas—glitz, business and tough times.

At the end of the block, she pulled into Fortier's lot and parked. After patting the inside pocket of her jacket to confirm the presence of the replica brooch, she exited the car.

The winds were picking up, but brooding clouds still hovered, as though unsure whether to take action or not. February forecasts were like crapshoots in Sin City—if the weather report called for fair skies, it might snow.

Heading toward the silver-tinted jewelry-store windows, she spied Enzo Fortier's Bentley, one of the inheritances from his late father, Alain Fortier. Enzo's siblings were angry their father had given the bulk of his estate, including the Bentley and jewelry store, to his youngest son, Enzo. The ongoing family drama, with its litigation, accusations of extortion, fraud and theft, had left Enzo distracted and vulnerable to criminals.

That was what she and Charlie believed, anyway. The person who stole the Lady Melbourne brooch had taken advantage of Enzo's distraction to fence the pin. Not that Enzo was innocent—he had to know he was receiving stolen goods, but was probably too frightened to say no.

Whatever the situation, Charlie had tapped her for this case because she knew about Georgian jewelry. Being a woman didn't hurt, either, he'd said, because Enzo had a roving eye.

So one reason Charlie had picked her for this case was because she was pretty enough to attract Enzo's attention.

Not much of a compliment, really, as it was her artifice, not her, that would attract him. Not to say she wasn't proud of her skill applying silicone gel and concealer. Sometimes she even wondered if she could market this talent, help other people struggling with facial scars.

And then sometimes, usually late at night when she'd run out of distractions, she wondered if any man could ever accept...touch...kiss the imperfection that lay beneath.

Stepping inside the jewelry store, she smiled pleasantly at the middle-aged security guard stuffed into a blue uniform accessorized with a shiny gold A-1 Security badge and gun holster.

She noted the surveillance camera in the ceiling to her right, which recorded her five-nine height—five-seven without the heels—as she strolled past the height ruler tacked on the inside of the entrance door.

A skinny middle-aged man in an Armani suit approached her. Despite his dazzlingly white smile, apprehension clung to him like a fog.

"Welcome. May I help you? I am the owner, Enzo Fortier," he said in a thick French accent, bowing slightly.

"Elise Crayton." On undercover cases, she always offered a name that couldn't easily be spelled. She absently adjusted one of her earrings, drawing his gaze to it.

"Exquisite," he said approvingly. "Antique, yes?"

"Georgian," she said casually, dropping her hand. "My favorite style."

"Oh, yes," he said, his face lighting up, "I just happen to have several Georgian pieces available." With a flourish, he gestured toward the back of the room. "This way, *madame*." He paused. "Or is it *mademoiselle*?"

"*Mademoiselle*," she murmured, letting her gaze lock with his for the briefest of moments, giving the illusion she just might be interested in him, too.

Nothing was more powerful, or more real, in life than the illusions people put forth. She guessed people didn't have the time, or inclination, to dig deeper, so they accepted whatever was presented on the surface.

Maybe because she was a magician's daughter, she understood that the best illusions were the result of weeks, often months, of practice, so she tried never to be overconfident in her own first impressions of others.

Moments later, she sat on a cushioned bench, eyeing a sparkling earring set and the Lady Melbourne brooch in the glass display case. As far as she knew, only the brooch had been taken from the museum. Later, she'd describe the earrings to Charlie, see if they could dredge up information about whether those had been stolen, too.

"What a lovely pin," she said. "May I see it?"

*"Absolument."*

As he retrieved the brooch from the case, she pretended to fix her hair while scanning the layout of the surveillance cameras. The closest one, in the ceiling almost directly overhead, captured a tight view of the two of them and this case. Another camera, positioned farther back in the ceiling to her left, recorded a long-range view of the back area of the store.

Fortier gingerly laid the piece of jewelry on a black velvet tray.

"Fourteen-karat yellow-gold pin stem," he said. "The center diamond is two carats, and the petals are covered with…one hundred and twenty diamonds."

Actually, there were one hundred and *fifty* diamonds, which was probably why he hesitated. He either hadn't done his homework or he'd forgotten whatever information the thief had provided.

He also hadn't mentioned that each stone had been mine-cut, one of the last hand-cut diamonds before the age of machinery took over. Although sometimes lumpy in shape, mine-cut diamonds reflected their natural shape, making each truly unique. A significant point to collectors.

"May I see the backing of the brooch?" She slid off an earring. "I'd like to compare it to the backing on this...."

As she handed him the earring, it dropped with a soft *fomp* onto the black velvet.

"Oh, *pardon!*"

He stood, his features pinched with worry. As he carefully lifted the earring, she leaned forward, angling her right shoulder toward the nearest camera. Her right hand slid into her left jacket pocket as the left plucked the Lady Melbourne brooch. The switch was complete within a few seconds.

Enzo, still examining the earring, murmured, "I do not see any damage."

She had purposefully let it fall on the velvet tray so it would land safely. Nevertheless, she frowned with concern.

"Thank goodness," she murmured. "So clumsy of me."

"No, *mademoiselle*," he said, returning it to her, "it is I who should have been more watchful. If you see a problem, you must bring it back and we shall repair it, at no cost, of course."

"Thank you." She slipped it back onto her ear.

"Even if you don't find a problem," he said, lowering his voice, "bring it back on your beautiful ear, and we shall take it out to a late lunch."

She smiled coyly. "How late?"

The look in his eyes darkened. "As late as you'd like."

She glanced at the brooch, back at him. "Maybe we can take the brooch to this late lunch, too."

He laughed uncomfortably. "I don't take my jewelry out to lunch or anywhere else."

"You think I'd steal it?"

He stared at her for a moment. "No, of course not. But someone else might."

"I was joking about taking it out," she said offhandedly, "but I am curious...." She inched her hand across the glass counter, her fingers almost touching his. "Where did you find this exquisite pin?"

He glanced at her hand. "A collector."

"Did he give you those Georgian earrings, too?"

"Yes."

So the "collector" was a man. Since the brooch had been stolen in Amsterdam, she asked, "A European collector, perhaps? Because I know a gentleman in Brussels who has an impressive Georgian collection.... Maybe we know the same person."

"No. Not Brussels."

One look at his wary expression and she knew he

wouldn't say more. Switching gears, she returned to a safer topic.

"So, is the backing on my earring the same as—"

Releasing a pent-up breath, Enzo picked up the flower brooch and turned it over. "This foil backing is similar to your earring, yes."

"How much for the pin?"

"Thirty-seven thousand."

Ten years ago, it had been valued at fifty. Which made it easily worth seventy or more today. He also hadn't referred to it as the Lady Melbourne brooch or mentioned its history. According to legend, it had been a gift from Queen Charlotte to Lady Melbourne, one of her ladies-in-waiting.

He obviously wanted to sell it, fast. Maybe he had been promised a cut.

"Let me think it over," she said pleasantly.

He gave her his card, and she left the store, smiling at the security guard on her way out.

As she drove out of the lot, she lightly touched the Lady Melbourne brooch, safely tucked into her inside jacket pocket. The replica now lay in its place at Fortier's, and unless his "collector" acquaintance checked it closely, no one would know about the switch. That was, until she, or maybe Charlie, returned to interview Enzo about his role in fencing the brooch. Depending on when, or if, she found the master thief, which could take days or weeks. Maybe months. Investigations always had their own timeline, based as much on the investigator's skill as patience.

Driving down the street, she saw the duplex ahead to her right. The young girl still sat on the porch steps, her eyes glued to the wedding chapel next door.

Frances pulled over and parked. Opening her clutch, she retrieved a bill that she'd tucked away a week or so earlier. Years ago, someone had given her such a gift. Now that she made a good income, she liked to give back in the same quiet way.

The girl's dark eyes widened with curiosity as Frances walked briskly up the cracked concrete walkway. The youngster scanned her linen pantsuit, all the way down to her Dolce & Gabbana heels, then raised her eyes to the glittering earrings.

Frances paused at the bottom of the steps and looked at the pile of old car parts stacked in a corner of the worn wooden porch, the bent metal frame of the screen door. They reminded her of a similar building she had lived in nearly twenty ago, and how for a few weeks she and her parents had spent their evenings in the dark because of an unpaid electric bill.

Not total darkness, though, because her dad lightened their moods, literally, with magic tricks. He'd light candles with a wave of his hand, make lightbulbs glow with a touch of his finger. She and her mom had seen the tricks dozens of times, knew the secrets behind the maneuvers, but they had laughed and clapped as though experiencing them for the first time.

Their responses had been real, not contrived. Although there was always trickery behind a magic act, something mystical bonded an audience to a magician.

They shared a belief, as far-fetched as it might seem, that everything would be all right. That the rabbit would reappear, the magician would escape the water tank, the lady sawn in half would be whole again.

Frances met the girl's gaze. "What's your name, hon?"

"Whitney."

She handed the girl a bill. "Whitney, do something nice for yourself and your family."

The girl's mouth dropped open as she looked at the fifty-dollar bill, then her eyes narrowed with suspicion.

"I don't do nuthin' for money."

"It's a gift."

"Why fo'?"

"For you to pay it forward someday." She saw the confusion on the girl's face. "Which means…when you're all grown up, give a gift to another young girl and her family."

As Frances headed back to her car, she heard the girl's barely suppressed squeal, followed by the thumpity-thump of feet running across the porch and the slam of a screen door.

WHILE DRIVING PAST the Clark County courthouse a few minutes later, Frances punched in the speed-dial number for her dad's cell, hit the speaker button and set the phone on the console. It was against Nevada law to make handheld cell-phone calls. In her opinion, that meant as long as she wasn't *holding* her phone, she stayed legal.

After all she'd been through, Frances was definitely keeping her life on the right side of the law. In five years, she would no longer be under court supervision, her payments would be completed for the necklace she stole and her felony conviction would be discharged. When that day came, she would have a second chance to live her life right.

"Hey, baby girl," her dad said over the speaker, "how'd it go?"

"Slick as glass."

"Get the brooch?"

"Of course."

"That's my girl!"

As she idled at a stoplight, a black cat dashed across the street in front of the Benz. She muttered, "That's not good."

"Something wrong?"

"I just saw a black cat."

"You and your superstitions," her dad said with a chuckle. "On your way to meet Charlie now?"

"He's in meetings until five. Figured while I'm downtown, I'll pull some files at the clerk and recorder's office to see if Enzo has recently used his jewelry inventory as collateral for a loan."

"This has something to do with the brooch?"

"Enzo's up to his teeth in litigation, probably having trouble borrowing money from banks right now. People in tight spots sometimes turn to questionable money sources, especially in Vegas. If Enzo took out a loan within the past week or so, which of course coincides with the brooch mysteriously surfacing, the identified lender might be the thief, too."

"My daughter, Sherlock—or should I say Shirley—Holmes."

In her rearview mirror, she saw swirling red lights from a white Crown Victoria hugging the bumper of her Benz.

Anxiety rippled through her. "Looks like I got company. Unmarked cop car's pulling me over."

"That's odd. Why an unmarked?"

Seemed odd to her, too, but she didn't have time to analyze the situation. "Charlie's office and cell numbers are written on the bottom of the whiteboard in the kitchen. Leave messages on both that I've been pulled over on Third, across from the courthouse. Gotta go."

After stopping the car, she eased the brooch from her pocket and set it carefully between the leather seat and the console, then rolled down her window and killed the engine. Slowly, she placed her hands on the steering wheel where they could be seen.

Exhaust fumes and the scents of hot dogs from a nearby street vendor wafted into the car as she watched the man in her rearview mirror unfold himself from the vehicle and swagger to her car. He wore jeans, white T-shirt, windbreaker—universal undercover-cop attire.

His steps crunched to a stop next to her window. Leaning over slightly, his blue eyes fastened on hers like steel shards to a magnet.

"Is there a problem, Officer?" she asked politely.

"Howdy," he said, all friendly like, "mind handing over your phone and car keys, ma'am?"

Not asking for her license and registration? "Uh... isn't this out of the ordinary?"

Looking around, he puffed out his chest while stealthily opening his jacket just enough for her to see his shoulder holster. Was this for real? The guy was acting like some kind of yahoo, showing off his big bad gun. If she wasn't so unnerved by being pulled over like this, she might laugh.

But even yahoos could be law enforcers, and she wasn't about to argue with a loaded gun, so she handed over her phone and key fob.

He powered off her phone and dropped it into his jacket pocket. "Step out of the car, please, ma'am."

Once she did so, he swiftly tied her hands behind her with a plastic handcuff, then leaned in close and whispered, "Where's the brooch?"

Maybe Enzo had been sharper than Frances had given him credit for, realized she'd lifted the real pin and left behind a look-alike. At least her dad was calling Charlie, alerting him to this snafu. He'd call the police department, get this ironed out. What a hassle.

Meanwhile, it'd be stupid to play dumb.

"Between the front seat and console," she said, more irritated than nervous at this point because she'd just blown the case.

Sure, Charlie would make nice with the police, and Vanderbilt would be pleased about the return of the Lady Melbourne, but she'd screwed up any possibility of tracking what Vanderbilt had wanted most—the fifth-century-BC coins. Although jewelry was her forte, she'd felt a connection to those coins after learning they were the last currency to be individually hammered, not minted. It reminded her of Georgian jewelry, the last to be made with hand-cut diamonds.

After the cop retrieved the brooch and her clutch bag, he thumbed the key fob to lock the car doors.

As he escorted her to his vehicle, she memorized the numbers on his license plate, mostly out of habit. Later she'd suggest to Charlie that the next time he wanted her to steal back Vanderbilt's property, at least give *somebody* in the police department the heads-up that she was working undercover and prevent a foul-up like this.

Of course, Charlie had his reasons for not alerting the police. He worried that details about her undercover work, as well as her true identity, would get disseminated too widely throughout the police department, compromising her ability to work.

He said it had happened before to other investigators.

"Watch your head, ma'am." The officer planted his hand on her skull as if it were a basketball and guided her into the backseat of the unmarked car.

Looking through the passenger window, she eyed the dozen or so people on the sidewalk who'd stopped to watch the arrest-in-progress. A middle-aged woman in a blue sweatshirt with the word *Lucky* in glittery letters licked her double-dip ice-cream cone, her wide eyes glued to the event as if it were a reality TV show.

After getting into the front seat, the cop held up her clutch bag. "I want you to know that I have not opened your purse. It will remain on the front seat of my car until I return it to you."

He was letting her know that its contents were safe, which protected him from any later accusations of theft. Definite police protocol. Yet he hadn't followed other standard procedures.

She shifted, trying to get comfortable, an impossibility with her hands bound behind her back. "So," she said, trying to sound unconcerned, "weren't you supposed to read me my rights?"

"Why, thank you, ma'am," he said, turning the ignition. "Guess I just plumb forgot. Lemme see…just like that Bud Buckley song about keeping secrets, you have the right to remain silent…anything you got any inkling to say can and will be used against you in a court of law…."

He drove, reciting her rights as if they were country-song lyrics, missing the turn to the detention center. Clearly, this wasn't a standard arrest, and the joker behind the steering wheel wasn't like any cop she'd ever known. A lot could go wrong while carrying jewelry worth seventy thousand dollars.

"Where are we going?" she asked, trying to sound calmer, stronger than she felt.

"I forget," he said, "did I mention the part about if you can't afford a lawyer? Hey, that reminds me of that ol' Willie Nelson song 'Mama, Don't Let Your Babies

Grow Up to Be Cowboys.' Has that line about lettin' kids grow up to be doctors and lawyers. And such."

As he started singing the song, she looked out the window, feeling more annoyed than scared. As insane as this ride-along was, she didn't have the sense she was in any danger. Her instincts told her something else, too.

She was on her way to meet the person who'd stolen the Lady Melbourne brooch.

TEN MINUTES, TWO country songs and one headache later, the unmarked car pulled into the parking lot behind the Downtown 3rd Farmers Market.

The building sat at the apex of Stewart Avenue and North Casino Center Boulevard, two streets that always bustled with traffic. Since the market only opened on Fridays, the lot was empty except for a sleek black limousine with darkened windows. In a corner of the lot, some teenage boys practiced their skateboarding moves, the wheels clattering and grinding along the asphalt. Across the street sat a bright red coffee hut.

The officer, flashing her a big ol' welcoming grin, opened the back door and helped her out. She closed her eyes against a gust of chilly wind as he undid the plastic binding. The scent of French-roast coffee drifted past. Opening her eyes again, she rubbed her wrists while watching the limo.

"After the meeting, I'll drive you back to your vehicle, ma'am."

So this had been planned. "Fine," she muttered, "just no more singing, okay?"

"Does humming count?"

She exhaled heavily. No wonder he didn't need to recite Miranda warnings—hanging out with him for a few minutes made anyone want to remain silent.

As they walked to the limo, her nerves kicked back in.

*No one is going to kill me in a luxury limo. Especially one parked in broad daylight, blocks from the Las Vegas Metro Police station.* Plus those skateboarding kids were close enough to easily describe her, the officer, his vehicle and the limo.

But even after mentally rattling off logical reasons that she was safe, she still wanted to throw up.

The cop opened a back door, and she leaned inside the limo, sliding onto a curved leather couch that faced a wet bar, leather chairs and small desk. Two men sat farther down the couch.

With the daylight spilling inside, she had a good view of the occupants. The man closest to her was in his early forties, with pronounced Slavic features, startlingly blue eyes and light, short-cropped hair. He wore leather loafers, slacks and a tailored blue shirt that revealed a muscled physique. On his far side sat a thirtyish man with a tight-lipped expression and wavy dark hair. His clothes weren't as nice—green-checkered gingham shirt, jeans, scuffed sneakers—and he wore an earbud, its wire connected to a smartphone.

The officer, quiet for once, handed the Lady Melbourne brooch to the older man, then shut the door without coming in.

"Hello, Frances," said a man with a Russian accent.

A ceiling lamp flicked on, lighting their seating area.

She wondered how he knew her real name. "And you're...?"

"An admirer...and a potential friend."

Considering how matter-of-factly he accepted the brooch, as though it were his, this had to be the criminal working with Enzo. The mastermind Charlie and Vanderbilt Insurance wanted her to find. And to think she'd been convinced she'd blown this case.

Great. She'd found him. But who was he? Apparently a Russian who had an undercover Vegas cop on his payroll.

The man picked a box off the couch. As he leaned forward, holding it toward her, she caught a whiff of his cologne, a potent mix of burned cherries and leather.

"Please help yourself," he said. "Chocolates from the Krupshaya confectionery factory of Saint Petersburg."

"Are you from Saint Petersburg?"

He made a clucking sound. "Don't be impolite, my dear. We've barely met and you're already asking personal questions." He gestured to the box. "I suggest the dark chocolates. They're creamy and sweet, unlike the dry, bitter variety one finds in America."

"No, thank you," she said. She vaguely remembered someone telling her that refusing a Russian's offer of food or drink was considered rude. "I'm allergic to chocolate."

"Allergic to vodka, too?" He helped himself to a piece of candy.

"Uh, no."

"Good. Would hate for you to miss out on all of life's pleasures." He settled back on the couch and, after popping the confection into his mouth, nodded to the other man, who moved forward, turning his smartphone so Frances could see the screen.

A video began playing of her and Enzo at the jewelry store, talking across the display case. It had been taken from the camera on her left, a good twenty feet away, yet it looked as though it had been shot from much closer.

Thoughts ricocheted through her mind. Enzo was either a terrific actor, emoting cluelessness as she lifted the brooch, or he had no idea she'd done it. Considering his current legal problems, she doubted he could pretend to be anything other than what he was—a troubled, weary man.

Which meant this Russian had somehow gotten hold of the surveillance film, but since he had the brooch again, why show this to her?

He said something in Russian to the younger man, who tapped the screen. The image froze just as she swapped the replica with the Lady Melbourne brooch.

"Nice work, Frances," the older man said. "You've obviously done this before."

"How do you know my name?"

"Your government has a marvelous facial-recognition database that contains every U.S. driver's license photo. My associate Oleg hijacked the signal from the surveillance camera to his smartphone, selected a clear image of you and ran it through that database. It linked to your license photo and gave us your name."

Hacking into a government database with such ease was mind-blowing. Either they had somebody on the inside or this younger guy was a computer genius. Good thing her driver's license had a bogus street address, courtesy of Vanderbilt and the state of Nevada.

"Oleg has been monitoring that surveillance camera for several days," he continued, looking pleased. "You see, I planted the Lady Melbourne brooch at Fortier's because I hoped to attract a thief—make that a *talented* thief—who is knowledgeable about Georgian jewelry."

This was a twist she wasn't expecting, although she had a good idea where it was leading. "You want me to steal something for you."

"Yes."

"I would have thought you already had such contacts...."

"Ah, I did have an experienced jewel thief lined up. An accomplished gentleman, but he's getting older and having health issues. Because I've been absent from your country for a while, I've unfortunately lost touch with other contacts." He shrugged. "My excellent team has been working hard for several months.... Silly to kill a project because one person drops out. You see, we are like a pirate ship, staying on course despite turbulent seas, determined to find the buried treasure marked with an X on our map."

"Seems risky to continue, though, if the person who dropped out is key to the plan."

"But a key can be forged. I found you, didn't I? As to risk...what beats in the heart of every thief is the thrill of uncertainty and peril. Without those, we lose our edge, our—" he rubbed his fingers together, as though touching a silky fabric "—*finesse.*"

His words resonated with her. She could still remember the rush after a successful pickpocket, a giddy high she had never gotten anywhere else in life. As an investigator, she sometimes felt that way after lifting an item, but it wasn't the same. The risk was there, but it was nothing like the thrill of the illicit hunt.

She shifted slightly. "What do you want stolen?"

"I'm sure you've heard of the Helena Diamond necklace...."

"Of course," she murmured.

The Helena Diamond was a heart-cut diamond necklace secretly commissioned by Napoleon with the help of friends during his exile on the island of Saint Helena in memory of his long-lost love, Josephine. Legend claimed that within the Helena Diamond was the pattern of two perfectly symmetrical hearts, only visible to the eyes of destined lovers.

The necklace disappeared after Napoleon's death, supposedly confiscated by his enemy, Prince Metternich, whose family hid the diamond after the fall of the Austrian Empire. Decades later, it resurfaced in the hands of a London diamond merchant who sold it for fifteen million dollars to an unnamed American businessman.

"That necklace is worth millions," she said.

"Twenty to be exact. It will be on display next month at the Legendary Gems exhibit at the Palazzo. We have the electronic know-how, locksmiths and muscle to grant you safe passage in and out. Your knowledge of Georgian jewelry—essential, as you will be mingling with antique-jewelry collectors and dealers—and your sleight-of-hand skills will do the rest."

Her stomach fell to somewhere around her feet. What he was describing confirmed to her that he'd also been behind the theft of the ancient coins that she was so eager to find. And more than that, he was reeling her into his next major heist.

For most of her five years as an insurance investigator at Vanderbilt, she'd worked garden-variety thefts. Mid-range jewelry and antiquities stolen from homes and small businesses.

This past year, though, Charlie had been pushing her to tackle tougher, big-ticket-item cases. A theft of jewels worth half a million from a Las Vegas entertainer's home safe. A briefcase of valuable coins stolen from a taxi. She'd solved both after weeks of investigative work, but tracking this mysterious Russian's shenanigans with the Lady Melbourne brooch *and* the ancient Greek coins was starting to feel as arduous as Napoleon's invasion of Russia.

This case was darker, more complex and frankly scarier than any she had handled before.

Part of her wanted to tell Charlie this job was out of her league and to get her out of it. But if Vanderbilt took issue with her backing out of this case and reported her insubordination to the court, the court could withdraw the suspension of her sentence, and she'd serve the remainder in jail.

"What do I get out of this?" she asked.

"Upon my receipt of the necklace, two hundred thousand dollars cash. And because of your fondness for the Lady Melbourne brooch, that, as well."

No jewel thief would work for such a measly percentage, but of course that wasn't what this was about for Frances. She had what most investigators worked weeks, months, for—she had an *in*. An invitation to the inner sanctum of her subject's world.

Charlie would be thrilled. Nailing a master thief would be a career coup. Vanderbilt would promote him and likely invite her to stay on after her probation ended. Or she could go into business for herself as a specialized antiquities investigator.

Which meant this case, if she succeeded, could skyrocket her career. But if she failed, cripple it. Maybe permanently.

Whatever the outcome, her life would be forever changed.

"I accept your offer," she said quietly.

## *CHAPTER THREE*

THE RADIO PERSONALITY had just announced the four-o'clock news as Braxton parked his old Volvo S70 in front of his mom's ranch-style home. He took a moment to look at the rock-gravel front yard, in the middle of which sat the desert willow his dad had planted on a long-ago Mother's Day.

Several years ago, after his mother informed Braxton he was no longer welcome in her home, his childhood home, he would sometimes drive by and look at that tree, envying it for having roots when his had been ripped out. More than once, he had parked down the street, trying to work up the nerve to go the front door and ring the bell. In his mind, his mom would answer, her hair fluffed in that short style she'd always worn. She'd stare at him, her eyes shining with joyful tears, and he'd say, *Mom, please forgive me.*

He'd probably seen too many sappy movies growing up, but that was what he'd envisioned. But it didn't matter, because he knew she couldn't forgive him. Hell, he still struggled with forgiving himself.

Then one night last August, after he'd helped the Las Vegas police, Drake and the arson investigator orchestrate the sting that put Yuri in jail, he drove straight here and knocked on the door. He knew his mother had already heard what happened, including how Braxton had severed all ties with Yuri's organization.

She'd opened the door, looking just as he'd imagined. Started crying, too. But before he could ask for forgiveness, she grabbed him in a hug and said, "Welcome home, son."

He was opening the front door when his cell rang. Recognizing Dmitri's number on the caller ID, he answered. After exchanging a few pleasantries, the Russian got to the point.

"That strip club you managed...it's been shut down for liquor violations and failure to pay local taxes."

Braxton walked across the living room, decorated in the same Swedish modern furniture his parents had picked out more than twenty years ago, and tossed his jacket across the back of the couch.

"Long time coming," he murmured.

He heard a faint ping from down the hall, the cue that his grandmother had started her electric wheelchair. He checked the red dice wall clock on the wall above the TV. A few minutes after four was close enough to five.

He headed to the kitchen. After he moved in last August, he'd been surprised how cold and clinical that room had felt with its white walls, white appliances and stainless-steel refrigerator. Hadn't been that way when he was a kid. Back then, the kitchen had been a mess most of the time, usually due to his recipe experimentations, and there had been family pictures everywhere.

Since moving back in, he'd taken it upon himself to bring some energy back into the room. He painted the walls a cheery yellow, hung curtains decorated with sunflowers and put family photos everywhere, including a picture of his dad with his favorite comedian, Jerry Lewis, at Bally's. The only time his dad had asked someone he'd just met to call him Benny.

But more important, Braxton cooked here almost every night, often with his mom, the two of them filling the room with delicious smells, a few recipe bombs and a lot of laughter.

He headed to Grams's special cabinet and grabbed a martini shaker while listening to Dmitri.

"Everyone I've talked to in the Russian community," he continued, "said you, Braxton, not Yuri, were the reason behind Topaz's success."

Braxton wasn't sure how to respond to that, because the compliment was a double-edged sword. Yeah, he'd been a good manager, in fact a *damned good* one, but he'd gotten dirty along with the business.

"Does this have something to do with what you wanted to discuss?" He nestled the phone against his shoulder and filled the shaker with ice.

His grandmother, wearing a shiny cocoa-colored caftan and gold shoes, glided across the linoleum floor in her wheelchair, her puf of white hair glowing like a sunlit cloud under the lights. Seeing he was on the phone, she halted and pressed her finger to her ruby-red lips, indicating she'd be quiet.

He winked at her, wondering how many other eighty-five-year-old women purchased half a dozen tubes of crimson lipstick after reading that "women of a certain age" should only ever wear more discreet shades. Grams, the makeup activist.

"Yes, it does," Dmitri answered. "I'm opening a club in Vegas later this year and wondered—"

"I'm not interested." It turned his stomach to even think of going back to such a job. In the six months since he'd stopped managing Topaz, he'd been inside a strip club only once, and that was for a buddy's bachelor party.

"I like you, Braxton," Dmitri said quietly, "but this is the second time you've gotten angry before I've had a chance to explain. It reminds me of a story my mother used to tell me about a frog who kept jumping to conclusions. He puffed himself up so much each time with his self-justified reasons, eventually he burst."

Braxton held the phone away from his ear, giving himself a moment to cool down. He didn't need some frog story to remind him he had a problem containing his temper when it came to Yuri.

He glanced at his grandmother, her jade-green eyes shiny with concern. Over these past six months, they'd shared many long talks over martinis about his guilt over hurting his family. Then one night she suggested his guilt might fade when he stopped being angry at himself.

He put the phone back to his ear. "Sorry, Dmitri. Please, go ahead."

"People have informed me that you have extensive knowledge in the field of security. What areas, may I ask?"

So polite, so sophisticated. Even had a better English vocabulary than most Americans whose paths Brax crossed. Dmitri might have Russian roots, but he was nothing like Yuri. Time to give him some credit, discuss this project as he would any legitimate business deal.

"Got my first job in hotel security at eighteen through my dad, who headed up security at Bally's—" he grabbed a jar of olives from the fridge "—followed by several years of business security consulting and personal protection gigs…then you know about Topaz." He set the jar on the small kitchen table, next to a bottle of vermouth.

"Personal protection… You mean, as a bodyguard?"

"Yes." He retrieved two martini glasses and held them up for Grams to see. She smiled.

"Ah, not only a man with brains, but brawn, too." He paused. "I might want to use you as a bodyguard soon. But back to my business venture—I will need a qualified head of security, which would also include living expenses, a car and substantial stock options."

Brax paused in front of the fridge, remembering how years ago Yuri had promised all those things, too.…

"Uh, one moment, Dmitri."

He opened the freezer door and placed the glasses inside, willing the blast of chilled air to knock some sense into him. He couldn't forget that life was good at Morgan-LeRoy Investigations. He had office space for his security consulting business and the best coworkers nepotism could buy, but damn, it would be a lie to say he didn't miss having plush digs, a slick car and a stake in a potentially profitable business.

He shut the freezer door and looked at a photograph on the fridge of his family at a sea resort years ago. He could still remember the soft splash of waves, the sun heating his skin.

His parents had one rule: no going into the water unless accompanied by adults. Which was like waving a red flag to ten-year-old Braxton. One early evening he sneaked down to the shore and waded in, only everything was different than it had been earlier in the day. The waves had churned, the skies had darkened. Then something pulled him underneath the water—later his dad said it had been a riptide—where he flailed in the dark, wet cold, fighting for air.

Strong arms jerked him out of the water. His father carried him back to shore, where they both fell onto the sand, gasping. After a few minutes, his dad had said, *On the surface, the sea can look like a beautiful dream. Now you know what lies beneath it.*

As good as Dmitri's offer sounded, Braxton wasn't sure he wanted to test what lay underneath it. The guy could be as straight-up as they came, but this was still Vegas, the sin capital of the world.

"Appreciate your thinking of me," he said into the phone, "but to be honest, I like my life right now. It's calmer, more predictable."

After a beat, Dmitri said, "I admire a cautious man. Before you make up your mind, I invite you to conduct a due-diligence check on my holdings and other business projects, because you will not find a single black mark. Better yet, I will save you the work and forward a recent due-diligence report conducted by The Dayden Group. Have you heard of them?"

"Yes." He had sometimes used The Dayden Group, a business-assessment service, to conduct corporate background checks.

"My associate will drop off their report along with the retainer check tomorrow morning."

After ending the call, he looked at Grams, who raised her eyebrows. "That sounded like a job offer."

"It was. But…I don't know. I've never met this guy, except by phone, but at least he's giving me some information to review."

"He's Russian, I take it."

"How'd you know?"

"That troubled look. You only get it when Yuri's name comes up."

He scrubbed a hand over his face, as though he could wipe off any remaining trace.

"I used to make snap decisions all the time, Grams,

rarely second-guessed myself. But these days—" he gave his head a shake "—I overthink everything to the point of wearing out the idea before it gets a chance."

"My darling—" the rings on her hand sparkled as she gestured toward the shaker "—let's make those martinis and talk."

THE FOLLOWING MORNING, Braxton arrived early for work at Morgan-LeRoy Investigations. Dmitri had said the retainer check would be delivered at nine o'clock and Brax didn't want to be late.

After turning on the lights and starting the coffee, he sat at his desk in the waiting room and checked email on his smartphone. At his old place, he liked to crank up the tunes first thing in the morning, his favorite bands being Green Day, Florence and the Machine, and anything by Maroon 5 and its lead singer, Adam Levine. Although sometimes nothing soothed his soul like an old country classic by George Jones.

But lately, he'd been keeping the noise down in the mornings so Drake and Val, who lived in the back apartment, could get some rest. His brother had recently been working some late-night surveillances, and Val, in the last trimester of her pregnancy, had been having trouble sleeping. Instead of blasting the office, Brax plugged in his earbuds and bobbed his head to the beat of "Moves Like Jagger."

A text message from his grandmother popped up on his smartphone.

We forgot to talk last night about the Magic Dream Date Auction on Valentine's Day!

Last night over martinis, they'd talked about everything *but* the auction—Dmitri's job offer; Braxton's dilemma over possibly leaving Morgan-LeRoy Investigations; Grams's crazy cat Maxine's bladder infection; and Gram's boyfriend, Richmond, whom she called her boy toy, although he was only six years younger.

But they'd forgotten to discuss the auction. Or maybe, subconsciously, he hadn't wanted to burst her bubble. Grams loved volunteering at Keep 'Em Rolling and made it a point to stay in contact with people who had received wheelchairs from the organization. Several times he'd driven her to people's homes so she could visit them in person. He *wanted* to support her.

It was just...he wasn't up for playing stud boy, *especially* on Valentine's Day at an auction catering to lonely hearts waving fistfuls of money as he sashayed down a runway in tight jeans and no shirt.

*Somebody shoot me now.*

Couldn't avoid the topic much longer, though. The auction was next Friday, February 14.

"Hello?"

He looked up, yanked the buds from his ears.

A woman, late twenties, stood in front of his desk. American accent, so he doubted she was Dima's associate; he'd mentioned something about having only a few Russian friends in the area. She wore a sophisticated gray pantsuit, lipstick the color of raspberry gelato and a bun knotted at the base of her neck. He glanced out the front window and saw a shiny lemon-yellow Mercedes Benz parked next to his Volvo.

Irked him that he drove that piece of junk.

Irked him more that she drove a Mercedes.

Pantsuit. Bun. Benz.

Oh, yeah, he got her number. Probably read *The Economist* cover to cover, or pretended to, wore sensible pumps and followed Hillary Clinton on Twitter. Her idea of a good time was to shop at Ikea, followed by brunch, where she ordered lettuce with a side of lemon.

"Are you Braxton Morgan?" she asked.

"Are you looking for a security consultant?"

Her eyes rounded in puzzlement. "No."

"Then why are you asking for Braxton?"

She stared at him for a long moment, as though he were a bauble she was thinking about acquiring.

That was when he noticed the color of her eyes. A light purple, like amethyst. Yet so clear, he could see into them, catch glints of gold in their depths. And something more, too. A wistfulness that didn't match the resolute lines of that pantsuit, the slick knot of that bun.

But it was more than what he saw. He *felt* her. A restlessness that swept over him like winds off the Mojave, as warm as they were unsettling. At the same time he sensed her vulnerability, which clashed with her business-power packaging, but fit right in with her flowery scent.

Distant yet close. Seductive yet standoffish.

He didn't think he'd ever met a woman who gave off more conflicting signals.

"Because," she finally said, "I have something for him."

He forgot what he'd asked her. Or why he was here, the day of the week, the current president of the United States. Oh, right, he'd asked why she wanted to see Braxton. Whoever that was.

A corner of her mouth lifted slightly, as though amused by his caginess. Although he preferred to think it was inspired by his overwhelming manliness. Anyway, it was a nice mouth. Soft, curvy lips. Their color so light and ripe, he could almost taste their raspberry sweetness.

He realized he was smiling back.

"So," she said, her voice turning husky, "do you know where I can find Braxton?"

Oh, now she'd done it.

He'd always been a sucker for women's smoky, raspy voices, and she'd just given it to him twofold. She was a young Lauren Bacall. Cool, unflappable, smooth. And he was Sam Spade, private eye, ready and willing to help the damsel in distress.

Ka-boom.

He straightened, laughing as he realized what he'd just fallen for.

"Oh, you're good," he said, giving his head a shake. "The hot blonde strolling in here, bringing trouble into my life. That pantsuit fooled me at first. Who's your stylist? Hillary Clinton? That uptight schoolmarm bun, whoa, we're talking *foxy*...like Frau Farbissina in the *Austin Powers* movies. But I have a thing for blondes, which they probably told you. And that husky, smoky voice. Wow. Tie me up and make me write bad checks all night long, baby."

He laughed. She didn't.

"So," he said, turning down the dial on his frivolity, "who put you up to this? Drake?"

A sly half smile played on her lips. "Right, it was Drake. He told me Braxton would be sitting at this desk at nine."

"Yeah, I open up most mornings."

She placed a manila envelope on the desk. "Then this is for you, Braxton Morgan. Have a nice day."

Neatly printed on the envelope were the words *To Braxton Morgan, personal and confidential* and *Dmitri Romanov* in the top left corner. The papers from Dmitri. And the check. Smoky-husky was his associate?

When he looked up, the blonde was walking away. No goodbye. Just a silky-smooth exit, like a trail of smoke from Lauren Bacall's cigarette.

Was that how the clichéd private-eye story ended? After the hot blonde walked into the detective agency and exchanged a few words with the P.I., who of course fell hard for her, she walked back out? Just like that?

Not in *this* movie.

Braxton grabbed his phone and headed after her.

HEADING TO HER CAR in the Morgan-LeRoy Investigations lot, Frances shivered as a chilly breeze flittered past. Two hours ago, the skies had been deceptively blue and the sun so bright she'd tossed her sunglasses into her purse. Now clouds were moving in, obliterating the sun, casting the world in a surreal, hazy light.

Footsteps slapped behind her.

"Hey, Babe!"

She looked around. The only other person nearby was a guy in a cap with earflaps and pom-poms ambling down the sidewalk, so "Babe" had to mean her.

She turned back to Braxton, who was walking briskly toward her. Hadn't bothered to put on a jacket or coat, so he had to feel the cold, but he seemed oblivious to it. Flashed her a smile and waved as though out for a stroll on a balmy spring day.

He was tall, a little over six feet, she guessed. That tucked-in fitted shirt emphasized his V shape—from the width of his shoulders down to his toned chest that tapered to a flat, lean waist. Although he wore his trousers stylishly loose, the material seemed to skim his muscled thighs as he walked.

A sensual awareness prickled over her skin.

Back in the Morgan-LeRoy office, she'd found him to be cute in a goofy kind of way, but he'd also been sitting down, so she didn't get an overall impression. Plus she'd been juggling other thoughts—trying to get a fix if this was Braxton, as she wanted to hand over the envelope to the right person, thinking about her brunch meeting today with her boss.

Her thoughts scattered as Braxton stopped in front of her. He blew out a breath and grinned—an infectious, sheepish smile that filled his whole face. Standing this close, inches apart really, she got the full force of his gray eyes, really more of a light gray-blue that reminded her of early-morning skies.

"I said some dumb stuff back there." He shifted his weight from one foot to the other. "I'm sorry."

His flustered boyishness—like a teenage boy worried about what to say to the girl—took her by surprise. Where'd the cocky, in-your-face guy go? The one who blurted that line about tying him up and making him write bad checks all night?

Sudden heat crawled up her neck, spreading to her cheeks. Shouldn't have thought about that.

"Must say," she said casually, willing the heat to subside as she looked over at an old pickup, its suspension squeaking, lumber along Graces Avenue, "I've never been compared to Frau Farbissina before."

"I thought someone was punking me—didn't know you were really here on business."

As she turned to face him, a gust of wind blew his soapy, masculine scent toward her. She held back a shiver, not from the cold this time.

"Don't worry about it." She meant it. Whatever had been going on back there in the office didn't make sense, but it was a small issue in a world of big ones.

"I don't deserve to get off the hook so easily," he murmured, his voice dropping to a low rumble she felt all the way down to her toes.

"No, you don't," she agreed, trying not to smile.

They'd only met a few minutes ago, but she felt the rhythm, the current between them, as though they'd done this dozens of times. Playing, teasing each other. Doubted any woman could resist his charm.

Braxton had what her mom would have called "matinee-idol good looks." Illegally handsome and exuberantly male. Plus he exuded an unlabored, playful sexiness that if left unbridled could gallop into full-on killer charisma. She imagined he had to hold the reins tight, practice some self-imposed restraint, try to wheel it out on special occasions only.

She glanced at the old Volvo, the only other car in the small lot. Had to be his. Why did a charismatic, good-looking guy with a sharp sense of style drive a rusting, bald-tired car?

"Piece of junk," he muttered, following her line of vision.

Everything within her froze.

She stared at a patch of peeling paint on the hood, a rusted dent on its side. Braxton couldn't see her imperfections, but if he did, would they be standing here, playing mental footsie?

She doubted it.

After all, he looked like the perfect male—classic good looks, sculpted bod, designer clothes. Maybe it wasn't fair to assume he'd seek the same perfection in life—be it a woman, car, house, whatever—but considering how he looked down on that poor Volvo, maybe he would.

"You should fix up your car," she said quietly, "then you'll like it better."

Pulling the key fob from her pocket, she headed to her Benz. Breezes whipped past, chilling whatever warmth she'd felt.

"Hey, did I say something wrong?" he said, following her.

Her heels clicked across the asphalt. She punched a button and the door locks on the Benz clicked open.

"I'll get it," he said, bounding ahead.

He looked so gallant opening the driver's door for her, those sparkling gray eyes seeking her approval, but she didn't want to play this game anymore because it was destined for a happy-never-more ending. He was the matinee-idol prince and she was the frog princess.

And no way that prince would ever want to kiss this frog princess.

Deliberately avoiding his gaze, she started to get into the car when their bodies bumped and she stumbled.

He grabbed her by the elbow, steadying her.

"Sorry," he murmured.

She could feel his eyes wanting to connect with hers, but she couldn't go there again. They'd experienced a few frivolous moments, and now it was time to get back to reality.

"I have a meeting," she said evenly, lowering herself into the driver's seat.

"What's your na—"
The rest of his question was cut off as she closed the door with a sharp clack.

## CHAPTER FOUR

TWENTY MINUTES LATER, Frances took a seat at the table, immaculately set with linen, crystal and a bottle of champagne—Taittinger, no less—chilling in an ice-filled silver bucket. The lights were moody low, the classical music softly romantic.

Her boss, Charlie Eden, was dapper in a charcoal Ralph Lauren suit that complemented his silvering hair. He looked at her with shining, attentive eyes from across the table.

She and Charlie had sometimes ordered cocktails during these meetings, but champagne on ice? This was a first. Made her uncomfortable. Did he think this was some kind of date?

She flashed on several women at the Vanderbilt Insurance office who'd run over their own grandmothers to be in Frances's shoes right now. In the company kitchen, they'd whisper breathlessly about his Porsche 911 and how its custom paint job matched its baby-blue cockpit, his Tuscan-style home on a golf course, his European vacations.

What they liked was his money, of course, not his withering looks when displeased or his condescending tone when addressing someone he viewed as an imbecile, which seemed to be half of the earth's population. It amazed her how some people, like Charlie's office groupies, viewed the almighty dollar as if it were the most important attribute in a potential mate, rather than traits like kindness and devotion.

Or maybe Frances was more attuned to what money *couldn't* buy based on her mom's stories of her privileged, but painfully lonely, upbringing.

So here Frances sat in a luxurious restaurant, feeling awkward. Maybe she wouldn't have thought twice about the decor and champagne on ice if her dad hadn't been so insistent that Charlie had a thing for her.

Did he?

She'd never picked up on any signals from her boss, but then she'd always related to his professional role, not the man behind it.

Something about Charlie she'd always picked up on loud and clear, though. He wasn't a gambler. His every action had a plan and a purpose. Nothing with him was ever simple or spontaneous.

Which meant his reasons for selecting this restaurant were more convoluted than his setting up a date. Eventually, he'd tell her what they were.

"Hope the bubbly wasn't too expensive, Charlie," she said, setting her smartphone on the table, "because I won't be drinking any. Way too early for me."

He flashed his Gordon Gekko smile. "It's almost noon."

"It's a few minutes after ten."

"Frances, as always, you are enmeshed in the minutiae. Observe, document, categorize."

"If everybody saw the forest instead of the trees, nobody would know how to plant a seed."

Charlie did a slight double take, but didn't say anything as the waiter appeared at their table. He wore a white jacket with *Chez Manny* stitched in blue on the pocket and gave them a practiced smile. After setting a basket of "hand crafted" rolls and butter on the table, he gestured toward the champagne. She noticed initials inked on the inside of his ring finger, which made her wonder why people got tattoos with personal messages, as though anything in life were that permanent.

"Now that your guest is here, shall I pour the champagne?" he asked.

She held her hand over her glass. "No, thank you."

The waiter bent his head in understanding and poured the bubbly into Charlie's crystal flute.

Her boss had wanted to meet at this restaurant last night, too, but she'd canceled, explaining she felt drained after the odd undercover-cop escort and limo meeting.

She was glad she'd gone straight home last night, because her dad had been worrying himself sick since their aborted phone call. He'd also thought he'd failed her because although he'd left messages for Charlie, he didn't know if Charlie had heard them, so her dad fretted about her possibly being behind bars with no one coming to her aid.

Wanting to ease her dad's concerns, she'd glossed

over what had happened during their dinner of Spam sandwiches and leftover Chinese food. Said the undercover cop had pulled her over for a broken taillight and let her go with a warning. That she would have called her dad after that but had been pulled into a last-minute meeting at a downtown coffee shop with a Vanderbilt client.

After dinner, she wrote an email to Charlie filling him in on all the details, including that she'd be conducting a delivery in the morning for the Russian, after which she could meet Charlie. He wrote back later that he'd be at Chez Manny by ten.

"Would you perhaps like a Baby Bellini, a non-alcoholic drink made with peach nectar and sparkling cider?" the waiter asked her.

She ordered one, plus an omelet. Charlie ordered the cedar-plank-roasted salmon special.

After the waiter left, Charlie lifted his glass of bubbly. "To my star investigator."

"Hardly a star. All I did was talk to the Russian."

He took a sip of champagne, set the glass back on the table. "But he trusted you enough to invite you into his inner sanctum, Frances, which is a coup. You've been an investigator long enough to understand the significance of that."

She caught an edge of apprehension in his tone.

"Pass the bread?" she asked pleasantly, studying his face, wondering what was going on with him.

He held out the basket and she helped herself to a "hand crafted" roll. She spread some of the butter—which the waiter had mentioned was "lavender laced"—on the warm roll and took a bite, savoring its herb-infused, yeasty taste.

For several moments they said nothing, listening to a gentle violin played over other diners' murmured conversations.

"I have good news and bad news," he finally said, "or possibly good news and good news, depending on how successful you are in this case, Frances."

"I'm not sure I like how this sounds," she murmured.

"I shouldn't call it bad news. More correctly, it is *potentially* good news for both of us."

"But you said this depends on how successful *I* am, so apparently my actions dictate how this...whatever it is...will affect both of us."

"Correct." He drew his lips into a tight, reflective grin. "I've been interested for some time in opening my own antiquities insurer company, but haven't found enough interested backers. Fortunately, the CEO of Vanderbilt—an old friend of mine, we attended Cornell together—has offered me the helm of a new Vanderbilt division that will handle all high-end antiquities insurance policies. I'll be building an elite team of appraisers, underwriters and fraud investigators whose focus will be to reduce claims fraud on our more valuable jewelry and antiquity items. Frankly, I haven't been happy with most of our investigators—their sloppy work has resulted in Vanderbilt paying extraordinarily hefty claims without recovering insured items. But you, Frances, have a solid track record of solving cases. I'd like you to join my team as my first investigator, but…"

But what? He was giving her high praise one moment, then seeming critical of her the next. She held his gaze for an awkward moment or two, watching the sparkle go out of his light brown eyes until they reminded her of dead leaves.

"Spit it out, Charlie."

She'd never spoken like that to her boss, but it was grating on her nerves he didn't just speak his mind. She might tell white lies to her dad so he wouldn't worry, fabricate stories and identities in the course of her investigative work, but sometimes the best way to deal with an issue was to put it out there.

As the violin music trilled in the background, Charlie stared hard at her, finally saying, "You can't fail at this case."

"Because you want to show Vanderbilt I have what it takes to be part of your elite group."

"Correct." He took another sip of champagne.

"I know how much Vanderbilt wants me to find those coins, Charlie, but there are never any guarantees. You know that."

"I do. Just bring your A-game, Frances. That's all I'm asking."

Which brought up the issue she'd tossed and turned over last night. Sometime between 2:00 and 3:00 a.m., she'd finally dozed off, still torn about whether or not to make this request.

"I'm not sure I should investigate this one," she said.

He frowned. "Why not?"

"It's out of my league. I can bring my A-game, but it's like asking a—" she listened to the violin warble "—a small-time fiddler to play first violin in an orchestra. You want me to find coins worth *millions* of dollars...but, Charlie, you seem to forget I was a teenage pickpocket who later lifted a few pieces of jewelry. My biggest theft was a diamond-and-ruby necklace worth eighteen grand retail, *and* I got caught."

Charlie obviously saw her concern because his expression turned soft, almost apologetic. "Let's table that discussion for a minute."

She nodded.

"Speaking of that eighteen-grand necklace, you've almost paid off the restitution, right?"

"Almost."

"I'm proud of you, Frances."

She didn't feel any pride over what she'd learned these past five years, but she definitely felt humbled.

It hadn't been easy paying the restitution. Besides the cost of the necklace, the court tacked on their case-processing fees, plus an assessment for the victims' compensation fund, which brought her financial obligation to just over $22,700. A hefty payoff considering her fence, a pawnbroker named Rock Star, paid her only $4,500 for the necklace, the standard 25 percent going rate.

At first she'd felt sorry for herself for getting into that mess. Then one day her probation officer called and said the victim, a woman named Leona, who'd recently lost her daughter in Afghanistan, wanted to meet her. Frances had balked, anxious about facing Leona's justified anger, especially as the necklace had never been recovered.

Her mother, in the last weeks of her life, although Frances and her dad didn't know it at the time, simply said, *You owe it to her.*

The following week, Frances had sat in a spacious, airy living room, eating chocolate cookies with Leona, a plump, fiftyish woman with eyes the color of water. She didn't get angry. Didn't mention the necklace, either. Instead, she talked for two hours about her daughter, Dena, who'd played the flute, raised bees and dreamed of being a veterinarian. She never mentioned Dena's death, only said she'd joined the army to help pay for her college.

Later, Frances thought how she'd gone to Leona's so the woman could yell and vent her justified rage. Instead Frances received something far greater. Forgiveness.

"But you weren't caught *stealing* that necklace," Charlie continued, "which is commendable."

Frances was surprised he'd used the word *commendable* about her theft. For all Charlie's education, sometimes he had the depth of a puddle.

"It was the fence that snitched you out, right?" he said pleasantly, as though this were a light, inconsequential conversation.

"The buyer of the necklace coughed up my fence's

name to the police, who in turn coughed up mine."

Loyalty among thieves.

"Which is my point—you've never been caught in the act," he said, "because you're good at what you do. Which our mystery Russian recognized after watching your brilliant audition on the surveillance feed."

The waiter returned with her Baby Bellini, poured more champagne for Charlie and informed them their food would be served shortly.

After he left, Charlie said, "You're not *out* of your league, Frances—you're stepping *up* to it."

As he paused to take another sip of champagne, she tasted her Baby Bellini, enjoying its peachy fizz, thinking she should call Leona and ask how her bee farm was going.

"Was the Russian at his office this morning?" Charlie set down his drink.

"Don't know. Oleg was in the front area, working on a computer, but the other doors were closed."

"Did Oleg discuss your work there?"

"Just to be there Monday morning around nine and to ask for him."

"Oleg," he mused, "is a very savvy hacker if he's breaking into a government facial-recognition database. If the feds were to nail him, he could spend up to ten years in prison."

"These people don't leave electronic tracks."

"No, they get caught after doing something stupid, like leaving behind a half-eaten sandwich covered with DNA."

A famously stupid mistake in one of the largest jewel heists in history. After several years of rigorous planning, a brilliant jewel thief named Leonardo Notarbartolo executed a meticulous break-in of the Antwerp World Diamond Centre and its supposedly impregnable vault. Afterward, he tossed his half-eaten sandwich, along with receipts for some of the break-in tools, in a farmer's field near the scene of the crime. The farmer called the police, angry people were dumping trash on his property, and read them the information on the receipts, which the police recognized to be the tools used at the crime. After running a DNA analysis on the sandwich, they identified Notarbartolo, who spent several years in prison, although he never divulged the whereabouts of the diamonds.

Cases like that taught investigators to never dismiss seemingly unconnected leads. That the jewelry was never located wasn't a surprise, however, as in nearly half of such thefts, the gold would be melted and the gems recut.

Which made intact historical jewelry pieces, such as the Helena Diamond necklace and the fifth-century-BC coins, all the more valuable.

"Think the big man's from Saint Petersburg?" Charlie asked.

"Chocolates were from there, but that doesn't mean he is. Saw a name—Dmitri Romanov—on the envelope I delivered this morning to Braxton.... Apparently that's the name he goes by, but I don't know... could be an alias, too."

"I don't think we know enough about him. What else did you notice?"

"I've gone over and over our meeting in my head. He wore no jewelry, had no visible scars from what I could see, but the lighting was dim in the limo. I described that other set of Georgian earrings at Fortier's in my email—learn anything about them?"

"The slight blue cast of the diamonds is unusual, but there's no record of their theft."

"And the license-plate numbers I forwarded?"

"Limo's registered to Konfety, which appears to be a bogus corporation. That undercover cop's vehicle is the real deal, though, as it's registered to the city. My guess is he checked it out. I won't subpoena the police for those records, because it would alert them that Vanderbilt has an interest in his identity, which of course would tie you to Vanderbilt."

"That guy was nuts."

"Maybe on purpose." He lifted his glass.

"To throw me off?"

"He's an undercover cop. You're an undercover investigator. Both of you are good at deceiving people in the course of your work, right?"

If the singing detective was a Dmitri gofer, he could have acted that way to hide his real personality. On the other hand, if he was one of the good guys, maybe he'd acted silly to put her at ease, which had worked. That also meant the Las Vegas Metro Police were working their own case against Dmitri.

"You said the Russian asked you to deliver something this morning—what was it?"

"A manila envelope that felt like it had papers inside, but I didn't want to open it and give myself away."

"Who's this private investigator?"

"Name's Braxton Morgan. Works at Morgan-LeRoy Investigations downtown, but his brother's the partner, not him. Apparently, Braxton is more of a security consultant."

"Private dicks," Charlie muttered, a look of distaste crossing his features. "Lowlife snoops in trench coats pretending to be Sam what's-his-name."

"Sam Spade?"

"Right, Sam Spade. Now, *that* was a private eye. Smart. Detached. Unflinching. Women wanted him, men wanted to be him."

She almost laughed. Did pompous, corporate-America Charlie secretly yearn to be a tough-guy Sam Spade?

But Charlie had Braxton wrong. He wasn't a lowlife in a trench coat. He wasn't detached, either, but he was definitely smart.

On her way over here, she'd quickly checked him out on the internet, impressed with a news story about his saving a politician's life years ago. Acting as a legislator's bodyguard, Braxton had perceived a threat at a political rally and taken action that saved the official's life. Such quick, calculated thinking proved his intelligence.

She'd have to do further research on Braxton Morgan.

"Most of those shamuses will do anything for a buck," Charlie said, buttering a roll, "including break the law. Which this guy Braxton must be doing, too, if he's hooked up with our Russian. How'd he react when you handed him the envelope?"

More like, how did he react to *her*.

"Seemed to be expecting it," she answered.

"What's your impression of him?"

"Early thirties," she said matter-of-factly, "dresses professionally, which tells me he takes his work seriously. Don't think he's dirty, though."

The last part slipped out before she'd given it any thought, but something about Braxton had struck her as honest.

"How do you know?"

"Just a sense I got."

"Interesting. You don't usually give much credit to first impressions." He let that hang in the air for a moment. "Anyway, as you get more involved in this Dmitri fellow's heist, keep your ears open for how Braxton fits into the picture." He checked his watch, a shiny gold Rolex.

"Are you late for something?" she asked.

"Told my ex I'd pick up the kids, take them to see a movie. Let me make a quick call."

He'd mentioned his exes before—there were two,

but only one lived in Vegas—and Frances had seen framed photos of several boys and a girl in his office, although Charlie didn't talk about them much, just passing references to having them for the weekend or taking them to some event.

Frances was surprised that he made the call at the table rather than stepping away, so she looked around the restaurant to give him a semblance of privacy. Scanned the brocade draperies that sealed off the far windows, listened to the beginning of a spirited piano concerto, caught scents of garlic and spices as waiters passed with steaming plates.

She couldn't hear Charlie's conversation as he kept his voice low, although at one point he snapped, "The credit card is *maxed out,* Cynthia!"

A few moments later he ended the call, slid his phone back into his jacket pocket. "Where were we?"

He looked pissed, but also confused, which was strange, since Frances had never seen Charlie betray any hint of vulnerability.

"Now that you're on the inside of this Russian's racket," he said, shifting back to business mode, "Vanderbilt wants you to learn the players on his team, their roles and, as we've discussed, anything you can find about the coin theft. Any dirt you can dig up will be smiled upon, too. Sometimes these guys get a lot chattier when faced with prison, and we'd like him to chat about those coins."

"What about the brooch?"

"Icing. This Russian promised you the pin as payment after the heist, but Vanderbilt is more interested in your finding the coins before then. It wants to sink this Russian and his crew."

An uneasiness swept through her as she imagined a pirate ship plunging to the ocean's depths.

"The jewelry show is March first," she murmured, running her fingertips lightly over the tight weave of the linen tablecloth. "A little over three weeks from today. What if I don't find enough evidence by then?"

"Vanderbilt will undertake a sting. Swap out the necklace with a duplicate, which you'd steal, the critical point being when you hand it over to Dmitri. You'll need to play this tight with Dmitri, get him to a spot you help choose—a hotel room, for example—where Vanderbilt technicians can be in the next room taking covert footage of him accepting the necklace, discussing the heist and so forth...."

Her nerves jumped. Those few videotaped minutes would make or break a multimillion-dollar case—the kind of high-stakes shakedown she'd never conducted, yet Vanderbilt thought she could pull this off in one shot? Even Meryl Streep needed more than one take to get a scene right.

"I'll do my best to find evidence in the next few weeks, Charlie, but please remember I'm an investigator, not a miracle worker."

"A *lead* investigator," he said, raising his glass. Whatever confusion or irritation she'd noticed before was gone from his face. He smiled his signature Gekko smile. "On behalf of Vanderbilt Insurance, I'd like to congratulate you on your *first* promotion, effective immediately, which includes a seven percent raise, more stock options…and I finagled an extra week of annual vacation time, but keep that to yourself."

"I'm being promoted?"

"That's what the champagne and the classy restaurant are all about."

"Really?" she said, feeling embarrassed that she'd wondered if this brunch was a date setup.

"Yes, Frances," he said. "Typically, other executives would attend, but since you're working undercover, Vanderbilt is keeping this celebration low-key. By the way, when you join my division as its initial investigator, your title will be Manager of the Special Investigative Unit."

The food arrived. As the waiter fussed over them—"Another Baby Bellini, *mademoiselle?*"—she unfurled her napkin into her lap, titles and money and her future swirling in her brain. She took another sip of her Bellini, its carbonation stinging her lips. From thief to investigator to manager? Was this real?

Of course it was. One thing about Charlie, he'd never lied to her. Now it made sense that he'd been handing her tougher cases this past year. He'd been testing her, grooming her to join his team.

He rapped his fingers on the table and leaned forward with a smile. "You need to stop doubting yourself, Frances. You're perfect—not only for this case, but also for manager of the special investigative unit."

She took another sip of her Bellini, thinking about

that word *perfect,* something she'd accepted long ago she could never be...unless she faked it.

BRAXTON SAT IN his Volvo on a side street next to the restaurant Chez Manny, one of those old-time Vegas restaurants that once catered to movie stars, famous singers and the usual assortment of high-living organized-crime types. These days it still had the reputation for great food, but the neighborhood had gone downhill. Rundown apartment buildings, empty lots cluttered with weeds and debris. An elderly man pushed a shopping cart, its wheels clattering over the broken sidewalk, eyeing Braxton as if he might jump out of his Volvo and try to steal the cart.

Not the kind of neighborhood that gave a person the warm fuzzies, but it was safer than a good third of Vegas's hoods, unfortunately. At least Frances was meeting someone here during the day.

Braxton had been sitting here, wondering who that someone was.

When he'd bumped into her back at the agency parking lot, he'd slipped his cell phone under her driver's seat. Then, after she'd left, he'd tracked his phone's location via his online "Find My Phone" software. Not exactly a classy move on his part, but how was a guy supposed to ask out a girl if he didn't even know her name?

Although that girl might not be too happy learning what he'd done. But if she were furious, he'd try to at least charm her into giving back his cell phone.

In spite of the cold, he'd rolled down his driver's window, hoping a few stray breezes might freshen the old, musty smell inside the Volvo. A previous owner apparently liked to smoke while driving, because there were lingering scents of stale cigarettes, too. Scents of cooking food wafted his way from Chez Manny... baked chicken and something yeasty-garlicky he imagined to be rolls or calzone or—

Click. Click. Click.

He heard high heels on sidewalk. It was probably her.

He'd parked on the side street so she wouldn't see him when she walked to her car parked in the lot behind the restaurant. Problem was, he couldn't see her, either, until she entered the lot. But the clicks of those heels sounded as if she were coming down the walkway from the restaurant's front door.

He pricked his ears, trying to identify other footsteps with hers. None. Good, she was alone.

Then she entered his line of vision, slim and gray, those hips swaying lightly as she headed to her Benz.

He jumped out of his car, taking care not to slam the door, then jogged across the street.

"Hey, Babe!" he called out, not wanting to scare her by running up too quickly.

She turned, a startled look in her eyes.

He stepped onto the sidewalk, slowing his pace as he crossed into the lot, trying to read her body language, but she stood so stiffly, that was impossible. Moving closer, he tried to catch a hint of her reaction to his surprise appearance and saw, well, surprise.

At least she didn't appear to be pissed off. Things were looking up.

She carried a paperback-size clutch purse, which she held tightly against her chest. Her gaze narrowed as he approached, those sparkling amethyst eyes clouded by suspicion.

Things weren't looking so up.

He stopped, held open his hands apologetically. "I, uh, accidentally dropped my phone in your car."

She tilted her head, flashing an *is that so?* look.

"So, I, uh..." His throat suddenly felt parched, as if he'd been sucking dirt.

"So you checked your phone-locator GPS program and realized with great surprise that you'd *accidentally* dropped it in my car."

Man, she was sharp.

"Something like that."

She made a noise that said more than most people could in a paragraph, mostly that she knew he'd dropped it on purpose to track her, so stop the bull.

*Really* sharp.

When up against that kind of smarts, it was time to stop peddling a story and offer the truth.

"You're right." He smiled.

She didn't smile back.

*At least she's still standing here, not getting into her car.*

"Okay, I admit it," he said, adopting a good-natured

tone, "I dropped my phone in your car so I could find you. Which I was wrong to do," he added quickly, "and I'm sorry."

She released a torrent of breath he could hear ten feet away.

"I don't like your stalking me."

"I'm not stalk—"

"Tracking my location with a GPS device, without my consent, is a crime in Nevada."

"Dumb move to track you, but I didn't want you to get away." That sounded bad. "I mean…"

A horn honked.

She looked over and waved at a light blue Porsche 911 that drove down the street. Glass was too tinted to see the driver's features, but from the size and lack of hair, Braxton guessed it to be a male. A rather well-to-do male based on his choice of vehicle.

As if he cared.

Okay, he did.

He looked back at Frances, who still stood in the same spot, clutching her clutch, staring at him.

*Handle this with aplomb. Don't show you're jealous over Porsche Guy.*

"Who was that?" he asked, trying to sound politely interested.

"What's it to you?"

He caught an intrigued look in her eyes, or maybe he was hoping for a positive sign that she'd stopped thinking he'd committed any felony class D actions.

"You're right. It's none of my business."

"He's an associate."

She'd dropped her edginess, which he took as a sign that she was open to talking more. "Dmitri?"

She hesitated. "No."

"How many associates do you have?"

An almost-smile curved her lips. "How many women do you talk this way to?"

"Only the ones I like. A lot."

He gave his head a shake, realizing vagueness wasn't going to help his cause.

"You," he clarified. "Only you."

She swept a strand of hair off her forehead, the shadows leaving her eyes as she relaxed, and this time that almost-smile made it to her lips.

And in that instant, he felt a mysterious kinship with her, a connection that defied words. He just *felt* it. Sensed the depth of her emotions in those eyes... her wistfulness, dreams, disappointments. And with a yearning that almost hurt, he wanted nothing more than to make this woman happy and satisfied.

To earn her love.

She blinked and the spell was broken.

But from the flush in her cheeks and the way she looked at him—a mix of disbelief and incredulity—he half wondered if she'd felt it, too.

"Let's get your phone," she said quietly.

*Let's.* He liked that.

Turning, she headed to her car.

"Let me get your door," he said, jogging ahead of her.

She pulled out the key and pressed a button. The doors clicked open, and he pulled on the driver's handle, opening the door for her.

She stood, giving him an expectant look. "Aren't you going to get your phone? I don't know where you tossed it."

He grinned, reached under the seat, found it.

Straightening, he dropped it back into his pocket, then stood next to the door as she eased herself into the driver's seat. This was going exceptionally well, so much better than he'd hoped. Time to find out more about this mystery lady who'd stolen his heart.

He leaned over and asked, "What's your name?"

She gave him a Cheshire-cat smile. "Babe."

The door slammed shut.

Stunned, he watched the car pull out of the lot, caught her wave goodbye before the Benz disappeared down the street.

Whatever mysterious kinship he'd felt just got more mysterious. Maybe she wasn't head over heels, but she felt *something* for him, and from those last looks he caught in her eyes, she felt more than mere curiosity. She liked him.

Well, there was only way to solve the riddle of the Babe.

Time to give Dmitri a call and let him know he was interested in that job.

## *CHAPTER FIVE*

IN 1976, BENEDICT MORGAN was hired as a security officer at the MGM Grand in Las Vegas, later renamed Bally's, retiring from there in 2004 as head of its security division. Respected by everyone from union bosses to the housekeeping staff, he had a reputation for being fair, never holding a grudge and quoting sayings, his favorite being, "Courage and a sense of humor is all you need to get by in life."

When he retired, Bally's gave his family lifetime discounts to their facilities. Several times a week, Drake and Braxton used that discount to work out at the Bally's fitness center. This Friday morning, they were grabbing a quick workout before starting their days.

"Let me get this straight," Drake said, grabbing a hand towel to mop the sweat off his brow, "the first time you met her—yesterday, right?—you said her hair looked like a prim schoolmarm bun?"

"Met her on Thursday," Braxton concurred, running on a treadmill, "and I said *uptight,* not *prim.*"

"Big difference." Drake tossed the towel onto a wooden bench. "Let me give you a word of advice, bro. Ladies like to be *complimented,* not insulted."

"After I catch my breath...remind me to laugh."

He pointed to his water bottle where he'd left it on the floor. Drake picked it up and handed it to him.

"Like I said...thought you'd set her up...to do that." Braxton took a swig of water.

"As if I'd waste my money hiring some hot blonde to play out your private-eye fantasy." Drake took back the bottle and dropped it on the bench on his way to a rack of barbells.

"Did you waste your money...paying the entry fee for the Valentine's Day auction?"

"I wanted you to get out of the house."

"To be a...stud muffin?"

Drake, carrying a set of barbells, headed back to his spot on the mat. "You wish."

Braxton had to smile. Yeah, he wished. Ever since meeting Miss Smoky-Voiced Bacall, he had wanted nothing more than to be her personal bakery item. And when Dmitri called him back and they set up a meeting to discuss this new security position, Braxton would finally find out Babe's real name.

"What else did you say to this mystery blonde?"

"You don't wanna know." Brax tugged up the edge of his T-shirt, using it to wipe a glob of sweat off his chin.

"Try me."

"Told her she looked...like Frau Farbissina."

His brother was one of those guys who could keep a straight face in the weirdest situations. The Three Stooges could be running amok in this workout room, giving each other noogies and eye pokes, and Drake would remain stone-faced. Not that it'd be easy, but he could do it.

But at the moment, he had a look on his face as though he'd just downed an entire pack of Warheads Sour Dippers candies.

"Can't believe your mouth kept going after that bun line." He straightened, a barbell in each hand. "She's Dmitri's associate, eh?"

Braxton nodded.

"Know what she does there?" Drake slowly curled the weights toward his shoulders.

"No idea, but she drives a Benz."

"Yeah, Grams told me."

"How'd she know?"

"Thought you told her." He lowered the weights to his sides.

No, but Brax had mentioned it to Val, who'd obviously shared it with his grandmother. Didn't these people have anything better to talk about?

Drake gave his brother a knowing look. "You did something to that Benz, didn't you?"

Sometimes Brax thought the two of them could have their own cable psychic show, except instead of reading other people's minds, they'd read each other's.

"Yeah...I did something." He walked, trying to catch his breath. "Threw my...phone in it."

Drake rolled his eyes to the heavens as though seeking divine intervention. "I can't believe how dumb you are. You tracked her to where?"

"Chez Manny."

"That place still open?"

Braxton nodded.

"What'd you do—walk into the restaurant and ask her out?" Drake kept lifting the barbells, never missing a beat, his biceps bulging.

"I have…more class…than that."

"Accosted her in the parking lot?"

"*Accosted*…is a…very strong word."

Drake snorted a laugh. "Please tell me she didn't call the police."

Braxton ran hard and panted. "She was…pleased to see me."

Okay, *pleased* might be pushing it, but it was close.

"But you still don't know her name."

"She had…to leave…quickly."

Drake glanced at the wall clock. "As do I. Hey, Val and I talked last night about that due-diligence report you showed us. If it were a report card, Dmitri would be an A-plus student." He kept lifting the bells, his breathing even. "He's got the business chops to help you carve a future. Just be sure you want it for yourself—not because you want to score with this blonde."

"Eighty percent, self…twenty, the blonde."

"Called him yet?"

"Left two messages…said I was interested."

"Good."

Braxton had been concerned he would be letting Val and Drake down if he left Morgan-LeRoy, but Val reminded him their invitation for him to join the agency as a contractor had always been with the understanding he could come and go as he wished. They'd never said it, but deep down he sensed they'd offered him that desk so he'd have a job to go to every day, a stepping stone to regaining his self-esteem.

At first he'd felt awkward sitting there like some kind of male receptionist. At least he made a damned good pot of coffee, and he liked clients meeting him in a real office instead of some coffee shop, but most of all he liked having a purpose again.

"Gonna miss you guys," he said.

"Not for long. Remember, you're our standby sitter after the baby arrives." He glanced at the wall clock again. "Mind holding down the agency until noon or so? Told Val I'd take her out to breakfast, then we're going birthday-gift shopping for Grams. Don't forget—we're all meeting at eleven-thirty Sunday for her birthday brunch. Cara's on the ground floor at Sensuelle. Can't miss it."

Cara was a new Italian restaurant at Sensuelle, the same casino where the Valentine's Day auction was taking place. Grams had selected Sensuelle to host this Keep 'Em Rolling auction fund-raiser, then asked for her birthday to be celebrated there, as well.

The auction would inevitably come up at the family get-together.

"After I get home…I'll tell Grams…I can't do the auction."

Drake gave him a look. "Can't believe you haven't told her yet."

Too difficult to talk, walk *and* feel guilt-ridden at the same time. Braxton punched a button to decrease the cardio program speed, and the treadmill started to slow.

"Wanted to the last…few nights, but…she was out."

"She and Richmond are out *every* night these days."

And all night, too, but Braxton didn't want to think about his grandmother having sex. Not that Grams was a fuddy-duddy. When he was ten years old, she'd slipped him a book about the birds and the bees, told him to feel free to ask any questions. He'd opened the book and asked why there were so many pictures of pollywogs swimming. She smiled and said, "Because they're *very happy* pollywogs, darling."

"Told Mom you're getting your own place?" Pushing out an exhale, Drake raised the weights.

More guilt. "No."

"Bro, you gotta stop putting off these talks."

*I'm not your kid brother, I'm your twin. Born four minutes before you, by the way.* Which Braxton would say out loud if he didn't have to pause for breaths every few words.

Pissed him off that his brother could pump iron and talk at the same time.

And that he was right.

Again.

Although, in Braxton's defense, it wasn't easy to schedule a face-to-face with his social-butterfly grandmother these days.

But his mom…he didn't want to tell her he was

thinking about getting his own place because it would upset her. They'd spent years not talking, losing time as a family, and she felt as though they were still making up for that loss.

She'd never said that, but he knew it. Because he felt the same way.

"I'm hitting the shower," Drake said, setting his barbells back in the rack, "then leaving to pick up Val."

"See you this afternoon." Brax caught his brother's look. "Look, I'll tell them, 'kay?"

After Drake left, Brax continued walking as the machine slowed to a stop, then stepped onto the floor and stood there for a moment, drying his face with a towel.

Coming back into the family fold hadn't been easy, but now that he was with them, he didn't want to start leaving again. Leaving Drake and Val at the Morgan-LeRoy agency. Leaving Mom and Grams at his childhood home. Hell, even leaving his grandmother's damned fund-raising event.

There'd been some lonely years when he had wished he could just hear his mom's voice. He wasn't ready to not hear her traipsing down the hall, asking if he'd mind taking out the trash, joking while they cooked dinner, even grumping around in the morning, muttering about the neighbors' barking dog.

He'd been her prodigal son who'd squandered his money, dirtied his reputation and shamed his family. And then one day, he realized he'd lost his way, lost the people who mattered most.

The night last August when he was finally man

enough to return home, he hadn't known what to expect, only what he hoped for.

Brax headed to the rack of barbells and selected two forty-pounders.

If he wanted to look good at that auction, he needed to shred some muscle.

On Sunday, shortly after eleven, the taxi pulled into the congested parking area in front of Sensuelle. A fat drop of rain splatted on the windshield.

"Ain't that sumpthin'," the cabbie said, looking up at the gray clouds. "Weather guy said rain yesterday, not a drop. Said sunshine today, we're gettin' rain." With a shrug, he turned off the meter. "Twenty-two dollars."

Braxton gave him twenty-five, tucked his birthday present to Grams under his suit jacket and exited the taxi. Cold drops of rain stung his face as he dashed between cars toward the front doors of the hotel-casino.

Inside the lobby, he paused to shake the moisture from his hair. Outside, thunder rumbled. Just a few hours ago, skies had been clear and blue, barely a cloud in sight. The only thing consistent about Vegas weather this time of year was its unpredictability.

He turned and headed toward the casino, then stopped. A sign—had to be fifteen feet high—hung over the entrance. Underneath a photo of some guy wearing little more than a hey-girl smile were the words:

**MAGIC DREAM DATE AUCTION**
*Ladies, Win a Date with the
Manwich of Your Dreams!*
Studs up for Sale, Starting Bids $10
Raise Money for Keep 'Em Rolling!
***Highest bid wins a car!***

Gritting his teeth, he kept walking, mentally reciting his new mantra. *I'm doing it for Grams. I'm doing it for Grams.*

After navigating his way through a small city of clanging, buzzing slot machines and taking a detour around a group of drunk guys wearing baseball caps that read Team Groom, he spied the sparkling green-and-red sign, Cara.

A few minutes later, a perky hostess wearing a name tag that said Sally from Boise, Idaho, ushered him through the restaurant to a large round table in the back, an arrangement of pink roses in the middle. At the table sat a chubby guy with wiry brown hair, nursing a drink with an umbrella. In front of him, an empty bread basket and a paper bag with a bow stapled on it.

Li'l Bit.

A thirtysomething process server who was good friends with Drake, although to Braxton they had about as much in common as Dick Cheney and Adam Sandler. But as Drake explained it, he and Li'l Bit shared a passion for their professions, and they always had each other's backs.

Braxton's grandmother and Li'l Bit were also friends after discovering their mutual hero worship of *Inner Sanctum Mysteries,* an old-time radio program that broadcast shows with ghoulish names like "Tempo in Blood" and "The Unforgiving Corpse." Every week or so, Li'l Bit would drop by the house and listen to a show with Grams while she sipped a martini and puffed her nightly cigarillo. Li'l Bit usually drank a beer or three and, from the occasional whiff of ganja Braxton detected, toked a joint.

"Nice threads, man." Li'l Bit, his eyes pinker than the roses, nodded approvingly at Braxton's oxford-gray suit and vest.

Braxton set his gift on the table and took a seat, eyeing the words on Li'l Bit's T-shirt, Life Goes On, Man.

Seeing Brax check out his T-shirt, Li'l Bit said, "Yeah, it's from *The Big Lebowski*. That was a killer movie. Jeff Bridges, man, he rocked as The Dude. 'Life Goes On, Man' is one of The Dude's sayings." Turning somber, he leaned forward, nearly knocking over his umbrella drink. "But it's more than that. That quote is like a vibe that resonates through time, man, touching people with its energy."

Braxton nodded, hoping other people would arrive soon. Perhaps someone from this decade.

"Hey, your mom told me you got some new gig. Head of security?"

"Yes," Braxton answered.

Li'l Bit made a power fist, pumping the air with it a few times. "That's righteous, dude."

"Thanks." Okay, he got that his brother and Grams were pals with Li'l Bit, but with his mom, too? She was so restrained, so conservative, so...un-ganjalike.

"Wonder where that waiter-dude went," Li'l Bit said, scratching his chin as he looked around the room. "We're outta bread, and I need a mai tai refiller."

"What did my mother say about the job?"

When Braxton had first told her about it a few days ago, she'd seemed more taken aback than happy, although she'd quickly recovered and said it sounded like a great opportunity. She had always been like that—preferring to show support for others rather than express her own opinions.

Li'l Bit looked at him. "Huh?"

"The job. Head of security. What'd my mom say about it?"

"Man, told her I'd not repeat a word." He made a motion of locking his lips and throwing away the key.

"Repeat—" Unbelievable. This Jerry Garcia wannabe was his mother's *confidant?* He was trying to come up with a next question that might open those invisibly locked lips when he heard a familiar woman's voice.

"Hey, you two, starting the party without me?"

Grams sat regally in her wheelchair, resplendent in a pink-and-orange caftan dotted with rhinestones whose sparkle paled compared to the diamond heirloom ring she wore.

Looking at the roses on the table, she touched the hand of the older gentleman standing next to her. "Richmond, darling, you ordered my *favorite* roses."

Richmond had always reminded Braxton of a balding version of Anthony Hopkins. He had a thing for bow ties—today he wore a burgundy one with a crisp white shirt and blue cardigan—lending him a studious air, fitting for the retired American history professor.

"How'd your sleuthing go?" she asked Braxton.

He shrugged. "No signs of you-know-who."

Earlier, he'd taken a taxi—didn't want to risk someone tracing his license plate—to a check-cashing business Dmitri had called him about, claiming a "compatriot" told him Yuri was fencing goods there. So Braxton visited the place, checked out the license plates in the lot, asked some innocent-sounding questions. Not a single indication Yuri was conducting any dirty business there.

"And you," Grams said, turning to Li'l Bit. "Still feeling tired?"

"A little bit," he said, pointing to the empty bread basket as a waiter walked by.

Braxton had heard that response was what had earned the stoner his nickname.

Satisfied more bread was on its way, Li'l Bit held up the paper bag, "Found those cigarillos you like, Glenda."

Why'd he bother to wrap the gift, or paper-bag it, if he was just gonna broadcast its contents before she opened it? But it didn't seem to bother Grams, who gushed about his finding her favorite cigarillos, which apparently were scarce.

"Your mother should be here any moment," Grams

said to Braxton. "She dropped us off at the handicapped parking spot—covered, thank goodness—then parked the car. Where would you like us to sit, dear?"

"Wherever the birthday girl wishes."

As Richmond guided the wheelchair to a spot, his mom arrived, her hair a little frizzy from the rain, clutching a white box with a big pink bow. Leaning over, she kissed Braxton on the cheek.

"I forgot to get a birthday card," she whispered.

"Me, too," he whispered back.

To him, it wasn't a big deal. But his mom thrived on order, tradition and responsibility. Which had always struck him as funny, considering she was raised by Grams, who was glitzier than Joan Collins.

Today his mom wore black pants and a white blouse, her only accessory a string of pearls, a long-ago birthday gift from his dad. She nervously clutched the gift as though unsure where to put it…or herself. Dorothy Morgan exuded confidence when it came to organizing potlucks for her bowling league or arranging dinner parties at the house, but grew uncomfortable in "showy" places, which she viewed this restaurant to be, nervous that she might break some rule.

Benedict Morgan had always told his wife she was too hard on herself. Nevertheless, whenever they were in public, Benny had been her protector. He'd walked close to her, ensured she had a comfortable seat, brought her drinks and anything else she wanted, so she never had to deal with crowds, rules or her own self-doubts.

"Let me help you, Mom." Braxton stood, took the gift from her and set it on the table, then pulled out the chair next to his.

With a smile of relief, she sat.

He looked around, didn't see a waiter. "Want me to get you a glass of white wine?" he asked.

"Thank you."

By the time Braxton returned from the bar with wine for his mom and a martini for Grams, Drake and Val had arrived.

Presents were piled on a chair next to his grandmother, and Li'l Bit was entertaining everyone with the story of the first time he met Val and how she'd threatened to throw a plant through his window. Everyone had heard it many times, but apparently this was the first for Richmond, who had a look of surprise on his face.

"So," Li'l Bit said, "I said to her through the closed door, 'Lady, you and your negative energy need to leave, man!'"

Val jumped in. "That's when, as my nanny used to say, the cheese slid off my cracker. You know, I went a little crazy. With good reason! I'd had a rough day tossing back vodka shots with Russian thugs, plus I was worried something awful about Drake, who'd been missing for hours, so *I* said to the door, 'I suggest you step back from your window, *man,* 'cause the glass is gonna fly!'"

Everybody laughed, except Richmond, who looked frightened.

Fortunately, a waiter appeared with more beverages and took everyone's food order. After he left, Grams tapped the edge of her water glass with her knife. Once she had everyone's attention, she smiled sweetly and said, "Richmond and I have an announcement."

Richmond cleared his throat and took Grams's hand in his. "I've asked this lovely lady to marry me, and she said yes."

As they kissed, everyone clapped.

"Being pregnant gets me so darn emotional," Val said, dabbing the corner of her eye with a napkin.

"Darling," Grams said to her, "I'm wearing the family heirloom ring because you asked me to, but after the baby arrives in May, it's yours again." She looked up at her husband-to-be. "The following month, this June bride will be wearing her own wedding ring."

Braxton stood, raising his wineglass. "I'd like to give a toast to the bride- and groom-to-be."

As he looked at his grandmother's twinkling jade-green eyes, he flashed on a long-ago memory of her moving into his family's house after the sudden death of her husband, Jack. For weeks afterward, Grams, never one to wear her pain, kept up a good front during the day, but at night he'd hear her softly crying in her room.

He glanced around the table, thinking about how each of them had weathered tough times. His mom losing her husband, he and Drake their father, nearly four years ago. Drake overcoming his gambling demons. Val surviving Katrina.

Li'l Bit...well, he must have weathered a scarcity of weed at some point in this life.

And Braxton survived the near loss of his family, the greatest loss he could imagine. To be here with all of them again, celebrating another milestone, was something he'd never take for granted again.

"Damn," he rasped, fighting to keep it together, "I must be pregnant, too!"

After the laughter subsided, he raised his glass once more. "To Grams and Richmond...there is only one true happiness in life, and that is to love and be loved."

As Braxton sat, Richmond stood. He gestured to the bouquet of flowers, his hand trembling slightly, then looked down lovingly at Grams's upturned face.

"If I had a rose for every time I thought of you, I could walk in my garden forever."

More clapping and a few sniffles.

"Welcome to the family, Richmond."

"Better learn how to make martinis!"

Then Li'l Bit stood, tears rolling down his face. He raised his Mai Tai, which now had two umbrellas, to Richmond and Glenda.

"You guys," he said, his voice breaking, "you're like the bomb, man."

As he downed the rest of his drink, everyone clapped.

Val started to stand, then sat back down as Li'l Bit continued talking.

"Glenda, I memorized some dialogue from our favorite *Inner Sanctum* show, 'The Skull That...'" He paused to wave his empty glass at a passing waiter.

Val shot a worried look at Braxton, as though he could stop this downhill train on its flaming collision course to hell.

He had to try. Nobody wanted a quote from the skull. "Li'l Bit," he said, "maybe you can share this later with Grams."

"It's okay, dude, I remember the words." He focused again on Grams. "Like I was sayin', this is from that primo show 'The Skull That Walked' because it reminded me of you and Richmond."

He closed his eyes and inhaled deeply.

"'I know it sounds strange…fantastic…but it's real, Helen,' he said in a deep, radio-announcer-like voice. 'This thing seeks to dominate, to possess me. Lately, I have begun to feel its presence in my sleep, during my waking hours. It controls my actions like a hypnotist controls his subject.'"

He opened his eyes and cast a proud look around the table, seemingly unaware that he'd done anything out of the norm.

Braxton shot a look at Grams. To his astonishment, she was staring fondly at Li'l Bit as though his walking-skull recitation was beautiful. Even Richmond looked moved.

"Of course, that was about the invisible monster," Li'l Bit said, back to his own voice again, "but I thought those words were right-on 'cause they describe—" his chin trembled "—the awesome power of your love." He raised his empty Mai Tai glass. "Richmond, I love you, man. Welcome to the family."

*Welcome to the family?*

Braxton raised his glass along with everyone else, not liking what he'd heard. Great if Li'l Bit wanted to hang out with his grandmother and Drake, but no way the dude was becoming a permanent fixture at their family get-togethers. He wasn't flesh and blood. He hadn't been there when Braxton was nine years old, sitting in the front row with his mom and Drake, bursting with pride as they watched Benedict Morgan accept an award from the mayor of Las Vegas for saving dozens of lives during a gangland shooting at Bally's.

Li'l Bit didn't know what it was like to be an outcast, to sit in the dark watching your childhood home that you couldn't go back into, aching to be part of it again. Why did he get to waltz in when Braxton had had to crawl back?

*Life might go on, man, but not with my family.*

A SHORT TIME later, everyone at the table was eating, drinking, chatting. As Braxton dug into his rigatoni with eggplant puree, he checked out the other Italian dishes around the table—chicken cacciatore, spaghetti, lasagna—and a thick-crust large pizza smothered with ham, jalapenos and pineapple for Li'l Bit.

"Hey, bro," Drake said, "did I see you in that dream-date poster hanging in the lobby?"

"Yeah," Braxton grumped, "Brad Pitt wasn't available, so they asked for me."

Li'l Bit, a chunk of pineapple stuck on his T-shirt,

did a double take. "Wow, Brad Pitt's gonna be in that auction, too?"

"No, dear," Grams answered. "They're joking. And that isn't Braxton in the picture, either."

"Oh, yeah, I knew that. Poster guy looks a lot younger. Hey, Brax, gonna shave your chest like that dude?"

"No." He stabbed his fork at his rigatoni. Irked him to be called Brax by anybody other than family. Especially *that* anybody.

"I think it's mandatory," Drake said, fighting to keep a straight face.

"Think again. And by the way, I'm not *that* much older than poster boy and his fake tan and digitally enhanced six-pack." He shoved the bite into his mouth.

"Getting kinda defensive, bro," Drake said.

"Maybe 'cause I'm getting kinda tired of you harassing me, *bro*," he shot back. "Like you'd be so easygoing if you had to strut you stuff wearing a pair of your hottie-whitie-tighties."

"*Harassing* you? Ouch!" Drake looked at his wife. "You kicked me."

She smiled sweetly at everyone. "Hormones. I do declare, being pregnant makes my body do the strangest things."

Ping. Ping. Ping.

Grams, tapping her knife on her water glass, got everyone's attention.

"Another announcement," she said. "This time to honor Braxton for being a guinea pig—I mean *volun-*

*teer*—for my fund-raiser." She waited for the laughs, which she got. "Last year we hosted a silent auction for Keep 'Em Rolling and raised twenty thousand dollars. This year I'm hoping the auction raises at least thirty."

"Hear, hear!"

"Let's do it, Grams!"

"Yes," she agreed, "let's do it!" She paused. "I'm one of the fortunate ones who can afford to buy an electric wheelchair with all kinds of goodies." She patted the chair arm. "This baby has a portable charger, adjustable armrests, swivel seat and maxes out at eight miles an hour."

"You said seventeen," Dorothy interjected.

"Yes, I did," Grams admitted, "because I just couldn't resist that bad-girl-on-wheels reputation." She sighed theatrically. "But the truth is I rarely go over five."

Dorothy gave a small smile. "You're incorrigible."

"I hope so. Anyway, there are people in Las Vegas who desperately need wheelchairs but can't buy them themselves, which is why Keep 'Em Rolling is near and dear to my heart. Our volunteers renovate wheelchairs for those in need." She looked around the table, her eyes shiny. "Makes me proud my family will be here next Friday night to support Braxton as he helps us raise money for this wonderful cause."

Braxton hadn't heard about this being a family affair until now.

"No pictures." He jabbed a finger at Drake. "I mean it."

Drake held up his hands in mock surrender. "Bro, thought never crossed my mind."

"Uh-huh." He glanced at Grams, whose sweet, appreciative look warmed him like sunshine.

Truth was, he'd do anything she asked. During those years when he'd been banned from the house and the rest of the family had treated him like a pariah, she'd called every week to ask how he was doing. After she started dating Richmond, he'd drive her to meet Braxton for dinner, once on his birthday. He'd never forget her singing "Happy Birthday" to him, tears shimmering in her eyes. Knowing how his lousy life choices had hurt her just about did him in. When he'd blown out the candle on the cake she'd brought—chocolate with cream-cheese filling, his favorite—his only wish was to fix his life so he could go home again.

He smiled at Grams, thinking she had to be one of the coolest ladies—young, old or anywhere in-between—on the planet.

She raised her martini to him in a quiet salute.

"Know the kind of car they're giving away?" Drake asked.

Braxton shook his head no. "Haven't heard."

"A cherry-red...Mustang...Shelby...GT500."

The world shrank to a distant memory.

As a kid, Braxton had a poster of that Shelby on his wall. That slick red 'Stang was the last thing he saw before falling asleep and the first thing he saw when he woke up.

He'd named his hamster Shelby.

Practiced drawing the Shelby, over and over, with red felt pen, putting his best sketch on homemade Christmas cards.

Begged his parents to let him change his name to...

"Did'ya hear me, Brax?" Drake asked.

"That's no car," Braxton murmured. "It's a road-eating monster."

Drake laughed. "So you still want one of those, eh?"

"Want? Bro, I *covet*. What does a guy have to do to win this thing? Because now that I know it's the giveaway prize, I'm ready to lose every ounce of dignity I've ever had and win that baby."

"Be like one of those strippers you used to manage at that club," Val offered. "As naked as the law allows and flashing moves that'll make those ladies hotter than a bunch of June brides."

He thought about those strippers at Topaz who'd lie on their backs and scissor-kick their legs in the air, or hang upside down on poles by the sheer strength of their thighs, doing contortions that were probably illegal in most states.

He, on the other hand, could barely keep time doing a two-step.

"I'll, uh, need to work on my moves." He looked at Grams. "How naked are guys getting?"

"You can't show your..." Searching for an appropriate word, she looked at Richmond.

"Hampton," he suggested.

She frowned. "Who calls it that?"

"It's a euphemism that originated in London, migrating to the states in the early twentieth century, I believe."

"Eighty-six years old," she muttered, "and I'm *still* learning new things." She looked back at Braxton. "You can't show your Hampton, dear."

"I have a G-string," Li'l Bit offered out of the blue.

Followed by a moment of stunned silence that lasted longer than the one after his *Inner Sanctum* speech.

"No, thanks," Braxton said.

"No, dude, I'm not offering it to *you*. I'm thinking of entering this gig myself. Helping people get wheelchairs, man, that's copacetic. Already got a car, so don't care if I win that Shelby. It's just...ever since Xela—" he swallowed hard "—broke up with me, I haven't had a date. It'd be nice to meet someone...."

He carefully folded a piece of pizza like a sandwich and wolfed down a bite.

Braxton had heard about Xela, a massage therapist Li'l Bit had met five or six years ago while attending law school in Brooklyn. When she left for Las Vegas, he ditched his plan to be a lawyer and followed her, only to be dumped when Xela ran away with a Cirque du Soleil acrobat. Although Li'l Bit was heartbroken, his process service business, Boss Services Inc., had started to thrive, plus he'd grown attached to the senior dogs at the Canine Retirement Ranch project where he volunteered, so he had decided to stay in Vegas.

"I think it's a wonderful idea that you enter the auction," Grams said. "With so many single ladies, there might be someone special who can help you forget Xela."

Li'l Bit chewed, nodding sadly.

"It's an opportunity for you, too, bro, to meet some new ladies," Drake said, "and get your mind off that blonde."

"What blonde?" his mom asked.

"Some Lauren Bacall type came into the office," Val explained, "and shook up Brax somethin' awful."

Still shook him up, too. More than that Shelby ever could.

He'd spent the past few days trying to find out her real name. Had read through Dmitri's background report several times, searching for any mention of an American woman in her late twenties who worked for one of his organizations, but found nothing.

On his way over in the taxi, tired of playing phone tag with Dmitri, he'd texted him, suggested they meet tomorrow, Monday, just name when and where. Wherever Dmitri was, she had to be; after all, they were associates.

He tugged his phone from his jacket pocket, checked if the Russian had responded yet. No.

Putting the phone away, he heard Li'l Bit asking, "Think I can get into Manwich shape by Friday? Not *total* Manwich, man, just Manwich enough."

"You'd need to cool it with the pizza, for starters," Drake answered, "as well as the popcorn and beer and…"

"Dude," he said, pushing away his plate, "I'm on it."

This had to be a joke. But no one was laughing. Not even smiling.

"This is what I've been waiting for," Li'l Bit continued, wiping his mouth with the back of his hand, "an opportunity to get righteous. Good news is I already have some killer dance moves. Just need to get into shape, man. Maybe I'll take up walking."

"Or," Grams said, "maybe Drake will let you use his discount at the Bally's gym this week. Braxton can work out with you, show you how to use the equipment."

What? How'd he become the sacrificial personal trainer? Oh, yeah, just how he wanted to spend his free time, getting Ganja Joe into shape.

"Discounts are for family members only," he said. "No substitutions."

Grams looked disappointed. "What a shame. Especially since Li'l Bit is just like a member of our family."

*Just like a member of our family.* Had she really said that?

"He sure is," Val chimed in. "I'll never forget how he gave Drake and his sweet dog a place to stay after his house burned down."

*Et tu, Val?*

"Tell you what," Drake said, all serious and helpful, "I'll call Pete—he manages the fitness center at Bally's—ask if he'll do us a favor. Tell him I'd like to give Li'l Bit my discount this next week...how we're trying to help him get into shape for Gram's fund-raiser. Pete's a great guy. I bet he'll turn his head on that family rule."

Li'l Bit looked as though someone just told him Xela had dumped the acrobat and was asking if Li'l Bit was still single. "You'd do that for me, man? Give up your gym pass for a week?"

"Yeah," Drake said, holding up his hand, "I'd do that for you."

As they slapped high fives, Braxton downed the rest of his wine. He'd finally gotten his head on straight about this auction, and now this. Since when did helping others also mean helping a chubby stoner get into shape? As if that was even possible in five days.

He looked around, wondering why every single person at the table was looking back. "What?"

"Li'l Bit just offered to teach you some dance moves," Grams said.

"Winner's gotta know how to shake it, bro," Drake said, "and if you want a chance at that Shelby…"

Had everyone at the table dropped acid? Because they had to be hallucinating if they thought *he* was taking *dance lessons* from Dude-Man.

"Look," he said, "no way I'm—"

A squeal drowned out the rest of his words.

"The baby's kicking again!" Val took Drake's hand and put it on her tummy. "Feel that, honey? He's gonna be a punter for the Saints!"

Everyone shifted focus to Val, who was excitedly gushing about every sensation.

"Been so bloated lately," she said, picking up her

glass of ice water and holding it to her flushed cheek, "sometimes I'm not sure if it's gas or kicks."

Li'l Bit began asking rapid-fire questions about what it was like to be pregnant, making Braxton wonder if the weed was wearing off, with Val answering in way more graphic detail than Braxton had ever wanted to know. Worse, his mother was offering tidbits about *her* experience when she'd been pregnant thirty-four years ago.

While that TMI Q&A session charged on, Grams started singing "One for My Baby," which inspired Richmond, Mister Reserved, to shed his introverted ways and join in. Which wouldn't have been bad except he sang about as well as Braxton danced.

Meanwhile Drake, his hand on his wife's belly, was describing the latest kick to total strangers at the next table. Surprisingly, they seemed interested.

Braxton looked around, wondering when the pod people had taken over his family. Li'l Bit, well…they'd taken him over a long time ago.

As though picking up on Braxton's thoughts, Li'l Bit looked at him, fresh tears welling in his eyes, and got up from his seat.

"Brax, man, you're like a brother to me," he said, heading around to Braxton's chair, opening wide his arms. "Helping me out like this 'n all."

"Don't you have more childbirth questions to ask Val?" he mumbled.

Stopping at Braxton's chair, Li'l Bit leaned over and smothered him in a hug. "I love you, my brother."

His face pressed against the words *Life Goes On, Man,* breathing in a funk-cloud of marijuana, Mai Tai and pizza sauce, Braxton knew he'd been beaten.

By his own family.

## *CHAPTER SIX*

THE NEXT MORNING Braxton was making scrambled eggs and toast when his mom shuffled into the kitchen, wearing the fluffy white robe embroidered with a large pink *D* on the front that he and Grams had given for her last birthday.

"That dog barked half the night," she muttered, staring blearily at the cuckoo clock, except it had a chicken instead, that clucked once every hour, but it hadn't clucked in years. "Nine-thirty. You're usually long gone by now."

"Got a meeting at eleven...going into the agency after that." He whisked some eggs in a stainless-steel bowl. "Want breakfast?"

"You know me," she said, ambling toward the coffeepot. "Go for the gold."

She'd always told her sons that breakfast was gold, lunch was silver and dinner was lead. Which meant they needed to eat a hearty breakfast to kick off the day, a nutritious lunch, but don't stuff yourself at dinner because it'll go onto your gut. He was pretty good with the first two, not so good with the last. At least he worked out regularly.

*Working out.*

After yesterday's brunch, those words were like lead, too. Li'l Bit had already texted him *twice* about exercising together. Same message—Dude, 530?—which Braxton assumed meant five-thirty today, but who knew what mysteries lurked in that stoner's brain.

He'd respond later. Hopefully, he'd be in a better mood about being railroaded into this personal-trainer gig.

"Didn't know we had chives on hand," his mom said, pouring herself a cup of coffee, "or sourdough bread."

"Got up early and went to the store." He retrieved a carton of milk from the fridge and set it on the small table. The kitchen was long, but so narrow that everything was within a few steps.

"Eggs, toast and strong coffee." His mom smiled. "Benny's breakfast special."

"The *only* thing he ever cooked for breakfast."

"That's what made it special."

They shared a laugh.

When Braxton had lived life in the fast lane, he'd loved the heady excitement, the constant rush of color, sounds and people.

Now he realized how much he'd missed back then. Now he valued taking it slower, sometimes wishing the people he loved would stay put and never change. To always be like they were in the photos here, frozen forever in sunlight, always smiling.

"Nice to have breakfast with someone," his mom

said, forks and knifes clinking as she retrieved them from a drawer. "With your grandmother spending every night at Richmond's, I'm on my own in the mornings. Felt odd at first...waking up to an empty house...."

"At least Grams and Richmond will be living on the same block. You can always walk down there, join them for a cup of coffee."

"Yes," she said brightly, heading to the table, "I can certainly do that. And they'll be dropping by to borrow my car off and on because Richmond's beloved BMW is acting up again. Anyway, tell me about this eleven-o'clock meeting—is it with that fellow who's offering you a job?"

"Yes."

"Demetrius?"

"Dmitri. Goes by Dima."

"Dima," she repeated, arranging the silverware on the table. "Almost sounds like *demon*."

"He comes across like a heavenly messenger in that due-diligence report. Worse thing he's done is get a speeding ticket two years ago."

She sat down and poured milk into her coffee. "Val told me this blonde works for Dima."

"Uh-huh."

"Drake says she's not the sole reason you're interested in the job, though."

"Uh-uh."

"You don't know her name?"

*Babe.* "Nope."

"Or anything else about her?"

Whisking the eggs, he slid her a look. "Are you worried that she works in security or private investigations?"

Her lips tightened. "Well, she did drop off that background report. Your father, your brother, your sister-in-law, even *you* have prepared such reports, and all of you work in investigations and security."

His mom had never approved of her husband's profession in security, always feared he'd get hurt on the job, but Benedict Morgan, a former Chicago cop, had loved his job at Bally's. Liked helping people, liked nailing the bad guys, liked making the world a safer, better place in his own small way.

Dorothy did, however, share her husband's idealism. When they'd met in the mid-seventies, she was considering going to law school to be a human-rights lawyer—the last thing she expected was to meet a rough-around-the-edges cop who asked her to marry him on their first date. Yet they fell madly in love, two people who shared a passion for justice, even if they quibbled over the details. When the twins came, Dorothy Morgan discovered a career far more rewarding than any she had imagined—being a mom.

"I don't know her job title," Braxton said, "but I didn't see the bulge of a gun under her jacket, so who knows…maybe she's a lawyer."

She made an approving noise. "Lawyer. Respectable profession. Good income. Wonder what her last name is…."

"Why?"

"Oh, just thinking how Val likes to combine her and Drake's last names. Morgan-LeRoy. Has a ring to it."

"Whoa, hold on." He turned off the burner, stuck two pieces of sourdough bread into the toaster. "I just met her, and you're hyphenating our names?" He crossed to the fridge. "Strawberry jam or blueberry?"

"Strawberry."

He grabbed it, set it on the table.

"It's just...from things your brother and others have said, you're so smitten. Don't know if I've ever seen you like this over a girl."

"Smitten is a world away from hyphenating my last name, Mom."

He turned away, busying himself with distributing the scrambled eggs onto two plates. Nice—his brother and other family members were yammering behind his back about being smitten, but since when did that mean a guy was ready to say "I do"?

"I've been meaning to talk to you about something," his mom said.

"Yeah?" He looked over his shoulder.

"Just because your grandmother's moving out—" she absently played with the collar on her robe "—doesn't mean you shouldn't, too. I'll be fine."

That hitch in her tone didn't sound fine, though.

Then it hit him. *Felt odd at first...waking up to an empty house.*

In the thirty-five years she'd lived in this house, she had never been alone. Not for more than a night, anyway. Had to be scary, facing a life of solitude at sixty-six years old. This was probably what she had confided to Li'l Bit in an unguarded moment. She'd no doubt regretted telling him the instant the words slipped from her mouth, so she insisted he keep it a secret.

Braxton knew why. Dorothy Morgan didn't like to let down her guard, because she didn't want people to catch a glimpse of her worries and hurts. If he'd learned anything from his past, it was that when you finally let down your guard and admitted your flaws and mistakes, people would stand by you. Those that didn't, eff 'em. You didn't want them in your life anyway.

He wished he could magically plant that philosophy in her heart and brain.

After cornering the eggs with toast, he served their plates and sat down opposite her. "Be present at our table, Lord," he said quietly.

As they ate in silence for a few moments, he mulled over how to ease her concerns. She had so much pride—*prides herself on her pride,* his dad used to say—so Braxton wanted to say this right, because God forbid anyone ever treated Dorothy Morgan like a pity case.

"Ordered something a few days ago," he said casually.

Actually, he hadn't ordered it yet, but he'd been thinking about it.

"What?"

"A five-foot outdoor Scrabble board." He took a sip of coffee, watching her over the rim of the cup.

She blinked. Several times. "*Five* feet?"

"Actually, it's a five-by-five square."

"Why? So it can be seen from outer space?"

He laughed. "It's made of concrete squares. Doubles as a patio floor. Figured I'd put it near the grill so when you throw your springtime barbecue parties, everyone can play outdoor Scrabble, too."

She nodded approvingly. "Inventive."

"Be a while before it's ready, though. Need to build a wooden frame, pour the concrete, score it into squares...."

"*You're* going to do this."

"Yeah."

"But...you don't like building things."

More like he sucked at it big-time, but trust a mother to cast it in a kinder light. "Maybe I want to make up for that D-minus I got in wood shop."

"Oh, my," she said, glancing at the kitchen clock, "I remember when your father found those report cards...."

As a freshman in high school, Braxton had tried to make a canoe paddle in wood shop. Several mangled pieces of wood later, he'd finally created one. While showing off for some girl, he'd wielded it like a sword and accidentally hit it against a wall, breaking off its shaft. Semester projects were due, so he sanded down the blade and called it a breadboard.

In the same class, Drake had created a cherrywood bumper pool table that placed first at the state competition.

When semester report cards arrived, Braxton, ashamed he'd received a D-minus in wood shop, especially as Drake, The Wood Shop King, got an A-plus, hid both cards in the back of the kitchen cuckoo clock. Not a well-thought-out plan, as within hours, the chicken stopped clucking.

Which led to his dad taking off the back of the clock and finding the crumpled report cards. One look at the grades, and Benny Morgan figured out the reason for the clock-stuffing. He didn't get mad, just told Braxton that if he ever felt embarrassed for not being as skilled as somebody else, he needed to focus on his own accomplishments. *Maybe your brother is a talented carpenter,* his dad had said, *but you can cook circles around him.*

His mom spread some jam on her toast. "I still have that breadboard, you know."

"I know." He'd seen it on her dresser, polished and on display as if it were some kind of art piece.

"Back to this supersize Scrabble board. How long will it take to make it?"

"I have to build the wooden frame—yeah, I know, but if I can build a canoe-paddle-breadboard, I can build a square frame—pour the concrete, score it, other stuff." He wrapped up quickly. "I dunno...a few months?"

She thought about it for a moment. "However long it takes, just tell me what needs to be done. I used to help your dad on his house projects, you know."

"This cement," he continued, glossing over her offer,

"needs to be checked often, like all the time, something about it drying just right because if it doesn't…" He grimaced at the horrific results, although he didn't have a clue what would really happen. "It'd be a hassle to drive back and forth all the time…cost of gas and all.… Makes more sense if I stay put until the Scrabble board is done. Think you can put up with me for a couple more months?"

He sprinkled some salt on his food, priding himself on how casually he'd tossed off that line, as if it were an afterthought. Damn, he was good.

When he looked up, he saw something he hadn't realized had been missing—a light in his mom's eyes.

"Well," she said, sitting taller, "I suppose I can put up with you for a while longer." She speared a bite of scrambled eggs. "These are excellent, by the way. You're quite the chef."

He wished he had a camera so he could capture this moment of her happiness, frozen forever, always smiling.

SHORTLY BEFORE TEN Monday morning, Frances parked her leased Benz outside a warehouse on West Sunset Road. This industrial park reminded her of the setting in some doomsday flick with its rows of mostly deserted concrete-block buildings, broken asphalt roads and barren desert. Okay to visit during the day as a few companies still maintained offices here, but only a fool would visit here at night when it turned into a dark no-man's-land.

The gray clouds looked ominous, although she questioned the forecast of snow.

Not sure what to expect on her "first day on the job," she'd dressed for comfort in slouch pants, a long-sleeved thermal shirt, beige quilted jacket and running shoes. She'd left her hair loose, which she realized was going to be a mistake, as the wind was going to whip it into a froth.

Grabbing her shoulder bag, she exited the car. Ducking against a blast of cold air, she told herself her shivers were from the chilly temperatures, not preshow nerves. But who was she kidding? She was scared.

She steeled herself with some mental attagirls.

*Of all the undercover jobs you've worked, you know this one—being a jewel thief—inside out.*

*These Russians found you, so there's nothing suspicious about your involvement.*

*You're not going into this alone.*

Last night over the phone, Charlie told her he was working on renting one of the empty offices in this warehouse. He hoped to give it some bogus business name and staff it with two Vanderbilt investigators who'd be there every day, Monday through Friday. If she ever needed help, all she had to do was hit 7 on her phone keypad, a speed dial to their phones, which also automatically generated a text message with her location in case she couldn't talk.

A few minutes later, she shoved open the heavy glass door and entered the warehouse.

Inside was a wide hallway with doors on either side.

No central heating for the cavernous building, only in the offices, so this corridor was on the chilly side. She paused, pulled a brush from her bag and attempted to tame her hair. Her hair won.

As Frances headed down the hallway, her running shoes squeaked against the linoleum tiles. She recalled the names on a few of the doors from her last visit—Quick-Silver Courier Service, Kings Natural Products, Bergstrom Exports.

Toward the end of the hallway was the door labeled 1F, the Russian's leased offices. Taped on the door was a computer-printed sign she hadn't seen last Thursday when she'd picked up the envelope for Braxton.

*Шоколад*-Russian Confections

She looked around. No surveillance cameras. She pulled out her smartphone and snapped a picture of the sign. Slipping the phone back into her jacket pocket, she glanced at the far end of the hallway, wondering if one of those offices might soon house her watchdog Vanderbilt investigators.

The waiting room area was heated, almost to the point of suffocation, and starkly furnished. Several folding chairs, a metal-tile reception desk, a tall plastic plant whose green leaves shone eerily under the fluorescent lights. The other doors—two to her left, one on her right—were closed, just as they'd been before.

Frances unzipped her jacket as she headed to the reception desk where Oleg had sat last Thursday. Today, a twentysomething woman was in his spot, her long, straight chestnut hair pulled into a side ponytail that cascaded down the front of her low-cut black sequined top. She took in Frances with heavily made-up almond-shaped eyes, a lit cigarette between her fingers. Her nails were dramatically long and red.

"Good morning," Frances said. "Oleg is expecting me."

"Oh? He not say to me," she said in a thick Russian accent. Eyeing Frances's hair, she took a long drag on her cigarette.

"Perhaps he forgot. Please let him know Frances is here."

"You need comb?" she asked on a release of smoke.

"No." Later she'd find a moment to go to the ladies' room and try to wrestle her hair into submission.

After setting her burning cigarette in the ashtray, the receptionist began tapping on her phone's keypad.

Frances took the opportunity to check out the girl's desk. A tablet computer with a shopping site on its screen, a makeup bag, a few ballpoint pens, an ashtray filled with cigarette butts, most with the girl's dark red lipstick imprint. The ones without lipstick were a darker, stubbier brand.

"He here soon," the girl said, her gaze gravitating again to Frances's hair.

"Is there a ladies' room?"

She frowned. "Ladez…?"

"Bathroom?"

The girl shrugged, took another puff.

Frances picked the most comfortable-looking folding chair and sat.

Twenty minutes later, the door on the right opened. Oleg, wearing a wrinkled blue-and-black-checked shirt, jeans and the same scuffed sneakers he'd worn the last time, walked up to her and extended his hand, giving her a tight-lipped smile.

"Hello, Frances."

He smelled like cigarette smoke and pancakes, and stood so close, she could see a tiny, ragged white scar above his eyebrow.

She turned her head slightly, so her right cheek was out of his line of vision, remembering something she had read. Russians were comfortable with a foot of personal space when talking to others, while Americans liked at least three feet. So he felt perfectly relaxed standing this close, while she felt uneasy. But when in Rome...

The girl said something in Russian. Oleg nodded.

"You want to meet more ladies?" he asked Frances.

Took her a moment. "No, I asked where the bathroom is."

"In hallway. Key behind desk."

He said something in Russian to the girl, who held up a key, attached by a jingling chain to a small red box of chocolates, which Frances hoped was empty.

"Ladez," she said.

"I'll borrow it later." She wondered if the girl understood. "No ladez," she added.

Oleg gestured for Frances to enter the office, and

she walked inside, her stomach clenching, nervous at what lay ahead.

Unlike the bare-bones waiting area, this room was large and inviting. Several floor lamps gave the room a soft glow. An oval cherrywood table ringed with matching chairs sat on a scarlet Persian rug. The only items on the table were a laptop, cell phone, pad of paper, which she guessed were Oleg's. A portable bar with a tufted-leather facade sat in the far corner, littered with an assortment of vodka bottles.

Natural light spilled into the room through a large window in the far wall, although the view wasn't that great—a mostly empty parking lot rimmed by desert, which Vegas lore claimed was pockmarked by shallow graves left by mobsters and hit men. Unfortunately, that wasn't just legend. In a housing development recently built in the desert, several home owners had discovered human bones buried on their property.

"Dima here soon," he said, closing the door.

Dima or Dmitri Romanov, the mystery man. She'd spent hours digging for details about that Russian and Oleg over the weekend, from internet searches to database queries. After finding next to nil, she decided Oleg must have erased electronic footprints leading toward them or away from them. Handy having a computer whiz like that around.

"Too warm," he said, scowling at her jacket.

She'd also read that Russians felt it their personal duty to offer advice, especially on matters of health.

"Thank you." She slipped off the jacket and draped it over the back of a chair.

He stared at her jacket as if it were an uninvited creature before meeting her gaze. "Drink?"

She thought he meant coffee, but as he was heading to the corner bar, she realized he meant alcohol. Probably vodka.

Shots for breakfast?

Lately, people kept wanting to tip the bottle early in the day. Not her thing, but she didn't want to look rude by refusing. Plus, as she ambled toward the bar, she could check out what was on his laptop screen.

"Sure."

She'd eaten breakfast, so at least she wouldn't be drinking on an empty stomach. And she'd keep it to one shot, no more.

Meandering toward the corner bar, she looked out the window at a commercial plane angling into the clouds. She'd forgotten how close they were to McCarran International Airport. Ten miles?

When Oleg leaned behind the bar, she glanced at his laptop screen.

Pictures of people's faces. Six—no, eight. Mostly men, a few women. Smiling, but in a staged way, not natural. Backgrounds were all a uniform color.

*Driver's license photos?*

"Hey," Oleg called out, "you snoop on me?"

Her pulse jammed in her throat. Keeping her face still, she turned, giving him a look that said she had every right to check what was on the screen.

"Who are these people?" Not a question. A demand.

He paused, a bottle of vodka in his hand, his eyes locked on hers.

She could hear herself breathing, ragged in-and-outs of air that seemed louder than the distant, low roar of planes taking flight from McCarran.

With a slight shrug, he looked away. "Employees at Palazzo," he muttered, pouring the vodka into a shot glass.

People she might run into during the heist.

He slid a drink toward her. These shot glasses had to be double the size she was used to.

He held up his glass. *"Naz dyroovnia!"*

They clinked glasses, downed their drinks.

When he started to pour her another shot, she waved it off. "Work," she rasped, followed by a cough. She blinked back the sting in her eyes.

He chuckled under his breath. *"Amerikantxy."*

Didn't need an interpreter to know that word. And from the chiding, teasing tone, she got the gist. *Weak-assed American can't handle a second shot.*

After another small cough, she whispered hoarsely, *"Dusha-dusha." Soul to soul.*

Something else she'd read. For Russians, sharing a drink was about forging a bond. Connecting soul to soul. She had practiced the pronunciation of the toast—*dusha-dusha*—figuring she'd need to know it at some point, although she hadn't expected that to be first thing Monday morning.

Oleg gave her an approving nod, poured himself another shot.

"What?" boomed a loud voice. "Drinking without me?"

Dima stood in the open doorway, grinning. He wasn't tall, not more than five-nine, yet had a large, commanding presence. He wore a long black overcoat, unbuttoned, which offered a view of neatly pressed slacks and a purple dress shirt.

Oleg said something in Russian that included the words *dusha-dusha,* at which point he gestured at her.

"Ah," Dmitri said, nodding enthusiastically, "our Frances is one of us!" Taking off his coat, he bellowed something in Russian out the open door.

The receptionist yelled something back.

With a boisterous laugh, he hung his coat on a wall hook, then slammed the door shut. Striding across the room, his burned-cherry-and-leather cologne filled the room. More Russian chatter to Oleg, who laughed and splashed more vodka into a fresh shot glass.

Passing Frances, Dmitri paused. "What did you think of Braxton Morgan?"

The question took her by surprise. *Boyish, goofy, handsome, cocky, intelligent.* But she didn't say any of those and simply answered, "Expressive."

"Expressive." He looked up at the ceiling as he pondered the term. "Interesting." He met Frances's gaze. "What did he do to earn that?"

"He—" *behaves like a crushed-out thirteen-year-old boy* "—reveals his emotions too readily."

"You think he's bad at his job?"

Just as she'd detected before in the limo, Dmitri had a very faint British accent in his excellent English.

"Wasn't what I expected from a security consultant."

"Not what you expected," he murmured, as though tasting the words. "So you think his being *expressive* impairs his ability?"

This conversation was starting to feel like a trek through a minefield. One verbal misstep, and she might detonate an issue that could blow up in her face.

"Merely my observations," she said, "which could be wrong—"

"Russians are expressive, Frances," he said, cutting her off as he strolled across the floor with a theatrical flourish. "Hardly a sign of weakness, although I can see why you would view it as such, being so—" his gaze traveled slowly down, back up her body "—closed-off yourself."

She felt a jab of irritation. He'd asked her evaluation of Braxton, then used it to judge *her* behavior.

"Security consultants are like jewel thieves," she said, refusing to be cowed. "Their successes hinge on remaining calm, controlled, professional. Emotions in a jewel thief can undermine a heist. For a security consultant, they can inflame an incident. Expressiveness, therefore, is *not* a beneficial trait."

Dmitri cocked an eyebrow, but didn't say anything as he continued walking to the bar. After embracing Oleg and kissing him on both cheeks, the two began chatting amiably in their native tongue.

She crossed to the window, watched another plane descend through the clouds. She guessed Dmitri's non-response meant she'd won that round, but why were they arguing about Braxton's ability to begin with?

Didn't matter. This conversation gave her an opportunity to learn more about his relationship to Dmitri. In her research, she'd learned a few more interesting facts about Braxton. Past problems with the law, linked to his ties to a Russian thug named Yuri Glazkov. Considering Braxton was a star witness for the state at Yuri's trial next month, the D.A. had probably offered him immunity, or reductions in other charges, if he cooperated.

When a criminal went from the dark to the light side of the law, a journey she well understood, a smart criminal *stayed* in the light. Going back and forth, which Braxton appeared to be doing, only invited trouble from both sides.

"Oleg," Dima bellowed, "time to get back to work! I must talk to my Frances now."

As Oleg took his seat at the table and began typing at the keyboard, Dmitri walked up to Frances, crowding her. She instinctively dipped her head, although it wasn't necessary. The waterproof silicone gel and camouflage makeup made her scar vanish. But as skin cells naturally sloughed off throughout the day, so did the makeup and gel, although her scar didn't become noticeable for twelve hours, sometimes less.

"Sorry I gave you a bad time," he murmured, his breath smelling of vodka and coffee.

"No problem."

"I might be tough on you at times," he said gently, pulling out a chair next to Oleg, who was engrossed with something on his computer screen, "because this is a major heist, and you're my star. Please, sit."

She did.

"There will be many things we'll be studying and practicing over the next few weeks," he said casually as he took the seat next to her, "reviewing the blueprints of the Palazzo, the setup of the jewelry exhibit, the hotel's security team, possible off-duty Vegas officers who might be working security, and so on...." He made a rolling motion with his hand. "I have a forger who will interview you over the internet, then create documents that identify you as an antique-jewelry collector. There is also a safecracker I have worked with before who will train you in opening digital locks, although this is purely a backup measure, as surveillance photos reveal the jewelry cases on this exhibit have metal locks."

Oleg said something in Russian, and Dmitri nodded.

"Oleg has already forwarded images of those locks to a key forger, who is making keys even as we speak. As you can see, you will be very busy these next few weeks." He smiled. "Plus, I'm hiring a part-time bodyguard for you."

*Bodyguard?* This was a surprise twist, one she didn't like at all. Someone hovering nearby, overhearing everything she said, could too easily compromise her undercover work.

Dmitri draped his arm across the back of her chair. She felt claustrophobic sandwiched between him and Oleg, plus the older Russian's sense-stunning cologne didn't help.

"He will not know you are a jewel thief," he murmured, "but will think you are my vice president of sales."

"This isn't a good idea."

He cocked that eyebrow again. "Why not?"

"Russian Confections looks like a small start-up company operating on a shoestring budget. Shoestring means it is operating on very little money—"

"I'm familiar with a lot of American slang," he snapped, "which I learned from watching your silly sitcoms. If I wish to know the meaning of a term, I shall ask."

This new piece of information gave her pause. The coins were stolen from a New York event two years ago. She wondered if she could place him in that region at that time.

She wasn't a fan of sitcoms, but her dad often watched them at night if no sports were on. A few years ago, he loved a show that was canceled after just one season. If Dmitri watched that sitcom as well, it could place him in the U.S. at that time.

What was the name of that show? *Something My Dad Thought.* No, *My Dad Says.* Had a cuss word in the title. Now she remembered....

"What a great way to learn slang," she said, flashing her best sincere smile. "Did you ever watch…" She said the title.

He released an exasperated sigh. "Yes, yes, funny show, but you were talking about our shoestring budget…."

She nodded, pleased she might have something more to go on.

"Right," she responded, returning to their prior conversation. "My point was people will wonder where Russian Confections got the money to hire a bodyguard. It will draw the wrong kind of attention."

"Ah, but looks can be deceiving, Frances. If anyone checks public records, they'll read that Russian Confections is the American arm of a lucrative chocolate factory in the Ukraine that makes dozens of sweet treats, including the Elegance Extra-Dark chocolate bar…." He pressed his fingers to his lips, giving them a small, reverential kiss. "Exquisite, really. I must bring you some."

She imagined a box of chocolates, realizing how perfectly a coin could fit at the bottom of a paper candy cup. Did he use this Russian Confections company to transport those ancient Greek coins? To where? she wondered.

"So I disagree with your conjecture," he continued. "Anyway, this bodyguard's primary job is to escort you after work to your car, which is a *smart* security measure, hardly a suspicious one." He lifted his chin, affecting a noble silhouette. "Think of yourself," he said, lowering his voice, "as a lovely damsel in distress I wish to protect."

What a ham. Probably envisioned himself as a swashbuckler type, swinging in on a rope, a cutlass between his teeth, a hero to the little lady's rescue.

Maybe by appealing to his blown-up ego, she could convince him to table this bodyguard nonsense. Shame she didn't know any heroic pirates to compare him to, although Dmitri's short-clipped hair, pronounced cheekbones and stylish clothes reminded her of another larger-than-life hero.

"Oh, my," she said, giving him a look, "has anyone ever said you look like James Bond?"

He paused, obviously delighted. "A child did, once, but…" He shrugged off the compliment, but she caught that tell-me-more look in his eyes.

"Oh, it's *true*," she cooed. "Both of you are handsome, charming and…well, *far* more intelligent than most people."

He raised his hand as though he couldn't handle more adulation. "You flatter me."

This was like hanging out with a beefy diva.

"And, uh…in shape. Both of you obviously work out." Time to drive her point home. "Although James Bond would *never* hire a bodyguard for someone."

He bolted upright. "Why not? An important, intelligent man like that can't be everywhere at all times."

"True, but Bond would never hire a bodyguard, especially for an important client." She frowned, doing her best to look worried. "Let's get real, Dmitri. What if this bodyguard figures out what we're planning and reports it to the authorities?"

"He will not do that."

"How do you know?"

"How do I know *you* won't deceive me?" he countered, jabbing his index finger at her. "You are obviously an experienced jewel thief who is knowledgeable about Georgian jewelry, but why is there not a *single* news account of one of your thefts? That bothers me!"

He glared at her, a vein in his forehead pulsing. She felt a bit dizzy from the way he'd gone from flattered to outraged within seconds.

On the streets in her teenage years, she'd dealt with her share of bullies who relied on tactics like explosive intimidation to make others grovel. After weathering a few confrontations, she'd learned the secret to managing bullies was not to show fear, even if they were scaring the bejesus out of you.

"There are no accounts of *your* thefts, either," she said, raising her voice, "but that doesn't bother me! Means you're very good at not getting caught, yet you refuse to give me that same respect!"

He lurched to his feet and kicked his chair like a two-year-old, toppling it over onto the rug with a soft thump. Flailing his arms, he barked something in Russian to Oleg, who jumped up and righted the chair.

With every spare ounce of steely nerve she could muster, she stared into Dmitri's blue eyes, which were frosty with rage. He tapped his index finger on the table, steady as a metronome, slicing out the seconds, one…by…one.

Then he stopped.

He hung his head for what seemed an eternity, during which time she mentally calculated the number of steps to her purse and how long it'd take to snatch her cell phone and punch the speed dial for help….

Then her stomach plummeted as she realized the bogus office didn't exist. Not yet, anyway.

Finally, he raised his head.

"Ah, Frances…" He drew in a colossal breath, releasing it with a heavy sigh. "How silly for us to fight." He thumped his fist over his heart. "I can be obstinate, I know. *Gordynya khorosho, chtoby ne dovodit.*"

Oleg, standing nearby, nodded somberly.

"Pride goes before good arguments," Dmitri interpreted for her, "or how you Americans say…pride goes before a fall. You and I, Frances, have much to gain in our business venture, so I will be less prideful because I want us to be friends. Truce?"

She could feel the tension seep from her body. Not that she could ever completely relax in these offices, but a truce would make this undercover job less uncomfortable.

"Truce," she said.

Rain began splattering against the window. Dmitri nodded to the younger Russian, who sat back down and resumed typing.

"You see," Dmitri said to Frances, "Oleg's research showed you had one felony arrest five years ago, here in Las Vegas, for which you did not serve time. Please don't take this the wrong way, my Frances, but no time for a felony sounds…*questionable.* As in acting as an informant…or testifying against a former associate."

Dmitri was paranoid, like most criminals. If something looked suspicious, he thought the worst. Of course, he was right on this one. If all went well, she *would* be testifying against him.

But she also knew that online criminal history Oleg pulled was relatively useless. In her work at Vanderbilt, she'd run hundreds of online criminal histories, which should be called criminal *sketches,* as they offered such sparse information. All Oleg could have learned from her criminal history was the date, city and felony charge. Clever of him, though, to run a separate check of Nevada prison records.

"It was my first offense," she explained, "and since I was young, the judge was lenient. Gave me probation and community service."

Nowhere, not even in court records, would it show the suspended sentence, her real court deal. Nor would any records, public or otherwise, reveal her true work history at Vanderbilt.

"I give you respect for avoiding prison," Dmitri said with a reverential nod. "Now…it is time for Oleg to take you to his office, where he will show you blueprints of the Palazzo, but before you go…" He reached inside his pocket and pulled out a wad of bills. "For putting up with my, pardon my Americanism, *bullshit.*" He peeled off four crisp one-hundred-dollar bills and handed them to her. "Do something nice for yourself. I insist."

She didn't want his guilt money, had half a mind to say as much, but she'd met her badass-girl quota for the day. Maybe the year. Plus she knew where bad money could do some good.

"Thank you." She slipped the bills into her pocket.

As she exited with Oleg, she reflected on how different she felt than when she'd first stepped into this room. Before, she'd been anxious entering Dmitri's inner sanctum. Now she felt as if she'd claimed a piece of its turf.

Which almost scared her more.

Shrugging off his trench coat, Braxton paused. He'd just walked into Dima's office, had barely handed him the manila envelope containing his investigation report on the check-cashing store, when the Russian asked him to be a…

"Did you say…*spy?*" he asked.

"Yes," Dima answered.

"I'm not sure if I should laugh or call the American consulate," Braxton joked, looking around the room for a place to hang his coat.

"What is so funny about that?"

From the Russian's dark glower, it was about as funny as a hangnail.

Braxton shifted his coat from one hand to the other, debating if he should just put it back on and leave. But he wanted that head-of-security job, *bad,* so he'd answer the question.

"It's just that you're a Russian, I'm an American, and the spy question struck me as humorous…like we were in some James Bond movie."

After a few seconds—five to be exact, because Braxton ticked them off in his head—Dima smiled.

"That name came up earlier," he murmured, tossing the envelope onto the oval table as he strolled to the window, where he eyed his reflection in the glass. "I've been told I look like him.…" He waggled a hand over his shoulder. "Coat hooks are next to the door."

Braxton headed over to them, mentally congratulating himself on that spur-of-the-moment movie reference.

"Have you seen many Bond films?" Dmitri asked.

"Not since I was a kid."

Hanging up his coat, he recalled a long-ago summer when he and Drake had watched and re-watched Bond movies until they could quote entire scenes in their sleep. Their mother hadn't been happy with their 007 obsession, fretting it was a sign they were overly enthralled with their father's security profession. She was right, of course; they *were* fascinated with their dad's career, and if there'd been hotel-casino-security-cop movies, they'd have watched those, too.

James Bond had looked cool in his tuxedo, but nine-year-old Braxton thought his dad looked even cooler in his security uniform—creased blue pants and shirt, gold badge, but best of all a leather holster with a real gun. Sometimes he'd help his dad polish his leather shoes, after which he'd put them on and try to walk, the two of them laughing as he clomped and slid, barely able to take a step.

Until this moment, he hadn't realized that this security position was a way to be close to his old man again. Stepping into his dad's career was like stepping into those shoes.

Maybe this time he could finally fill them.

"For all those gadgets Bond used," Dima said, pulling Braxton out of his reverie, "he had deplorable taste in weapons before he started carrying a Walther."

"Yeah, that Beretta belonged in a lady's purse."

With a spirited laugh, Dima turned to the table. "You are funny, my friend! Ah, remember when Bond escaped in a helicopter from a disintegrating plane?"

*Die Another Day,* Braxton answered, naming the film. He and Drake must have jumped off the roof a dozen times that summer, reenacting that very scene.

"Ah, if only such escapes were possible in real life, yes?"

The distant growl of another flight drew his attention. Through the window, Braxton watched a commercial plane lumber toward the clouds.

Dima pulled out a chair and gestured for him to sit. "What have you discovered about Yuri?"

Braxton had little to report. Yuri's businesses were closed down or had been taken over by others. His former boss was out on bail but keeping a low profile before the trial. "I'll email you my surveillance reports."

"I am more interested in your impressions."

"Yuri is wearing an ankle bracelet, and from my brief surveillances he's staying home, which is exactly where most people think he belongs."

"He will not cause interference for me?"

Braxton gave a who-knows shrug. "Apparently, most of his former pals have turned against him, and he has almost no support in the Russian community. But that could just be the story he wants people to believe. Plus you and I know those ankle monitoring bracelets are a joke—with the right electronics expert giving you a hand, they can be taken on and off at whim."

"So I should stay alert."

"Yes."

"In Russia, patience is a virtue, so I shall remain patient and see what else you learn about Yuri." He straightened. "Ready to discuss a new job?"

"Absolutely," Braxton said, crossing the floor. "I have some ideas about this security position I think you'll like."

"By the way, I've decided the title will be Security Director," Dima said, "which sounds more prestigious than Head of Security, don't you agree? Shakespeare may have questioned 'What's in a name?' to which I answer *everything*. But unfortunately we're not discussing that job until my overpaid lawyers finish hammering out the business details."

Classical music began playing.

"Ringtone," Dima explained, reaching into his

pocket. "Tchaikovsky's Violin Concerto in D Major. Excuse me—I've been expecting an important call."

As he spoke in Russian, Braxton crossed to the window. Rain pelted the glass. In the distance, lightning zigzagged. He looked down at his Volvo in the parking lot, hoped that weather stripping he'd put in the door seal would stop it from leaking again.

Parked near the Volvo was Babe's lemon-yellow Benz.

He'd noticed it the moment he'd pulled into the lot this morning, which wasn't difficult, as only twenty or so cars were parked in the large lot. Being early for his meeting, he'd sat in his car, contemplating her Benz. He also took interest in two shiny black Lexus models and a limo parked in a cluster nearby. Russians had a thing for black luxury cars, so he guessed they belonged to others in Dmitri's organization.

He'd already run her license plate, hoping to learn her real name, instead learning it had been rented a week ago from a car-rental agency downtown. For the hell of it, he ran the licenses on each Lexus and learned both were registered to a corporation named Konfety. Ran the limo's license. Konfety, again.

Why was her Benz rented, but the others registered to Konfety?

He looked up Konfety in the Nevada business database. Couldn't find it. Ran it through a translator program and learned that *konfety* was Russian for *candy*.

By then it was time to head inside, so he turned off his phone and exited the Volvo, taking a short detour past the Benz. Tidy leather interior. No books, addressed envelopes, nothing lying around to give a clue about her life. Seeing a small white receipt lying on the floor, he pulled out his smartphone and snapped a picture of it through the window.

"I apologize for the interruption," Dima said now, putting away his phone. "Shall we continue our discussion?"

A few moments later, they sat next to each other at the table.

Sitting this close, Braxton felt suffocated by the Russian's cologne, a leathery, fruity stench that could probably cure meat. He remembered Yuri and his pals wearing strong scents, too. For some reason, all the Russian men Braxton had met seemed to equate their masculinity with the ability to give others nosebleeds.

"I'd like to hire you to be a part-time bodyguard," Dima said. "I'm thinking ten to twelve hours a week, which leaves you plenty of time to conduct investigations on Yuri."

Why hadn't he mentioned this before? Plus, Braxton had never liked the term *bodyguard* because it made the profession sound like a bunch of knuckle-dragging goons. He preferred calling it *protection agent* or *executive protection,* but screw it. Call it *banana peel* for all he cared. They weren't talking about the real title he wanted—Security Director.

But rather than run off at the mouth, he kept it shut, forced himself to listen. He wasn't happy with this turn of events, but since he'd made the effort to come here, he might as well hear Dima out.

"Primarily, I would like you to provide an escort through the parking lot after work, as well as accompany her to any large events she might be attending—you two can discuss her schedule—and possibly a client meeting or two in the Russian community." Dmitri rubbed a spot on the table. "I'd also like you to gather intelligence about this person."

Here's the spy part. "What kind of information are you looking for?"

"What's said in conversations, identities of people visited, addresses of stopovers..." He gestured with his hand, which showed off his platinum Patek Philippe watch. Had to cost forty grand, at least.

"It's been a while since I accepted an executive-protection case," he said.

"But your reputation continues, Braxton. Your past clients speak highly of you."

He hadn't given Dima any references for his past protection work, but a quick Google search would find several newspaper stories.

"You mentioned my overhearing what's said in conversations," Braxton said, "but I speak very little Russian...."

"Does not matter."

"So this person's American."

Dima nodded.

Which made Braxton wonder... Nah, couldn't be Babe. Dima knew about The Dayden Group and had probably used them to run a background check on her. She'd obviously passed the test, because he'd hired her, so no reason to sic a spy on her.

"Is this a family member?" Braxton asked.

"No. A...vice president."

"Possible theft? Industrial sabotage?" When someone that high up was under scrutiny, there was usually something juicy going on.

Dima waved off any suggestion of impropriety. "I simply want confirmation this executive has no issues that could undermine a major project."

Braxton nodded, wondering what could undermine a Russian candy company. Stealing a recipe for Anna Karina's Creamy Fudge?

"I figure three thousand cash, paid weekly, for your services and expenses is fair."

"More than fair."

"Excellent. There's an envelope with your first week's pay at the front desk. *From Russia with Love*, yes?" he quipped, playing on the James Bond title.

Braxton smiled and meant it for the most part, too. He just needed to be patient—never one of his sterling traits—about the other job.

The door clicked open, and Dima turned. "Oleg, excellent timing!"

A lanky guy wearing a wrinkled, checkered shirt and jeans sauntered in. His wavy black hair needed a cut.

Braxton's gaze shifted to the woman behind Oleg, and his mouth went dry.

There she was…Babe, the blonde vision that had haunted his waking and sleeping hours ever since their last encounter in Chez Manny's parking lot.

She'd traded in her Hillary Clinton pantsuit look for some kind of lounge pants, a thermal shirt and sneakers. And that sleek, tight bun had unraveled into a mass of honey-blond hair that gave her a bit of a Wild-Woman-from-Borneo look. He didn't recall her ever wearing a lot of makeup before, but today it appeared she'd skipped it altogether.

Didn't matter. She was one of those women who didn't need to slather on the stuff to turn heads. Plus there was something about her—call it her Lauren Bacall mystique—that added layers of secrecy and depth, making her a puzzle he was dying to solve.

He shifted his gaze to Oleg, back to her, an uneasy realization dawning. Was his lovely, smoky, inscrutable Bacall actually a computer geek like her wrinkled-shirt buddy or, worse, his *girlfriend?*

"Braxton," Dima said, "this is Oleg Ivanovich, my computer wizard. He and his lovely wife, Raisa, recently moved to Las Vegas so he could be part of my team."

She was married. To Oleg Ivanovich.

His heart sank like the *Titanic*.

"And this is my vice president of sales, Frances, who is dressed like this—" he gestured to her clothes as though Braxton might not know what *dressed like this* meant "—because she's moving into her new office today."

*Her name is Frances, not Raisa.*

He felt a nudge of relief, followed by a jolt.

*She's the vice president I'll be spying on.*

He should've left earlier. So what if he got to hang close to her? He'd be deceiving the one person he wanted to impress. To think he'd spent months showing his family and friends that he was no longer a duplicitous jerk, and he'd just agreed to be one again.

But if he didn't take this part-time gig, Dima would hire somebody else to spy on her. No way Braxton could let some other guy play snoop, looking for dirt on her to report to Dima. Unless he discovered she was some kind of criminal, he didn't need to report squat to Dima.

He was staying.

Oleg wandered about the room, never straying far from Dima, though, like a satellite circling its planet. Dima draped his arm possessively around Frances's shoulders.

"She is my star employee," he said to Braxton, looking proud.

*If you're so proud of her, why are you surveilling her?*

"Congratulations on your new position," Braxton said, figuring if she was moving into her new office today, she'd just come on board.

"Thank you."

That voice again…smokier, sultrier than he remembered. Didn't matter what she said, she could read out loud the fine print on the back of his credit-card bills and he'd listen.

"Braxton," Dima said to her, "will be your part-time bodyguard."

A pucker of disapproval played on her lips.

Oh, great. He'd done something wrong *again,* although he didn't know what. Was she still nursing a grudge over his dumb Frau Farbissina comment from days ago? Okay, to be fair, that and the Hillary-bun-and-pantsuit remarks weren't exactly a gift basket of compliments, but still…at some point, she needed to let go, show a little forgiveness, right?

Just then, the receptionist walked into the room, diverting everyone's attention, although the look she slid Braxton indicated she was mostly interested in his. She slinked across the room as though working a catwalk before handing a white plastic card to Dima.

"Your access card," he said to Frances, showing it to her, "although the building is only locked from midnight to five in the morning. Please check that your name is spelled correctly."

"It's missing an *e*," she said. "Should be *J-e-f-f-e-r-i-e-s*."

So that was her name. *Frances Jefferies.*

Dima said something in Russian to the girl, who shot him a sullen look before snatching back the card and leaving the room. He made a shooing motion to Oleg, who left, too, closing the door behind him with a solid click.

Meanwhile, two words kept flashing in his mind like a Vegas neon sign.

*Morgan-Jefferies.*

Oooh, boy, not good. He'd blame it on his mother's hyphenation fantasy. He was attracted to Frances, but this boy was keeping his head on straight, his feet on terra firma. He didn't have a clue about her history or the emotional baggage she carted around. Hell, she could be divorced with five kids for all he knew.

Or maybe she was Dima's American girlfriend, the *real* reason he wanted her spied on, but wouldn't say, as there was the small issue of a Russian wife and four kids back in Yekaterinburg...a buried piece of history Braxton caught in a subsequent reading of that diligence report.

Report, yeah, that was what he needed. He'd run his own background check on Frances Jefferies. Treat his heart like a spacecraft on a launch pad and protect it with rigorous, practical research before allowing it to blast off.

"Braxton will be here when you leave work today," Dima was explaining to her, "to escort you to your car. This industrial park is no place for a woman to walk alone at night."

Those sparkling amethyst eyes turned to him. "Thank you, Braxton."

"Sure," he murmured, the only word his addled brain could latch on to after hearing her say his name for the first name. *Braxton.* He never knew it could sound so good, so imbued with meaning and promise....

*Focus! Ask what time she wants you back here, where you should pick her up.*

"Sure?" he asked.

Her face remained immobile, although he swore her eyebrows moved together a fraction of an inch. "Yes, I'm sure."

He nodded, trying to look like a man who would not only put his life on the line for her, but also knew how to not repeat monosyllabic words that made no sense.

A boom, like the roar of rocket booster, shattered the silence.

"Thunder!" Dima laughed. "If it is not loud, a peasant forgets to cross himself!"

Frances's eyes widened as she watched the rain lash the window.

Braxton looked at her hands, which she'd raised at the crashing sound. It struck him as odd how they hovered midair, the tips of her slender fingers almost touching, yet not, as though denying each other the comfort of being held. He imagined what it would be like to fill that empty space, to be her solace, to know the unbearable ache of her caress.

*Terra firma.*

As though sensing his attention, she looked at him, her hands floating back down to her sides. Her lips parted and she took in a quick breath, her breasts rising with the effort, and when she exhaled, he swore he could hear it from across the room, like a low, needy whisper.

And then she smiled.

That simple act seemed to send his soul skyrocketing and he felt all reason leave him.

Somehow, though, his feet remained rooted to the floor in Dima's office, but his eyes were riveted on the one person who both sent him flying and kept him grounded.

Frances Jefferies.

## *CHAPTER SEVEN*

FRANCES WAS SMILING on the outside, but she was seething on the inside.

She watched Dmitri stroll across the room, gesturing grandly as he went on and on about Braxton's "exceptional talents," "impressive record," "glowing references." He pretended to be speaking to both Frances and Braxton, but the show was really for her. Hard-sell advertising, in her book, was just another illusion.

Even from across the room, she could see that far-off, goofy look in Braxton's eyes as he looked at her.

Maybe on Thursday he'd found her attractive, but she'd been put together then. Nice suit, tamed hair, makeup. Today she looked like she cleaned aquarium tanks for a living. No makeup, except her gel-concealer combo. Slouchy pants that were really just baggy. She'd like to pretend she was having a bad-hair day, but it had turned into an atrocious one.

She flashed on a pickpocketing scam called the "sexy distraction." A hot-looking girl or guy distracts the mark so the pickpocket can steal a wallet or piece of jewelry. Was Braxton a sexy distraction so she'd let down her guard? Why?

Dmitri finally stopped extolling Saint Braxton's virtues. "Any questions, Frances?"

If Dmitri were being really honest, he'd ask, *Do you accept Braxton as your bodyguard now?* But then, the people in this room weren't exactly known for their honesty.

This was her chance to get rid of the guy. Part of her felt badly doing this—his crushed-out-teenager antics had made her feel attractive, desirable—but this was about business and the success of her case.

"I still have my concerns about him," she said, avoiding Braxton's gaze, "such as his expressiveness, but you already know that. Another issue is his car. It's, well...a rust bucket. Run-down. Bald tires. Peeling paint. I have concerns about its reliability. What if I were stuck somewhere and needed to rely on *that* for safe transportation?"

Dmitri actually looked a bit interested with that one. Good. Time to hit him with another idea she'd been mulling over.

"I just had a thought," she said, hesitating a moment as though weighing its value. "I happen to know a bodyguard, one of the best in Vegas, actually, who's skilled in state-of-the-art equipment *and* drives a sturdy new vehicle. He's between jobs right now and would be honored to work as a part-time bodyguard for you."

Charlie would *love* this idea. Her "experienced bodyguard" was a fellow investigator at Vanderbilt whom she knew had done some protection work, so he could convincingly play the part. It'd be great to have a buddy working this case with her, even a part-time one. Someone who knew the players, could brainstorm the case, was with her *inside* the enemy camp, not planted in some random warehouse office.

"You're leasing a car for the other investigation, right?" Dmitri asked Braxton.

"Yes."

"Then use it when you're guarding her, too." He turned back to Frances. "This friend of yours is Russian?"

"No."

"Braxton worked many years with others from the Russian community—does your bodyguard know my culture as well as he does?"

"But I'm not Russian, either, so why would that matter?"

"There will be times when you are meeting with a Russian customer, my dear," Dmitri said, ambling toward the table, his hands locked behind his back. "A bodyguard knowledgeable in Russian etiquette can save you the embarrassment of appearing rude or uncivilized...."

He paused at the chair over which she'd folded her jacket and looked at it.

"For example, Russians view it as bad manners to toss a coat over a chair. Goes back to our long winters.... Snow dripping off a coat can quickly become a small river on the floor. Braxton understands these things, and he can help you not look like an unsophisticated boor to my compatriots."

He turned his back to her and started chatting amiably with Braxton about a Russian restaurant in Las Vegas he'd recently eaten at.

She stood there, stinging from Dmitri's jab. *Unsophisticated boor.* What a jerk.

"When the receptionist leaves around noon each day," Dmitri was saying to Braxton, "she locks up our office, so I suggest you wait for Frances at the main building doors...."

Almost sounded as if Dmitri didn't want Braxton coming inside the Russian Confections office. Maybe they weren't as tight as she'd assumed.

"All right!" Dmitri clapped his hands together. "Time for my two American employees to get to know each other. It is close to noon, yes? I suggest you 'do lunch,' as you Americans love to say. While eating and drinking, give each other your contact information and schedules." He waved them out of the room. "Now go. I must meet with Oleg."

As Braxton grabbed his coat, she walked into the reception area, which was hazy with cigarette smoke. The receptionist, puffing away, shot her a resentful look that turned into a wide red-lipped smile when Braxton appeared, his trench coat folded over his arm.

"Braxton," she called out, "I have for you." She waved a white envelope in the air as if it were a surrender flag.

"Thanks, Ulyana," he said, walking over.

Frances wondered when the two of them had gotten on a first-name basis.

The receptionist leaned forward, giving him the Grand Canyon view down her neckline, as she pointed a long, red-painted fingernail at something scrawled on the envelope. "My phone number," she said, trilling the *r* like a purr.

*Subtle as a tank.*

"I'll be in the hallway," Frances muttered, wondering if Braxton really bought into that slinky Natasha Fatale act.

Frances opened the door a little harder than she'd intended. It flew open, smacking her big toe.

"Ow!"

She blinked back sudden tears at the stabbing pain. Damned sneakers. She'd worn them today because they were water resistant, but their "durable" canvas was about as protective as wax paper.

A hand gripped her arm.

"You all right?" Braxton asked, concern etching his face.

She strangled back a painful snort.

"Door hit your foot?"

She nodded. "Big toe," she managed to rasp.

"You like help?" the receptionist called out, sounding about as concerned as a fast-food server asking if she'd like fries with that.

"Let me get you to a chair," Braxton said.

Frances shook her head vehemently. No way was she

staying in this smoke-clogged room under the scrutiny of Uly the Benevolent.

"I can walk," she murmured. Toe still hurt, but it was better than that first excruciating flash of death-ray pain.

"We should take a look, make sure it's not broken—"

"No." She hobbled a step toward the open doorway.

"Frances—"

"Need to leave," she said between clenched teeth, taking another halting step.

He slid his arm around her back, bracing the side of his body against hers. "Lean on me."

She felt silly, but leaning against him helped her hobble better, at least.

"How's the pain?" he asked gently, his breath warm against her right cheek.

She ducked her head, fuzzily wondering when she'd slipped her arm around him. Her fingertips grazed the silky weave of his shirt, sensing his taut muscles underneath.

"Less."

The image of her and Braxton, their arms wrapped around each other, maneuvering their way out the door as one was undoubtedly stoking a certain chain-smoking Russian's green-eyed, homicidal fury.

"Shoe feeling tight?" Braxton asked.

"Not really."

"Because if your toe's swelling, that's a sign you might have fractured it."

They were in the hallway now, and she released an

unconscious sigh as the cooler air soothed her heated skin. She started to pull away, but he tightened his hold, causing her to tilt forward.

For a moment, her world rocked in place as they accidentally cuddled. She couldn't breathe, couldn't think, only feel. The strength of his body against hers, his masculine scent riding the woody, jasmine aroma of his aftershave, shot to some primal part of her brain, triggering a warmth she hadn't felt in a long, long time....

"Close door!" an angry female voice yelled. "Heat go out!"

"I need to shut the door," he murmured huskily, but didn't move. Just stood there, those gray eyes taking her in. "Are you okay to stand?"

Took her a moment to interpret his question. She vaguely realized her toe still ached, but not as badly as before.

"Of course." She shuddered from the chilly corridor and released a breath—her senses still reeling after that close encounter.

"It's cold out here," he said, pulling his coat off his arm and opening it for her.

"No..."

Too late. He wrapped his trench coat around her shoulders, enveloping her in its warmth. She looked past his shoulder at the receptionist, smoke seeping from her lips as she flipped Frances the finger.

"Be right back," he said, oblivious to the girl-on-girl smackdown brewing.

Frances nodded, forcing a small smile. As if this undercover job didn't have enough challenges. Now she had to deal with a psychotically jealous Russian girl who viewed her as competition.

Which would never have happened if she'd stayed focused on the case, but no, she'd let herself get caught up in a moment of... She gave herself a mental shake, not wanting to think about it, not wanting to feel, not wanting...

*Sex.* Was that it?

Her libido had been dormant for so long, she'd sometimes wondered if it had taken a permanent hiatus. It hadn't really bothered her, though, because she'd been pouring energy into so many other things—Vanderbilt, restitutions to the court, her dad and Teller, paying bills, upkeep on the condo.

Not that she hadn't dated. Three years ago, there'd been the high-school biology teacher, Alex. A great guy, but she wasn't into bicycling and camping, and he wasn't into watching Coen brothers films and magic shows. Eventually they admitted they were too different and parted amicably. A year after that there'd been Justin, the homicide detective, but that "relationship" ended after two dates when his ex-wife started stalking them.

The Russian Confections door clicked shut.

Braxton carried one of the folding chairs from the waiting area and set it against the far wall, then returned to Frances.

"C'mon," he said gently, taking her by the elbow, "let's look at that toe."

"This is silly—"

"Even sillier not to check it."

He led her to the chair, his arm circling her waist, as though her toe were the most important thing in the world. Was this the sexy distraction at work? If so, he was damned good at it.

She could play along. The closer they were, the more she could learn about Dmitri, Oleg, that other investigation Braxton was working for the Russian.

She sat down and he knelt at her feet, bending over her foot, the overhead fluorescent lights casting streaks of blue in his dark hair. She'd never been one to notice men's hair, besides the color or if the guy wore it short or long, but she found herself intrigued by the edgy style of Braxton's—neatly trimmed on the sides, combed forward off the crown into a peak. Self-consciously, she touched her own hair, embarrassed at its willfulness today.

She shifted her gaze to his hands, observed his long, tan fingers methodically loosening the shoelace. And when he gently slipped the sneaker off her foot—her white, thin, pale foot—she wished she'd gotten a pedicure, at least painted her toenails.

"Toe doesn't look swollen," he said quietly, cradling her foot, "and the skin around it isn't discolored. How's the pain?"

"Much better," she murmured, unsettled by the warmth of his touch.

Hands always told a story. Even when someone was lying or playing a role, unless they were a professional actor, their hands gave them away. His caress spoke of his tenderness, attention to detail, a reverence for others' suffering.... Maybe she was reading too much into that last one, but that was what she guessed.

He lifted his gaze to meet hers. "I think we can safely say you didn't break your toe."

Looking into his eyes, she held back, not wanting to fall into their soft, gray depths. Playing along with this sexy distraction was asking for trouble. She needed to hold on to the role-playing, the goals of the case...even as a thin shell around her heart cracked a little.

She leaned over and picked up her shoe, ignoring his offer to help. After tying the laces, she stood and headed down the hallway toward the main building doors, hearing the slap of his steps behind her.

"Frances?"

"Hmm?

"Want to do lunch?"

"Sorry," she said over her shoulder, "don't have time. Moving into my new office and all...." Didn't feel right lying, even if it was the one Dmitri set up, but she had to protect her case.

"Need help?"

"No. I'm just...unpacking boxes, figuring out where

I want to put stuff. Anyway, Dmitri asked me to share my schedule with you, so..."

FOR THE NEXT few minutes, Braxton walked alongside Frances, her sneakers squeaking against the linoleum floor, listening to her itemize her schedule. She didn't look at him once, just kept walking, looking straight ahead, explaining how she'd be going straight home tonight after work, so there was no need for his bodyguard services later tonight, obviously, and that tomorrow...

He tried to latch on to the words, but listening to her voice was like listening to music. Hers was like jazz. Slow and sultry. Sometimes he caught the faint growl of a jungle cat in it, which went with that mussed, tawny mane of hair.

"And on Thursday," she continued, "I'll be hosting my father's weekly bridge card game at our place...."

She lived with her dad? Small world—he lived with his mom. Probably for different reasons, though, as she obviously made good money and could afford her own place.

"On Friday night, I'll be cleaning the condo."

Friday. The auction.

He slowed, pulled out his cell phone to see if Li'l Bit had responded to his text, asking if 530 meant five-thirty at Bally's fitness center. There was a one-word answer.

Cool

Which he took to mean yes. Slipping the phone back into his pocket, he continued following Frances, who was talking about grocery shopping on Saturday.

"I like to go to Whole Foods Market, but my dad thinks it's too expensive. If we didn't argue about it we'd probably end up actually grocery shopping more often…."

His gaze slipped down to the seat of those baggy pants that seemed to skim and slip off her small, round behind. Maybe she thought loose clothing hid her assets, so to speak, but the hint of what lay underneath only intrigued him. The mystery underneath. He'd always been the kind of guy who found the suggestion of something far more enticing than the overt. Be it life or women, he preferred following clues, delving deeper to unveil the mystery.

Although sometimes seeking those answers backfired, like that long-ago summer vacation when he'd sneaked into the ocean. Pulled under those churning waves, he'd learned that secrets could be colder and harsher than the sparkling reality he'd hoped to find.

He felt a flicker of concern at what lay beneath Frances's involvement with Dima, but dismissed it. She was complicated as hell, but he wasn't picking up on any dark, churning waters under her surface.

"Anyway, it's basketball season," she continued, "so these days we prefer to sit in front of the telly and order in Chinese. Obviously no need for a bodyguard when I'm at home."

He wasn't sure if she was still talking about Saturday or had moved on to Sunday, but he'd sort it out later.

She stopped at the doors and turned to face him. Rain battered the glass behind her. A streak of lightning flared in the gloom of clouds.

With her back to the glass, her body outlined by hazy, gray light, she seemed like a shadow. He peered into her face, a dusky oval fringed by wisps of blond hair.

"What time do you want me back here?" he asked. When she didn't answer, he clarified, "To escort you to your car."

"I thought maybe you'd get the hint from my schedule," she said, her voice tight. "I don't need a bodyguard. To escort me after work or at any other time."

He did a small double take, surprised at her about-face. "What's with the cold shoulder?"

"I'm simply stating what I want."

"Meaning you want this *friend* of yours to be your protector instead?" Feeling a surge of anger, he decided to chill and count to ten, made it to three. "Who is this guy, anyway? I know *every* protection agent in town, especially the *best ones*."

She snorted something about know-it-alls.

"Yeah, well, it happens to be true. What's his name?"

"Doesn't matter."

"Does to me."

"Don't take this personally."

"How am I supposed to take it?" When she didn't

respond, he continued, "Look, just tell me what your issue is. Your *real* issue. Not that *expressive* bullshit. And what was the other one...? I remember, my *rust bucket* car. I've known a fair share of executives, because I happen to be skilled in *executive protection,* but I've never met one who resorted to personal attacks to make a point."

They stared at each other for a long, drawn-out moment.

"I know you can talk, Frances, because you've been doing it nonstop all the way down the hall."

She slumped against the glass door, the outside light casting a faint, silvery line down the length of her neck.

"I'm sorry for saying those things," she whispered huskily. "It wasn't fair."

He hadn't been ready for an apology.

"I've been called worse than *expressive,*" he murmured, shifting closer, liking her scent. Salty, clean. Not like the other day when he caught a more exotic, flowery fragrance. "What was that about?"

She peered up at him, a low, throaty sigh escaping her lips.

"You—" she swallowed, hard "—show your emotions."

"Is that a sin, Frances?" he whispered, slipping his hand inside his coat, skimming his fingers along the hem of her thermal top. "To reveal what I like?"

She gasped as he touched the bare skin of her stomach. A sound so soft, so quick, yet it struck him like a bolt of lightning, sending a hot, dark thrill through him.

"You haunt me," he murmured, stroking her impossibly soft skin, his entire body coursing with need, desperate to taste her. He angled his face, his lips almost brushing against hers....

"I can't," she whispered shakily.

He paused, felt a shudder pass through her body, her warm breath fanning his face.

He started to pull away.

She grabbed his shirt. "Stay."

Outside, lightning popped, turning the world a surreal blue, and in that instant he caught an outline of something on her cheek. Then the light vanished and the shadows returned. He blinked, unsure if he'd actually seen anything.

In those few fleeting moments, everything changed.

Frances had slipped away, like a trail of smoke, and now stood several feet to his left, her face turned away from the faint light seeping through rain-splashed glass doors.

She took off his coat and held it out to him.

He accepted it, fumbling for something to say, but it didn't matter because she was already gone, just like that, her shoes squeaking as she walked back down the long hallway.

He stood there stupidly, wondering what in the hell had just happened, then put on his coat.

Shoving open the glass door, he ducked his head

against a blast of rain and wind, thinking it was a helluva lot easier to deal with this storm than with Miss Frances Jefferies.

## *CHAPTER EIGHT*

FRANCES SPENT THE REST of Monday in Oleg's cramped office, which was furnished with an old metal desk littered with computer parts and cola cans, numerous cardboard boxes, a standing coatrack that held a black coat and several shirts, and a whirring rotary fan that clicked when it reversed direction.

On the wall was a banner in Russian:

*Сохранять спокойствие и перезагрузка*

Which Oleg translated to mean "Keep calm and reboot." So the computer nerd had a sense of humor. With his dour looks and barely there smiles, who knew?

After reviewing the blueprints of the Palazzo floor plan for several hours, he displayed the driver's license photos she'd seen earlier on his computer screen, identifying each person by name, background and security specialty.

He then mentioned two other people on Dmitri's team—Holt, who worked with alarms, and Aldo, a safecracker—and that neither needed to be physically inside the Russian Confection offices, as most of their work was accomplished remotely.

"I hijack feed at Palazzo, send images of alarms to Holt. He study, learn what kind they are. Early on day of heist, we disable."

"How?" she asked.

"Sometime we do remote."

"Remotely? You mean, over the internet?"

Oleg nodded. "Or other remote-access connections. If not possible, do old way. Dima's electrician friend makes visit."

"Not easy to gain access to alarm systems at a luxury resort such as the Palazzo."

"True, never easy. But is fun challenge, yes?" When Oleg smiled—the first time she'd ever seen him really smile—she saw he wore braces. The clear kind, so they weren't obvious when he spoke.

It dawned on her he wasn't as uptight as she'd assumed, just wary of grinning because he didn't want people to see his braces. Had to be difficult constantly fighting the urge to laugh, harder than it was for her to slap on gel and makeup.

Yet he'd decided to trust her with a smile.

She wanted to tell him braces weren't an imperfection and that lots of people wore them. But she knew too well that telling someone to accept something couldn't make the person magically do so. The person had to feel it inside, want to take a chance on acceptance for themselves, from others. Or so her therapist had repeatedly said.

For a moment, Frances envied Oleg. At least his imperfection would come off someday, maybe soon. Hers never would.

He grew serious again, talked about sending Aldo pictures of locks on the jewelry cases used in the exhibit. Frances realized computer-genius Oleg had hacked into surveillance systems in at least one other place where the Legendary Gems exhibit had been shown.

"From photos, he make keys," he explained. "Should exhibit change metal locks to digital, Aldo be nearby to…" He frowned, waggling his fingers in the air.

"Break into the digital locks?"

"Yes. Plus there will be…" He threw up his hands.

"A distraction? Interruption?"

He nodded enthusiastically. "Yes, interruption. *Boom!*"

Good God. Were they planning on using… "Guns?"

"No guns. Smoke."

"Smoke bombs."

"Yes."

What a circus that would create. But such a plan had been successfully executed a few years ago by a group calling themselves Ice—a slang term for diamond—who'd coolly walked into a French jewelry store and set off a few smoke bombs. In the chaos, they'd quickly slipped on gas masks, smashed several jewelry cases and walked out with three million in jewels.

Even if this heist actually took place, Vanderbilt and Palazzo security would be surreptitiously working with Frances so she'd have easy access to the case containing the Helena Diamond necklace. As Charlie told her at brunch, there'd be a replica there that she'd "steal." There'd be no need for crazy antics like smoke bombs and safecrackers manipulating digital locks.

Thank God Dmitri and Oleg weren't planning for her to bring a pickax into the jewelry exhibit, a favorite tool of the international jewel thieves the Pink Panthers, whose M.O. was to smash cases and grab jewels.

"You said no guns," she said to Oleg.

"*Nyet.* No guns."

"Good because I never carry one."

One thing she'd made clear to Charlie at the beginning was she'd never carry a firearm. He'd told her Vanderbilt had similar feelings on the subject—guns and people under stress were never a good combination. After all, an insurance company would be the last to want *that* liability.

Around four that afternoon, Oleg stood and plucked his jacket off the coatrack.

"I take Raisa to doctor," he explained. "She six months pregnant. Tomorrow, be here at nine. We discuss more security."

"Can I get a key for the office?" she asked.

He shrugged. "Ask Dima."

After he left, she continued reviewing the photographs of Palazzo security personnel. As much as she was dying to check out other files on his computer, she didn't want her snooping to be tracked by any keystroke-logging software Oleg might have downloaded. Plus she'd noticed one surveillance camera in the hallway and guessed there were others in these offices, so even taking pictures with her smartphone—if she'd had it with her, which she didn't—would be out of the question.

Close to five, she headed to Dmitri's office to grab her jacket and purse. She'd felt uncomfortable retrieving them earlier because he'd had visitors, but now his door was locked. She knocked a few times, called his name. No answer. She headed back to Oleg's office, looked out the window at the parking lot. The black limo was gone.

*Nice.* That egocentric Russian had left for the day without a second thought that her stuff was locked inside his office.

Heaving a frustrated sigh, she looked at Oleg's computer, debating whether to shoot an email to her dad to pick her up. No, didn't want Oleg analyzing the record of her keystrokes and learning about her email account, or her dad's for that matter.

Of course, maybe she wasn't stuck. Maybe Braxton was waiting to escort her to her car.... Oh, sure, like that was gonna happen today or ever. After she'd shot him down and walked away without a word, his next call was probably to Dmitri saying "I quit."

She looked up at the banner on the wall. *Keep calm and reboot.* When bits and bytes went awry, sometimes a quick computer reboot fixed everything. Like magic. She wished she could reboot the mess she'd created between her and Braxton. It was just...this case didn't need the complications of whatever was going on between them. Plus he saw too much.

Her heart thudding painfully, she recalled that moment. The flash of lightning. His face, the focus of his eyes, caught in that surreal light. He'd no doubt seen a faint line, the contoured edge of the silicone gel.

The tip of her secret.

And she'd bolted. An automatic response.

But it was more than his catching sight of her secret. It was also what he unraveled within her. He made her crazy with heat and wanting. Underneath that boyish charm was more hot male than she could handle. Than she'd *ever* handled. Stir in the demands of this case, and she was one confused, uptight woman.

A thud made her jump.

Her heart pounding, she stood stock-still, listening to a faint, high-pitched whining and realizing it was the wind. Another soft thud. She glanced outside the window, noticed a palm tree bending with gusts of wind, thumping the side of the building.

She needed to leave while there was still daylight.

A few minutes later, she headed down the long, chilly corridor, hugging herself for warmth, trying the doorknobs to the few companies on this floor. Only one, Quick-Silver Courier Service, was unlocked, but the place was dark, empty.

At least she had the four hundred dollars in her pants pocket. She'd go to Sunset Road, a ten-minute walk away, and head down it until she found a restaurant or gas station where she could call her dad.

Ahead, sunlight sparked on the glass doors. A man stepped into view.

Braxton.

She smiled, almost feeling giddy with relief. He'd come back, despite her snub. *A man of his word.* Which made her admire him all the more.

Couldn't have him drive her home, though. Like other investigators at Vanderbilt, her home address had been removed from all public documents, even assessors' property records, as a safety precaution. Not even super-hacker Oleg could dredge it up. She'd tell Braxton she'd had a change of plans, that she was meeting friends at a restaurant. Once he dropped her off, she could call a cab or her dad.

As she neared the doors, she saw Braxton more clearly through the glass. He stood tall like a sentry, watching her, his hands in his coat pockets. Sunlight cast a golden sheen on his face. Gusts of wind flipped up the bottom of his coat.

Maybe she'd thought him to be goofy before, but in that light, wearing that coat, he looked tough, uncompromising and hot as sin. A tremor passed through her as she remembered his hand sliding under her top, the shock of his fingers touching her. Like liquid heat. And when he'd moved closer, his lips almost brushing hers, Frances the investigator had murmured *I can't,* but Frances the woman had wanted desperately to give in....

He shoved open the door. Chilling breezes swirled inside.

"Where's your jacket?"

Her teeth chattering, she wrapped her arms tighter around herself. "Locked in Dmitri's office, along with my purse...."

He stepped inside, slamming the door shut behind him, and began removing his coat.

"I can't keep taking your—"

"Shut up," he murmured, slipping it off.

He wore a formfitting crewneck sweater that hinted at the muscled contour of his chest, the strength in his arms. Moving nearer, she noticed the hard line of his lips easing into a sensual curve.

Wrapping his coat around her, she relaxed into his familiar scents, his stolen body heat. Standing in front of her, he closed every single button, one by one, top to bottom, then tightened the sash, sealing her into his world.

For one crazy, heady moment, she imagined herself never leaving this sheltering cocoon, bundled into his warmth and smells, sequestered from the world and its problems. A place where she could finally let go, surrender...

Surrender to what?

A sense of melancholy rippled through her as she realized she had no clue how to answer that, only felt the yearning to relinquish something, the way a soldier might lay down arms, a longing that frightened as much as compelled her.

"Where do you live?" Braxton asked. "Wait, let me guess. Summerlin?"

She nodded. Hardly pinpointing where she lived, since Summerlin covered over twenty thousand acres.

"Your Benz tipped me off," he said. "Used to live out there myself, back in my *la vida* Las Vegas days. My mom's place—that's where I'm staying now—is near there, in the old Charleston Heights area." He checked his watch. "I have an appointment at Bally's in fifteen minutes—it'll only take half an hour or so. Lots of restaurants there, so take your pick. It's my treat. Afterward, I'll drive you home. How does that sound?"

He was trying to take care of her while juggling another commitment. *Despite* how she'd behaved earlier. It took guts to come back, but even more impressive, it took class to behave like a gentleman, as well.

If only they'd met at another time, under different circumstances...

As if wishing would get her anywhere. Time for the logical part of her mind to take over, say goodbye to that other person she repressed, the one who wrestled with her needs.

"Sounds good," she lied.

WHENEVER BRAXTON WALKED into Bally's, it was like walking back in time to when he was a kid visiting his dad at work. Even after twenty-some-odd years, the place was still loud with music and buzzing slot machines, the air laced with cigar smoke and cheap perfume.

He remembered the Chex Party Mix.

Their dad, being in security, had to be on the floor at all times, so he'd leave Braxton and Drake with his good pal, a bartender at the sports book, who'd sneak the boys into a back booth, where waitresses served them endless sodas and bowls of the crunchy, salty mix. Being a fledging chef, Braxton started bringing in extra goodies—corn nuts, Reesc's Pieces, pretzels—to add to it, calling his creations the Brax-Chex Party-Hearty Mix.

"What time is it?" Frances asked.

He pulled out his cell phone, checked the screen. "Six-fifteen."

They should have been here by five-thirty, easy, but traffic on the Strip had moved like sludge. When it moved at all. On the way here, he'd called Li'l Bit to explain he was running late, suggested they meet near the front entrance.

"See your friend?" Frances asked.

"No."

From the way she stood—shoulders hunched, head bent—she seemed to have withdrawn into his coat.

"You okay?" he asked.

She nodded unconvincingly while turning away slightly. Over her shoulder she shot him a wary look, her usually sparkling amethyst eyes now dulled.

"I'm going to the ladies' room," she murmured.

He watched her walk away, the overhead lights splashing reds and yellows on her form, half wondering if he should follow. No, when a lady excused herself to the restroom, a gentleman let her go. Only an idiot would follow. And he'd played the idiot enough lately with his open-mouth-insert-foot comments.

He was hoping he hadn't come across like an idiot again earlier today at their near-thermal meltdown.

On the ride over, he hadn't mentioned the subject, and neither had she. Hell, he was relieved they were getting along, even though they seemed to talk the weather to death. And the traffic. The kind of topics two nervous people babbled about as they avoided other, more uncomfortable ones.

After the weather and traffic, she'd asked about his meeting at Bally's, and he'd explained that he was helping a friend named Li'l Bit get into shape, but he didn't mention the auction.

Braxton kept waiting for an opening to ask Frances if he'd somehow offended her earlier, but none presented itself, or maybe he was too chicken to ask. Or maybe he wanted to show her he was one of the good guys, someone who, like his dad, didn't hold grudges, wanted to do the right thing, wanted to be there for her.

Wanted her to know that whatever she felt, experienced, needed was more important than anything else in his world.

Didn't stop him from worrying that he'd done something to make her suddenly walk away.

He kept mentally going over what had happened, beginning with when she'd hurt her toe. Things had started heating up when he'd guided her out of the office, their arms around each other, her hip snuggled against his side, the clean scent of her soap doing a wicked number on his senses. But he'd kept it together.

However, when he'd slowly slipped off her shoe, gradually exposing her pale foot, his fingers touching her skin, it had felt as though he were undressing her.

Maybe he shouldn't have asked her out to eat after that.

But then, the lighting wasn't so great in that hallway—a faint bluish-gray light from overhead fluorescents—so maybe she hadn't noticed that he was aroused.

Although she couldn't have missed it minutes later as they were feverishly pressed against each other, their body heat fogging the glass...thunder growling... his fingers daring to touch her impossibly soft skin... her rapid, choked breaths....

And in a pop of light, everything ended.

"Brax, dude, you made it!"

Flip-flops slapping against the marble floor, Li'l Bit lumbered toward him—his swaying gait, hairy legs and bushy hair bringing to mind a woolly mammoth. He wore plaid shorts and a tie-dyed T-shirt with the words *You Are Entering a World of Pain.*

With a lazy smile, he slapped to a stop in front of Braxton. "Hey, man, how's it hangin'?"

Braxton slipped his phone into his pocket. "Where's your workout bag?"

"Don't have a bag, man. This is how I roll."

"Well, you can't roll into the fitness center wearing

flip-flops. Fortunately, they sell workout shoes there, so we'll buy you a pair."

"*Rules,* man."

"Yeah, well, that's how the universe rolls." He looked into Li'l Bit's eyes, pinker than a Ruby Red grapefruit. "You're stoned."

Li'l Bit reared his head back. "Dude, I get the bad-attitude thing, but who died and made you the ganja police?"

Maybe he was worn down by one long, strange day, but the question hit Braxton's funny bone. Who cared if Li'l Bit got zonked out of his gourd? This weeklong workout was for a freaking *Manwich* auction, not the Olympics.

"Sorry," he muttered, "I've been under some stress lately."

Li'l Bit placed a meaty hand on his shoulder. "It's that blonde, right? Your mom talked to me about her, says you don't really know anything about her, not even her last name—"

"She's talking to *you* about Frances?"

What was it with his family? At least when they'd started gossiping about him, they kept it among themselves. Now it was spilling over to outsiders.

"Hey, man, we were just talkin' a little while playing slots. No big deal—"

"Slots?" Braxton looked around. "Mom's here?"

"Yeah, she's signing up for that contest thing...."

"What contest thing?"

"Poker contest."

"Poker tournament?"

"Tournament, yeah, that's what they call it." Li'l Bit scratched his double chin. "Dorothy's really stoked about doing this, man, been talking about it for weeks, so since I was cruisin' to Bally's to meet you, I asked her along, figured she could catch a ride home with you after our workout."

As a rendition of "Stairway to Heaven" started playing, competing with the symphony of whizzing, chirping slot machines, Braxton thought back to his mom playing poker years ago, mostly at Bally's while waiting for his dad to get off work. He'd had no idea she still played...or was *stoked* to enter a tournament.

It already rankled him that his family could talk *about* him, but to know they weren't sharing themselves *with* him? What was the point of returning to the family fold if he stayed outside the crease?

"She could've told me about the tournament," he groused, shooting a quick look toward the restrooms. No Frances.

"Dude, it's not like anybody's keeping secrets, man. It's just—"

"Just what?" Braxton snapped.

Li'l Bit shook his head sorrowfully, his woolly mane quivering a second or two longer.

"I'm saying this from a place of love, Brax, but you gotta shine life on, dude. Like the Eagles said, you gotta start taking it a whole lot easier."

"*Take it easy,* you mean."

"Yeah, man, you're getting the message." His pink

eyes got pinker as they started welling up. "Because I love you like a brother, dude."

"I'm not your..." The rest of his sentence faded away as he saw Frances heading toward them.

She held herself stiffly as she walked, her shoulders still hunched, but not as much as before, her mass of blond hair looking slightly different, as if she'd rearranged it or something....

She held her hand cupped close to her face, which made him think she was talking into a cell phone, then remembered hers was in her purse, locked in Dima's office. Then he wondered if she was eating something, but as she came closer he saw that wasn't the case. Yet her hand hovered near her face.

Twenty or so feet away she paused, her eyes locked on his, her hand, small and white, hovering near her cheek.

"Wow," Li'l Bit said, "that chick with the Lion King hair is wearing a trench coat *just* like yours."

"That's because it *is* my coat," he muttered.

Reaching them, she stopped, her body angled as though she were ready to bolt at a moment's notice. The way she was turned, he and Li'l Bit could only see half of her face.

"Sorry I took so long," she said quietly, "but you wouldn't believe the lines." She glanced at Li'l Bit's T-shirt and smiled. "That's one of my favorite lines. I'm a big fan of the Coen brothers."

He stared at her, his face slack with awe, the way the kid in the movie *E.T.* looked after the alien's glowing finger touched his forehead. Then, as though zapped back to life, he lurched forward and clasped her hand with both of his.

"My name's Nathan, but everyone calls me Li'l Bit."

"And I'm Dorothy," a voice said, "Braxton's mother."

His mother stood erect, dressed in gray pants and her yellow bowling league shirt with *Dot* stitched in red over the pocket. Her short-nailed fingers played on the strap of her shoulder bag as her hazel eyes focused on the trench coat, then took in the explosion of blond hair.

"I'm Frances Jefferies." Maintaining her angled stance, she dipped her head in greeting. "I'm wearing your son's coat because mine got locked in our boss's office."

"*Our* boss," Dorothy repeated, brightening. "So when do you start, Braxton?"

"It's a, uh, two-part venture," he said. "I'll tell you about it later."

"Are you a lawyer at this company?" she asked Frances, who looked momentarily confused.

"No."

"She's a vice president, Mom."

"Vice president of…?"

"Marketing," Frances answered.

"Sales," Braxton said at the same time.

"Marketing *and* sales," she quickly corrected, "although Dmitri just calls it sales."

Braxton thought it was odd for Dima to lop off part of a job title. The guy disagreed with Shakespeare, for

God's sake, for writing "What's in a name?" Couldn't simply say his ringtone was just Tchaikovsky—no, it was Tchaikovsky's concerto for violin in something major.

"Okay," he said, "time to get this show on the road. Mom, would you mind walking Li'l Bit to the fitness center while I get Frances set up?"

"Set up?" his mom asked.

"He's treating her to dinner while we work out," Li'l Bit explained.

"But...she'll be alone." Dorothy pressed the air with her hands in a this-is-how-we'll-do-it gesture. "You and Li'l Bit go to the fitness center while *I* take Frances to the sports book—left my jacket there with Ross, so I have to pick it up anyway—and she can grab a bite to eat there."

"Ross still bartends at the sports book?" Braxton gave his head a disbelieving shake. "He must be a hundred years old by now."

Dorothy scoffed, "Mid-seventies isn't old...well, much. Anyway, he only works a few nights a week and still makes the best Zombie in town."

"Sorry," Frances interrupted, starting to unbutton the trench coat, "but I can't stay. My dad's on his way here to give me a ride home."

Stung by the news, Braxton stared at her, or the half of her he could see. "But...when I asked to treat you to dinner..."

"I said yes, I know, but then we got stuck in traffic, and I didn't realize how late it was getting," she said, her words tumbling over each other, her hand fluttering up to her face again. "It just seemed, you know, easier to call my father, have him pick me up."

In the awkward, strung-out moments that followed, Braxton tried to contain his disappointment—and his hurt.

"When did you call your father?" he asked quietly.

"When I visited the ladies' room."

"Whose phone?"

"Don't know her name...."

"A stranger."

She nodded.

"Could've borrowed my phone at any time. On the ride over. Here...."

"Thought you needed it to call Li'l Bit—"

His gut flipped. "I get the picture," he murmured. "You borrowed some stranger's cell phone because you wanted to call your dad. Or a boyfriend—"

"I don't have a boy—"

"Look," he interrupted, "if you didn't want to do dinner, fine. Didn't want me to drive you home, okay. But you could have told me to my face."

He looked at Li'l Bit and his mom. "Yeah, I liked her, okay?" He laughed as though all this had just been some kind of joke, no big deal. "But I'll get over it. Feel free to share this end-of-the-great-love-affair-that-never-happened with Drake, Val, Grams, Richmond, your bowling league, your ganja pals, the *Las Vegas Sun*...." He paused, the reality catching up that he, the guy whose black book had been the envy of his buddies—who used to brag that he understood women better than they understood themselves—had missed the signs that Frances wasn't all that into him.

His mom reached out to him. "Braxton, darling—"

"I'm okay, Mom," he said as he strode away, half hearing Li'l Bit calling for him to wait up, but he wasn't slowing, wasn't waiting.

He probably should have taken his cue when Frances had slid out of their near-kiss earlier today, but that wouldn't have stopped him from returning later to escort her to her car, show her he could be a gentleman.

Good thing he had, too, because she'd been stranded in a desolate industrial park, only minutes of sunlight left. No jacket. No keys to her car. No phone to call for help.

Braxton toyed with the idea of calling Dima in the morning, explaining something else had come up, sorry, that he couldn't fulfill the part-time executive-protection gig. Suggest that Dima hire that best-in-Vegas bodyguard pal of Frances's instead.

Meanwhile, Braxton would fulfill the Yuri investigation, burn through that retainer. After that, his head and heart should be in better shape about Frances, making it easier to tackle that Security Director position.

"Dude, please…wait up."

Braxton stopped and turned.

Li'l Bit, trying to jog in his flip-flops, held up his hand as though hailing a cab. Seeing Braxton had stopped for him, he sank heavily against a slot machine, his face the color of a ripe tomato, gasping for air.

"Man, I haven't…run this much…since fourth grade…." He lifted the hem of his T-shirt and stared at the waistband of his plaid shorts. "Wow…I popped a button…."

The little old lady playing the slot machine stared, horrified, at Li'l Bit's round, hairy gut.

Braxton headed over before she called security. Tonight was bad enough without his family losing their lifetime discount, too.

"Check the button in the men's locker room," he said, taking Li'l Bit by the elbow and steering him away from disaster.

"But—"

"No buts," he said, "or showing guts. You can quote me on that."

"Dude, I'm sorry…about Frances."

"I'm sorry, too," he murmured.

FRANCES STOOD NEAR Dorothy Morgan, slowly unbuttoning the trench coat, unnerved by the woman's unflinching stare. Michael Jackson's song "Bad" pulsed over the speakers.

Frances felt badder, if that was even a word.

She understood how it looked, leaving to make a "secret" call, but she hadn't done it to deceive Braxton. Didn't mean she wasn't sorry that he'd felt hurt.

"My son might not be perfect," Dorothy finally said, keeping her eyes on Frances's face, "but he's a good man who's trying to live an honest life, and he deserves honesty—" her chin trembled "—from *all* of us in return."

"I didn't realize he'd take it this way. I'm sorry," she managed to say around the ache in her throat.

"Me, too." Dorothy released a heavy sigh. "I feel like a hypocrite. Always said I don't believe in gossip, told my friends I won't condone it, and then I go and blab about my son to others."

"Your intention wasn't to hurt him," she said softly, as much to herself as Dorothy.

"But I did."

A sadness engulfed Frances as she missed her own mother, who wasn't as tough as Braxton's mom seemed to be, but had been every bit as caring and loyal.

"Well," Dorothy said, rolling back her shoulders, "it's none of my business what you feel for him, but if you didn't want him to treat you to dinner, he's right, you should have told him up front, before you made your plans to leave." The furrow between her eyebrows deepened. "Do you have a boyfriend? Is that who you called?"

"No." She swallowed hard. "I really did call my dad."

"You needed privacy to do that?"

"Yes."

"If I didn't know better, I'd say you don't want Braxton to have your dad's phone number."

That was blunt and to the point. And partially correct. If Frances had made the call from Braxton's phone, her dad's cell number would have been stored as an outgoing call. Investigators had all kinds of tricks they could run with phone numbers, such as plugging them into proprietary and specialized phone-number databases. A really good investigator could take a seemingly insignificant result from one of those researches and extract new leads from it, and she didn't want to risk Braxton identifying her as a Vanderbilt investigator.

But mostly, she didn't want Braxton or anyone else to overhear her telling her dad her scar was starting to show, and to please come quickly, and bring her makeup bag off her dresser. She'd whispered all this to him over the stranger's phone while standing in a corner stall in the women's bathroom, the door locked. He hadn't questioned her shaky-voiced request, just said he'd be on his way.

"What time is it?" Frances asked.

After shooting her a quizzical look, Dorothy checked her wristwatch. "Six-forty."

She probably should have called a cab instead of her dad, but Frances had felt rushed, panicked. With the mess of traffic along the Strip, who knew when he'd get here. Her scar was already visible, would be more so as the minutes ticked past....

"Frances, this is already an awkward conversation, but it would help if you looked at me while we're talking. I feel as though I'm talking to your shoulder."

Frances nodded, knowing that her stance, mostly turned away, likely came across as rude. Cupping her hand over her scar, she turned toward Dorothy, her head bowed.

"I need special makeup," she whispered.

Dorothy leaned closer. "I'm having trouble hearing you...."

Frances raised her head a little. "I always keep special makeup in my purse, in my car, but I couldn't get to them." Her nerves wound tighter with each second, her worries bubbling and churning like boiling water.

She swallowed hard, wondering if she should go outside and wait for her dad, but it was chilly out there and she couldn't keep Braxton's coat, and who knew how long she'd be waiting, surrounded by crowds of strangers, and she didn't want anybody seeing, staring.

She glanced at the ladies' restroom, which, although a short walk, was packed with women standing in line.

Her panic rising, she looked across the casino at the swarms of laughing, chatting people, at the restaurants crammed with customers, more lines of people waiting to get inside.

There was nowhere to go....

"Special makeup," Dorothy said, gazing at her curiously. "I don't understand."

Frances nodded, a headache throbbing to life behind her eyes. She'd shared her darkest, ugliest secret with so few people in her life—five or six, maybe—but never with a stranger.

With her free hand, she gripped Dorothy's arm and tugged her closer, so close she could smell the older woman's rose-scented perfume.

Turning her head slightly, she uncupped her hand, holding her fingers stiffly at the side of her face, like a fan, so passersby wouldn't see.

"Oh, Frances," Dorothy murmured.

Cupping her cheek again, she met Dorothy's worried gaze.

"Please," she whispered hoarsely, "help me hide."

As Dorothy guided Frances—her head bowed, hand cupped on her cheek—across the crowded lobby, Frances felt like a kid being steered across a street by a no-nonsense crossing guard.

When she'd first met Braxton's mom, Frances had been hit with how different she was from her son. Rigid and critical, compared to his fervent charisma. Even her clothes were practical, whereas Braxton's were designer all the way. She'd kept her cool, while Braxton had a tendency to run hot.

But Frances saw one trait mother and son shared—they both had caring, protective natures.

The jingling slot machines and pop music faded as they entered the sports book, a theaterlike auditorium. People, many with drinks in their hands, sat in rows of seats facing walls embedded with screens silently playing different sports events. Occasionally there'd be yells and clapping, along with a disgruntled sports fan barking an expletive.

"You like white wine?" Dorothy asked.

"Sure."

As they passed the bar, she said to a silver-haired

bartender, "Two glasses of house white, Ross. Taking my friend to the boys' booth."

He nodded. "Haven't sold your jacket yet."

Moments later, Dorothy ushered Frances into a red vinyl booth nestled in the back of the sports book, quietly ensuring that her right cheek faced a wall. There were a few scattered tables nearby, all empty. Lights were dim back here, the area giving Frances an added sense of safety.

"Two chardonnays," announced a skinny waitress with pale skin whose name tag read Jan—Fresno, CA. As she set the glasses on the table, Frances noticed a silver tag engraved with a heart and the date 03-16-2009 dangling from a chain around her neck.

Dorothy reached for her purse.

Jan waved it off. "Ross says it's on the house."

"Tell him thank you," Dorothy said. "How's Denny?"

"Turns five next month. Has his heart set on going to Disneyland and eating lunch with Mickey Mouse, but the cost for gas, hotel, Disneyland... I'm trying to convince him Chuck E. Cheese's is as much fun as Mickey. Wish me luck."

She reached over to another table, picked up a small object and set it on their table. Frances saw it was a rock with writing on one flattened side.

"Menu for Rocky's Deli," Jan explained. "We started serving their food a few weeks ago. I recommend their pastrami on rye."

"Got a roast cooking at home," Dorothy said. "Hungry, Frances?"

She was starving, but wanted to wait to eat dinner with her dad. "No, thanks."

After Jan left, Dorothy said, "Jan's a single mom. She had it rough when Denny was diagnosed with epilepsy a few years ago, but fortunately medicine is helping control his seizures." She made an amused noise. "Lunch with Mickey Mouse. When Braxton was that age, he was all about Donald Duck. Bought him a pair of Donald Duck pajamas, which he insisted on wearing *every single day.* I explained they were *pajamas,* to be worn at *night,* but once that boy gets his mind stuck on something, watch out, world. I gave in—bought four more pairs of Donald Duck pajamas so there'd always be a clean set handy."

"Donald Duck," Frances mused, thinking of his classy clothes style. "The first of a long line of designer labels."

"Ha! Never thought of it that way, but too true. He also loves nice cars, nice restaurants…although he's a better cook than most chefs, if you ask me. The way he makes spaghetti *alla puttanesca,* you'd think he had an Italian mama. You like to cook?"

"I make a mean slice of toast."

Dorothy laughed, clinked her glass against Frances's. "We all gotta start somewhere, dear."

After they sipped their wine, Frances edged into a topic that had been weighing heavily on her heart.

"Did I blow it with Braxton?"

For all the times she'd told herself getting involved was a bad idea, now she was second-guessing herself.

Dorothy mulled that over for a few moments. "I'd love to say no, but I'd be lying. Once he's made up his mind about something, he tends to stick to it. Too much pride, like me." Pause. "Ever been married?"

"No."

"Neither has Braxton."

"Has he ever been engaged?"

Dorothy arched an "are you kidding me?" eyebrow. "Let's just say there was a time he made Hugh Hefner in his heyday look like a wallflower."

"Wow."

"Wow's right. He didn't get that playboy streak from his father or me. But those days are behind him." She paused. "Have to say, I've never seen him carry on about a woman the way he has over you."

Frances's heart shrank a little. *He won't be carrying on about me anymore.*

"What time is your father getting here?"

"It's a half-hour drive from my condo, but with Strip traffic being bumper to bumper…"

"Good idea to call him, check his estimated time of arrival." Dorothy rummaged in her purse. "I've got to stop buying monster-size purses," she muttered. "I can never find a damned thing… My other sock! Wondered where that was. Okay, found it…." She set her cell phone on the table. "Parking's a hassle, so tell him to wait in the loading zone across the street, and I'll walk you to his car."

Frances hesitated, again questioning the wisdom of

leaving a digital footprint on any device. Seemed silly to worry about it, but...

"Same problem using my phone as my son's?"

A bit stunned by the older woman's accurate assessment, Frances fumbled for what to say. But she couldn't lie. Not to Dorothy, who'd seen the scar *and* Frances's panicked reaction, without feeling the need to pummel her with questions. How'd it happen? When? Where? How do you feel, what is it like, will it ever go away....?

Who'd accepted Frances without conditions.

Not only did she trust Dorothy with the truth, she owed it to her.

"You're right," she finally answered.

"I like your honesty. As my husband, Benny, used to say, honesty is less profitable than dishonesty, but it feels better. Have to say, anybody who's this nervous about borrowing someone's cell phone is hiding something. So, let's start at the beginning. Is your name really Frances Jefferies?"

Frances almost laughed at the older woman's forthright approach, the exact opposite of her own mother, who'd had a tendency to be soft-spoken and overly polite.

"Yes, that's my real name."

"And...you really work at this company where my son interviewed today?"

She paused. "Yes."

"You seem unsure."

"It's complicated."

"Most things in life are, dear. Braxton's security position seems fairly straightforward, however."

"As part-time bodyguard positions go, I suppose."

Dorothy pursed her lips. "I didn't know that."

"I only know about the bodyguard position. There's another job Dmitri's hired him for, but I know nothing about it."

After the older woman took a sip of wine, she asked, "Are you really a vice president?"

"No. I'm an…insurance investigator."

"Oh, dear God." Dorothy downed several sips of wine in quick succession.

Of all the possible reactions, that was the *last* one Frances anticipated.

"I'll call my dad now," she murmured, picking up the phone.

A moment later, he answered. "Baby girl, you okay?"

"I'm fine, Dad. A friend is with me."

"Charlie?"

"No. Her name's Dorothy. I'm using her phone. When you get here, park across the street in the loading zone and call me. You should have the number in your call log."

"I'm glad you're with someone. I've been worried sick about you." He cleared his throat. "Hey, whatcha want for dinner?"

After a brief discussion about Spam, Chinese takeout or frozen pizza, the latter winning out, she ended the call.

"He should be here in ten minutes," she said, putting the phone down.

"Good." Dorothy paused. "Sorry about my outburst."

"Sorry about my meltdown earlier."

The older woman's eyes softened. "You're a naturally beautiful woman, Frances.... Don't let that scar get in your way of living life. Besides, we all have scars—most people's just aren't visible."

"Thanks," Frances said quietly, circling her finger around the base of her glass. "Since we're being honest, is there a problem with my being an investigator?"

Dorothy gave a wry smile. "Oh, I hate the profession and refuse to have another family member work in that field. But other than that, no."

"But...I'm not a family member."

Dorothy didn't say anything, just gently laid her hand on Frances's.

Frances looked down at the older woman's hand, so large it swallowed hers up, the skin threaded with veins, yet so warm. She imagined Dorothy's hands tending to her children, writing, cooking, caressing a loved one.

They finished their wine and headed toward the bar. Dorothy paused in a private area next to a fake palm. "I need to pick up my jacket from Ross—wait here for me?"

As Dorothy walked away, Frances smiled to herself, thinking about five-year-old Braxton wearing Donald Duck pajamas.

Hit with another thought, she quickly crossed the

few steps back to their booth, where she fished the four one-hundred-dollar bills out of her pocket and placed them under the rock menu, imagining another five-year-old boy's glee when he finally met Mickey.

Exiting Bally's, Dorothy and Frances scurried down the sidewalk packed with pedestrians, vendors hawking tickets and street performers. They paused at the corner of Flamingo Road to wait for the light to turn green, hunching into their coats as chilly winds blustered past.

"There's my dad," Frances said, pointing to a metallic blue Honda Accord parked in a loading zone across the street.

As they approached the Honda, her dad jumped out of the driver's side, jogged to the passenger door and opened it. Frances quickly introduced Dorothy to her dad, then kissed him on the cheek and slid inside the car.

He slammed shut the door and Frances sank into her seat. The motor chugged quietly, the heater on high, and she luxuriated in the warmth.

She looked through the windshield at Dorothy, who stood on the sidewalk, bundled in her brown hooded jacket, talking to her dad. With the windows up and the heater running, Frances only heard bits and pieces of the conversation.

"I insisted…coat home," Dorothy said.

Sounded like Dorothy was explaining she insisted Frances wear the trench coat home.

After an unintelligible exchange, her dad looked down at his bulky Miami Heat sweatshirt, then back at Dorothy. Frances swore he said *thermals*. Was he talking about his thermal underwear? Whatever it was, it made the older woman smile.

They exchanged a few more words before Dorothy waved and headed back to the crosswalk.

Her dad got into the driver's seat.

"Warm enough?" he asked, adjusting the heat settings.

"Yes, car's nice and toasty," Frances answered. "Thanks."

"Dorothy seems very nice. Appreciate her son loaning you his coat." He fiddled with the radio, jumping from station to station. "You like him?"

"Yes."

"You don't sound so sure."

"Some things happened today. Tonight. We can talk about it on the way home."

"Sure thing, baby girl. This station okay with you?"

He'd landed on some kind of new age music with airy flutes and chanting. "Isn't there a basketball game on?"

"Yeah, this stuff is getting on my nerves, too." He played with the dial again.

"So…you told her about your thermals?"

"Huh? Oh, yeah…after I expressed concern that her son was coatless, she said I was one to talk. So I explained I was wearing a T-shirt *and* my thermals under this sweatshirt."

Frances wondered if that was the comment that had made Dorothy smile. Her dad might be a man of mystery when it came to his magic, but in his everyday life he was a straight-up, no-nonsense guy.

"Here we go." He found the sports station and turned up the volume.

"Thompson on the drive...nails a three!" the announcer exclaimed against a background of music and cheers.

"Lakers versus Golden State Warriors," her dad said, pulling out into traffic. "Should be a dynamite game."

They drove for a few moments, listening to the rapid patter of the announcer, the yells of the crowd in the background. They drove past throngs of people on the sidewalks along the Strip, and the flaming volcano in front of the Mirage hotel and casino.

When they stopped at a red light, her dad turned down the volume and said, "I liked something Dorothy said."

"And that was?"

"When I thanked her for helping you, she said, 'That's what we're here for. Our kids.'"

An odd mix of emotions came over Frances...a momentary longing for her childhood, which had been a world where her family had shared an unshakable bond. She missed how it had been with all of them together, but at some point in the past three years she'd accepted it was gone forever.

Of course, there was still a wonderful closeness with

her dad, but she didn't want him living for her. He was barely sixty-four...had twenty, thirty more years to live...decades to discover new things, fulfill untended dreams.

That was when she realized that as much as he'd been living for her, she had been living for him, too.

And at some point, one of them would fly away.

LATER AT DINNER, Braxton took his seat next to Grams. Dorothy, wearing a powder-blue bib apron decorated with the words *I'm Not Aging, I'm Marinating,* walked into the dining room carrying a platter with prime-rib roast and potatoes.

Val closed her eyes and inhaled deeply. Releasing the breath, she murmured, "Mama D., that smells divine. I can smell the garlic...and thyme..."

"Rosemary, too," Dorothy said, setting the platter on the table. Straightening, she looked at Val's top. "Is that a vintage maternity top?"

"Yes. From the forties, I think." Val smoothed her hand down the tomato-soup-red fabric. "It reminded me of something Lucille Ball would've worn in those early *I Love Lucy* shows."

"Just like my '87 BMW, my entire wardrobe is also vintage." Richmond adjusted his polka-dot bow tie, which he'd paired with a button-down denim shirt. "Probably worth more today than when I bought it." He picked up a long, sharp knife. "I'm ready to do the honors, Dorothy. Is Maxine sequestered?"

"We can only hope." Braxton laughed. "Still haven't figured out how she made her great escape."

A smattering of chuckles as everyone remembered how Maxine, Gram's maniacal Siamese cat, had escaped her crate right before they sat down to Thanksgiving dinner and "took down" the turkey. When Dorothy discovered the star of the meal on the kitchen floor and Maxine feasting on a leg, she'd screamed. It had taken Richmond, Drake and Braxton nearly ten minutes to shoo away the cat, who hissed and bared her fangs at them, determined to keep her quarry.

"She's in her crate," Grams said, adjusting the sleeve of her fuchsia caftan, "with treats. I locked my bedroom door, so even if she gets out, she's stuck in there."

"Richmond, are you ready to live with Maxine?" Drake asked, spooning creamed corn onto his wife's plate.

The older man looked up from carving the roast. "In ancient times, cats were worshipped like gods. They have not forgotten that...and neither shall I."

"See why I love the man?" Grams turned her attention to Braxton. "Darling, mind getting that lovely silver canister over there on the bar cart?" She twiddled her fingers in the general direction, the diamond heirloom ring sparkling under the small crystal chandelier. "It's full of ice and gin. Just needs a shake."

As he headed to the cart, Braxton saw Val exchange a look with Drake.

"Now?" she whispered.

His brother, whose wolf-gray eyes, prickly hair and

brutish ways often intimidated people, suddenly looked like a shy kid who'd just been called on to give a book report.

"Everyone," he said, wrapping his arm around the back of Val's chair, "I'd like to share some news."

Braxton, heading back to his chair, stopped.

Drake, blinking back emotion, looked into his wife's eyes. "We've been keeping this news to ourselves for a while.... Selfish, I guess, but we wanted some time to enjoy our secret.... We're having a boy."

In the middle of the joyful exclamations from the rest of the family, Val cupped her hand to Drake's cheek. "Tell them the rest," she said gently.

Smiling sheepishly, Drake looked around the table. "But this next part we only decided last night. We're going to name him Ben," he said, his voice breaking, "for Benedict."

"Ben," Dorothy whispered, holding her hand over her heart.

Braxton had never understood when people said they'd experienced something so intense that "time stood still." He'd accept time feeling as though it had slowed down or sped up, but standing still? What was that supposed to mean?

At that instant, he knew.

As time stood still and silent, Braxton saw the smile of their father drift across his brother's face.

Then everyone began clapping and talking all at once. Scents of roasted meat and yeasty bread refilled the room. Braxton could once again feel the chilled canister in his grip.

"Congratulations, my darlings!" Grams said, dabbing the corner of her eye with a tissue.

Richmond resumed slicing the roast with the precision of a neurosurgeon while Val chatted to Grams about the new baby's room. Dorothy, holding Drake's hand, retold the story of when she and Benny learned they were having twins.

And Braxton shook the martini canister, the ice and liquid sloshing and rattling, grinning so hard his face hurt.

Finally, everyone settled down to eat, and for the next half hour the room filled with the clicks and scrapes of utensils, spurts of conversation and laughter.

Drake, waving off an offer for more roast, asked his brother, "How'd that first workout session with Li'l Bit go?"

"He got a little dizzy after a few biceps curls, but it passed. And he wasn't happy not being able to wear his flip-flops at the gym, but otherwise, fine."

Grams laughed, a happy sound like tinkling bells. "My, he does love wearing those thongs. I bet he has a dozen pairs."

"Plus a brand-new pair of Turbo cross-training shoes that set me back a hundred bucks," added Braxton, "and that's *with* the family discount."

Grams reached over and touched his arm. "Li'l Bit called me earlier, said he's texted you a few times about coming over tonight to teach you some dance moves, but hasn't heard back from you. I told him he didn't need an invitation, he's family, and to just come over."

*He's family. Here we go again.* "Grams," he said, trying to sound more benevolent than he felt, "Li'l Bit is a great guy, but he's not—"

"Brax," Val called out, "I know what can help you get some hot dance movies. Rent *Saturday Night Fever*. John Travolta does a hip-thrust action that could cook a chicken without an oven *while* lyin' down on the dance floor!"

He loved his sister-in-law, but sometimes he wished she'd keep some thoughts to herself.

"Can't I just stroll down the catwalk in tight jeans, no shirt and a smile on my face? Do I really have to do dance moves, too?"

"I agree," Richmond said, nodding sagely. "Half-dressed should be sufficient."

Everyone else grew quiet, preoccupied with eating their food. But they didn't fool Braxton for a moment. They'd latched on to that John Travolta idea, and God only knew what it'd evolve into.

He pulled out his phone and texted a message.

Dance lessons-COME OVER NOW

He started to put his phone away when a ping sounded.

MY BROTHER, I AM THERE

He made a mental note to later tell Li'l Bit they didn't need to text in big letters from here on out.

"Hey," Drake said, "what's the latest with your mystery blonde?"

"She's still a blonde," Braxton muttered, putting away the phone.

It'd been nice being distracted with the family dinner, talking about the baby, even the damned dance moves. But Frances? It hurt just to think about her.

He wasn't ready to talk about what happened earlier at Bally's because he still didn't understand it. Oh, he knew how he'd *reacted*—what Frances would probably call *expressive*—but he didn't comprehend why she'd agreed to spend time with him, then conspired to run away.

When he'd lived the *vida loca* life, women had been like a revolving door, and he'd been the same for them. Somebody took off? There was always another number to call, another party to go to.

But he was different now—tried to live with dignity, tried to be honest with himself and others. Which made it feel all the worse to be on the receiving end of someone else's deceit.

"I think Lauren Bacall and Sam Spade had a spat," Drake said. He took a pull on his beer.

"I think you should keep your thoughts to yourself," Dorothy muttered.

"I agree," Braxton said, shooting a mind-your-own-business look back at Drake.

"Well, I'm too old to keep my thoughts to myself,"

Grams said. "Anyway, what's so wrong with our asking about the blonde? She's hardly a secret, plus she sounds lovely. Li'l Bit said her name's Frances, has hair like a lion and loves *The Big Lebowski*."

"Braxton," his mom said, handing him the martini shaker, "would you mind making up another batch?"

"Happy to," he said, silently thanking her for an excuse to leave the room. He needed a moment alone to settle his thoughts, calm his heart. Yeah, his big ol' former-bad-boy heart. Who woulda thought it would crack?

*"The Big Lebowski?"* Drake snorted a laugh. "Lauren Bacall loves that stoner flick?"

"She's a fan of the Coen brothers' *movies*," Braxton corrected, heading to the kitchen, "not *stoner flicks*."

"Defending your lady's taste, Braxy Boy?" Drake laughed, followed by "Ouch!" He looked at Val, who demurely took a bite of her creamed corn.

Braxton didn't respond as he left the room, but in his mind that word *defending* released a torrent of thoughts.

Even as a kid, he had wanted to be a defender, a protector, like James Bond or Batman. Maybe that stemmed from his dad, who said he chose to be a cop and work in security because he wanted to "be the guy who ran toward danger, not away from it." Or his mom, who volunteered to be a human-rights advocate for his dad's casino union because she wanted to "help the employees articulate their needs for better working conditions."

Funny how she'd always disapproved of his dad's, brother's and his investigative and security careers, all defenders in a certain sense, when she had the same instinct, too.

Braxton filled the shaker with ice, gin and a splash of vermouth. After securing the lid, he shook the canister, looking out the far kitchen window at the moon hanging in the dark sky, so bright and alone.

Made him think of Frances.

It dawned on him that the part-time bodyguard gig was a far better job offer than a Security Director position because he got the role he really wanted. To be her defender, the man she turned to first, the guy who never let her down.

Despite everything, he still wanted to play that role in Frances's life.

But was it too late?

BRAXTON WALKED BACK into the dining room with the martini shaker and stopped.

His mother must have said there were to be no more questions about Frances because they all stared back at him with "we're not talking about *her*" looks in their eyes.

Well, he was going to change that because now *he* was ready.

"I want to apologize for being uptight about your questions. Of course you're curious about Frances. So am I, to tell the truth. But I don't need to get…"

"Meaner than a chicken," Val offered.

Another chicken comment. Was that a pregnancy thing or did he inspire that image for some reason? He hoped the former because his ego couldn't withstand the latter, especially now that he hoped for a do-over with Frances.

"And I want to apologize," Drake said, his voice low and somber, "for being a shithead."

"Which time?" Braxton asked.

"My brother, the comic," Drake muttered. "For making that 'defending your lady's taste in movies' crack. Sorry."

"Apology accepted. On the condition you watch a Coen brothers movie sometime."

"Bro, don't do this to me."

"Didn't say it has to be *The Big Lebowski*."

After a beat, Drake nodded grudgingly.

His grandmother raised her hand, waving a little to get his attention. Like a schoolkid wanting desperately to be called on.

Whatever his mom had said to them made a *big* impression. This get-together had morphed from a family dinner to study hall, and he was the teacher in charge.

"Grams? You wish to say something?"

She lowered her hand and smiled sweetly. "While you're standing up there giving a speech, would you mind if my handsome fiancé took that shaker out of your hands?"

"Of course," said the magnanimous study-hall teacher in charge.

Richmond wasn't a very expressive guy—*expressive*

now being a word in the top ten of Braxton's vocabulary—but the honor he felt at being her prince, his willingness to be at her beck and call, showed on his face.

Braxton felt a stab of envy.

Richmond the Lionhearted retrieved the martini chalice, carrying it with great pomp and circumstance to his Lady Grams and pouring it like a sommelier into her glass.

"My Lord," Val said, sniffing, "I do believe those two are like Romeo and Juliet in their eighties."

"He's only seventy-nine," Grams said, smiling like a fox as she lifted her now-full martini glass. "Still my boy toy."

Braxton clapped along with everyone else, wondering if he should start wearing bow ties.

After taking a sip, Grams turned serious. "Braxton, my dear grandson, may I make a few observations about Frances?"

He noticed his mother's posture stiffened, but she didn't say anything.

"'Kay," he said, "and while you're talking, mind if I sit down and help myself to some of that 'tini?"

Lady Grams nodded her acquiescence.

Braxton took his seat, poured a splash of martini. His mom and Frances had spent a chunk of time at the sports book earlier tonight. Considering how chummy they apparently got, he wondered if they'd talked about getting together for happy hour again sometime. Or maybe his mom had invited Frances to join her at that poker tournament. If so, they would have exchanged contact information, which would be handy, as he'd had no luck finding a number for Frances on his own.

If his mom didn't know her number, he'd show up at the warehouse doors again tomorrow, a remorseful prince ready to escort Frances safely to her Benz.

Of course, she might feel differently about him by then, after having hours to reflect on his bruised-heart response at Bally's. Maybe she wouldn't want him to escort her anywhere, ever again.

Didn't matter.

He'd wait for her at those doors every single day, even if he walked silently behind her all the way to her car, because at the crux of all this was his need to ensure her safety.

Even Batman probably wanted a night off sometimes, but he still put on the cape.

"Braxton," his grandmother said, her jade-green eyes glistening with sincerity, "we're eager—all right, obnoxious—to learn more about Frances because you've been living like a hermit for months, darling, and now we see you coming out of your shell, being happy, head over heels for this girl. Seeing how strongly she's affected you, we want to know more about her because…we love you so much, and…"

She cleared her throat, blinked a few times, took a healthy sip of her martini, then soldiered on.

"Because you deserve to be happy, my darling, more than anyone I know…except for your brother and my lovely granddaughter-in-law, of course."

"That's right, Brax," Val said.

"We love you, son."

"Got your back, bro."

"Man dies of cold," Richmond said, "not of darkness."

Braxton couldn't talk. His throat had tightened with emotion from all the love he felt. He also had the passing thought that Richmond and Li'l Bit should probably be screened ahead of time before giving toasts and commentary.

After his throat relaxed, he took a deep breath and said, "Look, here's the deal. You guys probably know more about her than I do, and that's the truth. But it probably doesn't matter because—" he gave a shrug "—I blew it tonight, and I doubt she'll give me a second chance."

"Oh, Braxton," Val murmured, looking concerned.

"It's okay, really," he said, sounding about as okay as a guy who'd just eaten his last meal and was ready to take that long, lonely walk down the prison hallway to the chamber of no return.

"Son," his mom said, "there's always hope."

Slumped back in his chair, he looked across the table at her, thinking how, as a kid, he'd thought she was a very serious person, realizing now that was likely due to her spending every last ounce of her energy managing the house and raising a couple of wild twin boys. Only after he grew up did he see different facets of her emerge. Her wicked sense of humor. How she sometimes sneaked dessert before dinner.

The box of platinum-blond hair dye she kept in her bathroom cabinet.

At this moment he saw something else he'd never noticed before, too. A childlike sweetness in her face, as though he might believe in magic if she wished hard enough.

"Mom," he said, "I want to hope. It's just she's so... complicated. So many secrets. Like why'd she rent a car last week when Dima's company leases cars for its employees? And I saw a receipt on the floor of her car—" he'd skip the part about taking a picture of it and blowing it up "—for camouflage makeup, the kind actors use." He gave his head a confused shake. "What's that about?"

Her eyes widened slightly. "Women use many different kinds of makeup, dear, including theatrical makeup. It's all personal style and taste."

"There's one way to find answers to the other issues," Drake said, pulling out his smartphone. He started tapping on its keypad.

Braxton knew what he was doing—running a background check on Frances. He'd wanted to do the same, but he'd decided against it. Call him crazy, but he thought he and Frances would have the chance to talk and clear up his questions.

But that wasn't about to happen, so he'd wait to hear what Drake found.

His brother paused, stared at the screen on his phone for a moment, then looked up. "There's a couple of Frances Jefferies in Nevada—anybody have another identifier, like her date of birth? Middle initial? Parent's name?"

"Her father's name is Jonathan," Dorothy said quietly.

"You didn't mention meeting her dad," Braxton said.

"I walked her to his car," she said, fussing with her napkin. "He and I talked briefly."

"Found her," Drake said. "She has a criminal record."

Val thumped her fist on the table. "I knew it!" She narrowed her eyes. "Just like *Chinatown*.... One day, out of the nowhere, a mysterious, hot-looking blonde walks into the detective agency with some story, asks the private eye to help her. He does...only her story is a sham, and the private dick, who's fallen hard for the blonde, gets sucked into her sinister world of lies, guns and death."

After a moment of surreal quiet, Grams said, "Darling, I love you, but this isn't *Inner Sanctum Mysteries*. We don't know what she did."

"That's right," Braxton said, "it could be speeding tickets."

Or it could be something worse. His gaze locked with his brother's, and he knew instantly it was worse. Much worse.

"Read it," he said.

Drake looked down at the screen. "One charge in 2009. Grand larceny of property valued at eighteen thousand dollars." He paused. "As you know, Brax, these criminal histories only show the charges. No details. I'll make a call."

Braxton leaned his head back and closed his eyes, letting the air leak out of his lungs. Grand larceny for eighteen thousand was the most severe charge for stealing in Nevada. A class B felony, just one class below murder, which showed how serious Nevada was about grand larceny. In Braxton's years working in security and investigations, he'd never once seen an innocent person charged with a class B felony—they'd all been found guilty, including his old boss Yuri.

To think he'd been tight with Yuri and his thugs for years, yet Braxton hadn't picked up on a single clue that Frances was a crook. Yeah, he'd listen to whatever details his brother dredged up about her charge, but in his gut Braxton already knew the answer. Frances was a convict.

*What a joke. I leave my criminal ways behind me, walk the straight and narrow, have the social life of a gnat, and I fall for a woman with a past more checkered than mine.*

"Braxton," his mom said, "are you all right?"

He opened his eyes, slanted her an appraising look. "You know about this?"

"No."

"You still like Frances?"

She smiled hesitantly, but nodded. "Yes."

Another thing he'd never seen in his mom before. Could it be that woman who'd always been too hard on herself was growing soft on the rest of the human race?

Was this what she called *hope?*

"Just got off the phone with Tony Cordova," Drake said, setting down his phone. "As an arson investigator, he has access to Nevada's criminal-records database, so I asked him to check that 2009 grand-larceny charge. Frances was convicted of stealing an eighteen-thousand-dollar diamond necklace at a society event. It was her fence, a pawnbroker called Rock Star, who snitched her out."

Grams gasped. "A jewel thief!"

"Whatever you want to call her," Drake said, his face turning hard, "Braxton's come too far to get hooked up with a felon."

"Whoa," Braxton said, making a down-boy gesture, "she and I never *hooked up*—"

"I agree with Drake," Grams said. "Braxton doesn't need to be cavorting with some jewel thief."

"We never cavorted—"

"Statistically," Richmond interrupted, "jewel thieves have very high IQs. A union between Frances and Braxton could produce highly intelligent offspring."

"You're kidding, right?" Braxton murmured, wondering if Richmond had tied his bow tie a little too tight.

"Just what this family needs," Grams said, the picture of righteous indignation, "a *brood* of genius criminals."

The doorbell rang. A sonorous pong-de-dong-dong that had always gotten on his nerves.

"Li'l Bit's here," he said.

"Lovely. Bring him in," Grams said, then continued a monologue about the family needing to keep Braxton from backsliding into darkness, where jewel thieves supposedly lurked, desperate to be impregnated. Drake was cheering her on while heading into the kitchen for another beer, while Val and Dorothy had forged some kind of alliance, the two of them fervently discussing women's rights, procreation and Braxton's right to date a convict.

Richmond held up his smartphone for Braxton to see. "Here's a picture of the notorious cat burglar Suzette Doyle. IQ of one-seventy. All her heists were completed within sixty seconds."

"Great," Braxton said. "I'll get the door."

Minutes later, he opened it, and his heart stopped.

Frances stood on the doorstep, bundled in a dark blue coat, the wind tousling her mane of blond hair, those amethyst eyes taking him in.

She held up his coat. "I wanted to return this."

The moonlight seemed to shift, play tricks. Her hair no longer looked blond, but the color of deep-yellow roses. Her amethyst eyes had deepened to a shade like late sunset. Her face, which she always worked to hold so still, so composed, appeared to come alive.

*She's the night.*

The thought bubbled to the surface of his mind, surprising him, yet it made perfect sense. Nighttime evoked mystery, paradox, secrets.

That was Frances.

And also everything he'd walked away from.

As sparkling and enticing as she might appear, he couldn't risk being pulled under, irretrievably lost in the churning, dark cold again.

A chilly wind gusted past, and she shivered, yet managed a smile that tugged at his heart. Made him think of the moon in the sky, alone and bright in the darkness.

That was when he understood hope.

It wasn't an answer or a guarantee, yet it would hover, like a smile, promising nourishment for something greater to grow. Like courage.

Or love.

Instinctively, he reached for her, guided her inside to the warmth and closed the door.

"I'm sorry," she murmured.

"Shh." He wrapped her in his arms, feeling the release of her breath as she relaxed against him, vaguely aware of his coat falling to the floor.

"I told my dad what happened. After we finished dinner, I decided to return your coat tonight because I was afraid you might not be there tomorrow after work—"

"Of course I'd be there."

"Thank you." She paused. "Going away to make that call wasn't about deceiving you, Braxton. I needed to call my dad about…something personal, that was all. Only after you got upset did I realize that my need for privacy looked suspicious, but we didn't get a chance to talk about what happened…."

"No, we didn't," he agreed gently.

There were other things they needed to talk about, too, like her felony conviction. It was only fair that he gave her the chance to explain, especially since he knew what it was like to be judged harshly because of past deeds.

But talk could wait.

"No more words," he whispered huskily, brushing his lips against the silky strands of her hair, taking in scents of a citrusy shampoo, then dragging his lips down to her temple, tasting her salty-sweet skin, trailing his lips slowly to the corner of her lips, ready, aching to kiss the mouth he'd dreamed of, craved….

A crashing sound jarred him out of the moment.

Frances stumbled out of his arms.

His grandmother sat rigidly in her wheelchair in the hallway, looking grim yet focused, like a homicide detective who'd just entered a crime scene. Shards of glass sparkled on the floor next to her chair.

Richmond stood behind her, blinking rapidly.

Val walked in with Drake. "Everybody okay?" he asked.

"We're fine, darling," Grams said coolly. "I accidentally dropped my martini glass."

Val walked a few steps closer, peering at Frances. "My Lord," she murmured, "is that the *jewel thief?*"

"Her name's Frances," Dorothy corrected, drying her hands on a dish towel as she entered the hall. "What broke?"

"Grams's martini glass," Val said.

"I'll get a broom and dustpan." Dorothy headed back to the kitchen.

It was as though his mother took all the air out of the room when she left. His family members stood so still, so silent, they reminded Braxton of the figures in a wax museum he'd visited on a sixth-grade field trip. Except most of the wax ones had been smiling.

Drake finally broke the silence.

"Braxton," he said in a deep, ominous tone, "like I said earlier, you've come too far to hook up with another felon. She'll only drag you down."

## *CHAPTER NINE*

GROWING UP, BRAXTON and Drake's dad had two rules about fighting. *Have enough self-control to keep it private, and let the loser retreat with dignity.* Braxton and his brother hadn't always followed the last one, but they tried to work out their differences one-on-one.

Even if they'd been alone, it would have ticked Braxton to hear Drake discredit Frances, but his brother had crossed the line by doing it in front of her and the rest of their family.

"You didn't need to say that here," he growled.

"I'm only telling the truth, bro."

"No, you insulted her." Braxton clenched his fists, half-ready to let them do the talking.

"Braxton, don't," his grandmother pleaded.

At the same time, he felt Frances's hand press lightly on his back, a gentle signal to reel in his anger.

He slowly relaxed his hands and blew out a gust of air. There'd been way too much melodrama in his life lately—no need to pile on more. Didn't mean he wasn't still massively pissed off at his brother, who stood across the room in all his self-righteous glory.

Val stood behind Drake, her wide eyes peeking over

her husband's shoulder, silently begging Braxton to bring peace back to the land of the Morgans.

He'd do that. After he cleared up a few things with his brother.

"Don't *ever* again refer to my seeing Frances as *hooking up*," he said in a low, threatening tone, "or call her a felon, or say she'll drag me down. You will treat her with respect."

The house creaked as the winds picked up.

"Had a heck of a time finding the dustpan," Dorothy said, walking back into the room with it and a broom, "then remembered I'd left it in the backyard after using it to scoop up gravel."

As Braxton leaned over to pick up his coat, he thought he caught his mom and Frances exchange a look, wondered what that was about.

"You look lovely, dear," his mom said to Frances.

"Indeed you do," Val said, flashing her husband a warning look before crossing to Dorothy and taking the broom from her. "Let me help, Mama D."

"Richmond, darling," Grams said, "steer me out of the way so they can clean it up."

Braxton had noticed lately that when his grandmother got tired these days, she'd put the chair on manual and ask Richmond to help her navigate it. Considering she was eighty-six, it was damned impressive she'd been managing on her own so long, but it also made him realize she was growing more frail.

As Val swept up the glass, Frances said to Dorothy,

"I should have called first, but I didn't know..." She glanced at Braxton.

*If I'd want to see her.*

After the way he'd carried on back at Bally's, of course that was what she'd think, but he was glad she'd shown up.

Anyway, his mom, who had a built-in barometer about people, found Frances likable and didn't seem bothered at all by her surreptitious call, so he needed to move on, too, and not dwell on the negative stuff or he'd end up a crusty old fart.

"Brax," Drake muttered, motioning him over, a grimace tightening his features.

Speaking of people in danger of becoming crusty old farts... But they needed to talk, clear the air, so Braxton headed over to his brother, who rubbed his eyebrow while keeping his attention focused downward, as though the hardwood floor was suddenly of monumental interest.

But Braxton was willing to wait this out because he was due a big, fat apology. And after he got his, Drake was going to give another apology to Frances.

Drake finally raised his head enough so his glowering eyes melded with Braxton's. A look that scared the crap out of most people, but only shook up Braxton a little.

The next instant, their twin psychic link kicked in, delivering the top story of the hour straight from Drake's gray matter, which in essence was *No way in hell am I apologizing for telling you the truth, and if you'd only wake up, you'd realize I'm right.*

Okay, Braxton was pissed again. Irked enough to share the conveyance of information in distinct, colorful terms. As long as his mom and Grams couldn't hear.

"So that's how you're going to play it," he muttered to Drake.

"If you mean sticking to what I said before, yes."

Braxton moved in a little closer, whispering emphatically, "You don't know her."

"Do you?"

"Yes."

"Really? What's her middle name?"

"Like that matters, and keep your voice down."

"What's her address, then?"

"Summerlin."

"That's not an address, Brax. That's a *region*." Drake gave his head a weary shake. "Look," he said, his voice gentling, "you got into trouble before because of your association with Yuri, remember? Live by the sword, die by the sword, bro."

"Frances isn't a sword."

"You know what I mean," he snapped. "I'm trying to watch out for you, Brax. Don't want to see you go down *again*."

Braxton heard the low-throttled hum of France's voice. He glanced over his shoulder, saw her talking to his mom, who was smiling as she gestured to the wall clock with glued-on dice on its face. Val hovered near them, staring like a besotted fangirl at Frances.

"We started telling time by dice slang," his mom explained to Frances. "If Benny said we needed to leave at Nina from Pasadena, that meant we needed to leave at nine o'clock."

When Braxton turned back, Drake was exiting through the door to the backyard. As he watched the door close, he felt disappointed that his brother was slipping away because he didn't want to deal with Frances. Or more correctly, deal with Braxton liking Frances.

*You dope. It's not just me who likes her. Mom's crazy about her. And Val can't wait to bombard her with questions about jewel thieving.*

A wait that was no more as Val, clutching Frances's hand, began excitedly asking if she'd ever seen *To Catch a Thief,* and what did she think of the reformed jewel thief played by Cary Grant?

His mom walked up to him, a conspiratorial smile on her face. "She fits right in," she whispered.

Obviously no one had filled her in yet on the showdown between him and Drake while she was in the kitchen retrieving the broom and dustpan.

"Kinda rushing things, aren't you?" he kidded.

She gave him a *Mona Lisa* smile. "Her father is outside, waiting in the car. I asked her to invite him inside, but she said he didn't want to interrupt our family dinner." A shy smile flitted across his mom's features. "I told her I'm going to fix a couple of plates of leftovers and take them out to her father. Meanwhile, why don't you take Frances to the TV room where the two of you can have some privacy for a few minutes?"

"Not before we're properly introduced to her, dear. Richmond, darling, next to my grandson is perfect."

Richmond guided Grams's wheelchair to a spot next to Braxton. His grandmother sat ramrod straight, petting Maxine the Terrible, who lay curled on her lap, a demonic glint in her crossed eyes.

After extricating Frances from Val's Q&A session, Braxton made introductions.

"Frances, this is my grandmother, Glenda Lassiter, and her fiancé, Richmond Housewright."

"Nice to meet you, Frances." Richmond bowed slightly. "I hope you don't find my asking this question too gauche, but what is your IQ?"

She blinked. "I took a test in high school—140, I think. But I've never really believed in numbers as labels. A person could have a high IQ and still be a fool."

"Brilliantly put," he murmured.

"Pleased to meet you," Frances said to Grams. "What's your cat's name?"

"Maxine."

"Hello, Maxine." Frances reached out to pet her.

Braxton put a warning hand on her arm. "I wouldn't—"

He watched, astounded, as Maxine closed her eyes, emitting a cooing purr while Frances lightly scratched her behind the ear.

"She doesn't take quickly to people," Grams said, her ring sparkling as she adjusted Maxine's collar.

Frances pointed to one of the larger diamonds. "That stone has a very unique cut.... Looks like the signature of a Belgian diamond cutter who lived in the southwest U.S. in the early twentieth century. Some people believed the way he cut diamonds imbued them with joy, so there was much demand for them in engagement and wedding rings." She gave a small shrug. "It's folklore, but I always liked the story anyway."

"I like stories, too. It's what we are, fundamentally, don't you think?" Grams held out her hand so everyone could see the diamond. "My great-grandfather purchased that diamond in Breckenridge, Colorado, for my great-grandmother in 1919, and they had a long, joyful marriage. Colorado is part of the Southwest, isn't it? Maybe that Belgian diamond cutter infused this diamond with joy." Lowering her hand, she smiled at Frances. "Do you drink martinis, dear?"

"Sometimes."

"Gin or vodka?"

"If it's not made with gin, it's not a martini."

"Don't sniff at your IQ, darling, because you're obviously genius material." She pressed a button on the joystick and the chair slowly pivoted. "Richmond, sweetheart, let's whip up another shaker for our guest."

A FEW MOMENTS later, Braxton escorted Frances into the family TV room.

"Welcome to 1994," he said, turning on the light in the TV room, which was awash in pastels, chunky sectional furniture and a teak entertainment center crowded with trophies Frances assumed he and his brother had won in high school.

"What's this?" Frances said, unbuttoning her coat while peering at a framed drawing on the wall.

"One of the dozens of pictures I drew of a red Ford Mustang Shelby GT500, my fantasy car. Even dressed like it for Halloween one year."

Slipping him an amused look over her shoulder, she headed to the couch and sat. "By the way, it was a bit of a shock to see another you. You should warn people you have an identical twin."

"Sorry about what he said."

"He's being protective of you," she said quietly.

Drake's words had hurt, but she wasn't naive about why he'd said them. Unfortunately, people sometimes made fast, harsh judgments about her past. She'd decided long ago the best way to deal with it was silence. No justifications, no arguments. How she lived her life now was her best defense.

"We're going to *love* having a home-cooked meal," she said, switching to a happier topic. "Dad and I are hopeless in the kitchen.... My mom spoiled us, I'm afraid. I sometimes still dream about a goat-cheese soufflé she'd make. Crazy, huh?"

He tossed his trench coat over the back of a chair and sat next to her. "Remembering people we love is never crazy," he murmured, brushing back a wisp of her hair, letting his fingers linger on the soft skin at her temple.

Frances stiffened slightly, overly aware of the bright

lighting in the room, how close his hand was to her cheek. She took his hand and set it on the couch. "We need to talk."

He looked at his hand, then back at her. "I seem to have a bad habit of doing or saying the wrong thing with you and not having a clue what it was."

"You didn't do anything wrong. It's just time for us to perform the Aquarium Illusion." She paused. "Sorry, I talk magic a lot with my dad—he's a magician—and sometimes I forget people don't know these references. Aquarium Illusion is a stage trick where first the magician's assistant and then the magician are trapped in a water tank. Of course, they're never really trapped.... It's what appears to be true, but isn't."

"You're losing me here...."

"I'd like to ask a few questions."

"Ask away."

"First, what's this investigation you're working on the side for Dmitri?"

"What does that have to do with—" He made a stopping motion. "I said ask, so here's the answer. I'm investigating a Russian, name's Yuri Glazkov, with whom I have a dark, convoluted history—you can read about it on the internet. Anyway, one day this guy Dima called our agency, said he was developing a high-end casino project, something about the Russian community concerned about their business ventures being hurt by Yuri's negative publicity, and he asked me to investigate if Yuri was fencing money. I haven't found anything. In fact, my Russian contacts say Yuri's always home, swilling vodka, moping about his trial next month. He probably slips in and out of that ankle monitoring bracelet, but—" he shrugged "—haven't seen any signs of him lurking around Vegas, not yet anyway."

A series of banging, thudding sounds made Frances jump.

"The outside window shutters," Braxton explained. "I need to secure them, otherwise they're at the wind's mercy."

She nodded, thinking how they, too, needed to secure their own feelings, and ultimately their safety, which led to her next issue. Not an easy one to bring up, especially considering what had happened when she'd arrived, but necessary.

And not easy because…she wanted him, although it would sound otherwise.

"Second, we can't do what we just did in the other room for a while."

He arched an eyebrow, giving her a look that said, *You liked it, but now it's off-limits?*

Oh, how she wanted to tell him that she didn't just want it—she craved it.

That just a look from him, like the one he was giving her now—dark, unrelenting—sparked feelings she'd never experienced before. As if her passions had been lying dormant all these years and now they'd been stirred awake.

She eased in a breath and let it out slowly, willing her racing heart to slow, her thoughts to settle. Because wanting was a world away from indulging. Too much was at stake. For both of them.

"Do you know how I found your address?" she asked.

"Figured my mom gave it to you, but what does that have to do with our not doing what we did?"

"Trust me, this isn't a non sequitur."

"Okay, I'll bite. How'd you find my address?"

"I ran a reverse on her cell-phone number."

*"Ran a reverse,"* he repeated, looking a little surprised. "You sound like an investigator. Most people have no idea what that means."

"Running a reverse" on a piece of data—a name, a street address, a phone number—was jargon investigators often used, meaning they'd plugged a piece of data into a search engine or database to see what information might pop up.

"That's because…I am an investigator."

For a stretched-out moment or three, they sat, their eyes locked, listening to the wind play with the window shutters.

Finally he murmured, "No wonder you're like the night. You work solo?"

"No," she answered, curious what that night comment was about, "I'm an investigator at Vanderbilt Insurance."

She could have said her new job title—Lead Investigator—but it still felt foreign. And a little pretentious. She'd mostly worked alone at Vanderbilt, had never really "led" another investigator, so as far as she was concerned, tagging on the word *lead* meant she made a little more money, not much else.

He gave a low whistle. "Vanderbilt's one of the heavy hitters. How'd you go from felony conviction to being— Oh, I get it. They wanted your jewel-thief skills." He gave her an appraising look. "You must have been pretty good."

"As a kid, I learned sleight-of-hand tricks from my dad, which I later segued into pickpocketing and a few jewel thefts, although my parents had no idea what I was doing. As for being good, it's all in the details. And the practice. If I'd been smarter, I would have practiced accounting. Pet grooming." She gave a self-deprecating smile. "Maybe jewelry making."

"How'd you get caught?"

She wasn't sure she liked his tone. Or even how he phrased his question. Or maybe it was her shame about her past that bothered her.

"A fence turned me in. I hated him at first, but it turned out to be the best thing that could have happened, although I wish my parents had been spared the embarrassment."

His gray eyes seemed to soften to the color of mist. "I hear you on that one," he said gently.

He relaxed against the couch. "So…you're pretending to be a VP of sales at Russian Confections in order to investigate a theft of jewels?"

"Vanderbilt suspects Dmitri stole some ancient Greek coins two years ago."

He gave a small, cynical laugh. "Gee, no mention of

*that* on his due-diligence report. Our boy did a masterful job forging a Dayden Group assessment."

"There's more. He's planning a jewel heist."

A beat of silence. "He never was developing a—" he held up his fingers like quotation marks "—*high-end casino.*"

"Right."

"And this Russian Confections is a front for planning the heist."

"Exactly."

"Wow," he said, staring off into the distance, "I feel like I've parachuted into a Bond film."

"How fitting," she muttered, "considering Dmitri has one serious Bond complex."

"Tell me about it."

"He'd probably call this heist *Diamonds Are Forever.*"

"Cute."

He held her gaze for a drawn-out moment, so long it was starting to feel like one of those see-who-blinks-first games, but what he didn't know was she was really, really good at that game. Not the blinking part. That was surface. The not-divulging part. Making her face a canvas on which the viewer could imagine his vision, and only his vision, because what lay beneath it was blank.

Braxton's face, on the other hand, provided an ongoing picture show. He could have been a silent-film actor, telling an entire story through looks. She was already interpreting the I-give-up cues on his face. A capricious arched eyebrow worthy of a vaudeville villain—a funny villain—whose charm was better than his bite, who used exaggeration to deflect defeat.

"Well," he said, "now that we know we're kindred P.I. spirits, give me the dirt on this heist."

She told him how the Helena Diamond was a heart-cut diamond necklace reputedly commissioned by Napoleon during his exile on the island of Saint Helena, where he pined for his long-lost love, Josephine. That according to legend, the diamond cutter crafted an image within this diamond of two perfectly symmetrical hearts that could only be seen by destined lovers.

"After Napoleon's death," she said, "the necklace disappeared. Some claim it was stolen by his enemy, Prince Metternich, and that for several generations Metternich's descendants hid the diamond. Then in the early 1960s, it resurfaced in the hands of a London diamond merchant, who eventually sold it for fifteen million to an unnamed American businessman."

That eyebrow again. "I take it this mystical diamond necklace is now in Las Vegas?"

"Almost."

"It's arriving soon."

"Yes."

"On the neck of some trophy wife?"

"No. In a jewelry exhibit."

"Is this one of those heists where the bad guys drill through the floor or wall, then sneak in when the exhibit is closed and steal the jewels?"

"No, this is where the jewel thief goes into the exhibit during broad daylight and pickpockets the jewels."

"Ballsy."

She shrugged. "Most jewel thieves are. Dmitri's no exception."

"This is his plan."

"Yes. With input from Oleg. Some hotshots—safecracker, electrician, alarm expert—are bringing their skills to the table, too."

He frowned. "Wonder why he hired me to investigate Yuri."

"My theory? Dmitri's paranoid about Yuri learning about the heist and wanting a piece of the action. After all, Yuri's better connected in Vegas, could put some serious muscle on Dmitri. I think your real role is to spy on him."

"I think you're right." He gave her an approving nod. "Got another one for you. My real role is to spy on you, too."

That one took her by surprise. "Dmitri hired you to spy on *me*?"

"Yep."

"Have you?"

"Nope."

"Does he suspect I work for Vanderbilt?"

"If he did, we wouldn't be sitting here. He's paranoid, not stupid."

"And as cagey as he is, sometimes transparent as glass." She flashed on the window in his office. "I find it interesting he picked an office with a view of McCarren Airport. Why? Even if no one ever caught on to his heist plans and he pulled it off successfully, there's no way he'd hop a commercial flight afterward. Authorities would be tracking tickets and passports for weeks, months to come."

Braxton stood, paced a few feet across the oatmeal-colored rug. "Maybe it's not McCarren he's looking at."

"Not much else is out there. Suburban home tracts, desert..."

"Dima said something the other day when we were talking about a flashy helicopter escape in a Bond film. 'If only such escapes were possible in real life.'"

"Wouldn't say that unless he's planning his own."

He paced a few more feet, stopped and gave her a slow smile. "From Dima's window, toward the southeast, there's an old, abandoned airstrip on several acres of desert owned by a crusty old character named Grover who was friends with my dad. Sometime in the '80s, he turned the dirt road in front of his place into a makeshift airstrip. Grover moved to Florida four years ago, around the time my dad died, but didn't sell his land."

"Can we drive there? See if there's still a viable airstrip?"

"Sure."

"Great." She pulled out her cell phone. "Let's get each other's numbers."

"Thought you'd never ask," Braxton murmured, retrieving his cell.

After typing his number into her phone, Frances said, "I should go."

"Before you do...I need you to know that...I'd do anything to help you, Frances. Any time of the day or night, if you need me, just call and I'll be there." He squeezed shut his eyes and groaned. "I sound like the lyrics of a bad pop song."

She laughed softly. "I like bad pop songs."

He squinted at her. "Okay, we're getting silly. Or stupid. Or both. Definitely time for you to go. I'll walk you outside."

He was kidding with her, but she saw through the teasing to what lay underneath. The tenderness in his eyes, the warmth in his voice...and she felt a shift in her heart. A melting. And an unexpected, hazy thought surfaced to the forefront of her mind.... Could this be...*love?*

The ridiculous possibility startled her. Made her feel vulnerable, exposed, how she felt earlier at Bally's without her scar covered.

She ran her suddenly trembling fingers down the buttons on her coat, wondering if a person could really fall in love after a only few days...except her own parents had. *The instant I saw him,* her mother used to say, *I knew we belonged together for the rest of our lives.*

Frances smiled, feeling a little giddy, a little scared, a whole lot confused. These past few days had been stressful and crazy....so throw a hot, irritating, flirtatious guy into the mix, and, well, what woman wouldn't go for it, maybe imagine it to be love?

It wasn't real, of course. This had nothing to do with love, and everything to do with needing some feel-good energy, a distraction in an otherwise tough, hard case.

But what if it wasn't?

"Shame you have to go," he murmured, "when I have so many more bad pop songs I could recite to you...." He inhaled a deep breath, looked around the room before meeting her gaze again. "For the record, I get why we're playing it cool. If we don't, it puts you—us—at risk...." He closed his eyes and released a long, ragged groan, then looked at her. "I promise you I will abide by your wishes. When's this jewelry show?"

"March first."

He moved closer and whispered in her ear, "I can't wait for March second."

As Braxton walked Frances through the living room, an old Frank Sinatra hit, "Come Fly with Me," was playing. Grams and Richmond sat at the dining-room table, her head on his shoulder, the two of them singing along.

Val, clearing the table, looked up with a funny expression on her face. She mouthed something with great earnestness to Braxton, nudging her head toward the front door.

He'd never been a lip reader, especially from twenty feet away, but obviously she wanted to convey a message of great importance about…the front door?

Moments later, he and Frances stood in front of it.

Listening to the off-key Sinatra sing-along in the background, he checked out the wooden panel door. Like the TV room, it hadn't changed much over the years. He could still make out the sanded-down scratch marks of their long-ago beloved family dog, Buddha, a black Lab with the heart of a giant, who'd politely scrape at the door whenever he wanted go outside.

As he opened the front door, he finally understood Val's mimed alert.

The porch light cast a yellow glow over the concrete driveway, where a blue Honda sat. His mom leaned into the open driver's window, her voice lilting through the air, interspersed with a man's lower octave.

He flashed on the girlish look he'd seen on his mom's face when she'd learned Frances's dad was outside.

He wasn't ready for this.

"Oh, hi, you two," his mom called out, her head rising over the car roof, her voice sounding light and happy.

A breeze fluffed her hair, which she didn't bother to pat back down.

Braxton didn't want to deal with this.

Frances started walking to the car. "I'd like you to meet my dad."

*My dad.*

God, how he missed his.

No one was supposed to take Benedict Morgan's place. Not as a dad, a husband, a friend, a boss.

Growing up, his father had been like a giant tree, always rooted, fiercely strong, his wide-reaching branches green with leaves. A powerful presence that always offered shade, a place to rest, a quiet lesson. Such mighty trees were never supposed to fall, yet one day his did, the slow, silent crash to earth shattering the world into a million jagged pieces that would never fit together again.

And yet, somehow they had.

Time softened the edges, memories filled the spaces and the wide-reaching, quiet lessons gradually blossomed with new life.

"Braxton?" His mom waved to him, the wind ruffling her hair.

There was a giddiness in her voice, shiny and bright as a new leaf.

Which was all that really mattered, right?

He thought of Grams earlier tonight saying that stories were fundamentally what people were, then thought about how many new stories were starting in his family...including the one between his mom and Frances's dad.

As Braxton approached the car, the driver's door creaked open, and Mr. Jefferies got out. The inside dome light spilled into the night, highlighting his polished black lace-up shoes, slacks, Miami Heat sweatshirt. As Frances made introductions, the two men shook hands, and Braxton sized him up. About five-ten, a gut that showed his love of food, a grip that signaled confidence.

"Thank you for loaning your coat to my daughter."

"Anytime."

He glanced at his mom and did a double take. She wore a faux leopard-print coat, the one he recalled Val wearing earlier that evening. Apparently his sister-in-law had helped his mom primp for this encounter.

A car rumbled down the street, its tires crunching on the asphalt. Rap music thumped from inside. A dog howled. And howled.

"Neighbor's beagle," Dorothy muttered. "One bark is never enough."

"A howling dog is bad luck," Frances said. "Means the spirits of the dead are out walking around."

"Don't worry, baby girl," her dad said. "I won't let the ghosties get you."

"We should go," she said.

Braxton headed around the car to the passenger door, opening it for her. "I'll be waiting at the warehouse doors tomorrow, same time."

"Thank you, Braxton," she murmured, slipping inside.

He slammed shut the car door, double-checked the handle to ensure the door was locked. Satisfied, he turned, surprised to see Jonathan standing on this side of the car, belatedly realizing he probably always opened the door for his daughter, but tonight Braxton had instead.

And that Jonathan might not be ready for this change, either.

As he walked back inside the house, Braxton heard his mom's laughter behind him, a happy sound like wind chimes, and smiled.

## *CHAPTER TEN*

TUESDAY MORNING, FRANCES arrived at Russian Confections a few minutes after nine only to find that the door was locked.

She knocked. Knocked again. Pressed her ear to the door and thought she heard footsteps inside, along with muffled voices. So people were inside, but the door was locked?

She knocked again, harder this time.

At least she'd worn her beige quilted jacket today, over her light camel wool Dolce & Gabbana jacket and pants, so she wasn't freezing in the hallway, but still...it was a pain in the butt to have to stand out here, knocking and waiting, hoping somebody would let her in.

Somebody being Mistress Ulyana, the Gatekeeper. Unless Frances lucked out and Oleg or Dmitri happened to wander through the waiting area and hear someone knocking at the door.

She didn't have Uly's cell-phone number, and even if she did, that Russian dominatrix wouldn't respond. And although she'd had Oleg's number yesterday, he said he changed it every day...which didn't make a lot of sense to her, but she didn't have today's number, so that took care of that.

She knocked again, her knuckles starting to hurt from rapping on the cold metal door.

*Thanks, Dmitri, for being too fricking paranoid to give me a fricking key.*

She couldn't text Dmitri and let him know she was out here because he didn't like to be texted unless it was an *emergency,* which he'd told her three times yesterday after Uly-Byotch gave her the men's bathroom key, which Frances didn't realize until she'd walked all the way down to the women's bathroom and noticed the key with the clunky chain was attached to a *blue* candy box, for men, and not a *red* candy box, for ladez, so Frances had to schlep all the way back to the office, her bladder screaming, only to find the Russian Confections door locked and no response when she knocked and knocked.

She probably should have just schlepped back to the men's bathroom, but she was nervous about running into Dmitri or one of his Balkan safe cracker thugs at the urinals, so she'd texted Dmitri, asked if he could please open the Russian Confections door as she was locked out.

He'd opened it all right.

Looking like a pissed-off James Bond after wrestling with the metal-toothed assassin-villain Jaws, as though Frances had purposefully locked herself out just to irritate him.

After giving her a lecture about never texting him unless it was an emergency, he snapped his fingers and Ulyana, looking surprised and concerned—an acting role that should earn her a Best Supporting Actress nomination in the Duplicitous Receptionist category—ran over with the key to the ladez room.

Frances checked the time on her smartphone. Nine-fifteen.

She thought of that English band The Clash's song "Should I Stay or Should I Go?"

Thinking of funny old songs made her think of Braxton last night with his bad old pop lyrics.

She pulled out her phone and texted him.

Uly locked me out of office

He texted her back immediately.

I'll be right there to break down the door

She heard a sharp click and tested the knob, which now turned easily. Apparently Uly had decided to allow Frances inside. She texted back.

Door open

Good. Lunch?

She was meeting Charlie over coffee at two this afternoon, which she'd told Dmitri was a doctor's appointment. Plenty of time for lunch before that.

She texted him back.

11:30?

She paused, not sure where to suggest they meet. She didn't "do lunch" with her Vanderbilt coworkers, except for occasional meetings with Charlie at restaurants, and she didn't want to suggest any of those places. Her best choice was to meet Braxton at Morgan-LeRoy. They could figure out where they wanted to go from there.

She finished her text message.

11:30? Meet you at M-L?

She hit the send button, feeling a little tingle at the thought of seeing him as she slipped her phone into her jacket pocket. Then she stood in front of the Russian Confections door and took in a deep, life-affirming breath before entering.

Her last breath of fresh air as the waiting room was already hazy with cigarette smoke. Ulyana sat at the metal-tile desk, puffing away, observing Frances as she walked inside. Today she wore her usual business attire. Another sparkly plunging-neckline top, a red one that barely restrained her breasts. As Ulyana was sitting down, Frances didn't know what else she was wearing, but guessed it to be a pair of skintight pants— shiny or lizard print—and stiletto heels.

To top off the office look, Uly's chestnut hair had been back-combed over her head, from where it tumbled down the side of her face and spilled over her shoulder onto her chest, the curly ends shellacked into place with hairspray.

"You late," she said, her eyes narrowing into two thick lines of black eyeliner.

Frances didn't expect everybody she met to like her, but she'd never encountered someone who expressed such instant venom toward her. She could chalk it up to jealousy over Braxton, but Ulyana's intense dislike had started before he'd even entered the picture.

Some things were too complicated, or crazy, to waste brain matter on.

"The door was locked," Frances said, as though that was news.

"Door, really?" Uly took another puff on her cigarette, feigning a look of incredulity. "Maybe Dima or Oleg lock when they go."

"This morning?"

"Yes," she said on the exhale, smoke seeping out with the word.

"Where'd they go?"

She shrugged. "Have thing for you," she said, setting her lighted cigarette on a white ashtray, a cursive gold *B* visible underneath several cigarette butts stained with Uly's berry-red lipstick. The *B* looked familiar, but Frances couldn't place it.

Uly retrieved a letter-size white envelope from a stack of papers held down by a rock paperweight and handed it to her. "From Dima."

*Frances* was written in blue ink on the front of the envelope. She'd never seen Dmitri's handwriting before, and it surprised her he wrote in such a tight, small script instead of big and bold, the way he was.

Frances turned the envelope over. It had already been opened, rather hastily, she guessed, as the flap had a small rip.

"Did you open this?" she asked Uly.

"No." The receptionist took another drag off her cigarette.

"What time are they expected back?"

Uly shrugged again. "Dima say use his office. It open."

A moment later, Frances opened Dmitri's door and stepped inside, catching a healthy whiff of his cherry-leather cologne that permeated the room. As she started to close the door, Uly spoke loudly.

"*Nyet*. It stay open!"

"Door, really?" Frances said while closing it, letting it shut with a loud thunk. She pushed the lock button on the knob.

Turning, she looked around the room, her gaze settling on the far window. Crossing to it, she looked in the direction where Braxton said the airstrip lay. It had to be in that small, undeveloped square of land. She scanned the patch of greenish-brown, settling on a faint, grayish line—that had to be it.

She sat down at the large oval table, wondering how Dmitri had learned about that abandoned airstrip as she pulled a piece of paper from the envelope.

On it was a two-column printed table. In the left column were two-digit numbers, and in the right column were two- and three-digit numbers. Below it was a handwritten message: "What's your number?"

*Her* number? What was that supposed to mean?

Something that mattered to Dmitri, obviously, although why he made it into some kind of riddle escaped her.

She looked at the torn envelope again. She suspected Uly had opened it, but maybe Oleg had. Or maybe Dmitri had sealed it, then reopened it to add his handwritten message.

She flipped the envelope over, looked at his compact handwriting. A handwriting analyst she'd worked with on several investigations had evaluated a similar cramped style of writing in a case, identifying the writer to be someone who was intensely focused and handled pressure well…all of which turned out to be true.

So it appeared Dmitri was intensely focused on her answering this riddle…but if she didn't, at least she could count on him handling the pressure of her failure.

If he was even the one who wrote this note.

At 11:30, Braxton, sitting at his desk, experienced a sense of déjà vu as he watched Frances stroll through the front door of Morgan-LeRoy. The last time she'd come here, she'd been the mysterious blonde visiting the private eye's office. Seemed like a lifetime ago, and yet it had only been a week.

And in those seven days, Frances had changed.

If he'd had to sum her up in a word that first day, it would've been *strict*. Like a librarian who'd shush you for even thinking too loudly. Tailored gray pantsuit, tight bun she was passing off as a hairstyle. Not so strict she didn't radiate sex appeal, but a guy had to think outside the box to pick up on it.

But looking at her today, the word that came to Braxton's mind was *soft,* although *sweet thing* fit the bill, too. Even though that was two words.

She wore light tan slacks and a matching jacket that combined with her blond hair made her look like a stick of walking butterscotch. She still went for the bun look, but this one was so relaxed at the nape of her neck, it looked as if it might shed its inhibitions any moment.

"Hi, you," she said, sitting in the guest chair in front his desk.

Her low-throttled voice reverberated through him like heated sonic waves. She'd put on a darker lipstick, this one a reddish-pink that reminded him of ripe strawberries. More eye liner, too, and a bronze shadow that emphasized the sparkling amethyst of her eyes.

"Hi back," he murmured. "You look pretty."

She smiled her pleasure at the compliment. "Not so bad yourself. Like your shirt."

"Oh, this old thing?" He adjusted the sleeve of his navy-striped French-cuff dress shirt. "Ulyana treat you any better the rest of the morning?"

"Only saw her again as I was leaving, and she made it clear she wasn't happy that I had shut Dmitri's office door. But then, she's not happy with me in general. I don't get that girl."

"Think she's Dmitri's girlfriend?"

"From what I've seen, they never flirt, and they squabble in Russian all the time, which makes me wonder if they even like each other all that much."

"When I was there, seemed all she did was smoke and shop online."

"She also guards the bathroom keys.... Oh, I just realized something!" She gave her head a disbelieving shake. "Today I saw an ornate gold *B* at the bottom of her ashtray. It looked familiar, but I couldn't place it."

"The old Bally's logo?"

"That's it! And you know what else? I saw a rock paperweight on her desk that I'd never seen before... but now I realize it's the exact color and shape as the Rocky's Deli menus. I saw one that night when I was at the sports-book bar with your mom."

Braxton mulled this over for a moment. "We both know how paranoid Dima is. I'm starting to think he has me checking up on Yuri because Dima doesn't want him near something he's protecting."

"Something to do with the heist?"

"My gut feeling is no. For the most part, those activities are contained within the Russian Confections office."

He stood, plucked his jacket off the back of his chair. "I know where we're going to lunch."

"Bally's?"

"You're a mind reader."

In the background, a door shut with a thud, followed by heavy footsteps down the hallway. A moment later, Drake entered the room. Seeing Frances, he stopped and glowered at her, the muscles in his jaw clenching.

"Hi, Drake," she said softly.

Drake turned his attention to his brother. "I'm heading out to interview the manager at that trucking company about a recent hijacking. Be back around three."

A prickling started at the top of Braxton's scalp. Fighting to keep his voice even, he said, "Frances said hello to you."

"It's all right," she murmured.

"No, it's not," he said, locking eyes with his brother.

"You start a fight in here, bro," Drake said, his voice a dark rumble, "and you're fired."

Braxton laughed. "I'm a consultant! You can't fire me."

Which he realized made no sense, but he'd said it, so he was sticking to it.

"I'll meet you outside," Frances said softly.

Braxton watched as she headed to the front door, her heels clicking across the floor. When the door shut behind her, he turned back to Drake.

"I told you to treat her with respect," he said.

"And I told you she's going to drag you down."

"Because she's made mistakes in her past? So did I! Does that mean *I'll* drag down any woman I get involved with?"

"Her crime," Drake said, his scowl deepening, "makes yours look like child's play. She got a ten-year felony conviction—you got a slap on the hand. She's bad news. If you're smart, you'll cut her out of your life. If you don't, your family will start cutting you out. It's inevitable, bro."

Without another word, Drake headed back down the hallway. Seconds later, the adjoining door banged shut.

Braxton stood there, his anger dissolving into a gut-deep ache at the thought of losing his family again. But they wouldn't cut him out. Drake was overreacting to Braxton's past, that was all. Yet he'd thrown down the gauntlet, voiced the threat.

Frances...or his family?

He hated his brother for making him even entertain that thought.

Thirty minutes later, Braxton and Frances walked into the sports-book bar at Bally's. A silver-haired bartender set a drink in front of a customer who was intently watching a horse race on an overhead screen.

"Well, if it ain't Mister Party-Hearty Chex Mix!" the bartender called out.

"Hey, Ross," Braxton said, walking up and shaking his hand. "Good to see you again."

"I remember this lovely lady," Ross said, referring to Frances. "House chardonnay. You came in with Benny's best gal, Dot."

"Yes," she said, "nice to see you again."

"Your dad, Benny," Ross said to Braxton. "They broke the mold with that guy, I tell ya. *Courage and a sense of humor is all you need to get by in life.* I musta repeated that sayin' of your dad's a thousand times to customers."

As Ross and Braxton caught up for a few minutes, Frances wandered over to a TV screen, wondering if courage and a sense of humor were guidelines for dealing with Drake's intense dislike of her seeing Braxton. Courage to face Drake's loathing, and adopting a sense of humor the next time he dissed her?

Maybe it'd help her cope—and that was a big maybe—but it wouldn't fix this problem.

"Frances?" Braxton, smiling, waved her over to join him at the bar.

She could hardly breathe for the way he looked at her, his warm smile dissolving her concerns and worries. Even from ten feet away, she swore she could feel his breath on her cheek, the heat of his hand cupping her face, the strength of his arms around her, protecting her.

She gravitated toward him, wondering if she could ever break away.

When she reached him, Braxton gave her an I've-got-a-secret look.

"Guess what Russian receptionist Ross has seen around here every Thursday afternoon for the last month?" he asked her.

"Like clockwork," Ross added, "two on the dot."

"I suggest we sit at the bar and eat some Rocky's Deli sandwiches," Braxton said, pulling out a stool for Frances to sit on, "and chat with Ross."

After Ross handed their order for pastrami sandwiches off to one of the waitresses, he told them Ulyana sat in the same seat in the sports book every Thursday from two to three, sometimes three-thirty. A few guys would drop by and talk to her, but Ross never saw any money exchanged, nor did she leave with any of them, although she typed a lot on her cell phone.

"Gotta be fair, though," Ross said. "She might just be a nice girl who likes to bet the horses."

After their sandwiches arrived, Frances and Braxton ate in silence for a while. Occasionally there'd be a loud yell or clapping from the sports book.

Frances shook some salt on her fries, set down the shaker. "Ulyana handed me an envelope from Dmitri this morning that had already been opened. Claimed she didn't do it, but who knows. Anyway, let me show you what was in it."

She pulled the envelope from her purse and showed Braxton the cryptic assignment Dmitri had left for her.

After looking at it for a while, he said, "All the numbers in the left column start with either zero or one. Those could be months."

"Good point." She took a bite of fry.

"Thank you. Let's see...the numbers in the right column... I don't know. There's no pattern." He met her gaze. "How could a bunch of different three-digit numbers apply to the heist?"

"Whatever those numbers represent, he seems to think I have one, too." She pointed to the handwritten message "What's your number?" at the bottom of the page.

"Let's run a Google search on a month and its corresponding number," Braxton suggested.

She retrieved her smartphone. They tried June and 278.

"Three years ago in June," she said, reading the search results, "a man walked into the Peregrine Hotel in Cannes and stole fifty million dollars in jewels in two-hundred seventy-eight seconds."

"'What's your number?' sounds like Dmitri wants you to estimate how many seconds it will take to accomplish this heist."

"First a riddle, now math," she muttered, putting away her phone. "How'd I get so lucky to get an undercover job with homework assignments?"

AT TWO, FRANCES met Charlie at Ronald's Donuts, a mom-and-pop business located in a strip mall off Spring Mountain Road. They sat in the back at one of the small Formica tables. The air smelled like coffee and cinnamon.

A slim middle-aged man with clipped dark hair stood behind the glass counter filled with trays of doughnuts and pastries. As customers entered, he'd greet them with a slight bow.

"This place," Charlie grumbled, "is a hole-in-the wall."

"It's conveniently located," Frances said, ripping off a piece off her apple fritter, "and I figured a safe spot to meet, as Dmitri and his associates probably don't eat vegan doughnuts."

"*Vegan* doughnuts?" He snorted a laugh. "Isn't that an oxymoron? At least this place is cheap."

His comment seemed so…un-Charlie. "Since when do you care about cheap?" She put the piece of fritter in her mouth, savoring its gooey sweetness.

"Since my ex-wife took me to court to bump up her alimony and child support *again*. After quitting her personal-shopper job at Nordstrom because she doesn't like the new spring line or some such nonsense, I've taken over mortgage payments on a vacation condo in Tahoe that's in *her* name, car payments on her Lexus, plus I'm paying for a trip to Italy for her, my kids *and* a nanny for some bullshit 'intensive language program.'"

His sullen gaze turned inward, into what she guessed was more mental seething.

She took another bite of her fritter, thinking about how her boss had always seemed like a guy who wallowed in money. Tossing a grand here or there the way others tossed pennies into water fountains when making wishes. Guess she got that wrong.

He finally looked up from his reverie. "I'm sorry for that diatribe."

"I, uh, hope things work out."

She wiped her sticky fingers with a napkin, feeling uneasy hearing about his personal issues, especially as they made him so angry.

Setting the napkin aside, she met his gaze, taken aback at the pleading look in his eyes, as if he sought some kind of understanding from her.

"You wanted to meet because there's something critical I need to know?" she asked, steering their conversation to business.

"Yes, that's right." He pressed his fingertips together and affected a somber air. "Remember the two investigators I wanted to set up in that warehouse business office? Unfortunately, I've had to pull them onto another critical fraud case. I'm sorry."

She hadn't thought about those investigators in a few days, but hearing they wouldn't be nearby, she felt a trickle of cold panic realizing how isolated she'd be in that Russian Confections office.

He frowned. "You're upset."

She tried to flatten her face, make it a blank canvas, then thought, *Why pretend I'm not upset? This situation needs to be corrected.*

"Right now," she said quietly, "I'm treated reasonably well at the office, but if Dmitri were to suspect anything...well, that scares me."

Charlie spread his hands helplessly. "I didn't mean to leave you high and dry, Frances. Maybe I can pull McKenzie off his case early...."

"Please, not McKenzie. He graduated from college, what, six months ago? I need an experienced investigator. Someone who can help me sift through details, be there when I call...."

*Braxton.*

No, Charlie wouldn't go for this. He despised private investigators. She remembered his words at their brunch. *Most of those shamuses will do anything for a buck, including break the law.*

On the other hand, they were under a time crunch, no one else was available, and despite what Charlie claimed, he *was* leaving her high and dry.

"I have an idea." She paused. "What about hiring Braxton as a—"

"Braxton," he muttered. "Did you tell him you're working undercover?"

"Of course not."

A white lie, but Vanderbilt didn't like its investigators revealing their identities while undercover except under extraordinary circumstances—and she doubted that Charlie would think these qualified.

"Anyway," she continued, "what about hiring him to—"

*"No."*

"Charlie, please, hear me out."

"I'm not bringing some Vegas private dick into a Vanderbilt case."

"But he's knowledgeable about the Russian community, which is a big plus."

"Does he speak Russian?"

"Yes," she said, recalling his understanding some things Dmitri had said the other day.

"Fluent?"

"I don't know. But another point in his favor is that Dmitri already trusts him, so it's not like we're bringing in as an unknown."

"But I thought he didn't want Braxton in the offices. How can he help you if he can't get inside?"

She never thought she'd view Ulyana as an asset,

but she did now. "For starters, the Russian receptionist has the hots for Braxton and would open the door for him while she's there. If possible, I could also let him in, which would irritate Dmitri but at least he knows and trusts Braxton. If I were to let a total stranger in, Dmitri would implode."

He thought about it for a moment. "I don't know...."

"We're under an insanely tight time constraint, Charlie. Braxton's not just our best option, but our *only* one. If Vanderbilt was willing to put two additional full-time employees on this case, seems they'd be happy to pay a lot less to an investigative consultant."

"Investigative consultant." He smirked. "They're *private dicks,* Frances. Most being ex-cops who quit or were fired, which says it all right there. By the way, I did a Google search on Braxton...need I say more?"

A loud burst of giggling distracted her. At a nearby table, a red-haired teenage boy fed a maple bar to a girl who managed to giggle and nibble at the same time. Frances had a fleeting ache to run away with Braxton, away from their problems and worries, just be the two of them doing something silly and fun....

She looked back at Charlie, entering the ring for the next round.

"If you looked him up on Google," she said, "you must have also read that he worked closely with the Vegas police last summer in a sting that brought down a Russian mobster and that the D.A. has tapped Braxton to be his star witness at the trial next month."

"So you're saying he's reformed."

"It's possible people can be, you know. You've acknowledged my rehabilitation yourself in reports to the court." She paused. "Anyway, I could use his help on this case."

"What kind of help?"

"Field investigations."

Braxton had already helped her this morning when they went to Bally's, but Charlie wouldn't like hearing she'd already involved him on case work, so she'd keep that one to herself.

"For example," she said, "there's an abandoned but supposedly still functional private airstrip I'm interested in checking out. It's near the Russian office, which makes me think Dmitri might be planning to use it for his great escape after the heist. The location of the airstrip isn't exact—somewhere on acres of uninhabited desert—so I'd like Braxton to accompany me."

He frowned. "But if you find evidence of Dmitri stealing coins, he'll be in jail instead of making a great escape."

A roundabout way of saying he didn't want to bring Braxton on board, but he hadn't said no this time. Plus, Charlie had brought up something she'd been thinking about ever since visiting Bally's.

"There might be other evidence that could put Dmitri in jail," she said. "Unrelated to the coins, but it could lead us to them. Like you said, criminals behind bars can get chatty, thinking the more they tell, the less their sentence might be."

From the glint in his eyes, she knew she'd sparked his interest.

"Do you know about something else?"

She thought about Uly hanging out at Bally's on Thursday afternoons. Where else was she hanging out on her other afternoons off? Was she conducting business for Dmitri? That bartender Ross said maybe she was just a bettin' girl, but Frances would bet otherwise.

"I have a hunch about something," she admitted, "but nothing concrete."

Charlie gave her an assessing look. "Keep your priorities straight, but if you learn something that backs up that hunch, let me know. Now, tell me about this airstrip."

"Don't know much about it yet, just that it exists on property owned by an elderly gentleman who now lives in another state. Apparently he cowboyed this landing strip on his own, literally flew below the radar, so McCarren never detected it."

"How'd you learn about it?"

Better to slide into the truth sideways, cloud the fact Braxton had first told her. Otherwise, Charlie would wonder why Brax mentioned it out of the blue.

"Dmitri has a thing for James Bond, and while he was looking out his window at something in the distance, he started talking about a dramatic escape Bond once made by airplane from some secret airstrip. I mentioned this to Braxton...as he was walking me to my car...and he told me about a small abandoned airstrip near the warehouse.... When I looked out Dmitri's office window today, I saw it."

"How did Braxton know about it?"

"Seems his dad and the guy were friends."

He nodded slowly. "Check out this airstrip, give me a report."

"I'll need Braxton's help finding it."

Another round of quiet.

"I'm not happy about this," Charlie finally said, staring hard at her. "But under these circumstances, bringing Braxton in makes sense. But I'll have to hard-sell him to management, since I can't hide his past from them. But...I'll explain why he's our best option right now and that he will *never* work an investigative task alone but always in tandem with you. Which makes you responsible for his actions, Frances."

"Thank you, Char—"

"It bears repeating," he said, his expression darkening, "that you will be responsible for his actions. If he slips up, it's on you."

She knew exactly what he was saying—if Braxton messed up, Vanderbilt would terminate her employment, which meant the court would revoke her suspended sentence.

Apprehension prickled her skin at the thought of serving out her sentence in prison. But she trusted Braxton, believed without a doubt he'd work hard and smart on this case with her. Minor slipups happened all the time in investigations, but she could easily smooth those over, and no one would be the wiser.

Charlie was talking *major* snafus, and she'd ensure none happened by anticipating potential problems ahead of time and working them herself.

"I understand what you're saying, Charlie. You can reach Braxton at—"

"Morgan LeRoy Detective Agency," he said, as though the name itself disgusted him.

Which almost made her laugh. That and the childish pout on her boss's face, like a prep-school boy forced to make nice with some dirty hooligan. Poor Charlie. Soiling his lofty standards by associating with a private dick.

"I need something to lift my spirits," he grumped. "Maybe I'll try a vegan doughnut."

"You won't regret it, Charlie."

"The doughnut or the shamus?"

"Both."

She'd make sure this worked, no matter what it took. Because failure was not an option.

At six on Tuesday evening, after a bumpy ride in the dark across several acres of barren desert, Braxton braked his rented Jeep Cherokee in front of a wide strip of concrete, which had an otherworldly glow in the headlights.

"There it is," he said to Frances, "Grover's old airstrip. The last of the renegade runways."

The gloomy skies and winds of the past few days had finally dispersed, leaving a clear night sky dotted with stars.

"How wide is it?" she asked.

"Probably sixty feet. Pretty narrow for an airstrip. I was going to kill the engine, but I won't if you still want the heater running...."

"Please, turn it off."

After Braxton escorted her to her car after work, she'd rushed home and changed into jeans, a turtleneck and her down jacket for their investigation tonight. Perfect attire for the chilly outdoors, but bordering on a sweat lodge inside a well-heated vehicle, so she'd peeled her jacket off on the twenty-minute ride over and tossed it into the backseat.

He turned off the ignition. Except for the distant hum of traffic from Interstate 15, it was eerily quiet.

"Should've told me you were uncomfortable," Braxton said. "I would have turned off your heated seat."

Heated seat. She felt a rush of warmth fill her cheeks. Couldn't seem to escape being overheated in one way or another tonight.

"Your *car* seat," he elaborated.

"I know what you meant."

"Didn't want you to think I was flirting with you or anything. I'm playing by the rules. Not exactly what I've been known for in the past, so this is an exercise in character building. For me, I mean."

Frances wasn't sure how to respond, so she decided not to. Talking about denying their sexual chemistry was like being on a diet and talking about not eating chocolate truffles.

It was probably good that the vehicle's interior was

so dark she couldn't see the play of emotions in Braxton's gray eyes. Or that way he had of quirking an eyebrow, which always made her want to laugh. Or the sexy, teasing curve of his lips when he smiled. Or that brown leather bomber jacket he'd worn tonight, giving him an edgy, motorcycle-gang look that could make a nun kick out a church window.

Clasping her hands tightly in her lap, she forced air into her lungs. *Should've stuck with thinking about truffles.*

"After you went back to work this afternoon, I came out here to check the airstrip while there was still light," Braxton said. "Didn't see any fresh tire marks, and farther down the strip there's brush growing up through some cracks in the concrete, so I'm guessing it hasn't been used in a while." He paused. "Drake and I were teenagers when we visited Grover with our dad. Kind of sad seeing his old house boarded up—it's a quarter mile or so to the north. And the hangar is totally gone. I mean, not even a stick of wood where it used to be, like it vanished into thin air."

His comment struck a chord with her.

"Lately," she said, "I've sometimes thought how people work so hard to gain things. Money. Cars. Houses. When really, life is about letting go, hopefully gracefully, of everything."

"Are we doing deep thoughts now?"

"Don't make me slug you."

"Yeah, wouldn't want to do that. You could probably take me mano-a-mano."

She laughed softly. "Why do I put up with you?"

"There must be *some* reason, because according to Charlie Eden, you highly recommended me to be your investigator underling."

On the drive over here, they'd discussed Charlie's call to Braxton earlier today in which he'd offered him a consulting contract. Braxton said their conversation had been "stilted" but professional. Frances took that to mean her boss had been on his best behavior, which was a good sign.

"Did he really say *underling?*" she asked.

"No, I added that part. He said you would be the lead investigator on this case, and I was to work in tandem with you, never alone. Which is stated in the contract he emailed to me, as well. Three times."

"He's worried about you taking on something solo, messing up the case."

"I would never do that, Frances," Braxton said, his tone serious. "Like I said before, I want to help you."

She looked out into the night, irked that Charlie had put the requirement for their always working in tandem *three* times into the contract. Did he think Braxton was an idiot?

*Charlie thinks most people are idiots. Probably treated his exes like that, too. And they're going to make him pay and pay for it.*

"Awfully quiet over there," Braxton said gently. "Something wrong?"

"Charlie," she muttered. "He can be such a…" She blew out an exasperated breath.

"Pompous asshole?"

She smiled. "Yes. He made it clear today that should you slip up, it's on me. He had his reasons, of course, but it's more about keeping his reputation shiny at Vanderbilt. I told you he'll be heading up a new division soon, right?"

"Yeah, and that you'll be his star investigator-manager." He made a concerned noise. "What did he mean, it's 'on you'?"

"I'm responsible if you mess something up. Which I know you'd never do, of course," she added quickly.

"I know that, Frances." He paused. "Responsible as in…they'd fire you?"

"Probably."

"But that could mean…prison."

She felt as though she'd swallowed ice cubes. "I have to admit, there was a minute or two after I first met Dmitri when I wondered if prison were preferable to working this case," she said quietly. "But the thought of losing my freedom—losing the chance to be with you—terrifies me more than anything else."

"Baby," he murmured, pulling her close.

Sinking against him, she snuggled into his warmth, taking in his familiar masculine scent.

She felt him shift as a groan, guttural and needy, escaped his throat, shooting a thrill through her.

His hands moved up to her face, cupping it and tilting it slightly so she looked up into his shadowed features. In the ambient glow from the headlights, she could almost make out his dark eyes and the shadow of his mouth, so close she could feel his breath on her face.

"Sometimes I've imagined you to be like the night," he murmured huskily, "mysterious, full of secrets. And then sometimes like the moon…beautiful, bright, alone. But you're not alone. I'm here, and I will always be here."

She felt hypnotized by the roughened quality of his voice, the heat of his palm cradling her cheek, almost as if protecting the scar, shielding it for her. She closed her eyes, imagining how it would feel to let go, finally let go, never worry about probing stares, whispered comments…to really be his beautiful, bright moon.

"But I promised you no frisky business," he said in a strangled whisper, "and I will keep my word, even if it kills me. And that means not even a kiss. I'm being strong for both of us, Moon."

With a soft laugh, she reluctantly pulled away. Settling herself back in her seat, she gazed out at the airstrip. "Looking out Dmitri's window today, I wouldn't have been able to find this unless you'd told me where to look. Would anyone else have a better view?"

"It's visible while driving along a short section of Interstate 15, but without planes or a hangar, it doesn't stand out as an airstrip."

She stared into the inky night, imaging Grover living alone on five acres of desert, playing hide-and-seek with the airport.

"How'd Grover keep it secret? We're, what, eight

miles from McCarran? Wouldn't air traffic control have noticed?"

"Grover never called for takeoff or landing permission, so there was no reason they'd find out."

"What about radar?"

"That doesn't always detect small, light airplanes, especially if they're flying at a low altitude."

Something moved in the dark.

She froze.

"Somebody's out there," she said. Or tried to, but it was as if her throat had locked, with only a garbled wheeze coming out.

"Frances?" Braxton asked.

Nodding like a bobblehead doll, she pointed in the direction of the movement, half realizing Braxton couldn't really see her in the dark.

"Something," she rasped, "is out there."

"Where?"

Frances leaned back, her pulse pounding in her ears, and scanned the night for a shape, a movement, but only saw darkness beyond the bright strip of concrete. "Are the doors locked?"

"Yes. What'd you see?"

A shadow broke from the night and stared at their vehicle.

Her heart racing in panicked fits and starts, she pointed madly at it and shrieked.

"Frances, calm down, it's only a coyote."

The animal skulked the periphery of the headlight's

reach, its eyes glinting as it looked back one last time before slinking away.

Frances sucked in a shaky breath, dabbing the back of her hand against her forehead. "Sorry. Obviously I'm a city girl."

"Didn't you know it was a coyote?"

She knew he probably meant well, but that comment made her feel even more pathetic.

"No," she said tightly, "I thought it was a poodle."

He laughed.

"I was kidding."

"I know, Babe. That's why it was funny. You have a great sense of humor—should let it play outside more often." His voice turned serious. "That coyote's got me thinking. If Dmitri really wants to use this airstrip, somebody will be checking the runway and landing conditions. I'll come back tomorrow and set up a motion-detector camera. Drake can help me set up apps that'll run feeds to my smartphone and yours."

The analytical part of her mind took over, easing out the frantic, worried part.

"Sounds good. I'll let Charlie know."

"Hungry?"

"Starved."

"I know a place that serves killer roasted-pepper-and-goat-cheese sandwiches."

"Goat cheese," she murmured. "You remembered my mom's soufflé."

"We'll get a few sandwiches to go, and I'll drive you back to your place."

"Great. I think we have some wine that'll go great with goat-cheese sandwiches."

"Sorry, I can't stay to eat. I have a dance lesson."

"I didn't know you were taking dance lessons."

Braxton turned the ignition key, and the engine growled to life. "It's a temporary thing."

And that was that.

AT FIVE ON WEDNESDAY, Frances exited the Russian Confections office, relieved to finally be leaving. Not that things weren't going well. Dmitri had been exceptionally polite, constantly asking how she was doing, if she wanted anything—coffee, chocolate, vodka?—complimenting her clothes and hair.

After her dressed-down, bad-hair first day, she'd returned to wearing tailored pantsuits, sleek chignons and more makeup. Her efforts apparently made an impression on Ulyana, who eventually toned down her surly act. Not to the point of being *pleasant,* but at least there were fewer eye rolls and she willingly handed over the key to the ladez bathroom.

In a phone call with Charlie last night, Frances had relayed these positive changes, after which he asked if she'd picked up any clues about the stolen coins.

She'd bit back the urge to say, *Without injecting Dmitri with truth serum, no.* It wasn't as if she could suddenly ask, *What about those Greek tetradrachm coins stolen from the New York numismatic event several years ago? Seems you were living there at the time. Have any idea what the heck happened to them?*

Instead, she told Charlie no, she hadn't picked up on any clues and that unless she mentioned them in some context—which would only spark Dmitri's paranoia—the chances of tracking leads to their whereabouts were nil. Without the coins, she questioned Charlie about the necessity of continuing her undercover work—could her testimony about what she'd learned so far about the heist be enough to put Dmitri away?

At which point Charlie launched into a spiel about the pointlessness of such testimony as it was circumstantial evidence, way too thin for prosecutors to file and juries to convict; therefore, if she couldn't find a lead to the coins, Vanderbilt needed a confession.

Meaning that unless she came up with concrete evidence, the sting was on.

All of which she thought about as she headed down the building exit, the click of her heels echoing in the empty corridor. But the thoughts scattered, blown away like dust in a wind, as she approached the glass doors.

Braxton waited outside for her, dressed casually in jeans, a gray T-shirt and shades...but his demeanor was anything but casual. Maybe it was his nonchalant, cocky stance or the way his toned chest and arms seemed to strain against his shirt, but even separated by heavy glass doors, she could *feel* his sexuality stoking her internal temperature.

He...was...so...damned...hot.

Slowing her steps, she took a steadying breath, working to empty her mind of their heated encounters—the way he'd pressed her against those very glass doors, their passion as fierce and turbulent as the storm outside…the way he'd pulled her into his home and into his arms, his warm, full lips dragging a trail down her face, lingering at the corner of her mouth…

*Hard to diet if you're thinking about truffles.*

So much for emptying her mind.

With Dmitri's and Oleg's offices having views of this parking lot, she and Braxton had agreed to keep it low-key and professional during these walks to her car, not do anything to raise others' questions or doubts.

Easing in a calming breath, she proceeded to the door.

"No purse today?" Braxton asked as they started walking across the lot.

The warm breezes and clear blue skies hinted of spring, but locals knew better. Just because February weather flashed a smile didn't mean it wouldn't be brooding later.

"I've decided not to bring a purse to work anymore—don't want it locked in somebody's office again." A passing breeze lifted wisps of her hair. She smoothed them back into her chignon. "I'm keeping my phone and keys in my jacket pockets. Anything else can stay in the car."

They stopped next to her Benz. She retrieved the key from her jacket pocket and unlocked the doors.

"I've got the motion-detector cameras set up at the airstrip," Braxton said casually, glancing up at the skies. "Tomorrow I'll download the app to your phone so you can view the feed."

"Tomorrow?"

"I'm busy tonight."

Something flickered in his eyes that made her uncomfortable. Was he hiding something?

"Another dance lesson?" she guessed.

He hesitated, then nodded.

She flicked a glance at Oleg's office window. Time to cut this short.

"Have a good class," she said, reaching for the door handle.

"I'll get that." He opened her door, shutting it behind her. Leaning over, he peered at her through the tinted driver's window, jabbed a finger at the door latch while mouthing, *Locked?*

She started the engine, rolled down the window.

"Yes indeedy," she said brightly, gaily punching the lock button on the arm console. "See you later, Fred!"

Ignoring his baffled look, she closed the window and took off, peeling a little rubber in her not-exactly-smooth exit.

There was a lot on her plate these days. Thwarting Russians, finding coins, dealing with bosses, solving mysterious transactions in sports books, monitoring mysterious airstrips, calculating seconds....

But there was room on that plate for one more task.

She was going to get to the bottom of this dance-lesson thing.

On Thursday, as Frances walked down the corridor at five, she saw Braxton waiting outside the warehouse doors again. He'd texted her once today, just one word.

Fred?

Yesterday she'd called him Fred, as in Fred Astaire, which had been a spur-of-the-moment whimsy on her part, mostly because she was afraid if she didn't say something light she might say something heavy like *Are you seeing somebody else?*

Which probably would have come out very badly, making her appear to be some kind of jealous girlfriend. Which she wasn't, not really. They'd never called themselves anything like boyfriend or girlfriend, just Babe and Braxton, or he'd called her Moon, and then there were his early endearments, Frau Farbissina and Hillary Clinton...

But never girlfriend.

She wondered why.

Not that it mattered. Babe had a sassy ring to it and Moon was beautiful and bright and alone. On second thought, she wasn't so sure she wanted to be called Moon anymore—that alone part was too depressing. Frances didn't like feeling this vulnerable, either...and insecure...and jealous...

Braxton opened the glass door for her, and she stepped outside into the last golden light of the day, felt a cool breeze on her face and caught a scent of his musky cologne. She liked how his navy blue shirt deepened the color of his eyes to a shadowy blue and how its top button was undone, revealing a few wiry strands of chest hair. She even liked his brown oxford shoes.

She didn't feel so alone now.

"You look very pretty," he said quietly.

"Thank you."

She'd prepared for this encounter by wearing strappy sandals with a filmy print dress topped with a flowy blazer. It had taken her forty minutes this morning following step-by-step instructions for a "sexy updo" hairstyle, which she'd anchored into place with half a dozen flowery barrettes. A few weeks ago Frances would never have worn them because they were too girlie.

Almost thirty, and she was embracing her inner girlie for the first time.

As they walked to her car, Braxton asked, "Fred?"

Ignoring his question, she asked sweetly, "Shall we download the app now?"

"Sure. Your place?"

She nodded. "I was going to order Chinese. Interested?"

He paused. "I, uh…can't stay for dinner."

"Dance lesson?"

"It's over after tonight. Well, tomorrow night."

"Over?" She paused. "That almost sounds as though you're breaking up with someone."

He did a double take. "What?"

He looked so surprised, she wondered if she'd been worrying over nothing. But he hadn't really given her an answer, either. Well, she'd opened the door—

might as well charge right on through and ask the big question.

"Is there someone else?"

"You mean, am I seeing anyone else?"

She nodded.

Braxton glanced up at Dmitri's office windows, then back to her. Lowering his voice, he said, "Frances, this is a heck of a time to have this discussion, but trust me, my playboy days are over."

She forced a small smile, but she felt more uncomfortable than ever. He could have said no, but instead he let her know that he was no longer a playboy.

That word *over* had started this conversation and ended it, but it wasn't an answer. It was a dance around the issue.

"What does that mean, 'it's over after tonight'?" her dad asked.

"No idea." Frances turned on the kitchen faucet and held a dish towel underneath it. "After that he said, 'Well, tomorrow night.'"

"And what does *that* mean?"

"Like I said, we were in the parking lot, and I didn't want to get into an awkward conversation."

And she didn't want to tell her dad that she'd asked Braxton if there was someone else and hadn't really gotten an answer.

She turned off the faucet and faced her dad. "Maybe I shouldn't have told you. With you seeing Dorothy tonight for dinner and all…"

Her dad wore a chambray shirt and trousers he'd purchased today in "some mall," along with the shiny black lace-up shoes he usually only wore to his monthly International Brotherhood of Magicians dinners, but had worn twice this week when visiting Dorothy.

She caught a scent she'd hadn't smelled before—a light mix of spice and citrus—apparently another purchase he'd made today, as he hadn't worn cologne in years.

"You know I won't say a word about this to Dorothy, baby girl."

"I know."

One thing about magicians, they knew how to keep secrets. Without secrets, there'd be no magic, just cheap tricks.

She hesitated. "Are you thinking what I'm thinking?"

"I'm no mentalist, but…yes, it makes me wonder if…"

"There's somebody else," she finished.

He looked uneasy. "But it could be…"

"He's trying to end it with her."

He nodded solemnly. "Still…"

"He should have told me."

It wasn't as if she and Braxton had been seeing each other for weeks or months. It had only been a few days, so it was understandable there might be someone else hovering in the background. Maybe someone he'd been casually dating, but because of his developing relationship with Frances, he wanted to make a clean break with Miss X.

*Relationship.* That word was haunting her as much as *girlfriend* right now. And to think the other night she'd actually thought she was maybe…in love.

Braxton had never indicated he felt that way about her, though.

A nauseous feeling settled in her stomach. Had she been trying to sell herself an illusion, one where she loved and was loved in return? Where there was a shared life together, through richer or poorer, in sickness and in health, till the end of their days?

Because if there was no truth behind this illusion, there could never be magic.

"He'll be here any minute, so I'm going to wipe down the table," she said, heading toward the dining room. "It's caked with dust."

Braxton had never been inside her condo. When he'd picked her up the other night for their airstrip investigation, they'd left right away. Tonight she planned to sit in the dining room, as it was roomy and convenient to work at the table. But more than that, she didn't feel comfortable inviting him farther inside her home, her private world.

The last light of day sparkled through the small square windows on the far wall, casting hazy patterns of gold and orange light around the room. This room had been one of the reasons she bought the condo. At the time, she had the wild idea she'd throw dinner parties or host soirees filled with lively conversations about books and film, although she'd never thrown a dinner party in her life and only knew the people in her Yahoo film buffs group by their login IDs.

Funny how introverts indulged in extroverted fantasies.

As she began wiping the table, her dad entered, a wad of paper towels in his hand.

"Figured I'd help out," he said, ripping off one of the towels, "I'm not leaving for another fifteen minutes."

"Taking Dorothy to dinner?"

"I asked, but she insisted on making her famous meat loaf, which apparently has won some awards."

She swirled a few circles on the table surface, thinking how tonight's home-cooked dinner might also turn into breakfast. Should she ask if he was planning on staying out all night? Or not ask and wonder when he'd be getting home?

Maybe it wasn't any of her business. Wasn't as if he was a teenager going out on a date and she was the parent, but in an odd way, that's how it felt.

"So, uh…" She rubbed at a spot. "Planning on staying out late?"

"Don't know."

Which she guessed meant *Yes, if things go well.* "Dorothy likes you. I mean, she hasn't told me that, but I can tell."

He carefully refolded a paper towel. "And I like her."

She straightened, figuring it was time to put this next topic out on the table, so to speak.

"I like her, too, Dad."

For several moments, they stood on opposite sides of the table, reading each other's gazes, listening to a bird twittering outside.

"I sometimes feel like I'm cheating on your mother," he said quietly.

The comment surprised Frances at first, but one thing she'd always known about her dad was that he owned his truth. He never talked around it, or pretended it was something else, just acknowledged it. Deception and secrets were for magic, not real life.

"Have to admit," she said, "it feels odd imagining another woman in your life…but it's time, you know?" She paused, wanting to be sure her voice remained steady for what she wanted to say next. "Finding love again doesn't mean you need to cut Mom out of your heart. She can still have her special place."

"She'll always be my Zig Zag Girl," he whispered.

Frances blinked back her emotion. For a moment, that fathomless void that could never be filled threatened to overwhelm her, but she held it off.

Because what truly mattered right now was for her to be supportive of her dad, let him know she stood behind him.

"Maybe Dorothy," she said, trying to infuse some lightness into their talk, "can be your Aztec Lady." A reference to a famous stage illusion where the female assistant magically survives swords and spells.

With a gentle laugh, her dad returned to his polishing. "Did you know only one magician in the world is allowed to perform the Aztec Lady illusion? He purchased the exclusive rights from the magician's family after his death."

"I didn't know that."

The doorbell rang.

Frances's insides flip-flopped. Braxton. Was she ready to embrace her own truth? Tell him how his hesitancy to discuss these dance lessons had confused her, made her anxious. Or maybe she'd skip that and go for the big question. Was there someone else?

*God, I sound so insecure.*

"You toss the rags, I'll get the door," he said, setting his paper towel on the table.

"Dad," she whispered frantically.

He stopped, turned to her.

"I don't know if I can do this...."

"Yes, you can. Plus you look so pretty, those flowery things in your hair, that dress." He gave her an encouraging smile. "And don't forget, answers are sometimes right at our fingertips."

When Braxton stepped inside the small entranceway of Frances's condo, his first impression was "detached."

The walls were a misty color, like fog, reflected in several silver-framed antique mirrors. To his right was a small white half-table on which sat a pale yellow bowl painted with bees, a set of keys inside.

"She'll be out in a minute," Frances's dad said.

Braxton shifted his attention to Jonathan Jefferies. Although they'd met the other night, it had been outside in the dark, so this was the first time he'd seen his face clearly.

Glints of gray showed in his trimmed dark hair, with a sharp side part that told him where Frances got her perfectionist streak. His eyes glistened with curiosity, which also reminded him of Frances. But the rest of his face—blunt, ruddy, open—was his alone.

"Let's go to the dining room," Jonathan said, leading the way.

Maybe it was the soft lighting or the pale yellow walls, but the room made Braxton think of afternoon light. In the center was an oval oak table, its surface gleaming like honey.

Except for one fat, bushy spot in its center.

"What's that?" he asked.

"Frances's cat. Name's Teller."

"He's...large." Gargantuan was more like it.

"He likes to eat. Get you a beer?"

"No, thanks. I've got another appointment in a few minutes."

"Oh?"

Braxton looked at Frances's father, wondering if that was a question or verification that he really had to leave soon.

"Yes," he answered, figuring that covered both.

"An appointment this time at night?"

"It's barely six, right?"

He looked around for a wall clock. A display of fans were on one wall, a framed poster of Penn & Teller's Magic and Mystery Tour on another. No clock.

"It's exactly six o'clock," Jonathan said, glancing at his wristwatch, stating the time with a fatalistic cynicism Sherlock Holmes might use to address Professor Moriarty.

This wasn't going well.

Not that Braxton expected to win over Frances's father at their first man-to-man chat, but from the suspicious looks he kept giving him, and the sudden chill in the room, he'd obviously done or said something offensive.

Had to be the cat. *Shouldn't have asked what it was.*

People tended to take any comments about their pets personally, not understanding why others might not find their furry children adorable and loving. Like Grams, who believed Maxine was merely misunderstood, not a psychotic she-cat from hell.

"Hi," murmured a familiar, smoky voice.

Frances stood in the doorway, smiling at him, a glass of white wine in one hand, her cell phone in the other.

Whatever worries or concerns he had drifted away, leaving him feeling warm and happy, the way he felt after a long, hot soak or a perfectly chilled martini, only better. She hovered in the entrance to the dining room, awash in the afternoon light, as beautiful and intriguing as the vision of her that haunted him every single waking moment.

"I need to go," Jonathan said, kissing his daughter on the cheek. He paused, turned to Braxton. "My daughter's a beautiful woman, inside and out, and if anybody hurts her..." His voice dropped to a threatening growl. "They're going to answer to me."

*"Dad,"* Frances said.

He smiled brightly at her. "You need anything, baby girl, just call." After they exchanged "I love you's," he left the room.

After the front door clicked shut behind him, she shrugged apologetically. "What can I say? That's how dads are."

"Ready to kill men their daughters are seeing?"

"Don't be silly, it's not like that. Can I get you anything? Beer? Wine?"

"No, thanks."

"Good," she said, entering the room, "because this is the last glass of wine, and I'm not sure if there's any more beer."

As Frances sat in the chair next to Braxton, she had to admit he was right—her dad had sounded as though he was ready to hunt down Brax with a shotgun if he broke his little girl's heart. She'd never seen her father act like that, but then he'd never seen his daughter all inside-out, upside-down over a guy, especially one who had some kind of smoke and mirrors act going on.

She handed Braxton her smartphone. "Ready when you are."

Beep. Beep.

"Got a text," he said, pulling his phone out of his shirt pocket. "I should check it."

As he read the message, she thought she detected

an irritated look on his face. Which made her feel better. Had to mean he wasn't that into the other person, whoever it was.

And then he smiled.

Her insides clenched. What did that mean? The other woman amused him? Had a talent for writing pithy, witty text messages?

"I need to leave soon," he said, slipping the phone back into his pocket. "Let's get this app rolling."

While downloading the app onto her phone, Braxton explained how he'd set up two motion-detector devices at each end of the airstrip, one in a cactus, the other in a fake rock—and how she could see views from both using this app.

Then he slid her phone between them so they could both look at the screen.

"When you open the program," he said, tapping the screen, "it asks you to make a selection. See?"

"Yes." She took a sip of wine, wondering if Braxton was in the middle of making a selection, too.

"You can choose Option 1, this blue icon, or Option 2, the red one. If you want to look at the north end of the airstrip—"

"Oh, no!"

"What happened?"

She stared, aghast, at the wet patch on her dress. "I just bought this!"

He took the empty wineglass from her hand, set it on the table. "At least it wasn't red wine. If you get it cleaned quickly, it shouldn't stain. I know a great dry cleaner if you need a recommendation."

"Thank you, but I have a great cleaner, too, and it's only a few blocks away." She looked down at the spot. "How clumsy of me. I was leaning forward to get a closer look at the screen, and wasn't paying attention to my glass." With an exasperated sigh, she stood. "I need to change. Be right back."

A few minutes later, she stood in her bathroom, wearing jeans and a baggy sweatshirt, Braxton's cell phone in her hands. When her dad said answers were "right at our fingertips," she realized there was one sure way to learn if there was another woman. Check Braxton's cell phone.

She could contact Dorothy, but his mom had already said she'd learned her lesson, and wouldn't be talking about her son's personal life anymore. And Frances wasn't comfortable enough to ask anyone else in Braxton's family.

When Frances sat next to Braxton tonight, she wasn't sure if she'd really pickpocket his phone. Weren't deception and secrets for magic, not real life?

But after observing him read those text messages, and feeling her heart twist again, she changed her mind. Maybe deception was sometimes the best way to deal with deception. Fighting fire with fire, so to speak.

During the distraction—spilling her wine—she had quickly lifted Braxton's phone from his pocket. The spilled wine also provided an excuse to leave the room and check his phone in private.

She tapped the message icon and read his most recent incoming text message.

WHERE ARE YOU?

She stared at the words, wondering why they were capitalized. Seemed...demanding. A formidable dance instructor?

Or an impatient girlfriend?

The last thought made her feel shaky inside. She didn't want to think he was deceiving her, but after his evasiveness this afternoon, she couldn't help but wonder.

Hard to believe this was the guy who felt betrayed when she'd called her dad at Bally's. The guy who said he wanted her to tell him the truth to his face.

What a hypocrite.

What had he read that made him smile? She bit her lip. *Maybe I don't want to know.* This could be the dagger to her heart.

But also the definitive answer to her question.

Steeling herself, she checked the other most recent message.

Darling, I'm out of vermouth. Grams

She stifled a laugh.
Then closed her eyes and drew a deep breath.

Her emotions had been on a bumper car ride, bouncing from shocked to devastated to furious to amused. More emotions in a few minutes than she'd probably experienced in the last six months!

She had to remember that she hadn't been promoted to lead investigator because of her feelings, but for her ability to analyze facts.

She re-checked the first message and identified the sender's ID. Boss2.

That's all she needed to solve this case.

THE INSTANT BRAXTON left, Frances went to her computer and plugged *Boss2* into a proprietary database, learned the ID was referenced in a medical marijuana forum. She checked it out, found a posting about a Green Meet-and-Greet, and to contact Boss2 at a certain phone number for reservations. Running a reverse on the number, she found an address for "N. Davidovitch."

Then she grabbed her dad's black hooded canvas jacket and Miami Heat baseball cap, and headed to her car.

Twenty minutes later, Frances parked in the lot behind a senior citizen center and headed across the street to the Willow Creek Apartments, a stucco complex with a few scraggly palm trees instead of willows, and the noisy U.S. 95 interstate behind it instead of a creek. N. Davidovitch lived on the third floor, apartment 3B.

Braxton's rented Jeep was parked in a Willow Creek Visitors Only spot.

*Some dance lesson.*

A blue funk crept over her. Nothing like the wretched, kicked-in-the-gut feelings she'd had before, but a kind of a meandering melancholy laced with disappointment.

*If he'd really wanted to end it with this other woman, he should have told her. Instead, he popped in at this tawdry apartment complex for "free-form dancing" night after night. This wasn't some casual dating scenario, but somebody he kept returning to.*

Frances had never felt this deeply about anyone before, had never put her heart out there the way she had with Braxton. It wasn't going to be easy reeling her heart back in. It'd gotten a little too free-spirited, pumped up with dreams and ever-afters....

Heading back across the parking lot toward the senior center, she thought about picking up some takeout on the way home, eating it at the dining room table for a change. Time to start using that room. Afterward she'd spend some quality time with Teller, give Charlie a call, and try not to think about Braxton and N. Davidovitch.

*Wonder what she's like...*

Frances stopped, turned and looked up at the third floor of the Willow Creek Apartments. Was she blonde, redhead, brunette? Thin, medium, a little extra? Sexy, studious, laid-back?

She'd always wonder what N. Davidovitch had that Frances didn't...and there was only one way to find out.

Her dad's jacket was way too big for her, but its

bulky shape hid hers. And the beauty of baseball caps were they disguised key features, like the shape of the head, hair color, and when pulled low enough, the shape and color of the eyes. No wonder they were bank robbers' disguise of choice.

Before getting out of the car, she'd pulled her hair up in a topknot so her hair wouldn't be visible under the baseball cap. Tugging its bill lower, she headed back to the Willow Creek Apartments.

After climbing three flights of stairs, she paused to catch her breath, embarrassed she was this out of shape. Not even thirty and she was huffing and puffing like someone twice her age. Probably time to start some exercise regime. Daily walks or exercising along with some TV program.

Which sounded as much fun as wearing pantsuits every day for the rest of her life.

On the third floor, four apartments lined a narrow concrete walkway with a metal handrail. An aging palm tree leaned against the midsection of the railing, its bushy fronds providing a natural cover over part of the walk. The area outside 3B's door was crowded with clay pots. *She's a gardener?*

Frances stood there, eyeing the walkway, listening to the rattle of dry frond leaves, the distant buzz of traffic on Interstate 95, smelling a smoky scent of barbeque.

Where should she station herself to conduct this surveillance? Although she was tempted to stay in this spot, a shadowy niche in the stairwell thanks to the overhead burnt-out bulb, a dark form loitering up here only invited trouble. Couldn't hang out on the walkway near 3B. That would be way too obvious, although she could stroll down it once without drawing attention. She glanced at the adjacent apartment complex, a gray cinder-block building with bars on most of its windows. No options there.

For now, she'd take that stroll, and see what she could learn.

Walking casually down the walkway, she glanced up at the half moon in the sky as though that's all that held her interest. Approaching 3B, she heard the thump thump of a vaguely familiar song. A few steps more, she recognized the funky, bass-heavy seventies disco song "You Should Be Dancing" by the Bee Gees, their voices soaring in a vibrato rift about keeping a woman warm.

She stood outside 3B and gazed down at the clay pots…five of them, different sizes, filled with dirt, but nothing was growing. Stuck in one pot was a small flag with a picture of a pink bear wearing some kind of boa, a red star in the corner, with the words DEADHEAD REPUBLIC.

Deadhead? Seventies disco music? How old was this woman? Seventy-five?

The music stopped abruptly, the silence filling with the clatter of dry fronds in the breezes…and the grating slide of a latch.

A jolt of adrenaline slammed through her.

*Shit!*

Frances thought about running, about walking, even about throwing herself over the metal handrail into that palm tree.

But she didn't do any of those things.

Instead she ran in place, the rubber soles of her Keds smacking softly against the concrete, too freaked to think about a direction, having the crazy thought that when that door opened maybe she'd run right past them into N. Davidovitch's apartment....

The knob rattled.

As though woken from her trance by the snap of a hypnotist's fingers, Frances's entire body relaxed. And with a cooler-than-Bacall swivel, she walked away.

Behind her, the door creaked open.

"Brax, you're gonna be fine, man," said a male voice. "Just remember to do the heel spin *after* the second 'dancing yeah' part, and practice your moonwalk. Like, a lot."

"I don't know if I can do this, Li'l Bit."

*Li'l Bit was giving dance lessons to Braxton?* Frances slowed her pace, her ears perked up.

"Dude, stay with the flow and you'll be fine. I didn't know if I could do those leg squats you showed me, but learned I could. By the way, man, I really appreciate your helping me out at the gym. Meeting me there at different times this week 'n all."

"No problem."

"Val said she's almost done with your costume. It's

gonna be righteous, dude…gonna help you win that Shelby."

*Costume? Win a Shelby?*

"We'll see," Braxton said. "Anyway, we're helping Grams's cause. That's what matters."

Frances had leaned against the handrail to look up at the sky, far enough away to not look like a lurker but close enough to still hear their conversation. *So this dance thing is some kind of fund-raiser connected to his grandmother.*

"Glenda, man, she's the bomb. Makes me feel like I'm one of the family. Which brings me to somethin' I've been wanting to say to you, Brax." He cleared his throat. "Sometimes the truth comes down to a moment…and this moment is it for you and me."

"It's been a long day, maybe we can talk later—"

"Brax, you're my brother, man. I mean it. *My brother.* I'd kill for you."

"Okay, I'm going now—"

"But I could never really kill."

"Good to know. See you tomorr—"

"But I'd go right up to that line, man, because you're *my brother.* I know, you already have a twin, which is way groovy in a random universe, but if I could have one wish—" he sniffed loudly "—I'd ask to be—" his voice broke "—your triplet, man."

After a drawn-out silence, Braxton said, "This brother thing. Like you said, I already have one, so how about you and I just be friends. Not brothers. Not triplets. Deal?"

Pause. "Sure, Brax."

"Have I upset you?"

"Yes. But I'll get over it. Like Celine Dion said, life goes on."

"You mean 'My Heart Will Go On.'"

"Yeah, man, that too. See you tomorrow night. I hope you win."

The door clicked shut.

She continued looking up at the sky, listening to Braxton's footsteps as he walked down the walkway, passed behind her, his steps fading as he headed down the stairs.

Frances looked at the half moon, thinking how she came here tonight to learn if Braxton was toying with her heart, and then to see whose heart he preferred.

But what she really learned was that it took courage to give love.

## *CHAPTER ELEVEN*

THE COFFEEMAKER bubbled and hissed as the dark brew dripped into the glass pot, the aroma filling the kitchen. Frances, her cell phone wedged between her ear and shoulder, dropped a piece of wheat bread into the toaster, pushed down the lever.

"That's right, Charlie, both feeds go to my phone." She opened the refrigerator and peered into it. "A motion detector at each end of the airstrip, yes."

She pushed aside a jar of pickles that had taken up permanent residency in the fridge, wondered why they had three jars of strawberry jam but no butter.

"I don't know where he set the other motion detector...." Was that a Tupperware container? "Maybe he scooped out a chunk of cactus and put it in there."

She took the container out of the fridge and peeled back a corner of the lid, which opened with a soft pop. Inside were several thick slices of meat loaf with cut potatoes and carrots. She smiled.

"It's just a hunch, Charlie," she said, reclosing the container and placing it back in the fridge. "Doesn't hurt to keep an eye on that airstrip, just in case."

She smelled the bread toasting, made a mental note to pick up butter on the way home tonight.

"I mentioned my uncle collected rare coins…." She poured steaming coffee into the mug. "No, Dmitri said nothing…looked disinterested…Oleg? Hard to say. Made a comment to me about meeting his wife in Saratov two years ago, so he probably wouldn't have been in New York when they were stolen, but…right…a computer whiz can work from anywhere in the world."

She picked up her mug, blew on the steaming coffee. "Yes, he's there every day by five…uh-huh…giving Dmitri reports on what I say and do, all of it inconsequential of course…yes, absolutely I trust Braxton."

After ending the call, she felt a little guilty about *why* she now absolutely trusted Braxton. Skulking about the Willow Creek Apartments, tracking him like some kind of stalker, wasn't one of her finer moments.

But it had sure made her happier. Now she knew there wasn't some mysterious other woman, just a deadhead process server with a big heart who obviously wanted Braxton's approval so much, he was almost begging for him to call him brother. But Brax had pushed him away. She wondered what that was about.

She glanced at the wall clock. A few minutes past eight. Her dad must have come home late last night because she still hadn't heard a sound from him. Not that he'd ever been a morning person. At best, he'd stagger out of bed, make coffee and plunk himself down in his chair to watch TV. But he usually got up in time to at least say goodbye before she left for work.

She hadn't heard him come in last night, hadn't heard the hallway floorboards squeak as he made his way to bed, but such noises would've been drowned out by the screams and ominous music from the film she'd been watching in her room. Scary movies weren't her thing, but after reading that a 1944 noir classic, *The Uninvited*, was starting at nine p.m., and that a curmudgeon film critic had enthusiastically called it "riveting," how could she not try it?

It had been riveting, all right. She should've turned it off, but she couldn't make herself. Had to follow the couple as they investigated the deep, dark secrets of a haunted house, which made her think her of hers and Braxton's investigations at Russian Confections... although, hopefully, their case didn't have a heart-pounding, sinister twist at the end.

After finishing her coffee and toast, Frances grabbed her jacket, stuffed her keys and phone into its pockets, grabbed her purse, which she'd lock in the trunk of her car, and headed for work.

As she closed the front door behind her, something on the porch caught her eye. A small pile of cigarette ashes, as though someone had stood here, smoking. She looked around for a cigarette butt, didn't see one. So this person had stood here, smoking...long enough to take several puffs at least, then left?

She and her dad didn't smoke, and their only recent visitor had been Braxton, who didn't either.

Could be the groundskeeper, an old guy named Jay, who maintained the trees and shrubs around the compound and almost always had a cigarette dangling from his mouth. Sometimes he'd stand up here to clip the top branches of her sissoo tree that crowded the porch. She looked at its leathery green leaves, trying to assess if it had been recently trimmed, but what did she know? Gardening ranked right up there with cooking in her life skills.

Frances shifted her gaze back to the ashes on the concrete, just beside the round welcome mat on which she stood. An old wives' tale flitted through her mind, something about evil spirits being unable to harm a person standing within a circle.

Silly stuff. Just as it'd been silly to stay up late, scaring herself half to death watching that movie.

As she stepped off it the mat, a gust of chilly air swept past, rattling the leaves of the sissoo tree.

"AND NOW," VAL said, reaching into a cardboard box lying on the marble floor, "the cutlass!"

Braxton reared back as his sister-in-law held up a small sword. "Is that thing real?"

"No, it's plastic, but sure as heck looks convincing, doesn't it?"

He and Val stood behind a large potted palm, which served as a barrier of sorts, in the tent acting as the backstage area for the Magic Dream Date Auction in the massive lobby at Sensuelle.

The inside of the tent was buzzing with activity. People carrying clothes, clips of music as guys practiced their moves, hangers-on laughing and drinking cocktails. A popcorn machine sat in the corner, offering a sideshow of popping kernels that filled the air with their buttery scent.

"Avast, ye varmint!" Val swished the play sword in the air a few times, its blade silvery bright under the lights. "Handy for slashing, hacking and stabbing." She handed it to Braxton. "Slip it in your scabbard."

"My what?"

"Your sword holster."

"Oh." He slipped it into the plastic sheath hanging off his belt.

"I bought these boots, too." She held up a pair of high-heeled, calf-high boots. "I called Dorothy to double-check your shoe size. Didn't want to assume you and Drake had *exactly* the same size feet, but guess what? You really do! Try them on, see what you think."

Braxton put them on and walked a few steps, thinking about how he and his brother had exactly opposite attitudes on some things, though. Like Frances. Since he and Drake had exchanged words on Tuesday, they hadn't discussed Frances again. He figured his brother just needed some time. Maybe after he got to know Frances, saw she wasn't some kind of threat, he'd accept her.

"Boots are comfortable," he said.

"Good, 'cause they look *freaking awesome* with that outfit." She pawed through the cardboard box. "Pirates were quite the clothes horses, Brax, which reminds me of you. Except they stole theirs off their victims."

"Yeah, I prefer shopping." He frowned. "Peacock feather?"

Val lightly waved the brilliant blue-and-green feather. "Thought we'd stick it in your hat. I've written a little introduction the announcer will read before your dance. He'll say this exotic peacock feather was in the treasure chest you pillaged from the Isle of Kasbah, and you're giving it to the first lady who bids one hundred dollars."

He and Val had clashed when they first met last August. Braxton and his brother had swapped identities so that Drake, pretending to be Brax, could gain access to Yuri's office. Things were moving so quickly that day, there hadn't been time for Drake to inform Val of the swap, so the first time she met Braxton, she'd thought he was Drake.

And as the twin brothers' six-year rift had only started to mend that same day, Brax didn't know Val was involved with his brother, so his first words to her were some of his less artful pick-up lines.

Which had instantly clued Val in that this guy had to be Drake's identical twin because Drake had more class than that. The kind of class Braxton now emulated as he'd put his bad-boy days behind him for good.

These days, he and Val got along fine. She was one of those people who loved to help others, so she'd volunteered to help Grams with this Magic Dream Date

Auction. One of her tasks was to prep Braxton for his first and only dance performance. When Grams suggested that he'd have a better chance to win the Shelby if he were dressed like a pirate, Val was all over it.

"Let me slip this into the fold of your hat," she said, sliding in the feather. "Perfect! Just reach up, pull it out and hand it to the first lady who bids a hundred." She picked up a large oval hand mirror and handed it to him. "Check yourself out, Captain Brax Sparrow."

He gave her a look. "Let me guess…Captain Jack Sparrow's brother?"

She nodded. "Long-lost brother. Last seen, you were sinking into the murky depths of the Roppongi Ocean, cutlass in hand, frantically hacking at the iron-weighted rope pulling you under."

Had to be the hormones. Val had a creative streak, but this and the private dick story she told at the dinner table the other night were going beyond the yellow brick road.

But the baby would be here soon, and things would settle down to normal. Or as normal as they ever could be in the land of the Morgans.

"Drake said something about the two of you starting a childbirth class tonight," Braxton said.

"That's right. We'll have to leave around seven-thirty to get there on time, so we'll probably sneak out after you do your thing."

He held up the mirror, checked out the three-cornered hat with the peacock feather, his jaw darkened with five o'clock shadow. The only body part over which they'd had a "creative difference"—Val's words—were his eyes when she tried to apply eyeliner and he refused.

Vehemently.

Then she mentioned how Johnny Depp had worn kohl around his eyes as Captain Jack Sparrow in the movies, and to this day, women all over the world swooned over his smoky eyes.

Braxton had agreed to a dash of kohl.

Angling the mirror, he looked at his bare chest. When Val had suggested he shave it, he responded over his dead body, which ended that creative difference. Below were the low-cut, tight-fitting red velvet breeches Val had found at a secondhand store, the scabbard and calf-high boots she'd purchased at a costume store.

"What do you think?" Val asked.

"I have a sudden urge to swill rum, weigh anchor and hoist the mizzen! I think you should be Johnny Depp's stylist in his next pirate movie."

Val didn't just smile, she glowed.

"It's six-forty, people!" bellowed a middle-aged guy with a cookie-duster moustache. "Auction starts in twenty minutes! Manwiches, I'm handing out numbers in the order you'll be performing. Don't swap numbers or we'll get more confused than we already are."

"Are they really calling us *Manwiches?*" Braxton muttered.

"Okay," Cookie Duster continued, looking down at his clipboard, "where's Michael Benning?"

"Over here!" A shirtless twentysomething guy, his

ridged abs visible from thirty feet away, waved. He wore tight blue jeans, a bulging thigh muscle trying to escape through a rip in the denim.

Braxton looked around, noticed other buffed twenty-somethings were dressed similarly, most also absurdly tan for February with no qualms about shaving their chests.

Apparently, nobody had told them wearing costumes gave them an edge.

Yo ho ho. Looked like the joke was on him.

He felt dumber than the year he'd dressed as a spider for Halloween. After reading how to make a spider costume, his eight-year-old self decided to tackle the project solo, refusing any adult help. After stuffing nylon stockings with black tissue paper, he attached them to a black sweat suit, smeared black makeup on his face, and voilà. A spider.

As he, Drake and some of their pals were trick-or-treating around the 'hood, one of the boys asked if Braxton was an insect 'cause he only had six legs. Or were they wings? Another kid said Braxton's favorite comic hero wasn't Spider-Man, but Spider-Insect, and the jokes just kept rolling, all night long.

Tonight, he had all his pirate parts in order, but Captain Brax Sparrow looked as though he'd crashed a private Chippendale party.

"Just got a text from your mom," Val said, "Grams is sitting with the Keep 'Em Rollin' board members, and your mom and Drake are taking their seats now. She wants to know if she should save one for Frances." Val paused. "Oh, bad idea. We can't have her anywhere near Drake."

"Tell me about it. Not an issue, though, as I didn't tell Frances about this."

"I'm sorry about Drake being so..." She gave her head a shake. "That man can be fierce sometimes, but he has a good heart. Like those camera feeds he helped you set up at that airstrip—told me he ran a feed to his phone too, as a backup, in case you need help on the case."

"Great."

"Back to Frances, though. It's probably good she isn't here, seeing a bunch of drunken women shoving bills down your breeches."

Women could donate money to the Wheels auction in several ways. Pay electronically through the website, bid at the auction or stuff cash into a hunk's clothes. It was the last one that unnerved him. Which also made him feel like a hypocrite as he'd managed a strip club for years. Guess he would learn tonight how it felt to be on the receiving end.

"I hope no one really *shoves* money," he murmured.

"All that free booze, estrogen and too few men in one room? Money-shoving might be the least of your worries. This place is just beggin' for one helluva hissy fit." She looked approvingly at his costume. "I expect you to take in lots of pieces of eight tonight, Captain Brax. Word to the wise, you should tell Frances about this soon 'cause you'll be going on a date soon with your highest bidder."

Val was right. If Frances heard about this from someone else, she'd wonder why he hadn't said anything. He'd already lived with way too many secrets, and knew how damaging even the little ones could be.

Plus he didn't want her father hunting him down.

"Maybe I should call her now."

Val shook her head vehemently. "Darlin', there's a time and a place for everything, but trust me, this one isn't it. Pick a quiet time when the two of you are alone—"

"Whoa, dude, you got the pirate thing goin' on!"

Li'l Bit stood there, wearing a bathrobe and flip-flops, a pair of sunglasses stuck on top of his frizzy mass of hair. He looked like a guy you'd see wandering around the supermarket at three in the morning looking for a box of honey-nut cereal.

"You okay?" Val asked him, looking concerned.

"A little shaky, but I'm good," he answered. "No weed, no Cheetos for five days... Man, hasn't been easy. But I've lost five pounds. And thanks to Brax, gained some muscle."

"Better get your costume on," Val said, "auction's starting soon."

Li'l Bit looked surprised. "This *is* my costume. I'm dressed like The Dude in *The Big Lebowski*." With a proud grin, he pulled open the robe to reveal his T-shirt with the words *Is This Your Homework, Larry?* and baggy plaid shorts. "Plenty of give in the waistband to hold the ladies' bills," he said, snapping the elastic.

Braxton looked at Li'l Bit's eyes. Clear and bright

without a hint of pink. Could it be possible Li'l Bit sober was stranger than Li'l Bit stoned?

"Time to start lining up, Manwiches!" boomed the male voice.

"Brax, my...friend," Li'l Bit said, "the time has come."

THE MANWICHES SAT in folding chairs lined up against the side of the elevated stage. The guys couldn't see the audience, unless they stood and looked out over the performance area.

Which Braxton was doing now. The stage floor looked to be about the size of his mom's living room. On the far side of the stage, a tired-looking guy wearing headphones sat hunched over a podium, reading something on a sheet of paper.

From the edge of the stage, a catwalk extended forty or so feet into the audience of several hundred women. One section in front of the stage was roped off for wheelchair access where six or so women sat, chatting and drinking cocktails.

Beyond the audience, blazing red under spotlights, sat the Mustang Shelby GT500.

He stared at it for a long moment, coveting it with the heart of a twelve-year-old Braxton. All those drawings, all those dreams, and here it was, teasing him all these years later.

He felt a fortifying rush of determination. An almost surreal belief he could do anything—climb Mt Everest, swim the English Channel, win the Magic Dream

Date Auction. Why not? He'd been paying dues, making amends, fixing his life—maybe he'd earned one night to dream big.

*Tonight, 'Stang, you're gonna be mine.*

After he sat back down, Li'l Bit—who'd switched numbers so he and Braxton could sit together—said, "Think I ate too much popcorn. Feeling a little queasy. Kinda dizzy."

"Need some water?" Braxton asked.

Li'l Bit waved him off. "No, man, but thanks. After all the food denial this week, I kinda lost it at the popcorn machine." He belched, infusing the air with its buttery scent. "Ate three bags."

A hissing static-y sound crackled over the speakers. "Is this on?" said a man's voice.

The chatter level decreased. Beeping slot machines could be heard in the distance.

"Welcome, ladies," the announcer's voice boomed, "to the Magic Dream Date Auction! Are you ready to see the fifteen hunky guys who want to be *your* dream date?"

After the deafening response of screams and squeals died down, the announcer went through the rules, including the warning that if anyone inappropriately touched any of the hunks, security personnel would escort them immediately from the event and there would be no refunds.

Once he'd given the audience a chance to boo and hiss, the announcer said, "And now, let me introduce our first Manwich."

Michael Benning, bare-chested and tight-jeaned, stood, gave the other Manwiches a thumbs up, then climbed the stairs. Wolf whistles and clapping drowned out the rest of the introduction.

Then Mötley Crüe's badass, guitar-growling metal hit "The Animal in Me" began playing.

From the howls and screams and women begging Michael to take their money, Braxton got the sinking feeling his pirate moonwalk was doomed to walk the plank.

"Dude is killing it," Li'l Bit murmured.

Captain Brax Sparrow solemnly nodded his agreement.

Manwiches Two through Seven were hit and miss, several cresting the scream factor of Michael Manwich Number One. As each guy, sweaty and flushed from exertion, left the stage, auction volunteers gathered the stuffed bills. Braxton watched as they retrieved at least six hundred dollars off one guy.

Rules were that the women who tipped cash had to document it via photo, and forward it to Keep 'Em Rollin' with their names and contact information. So there was a lot of camera and cell phone photo-taking action along the catwalk. Flashes to challenge the red carpet at the Oscars.

"Manwich Number Eight!" The announcer's voice reverberated over the speakers. "Captain Brax Sparrow!"

Li'l Bit turned to him and grabbed his shoulders. "Listen, man, you can do this. If you forget a step, just swirl your hips. Drives women crazy."

Braxton climbed the steps, his peacock feather waving in his peripheral version, wondering if *swirl your hips* meant what he thought it meant, and that no matter how bad things might get, no way was he swirling.

"Ladies," the announcer said, "let me introduce you to Manwich Number Eight, Captain Brax Sparrow, the long-lost brother of Jack Sparrow."

He stood there, his hand on his sword holster, wishing Val had told him he was actually being introduced as Captain Brax Sparrow. He didn't like people outside of family calling him Brax, but so much for that.

"Captain Brax Sparrow," the announcer continued, "whose breeches no woman could resist, was last seen sinking into the murky depths off—" a pause "—Rop-o—" another pause "—off some exotic ocean, cutlass in hand, frantically hacking at the iron-weighted rope pulling him under."

"Can the words—start the dancing!" a woman yelled.

Clapping and whistles.

Braxton waited for his music to start... Nothing. He glanced over at the tired-looking guy wearing headphones who gave him a don't-ask-me look back. Brax turned back to the several hundred bored, confused-looking women who'd turned sullenly quiet. No one even cared to boo.

He was getting the feeling that the Shelby was always going to be out of reach.

Time for this pirate to exit the Chippendale party.

Anyway, his moonwalk sucked.

As he turned to leave, one brave soul started clapping.

"Bravo, Captain Brax," yelled his grandmother.

Someone else started clapping with her. "Go get 'em, son!"

He paused.

Then smiled.

He'd always pushed the boundaries, broken the rules. Been a six-legged spider, the inventor of Brax-Chex Party-Hearty Mix, a pirate bucking the trend. But the most important thing of all, he finally had what he'd fought hard for years to earn back. His family's devotion.

Sometimes life was about making breadboards out of shattered paddles.

Walking to the edge of the stage, he whipped the peacock feather out of his hat and loudly announced, "Captain Brax Sparrow will be giving this exotic peacock feather he brought back from...." What the hell had Val called it? He'd wing it. "...the Land of the Morgans, to the first lady who bids...two hundred dollars!"

Once a hot dog, always a hot dog.

The funky percussion intro of the seventies hit "You Should Be Dancing" began playing, and Captain Brax started dancing. Or the steps he'd practiced, anyway, doing his best to keep pace with the music. A few women stood, swaying to the music, bills in their hands.

The Bees Gees hit a spine-tingling vibrato, his cue to do what Li'l Bit called a free spin. He did it, ended up facing forward, a good sign, and started his strut to the catwalk.

Maybe he didn't have the throngs of screaming devotees like the previous Manwiches, but he had a handful of pirate groupies crowding the catwalk, waving bills. Money for Grams's charity, which was all that mattered.

He remembered to hit the heel spin at the second "dancing yeah" part, but when it came time to do the moonwalk, screw it. He was free form, baby, from here on out.

Time to hit the catwalk.

He strolled toward it, giving his step some of the ol' bad-boy Brax *attitude,* sliding eye contact to her and her and her, tossing smiles like Halloween candy.

More women were standing, waving the green. He could feel the excitement rippling through the crowd. He glanced at the Shelby in the distance, wondering if it was too late to dream.

He'd never know unless he tried.

He waved the two-hundred-dollar feather like a wand over his pirate groupies, whose cult was growing. Red, brown, gray hair. Pre-cougar, post-cougar. Clapping, dancing and singing along, they pressed against the sides of the catwalk like barnacles to a pirate ship's hull.

"Captain Brax," one yelled, leaning provocatively against the side of the catwalk, holding both arms straight up into the air, a Benjamin in each hand.

She looked mid-cougar, curly brown hair, eyes too

blue and a top cut too low. He stepped toward her, pretending it was dancing, holding the feather toward her like a divining rod. She smiled, straight white teeth framed by slick red lips. As he step-danced closer, she slowly lowered her arms, giving a little shimmy as she shook the Benjamins.

As the Bee Gees hit a trilling note, she dipped one bill, then the other, into the waistband of his red velvet breeches, her fingers staying, her body swaying, those red lips pursing....

Two other hands reached up and grabbed the hundred-dollar-clutching ones, and yanked them away. Mid-Cougar, nostrils flaring, took a fighting stance, ready for battle.

Just as Val had warned. Booze, estrogen and too few men were trouble. He went into security mode. Time to separate these two before things escalated.

Making a back-off-and-take-it-easy gesture to Mid-Cougar, he turned and looked at the instigator.

"You need to leave—"

His heart stuck in his throat as he looked into a pair of familiar amethyst eyes.

## *CHAPTER TWELVE*

LOOKING UP AT Braxton on the stage, Frances's heart thumped against her rib cage. Removing that woman's hands from his pants made Frances look like the poster girl for Miranda Lambert's song "Crazy Ex-Girlfriend."

An ex. Before she ever got to be the girlfriend part.

Pulling her sweater jacket tighter around her work dress, she shifted her weight from one strappy-heeled foot to another, wanting to tell him that the real reason she was here had nothing to do with jealousy, but being damned scared since finding a GPS tracking device attached to her car a few hours earlier.

With her dad out for the evening at his monthly magicians' dinner, she hadn't felt comfortable staying in the condo alone, especially knowing someone had been on her front porch in the last day or so. So she'd reapplied her gel and makeup, ran a few Google searches based on bits of information she overheard last night, and learned all about the Magic Dream Date Auction, including that Braxton was one of the bachelor hunks.

When she'd walked into Sensuelle a few minutes ago, her frame of mind had been scared, but determined to find Braxton and tell him about the GPS. She wasn't born yesterday, knew all about bachelor auctions. That part didn't bother her at all; obviously, he'd been part of his grandmother's event before he met Frances.

Then she'd seen that woman fastened on to Braxton's pants, looking like a lonely abalone seeking its shell.

That's when Frances snapped.

Before she knew it, she was reaching up and not-so-gently detaching those shifty, scheming, badly manicured digits off her man's red-velvet privateer privates.

Now she stood here, looking up into Braxton's bewildered expression, mortified by her actions and ashamed she'd hurt his chance to raise money for his grandmother's charity. She was going to make it up to Grams and Keep 'Em Rollin' with her own donation.

"I'm sorry," she said, and she was, but that didn't change why she was here. "I found something. When can we talk?"

His confusion shifted to concern. "Meet me at the tent. You okay?"

She nodded yes as static crackled over the speakers.

"Captain Brax Sparrow?" boomed the announcer's voice.

"Present!" Braxton raised his hand as if responding to roll call.

Laughter rippled through the area.

"The Bee Gees have left the building, and the next

Manwich, Li'l Bit Goes a Long Way, is in the wings, ready to take the stage."

"Tell him I surrender the stage to him." Braxton looked back down at Frances. "You know where the tent is, right?"

"Yes."

"Whatever it is, Frances," he said solemnly, his hand on his heart, "I'm here for you."

His gaze held hers, and in that moment, she believed his words, believed that he would stand beside her no matter what came her way. She could almost believe he might care for her the way she was coming to care for him.

A screech jolted her out of the moment.

"What's your problem, bitch?"

Frances turned to see who was talking…and every muscle in her body froze.

The curly-haired, stealthy-fingered woman stood a few feet away, glaring at her.

"You had no right to grab me like that," she said, jabbing her finger at Frances.

"Hey," Braxton said, "let's take it down a notch."

"I'm sorry," Frances said. "I was wrong."

Frances had learned one important thing about people over the years. Defending her actions to someone this angry was useless. Things were likely to explode.

But a simple apology could usually soothe even the most ruffled ego.

But not this woman's. She held up both hands, giving Frances the bird with each.

"Captain Brax Sparrow," the announcer said over the speaker, "it's the crow's nest for you, sir!"

"Coming, coming...." Braxton looked at the other woman, then back at Frances. "I suggest—"

"I've got it under control," she said, her voice cool and steady. "See you in the tent."

She'd caused enough problems; wanted to show him she could handle this quietly. Anyway, the woman had turned away, was chatting with her pals.

After a slight bow to her, Captain Brax Sparrow headed backstage.

Frances heard a woman swoon behind her. "I'd love to visit that Davey's locker."

"Tell it, girlfriend," murmured another. "When I get home, I'm gonna log on to that website, send a donation in Captain Brax's name."

Frances felt relieved. *Maybe I didn't blow it that badly for him.*

A blur of movement caught her eye. The bird-flipping woman sidled closer, flashing Frances yet another energetic one-fingered salute as though to say, *Whatcha gonna do about it?*

What was it with women flipping her off lately? First Uly, now Abalone.

Big deal. Time to meet Braxton in the tent. She started to walk away.

"What's he see in you?" screeched Big Bird.

*Take the high road,* Frances told herself. *Keep walking.*

"Didn't your mama teach you any manners?"

Frances stopped. *Sticks and stones. Don't take the bait.*

"Or did your mama have bad manners, too?"

Frances was damned tired of running away.

Tired of reacting instead of acting.

Tired of playing nice with Dmitri.

Tired of Charlie giving her cases that didn't feel right.

And really, really tired of waiting to have a complete relationship with Braxton, one where they spent more time together being themselves than being undercover. One where they took walks, watched movies, and made love whenever they wanted.

But as tired as she was of putting up with other people's crap, she'd try one last time to make amends.

She turned, wishing she'd thought to at least change her shoes when she had the chance because these heels were starting to hurt her feet.

"I'm sorry you don't believe me," Frances said, "because I meant what I said. I apologize. And by the way, my mother was one of the kindest human beings who ever graced this planet, so why don't you cool your mouth-jets on that one."

All right, the mouth-jets comment wasn't exactly taking the high road, but it felt good to say it.

The woman curled her hands into fists, her face scrunching into a tight, ugly mask.

The announcer's voice came over the speakers. "And now, ladies, it's time to introduce our next Manwich, Li'l Bit Goes a Long Way!"

As the announcer continued his introduction of Li'l Bit, who liked bowling and area rugs, Frances turned her back on the woman and continued her trek to the tent.

She made it all of three steps when something slammed into her, throwing her off balance. Staggering sideways, she fell against a table laid out with plastic utensils and a platter piled with fried won ton, causing the items to crash to the floor.

The area around her grew surreally quiet. Even the announcer stopped talking.

Frances slowly straightened, meeting the woman's furious gaze, and wondered why her gal-pals didn't drag her away.

A hundred years of silence passed as they continued their stare-down like a couple of cowgirls at high noon. The air reeked of oily won tons and wine.

The woman lowered her head, bunched her fists, and ran at Frances like a human cannonball.

As women screamed and shouted, Frances decided maybe running away wasn't such a bad idea after all. She didn't go far before slipping on a won ton and falling smack on her butt, rolling over in time to see a blur of curly brown hair descending upon her.

Frances threw a wild punch, her fist connecting with a sickening thud on flesh and bone.

Emitting a stifled grunt of pain, the woman fell backward with a loud *fwomp*.

And lay on the floor, blinking up at one of the

dangling red hearts with the words "Happy Valentine's Day!"

Women ran over, hands fluttering over the fallen woman. Someone plucked a won ton off Frances's shoulder.

Rubbing her aching hand, Frances looked over at the curly-haired woman who was sitting up and rubbing her jaw, staring blearily at her pals who were asking her if she knew what day it was and did she want to see a doctor?

Frances had never hit anyone in her life. There'd been some words exchanged with girls at school, but never a physical fight. She'd had no choice but to defend herself with that wild punch, but hurting another person made her feel sick.

And to think she'd just gotten in touch with her inner girly.

A man's shiny black shoes stopped next to her.

Her gaze travelled up a crisp blue police uniform to steely blue eyes that looked oddly familiar.

The realization came in a horrific rush.

Dmitri's go-for, the singing detective. The undercover cop who'd pulled her over after she stole the Lady Melbourne brooch. Maybe he'd seemed like Kindhearted Andy of Mayberry then, but he looked like Dirty Harry now.

Last time, he'd driven her to a chatty meeting in a limo.

From the look on his face, she was headed somewhere more remote, lonely and cold.

As Braxton headed to the backstage area, he gave a last look at the Shelby in the distance, glistening cherry red and perfect, never to be his.

To say that losing the chance to win that car didn't hurt would be a lie. It definitely hurt. Like the girl who got away, that 'Stang would always be more beautiful, more perfect, have a better bod than any other car he'd ever own. He'd still dream about it, compare other cars to it, hanker for it, but it was gone, baby, gone.

*Whoever wins that car tonight better treat it right.*

As he walked down the steps to the backstage area, one of the Keep 'Em Rollin' volunteers, a friend of his grandmother's, Betty-something, strode up to him, her mane of salt-and-pepper hair floating with her. Grams had told him that Betty had been one of the organizers of the Women's Strike for Equality in the seventies. In her khaki skirt, Lennon glasses and socks-with-Birkenstocks, Betty looked as if she were *still* leading that movement.

"Let's document your tips," she said matter-of-factly, opening a black notebook. She plucked a ballpoint pen from behind her ear. "Name?"

"Captain Brax Sparrow, and I'm afraid I didn't make any tips."

She arched a gray eyebrow. "None?"

"Zero."

She looked at his hat, down his chest—which didn't seem to impress her—past his red velvet breeches to his boots, then quickly back up to his eyes.

"Not a year for pirates, eh?"

"Something like that."

"Hold this please," she said, handing him the pen.

Reaching into a pocket, she pulled out a ten-dollar bill and tucked it neatly into his waistband. She held out her hand.

He passed her pen back to her.

She spoke out loud as she wrote. "Captain Brax Sparrow, ten dollars." She smiled at him. "Maybe you didn't win today, but you're an outstanding loser. Now, please give back that ten-dollar bill."

He did.

And as she marched away, her Birks slapping, Braxton felt like a winner. Maybe not a winner-winner, but a guy who'd gained a lot today despite losing. Learned that real men could wear red velvet, and that even a guy with two left feet could do a mean free-form dance.

And when Frances had shown up, looking to him for help, he'd risen to the occasion. He'd made her needs his priority without getting wrapped up in their surroundings. Maybe he'd never have Drake's class, but he'd proven today that he could still be a stand-up guy. He could still be the person Frances needed him to be.

Li'l Bit shuffled up to him, making smacking noises with his mouth. "My mouth is, like, mothball-dry, man. I'm laying off the popcorn for a while."

And he'd re-learned that he'd never, *ever* understand this guy. At least he wouldn't have to hang out with him anymore after tonight.

"Gotta learn some self-control, Li'l Bit. Get some healthier eating habits."

"Yeah, I dig what you're saying. Was watching an *Oprah* rerun the other day…and Dr. Oz was talking about a forty-eight-hour cleansing diet that keeps your colon flowing regularly. Lots of strawberries and flax-something, can't remember. Anyway…while we're here sharing this moment, I wanted you to know I'm not bringing up the brother thing anymore. It's enough that we're, like, harmonious opposites that interact within a greater whole."

Whatever that meant. "Aren't you supposed to be on stage right now?"

He nodded. "There was some kinda chick smackdown with wontons…. After the cleanup crew finishes, I'm on." He dragged his hand through the mass of frizz on his head. "Not trying to spread bad vibes 'cause I dig being an auction hunk 'n all, but some of those ladies are a little out there, know what I mean?"

"Too much estrogen and booze," he said, thinking of Val's comment.

"Woodstock meets menopause, man." Sadness flickered in his eyes. "Sorry you had a bad dance day. Losing the Shelby 'n all."

"Yeah, well, probably a reminder to me that my fast-lane lifestyle is a thing of the past. Time to slow down, appreciate life more." He was surprised to realize that he actually meant it. For the most part.

"What matters is how we look at things, not how they are in themselves."

"Yeah, well…" Time to leave Planet X. "Told Frances I'd meet her in the tent, so…"

"She's not in the tent, dude." He pointed somewhere past Braxton's left ear. "She's with the fuzz, over there."

Braxton turned.

Frances and a police officer stood near the entrance to Sensuelle. She stood stiffly, listening intently to whatever he was saying, her hands clutched together. Nervous and pale, but focused.

The officer walked away and Frances stood there, alone, seeming to shrink into herself. Less bright, less sure. As though the moon had fallen to earth.

"I'll be right back," Braxton said.

"My first thought when I saw the cop," Frances said to Braxton, keeping her voice low, "was that he was going to arrest me, which would've violated the terms of my suspended sentence and…and, well, you know what that would've meant. Seems every time I turn around lately, prison is staring me in the face."

She gulped a calming breath, still stunned at the surreal events that had transpired in the last fifteen minutes. Things had only begun to normalize when, moments after Detective Parks walked away, Braxton had appeared and folded her into his arms.

Walking to the backstage area, their arms still around each other, she told him about the crazy woman charging her, the won tons, her wild sucker punch, and now, as they sat on folding chairs behind the stage, the latest twist in the case.

"Remember my telling you about that goofy undercover cop who sang country songs while driving me to that first meeting with Dmitri in the limo?"

He nodded. "The dirty cop on Dmitri's payroll."

"Except he's not dirty. His name's Detective Parks, and he heads up the Las Vegas police department's narcotics section. They've been investigating Ulyana's involvement in a drug distribution ring."

"He knows you work for Vanderbilt?"

She nodded. "After he dropped me off at my car following my limo meeting with Dmitri, Parks ran my ID through some government databases and learned about my real job."

"Did he call Charlie?"

"No. Parks said that he wanted to contact me directly because of the sensitivity of his case. He didn't feel comfortable calling me or showing up at my condo in case Dmitri was keeping tabs on me, so he followed me here to talk about his investigation and how we might help each other."

"Does he know about me?"

"No."

"I'm surprised he didn't arrest that nutcase who started the fight."

"He didn't see how it started and I didn't tell him. Besides, if he'd gotten caught up in making an arrest, he and I wouldn't have had a chance to talk. Plus, that woman's friends were taking her home, so it's not like she was going to hassle anyone else."

"So, is this Ulyana case too sensitive to discuss with me?"

"You're my Vanderbilt coinvestigator, so I can tell you. They suspect the dealers work in gift shops that sell those Russian chocolates."

Braxton thought about that for a moment. "I'm going to guess those guys who talk to her at the Bally's sports book are runners placing orders. They go to the shops, get the numbers, come back and give them to her."

"Drug Order Central."

"Right. The gift shop employees never meet her, just the runners."

"Runners go with her to each casino?" she asked.

"Probably. So Detective Parks is investigating her involvement, but not Dima's?"

"He said they can't tell yet if she's running her own operation, or if Dmitri's involved."

A group of laughing teenage girls walked past, a collage of creamy, perfect skin, glossy hair, long limbs. Several ate thick slices of pizza, the smell of melting cheese and tomato sauce doing a wicked number on Frances's concentration. Even with the craziness of the past few hours, and the other things she should be focusing on, all she could think about was a deep-dish pepperoni-and-mushroom pizza, heavy on the sauce, and a diet cola with lots of ice.

"I'm starved," she said. "Shall we continue this over pizza?"

"We're back!" boomed the announcer's voice.

Frances jumped.

"We apologize for the break in the evening's festivities, but now we're ready to continue. Are you ready, ladies, to start bidding for a date with a hunk?"

Squeals and clapping.

"Our next Manwich is Li'l Bit Goes a Long Way...."

She watched Li'l Bit head to the stage in a robe and flip-flops.

"He's not dressed," she murmured.

"No, that's his costume."

She got it. "The Dude."

"Who else?"

"They're going to eat him alive." She half-shrugged. "Or love him to death. Whatever happens, we need to give him our support, then get pizza."

"Sure." He took her hand. "C'mon, I'll take you to a spot where we can watch."

As they walked, Frances thought about Braxton's lack of enthusiasm. She had heard his grudging tone, saw a put-upon look cross his features, and wondered again what his issue was with Li'l Bit. Granted, she didn't know Li'l Bit all that well, but he seemed close to Braxton's family. Maybe he was a bit eccentric, too hung up on *The Big Lebowski,* but there were worse things in life to get hung up on.

Last night, she'd heard Li'l Bit get choked up when he told Braxton he wanted to be his brother. His triplet. He'd sounded like a child asking to be accepted, to be loved.

Braxton had offered to be friends instead. But she knew him well enough to hear that he didn't mean it.

She hadn't grown up with a sibling, so she didn't

understand all the complexities in those relationships. But she understood loneliness as much as she understood putting up walls. Which was the real dance those two were acting out.

Braxton led her to the side of the stage and stopped. "We can see everything from here."

In the center of the stage, Li'l Bit stood duck-footed in his flip-flops, the sunglasses perched on his nose. The robe hung open to reveal his baggy plaid shorts and tee. He was a furrier, chunkier version of The Dude, but with the same life-goes-on-man Zen.

"Honey, did you take out the trash?" someone yelled, followed by laughter.

An ominous guitar riff screeched over the speakers.

"Can't believe he chose this song," Braxton muttered.

A heavy guitar riff kicked in. Li'l Bit began snapping his fingers and rolling his shoulders.

"Bring back the firefighter!" a woman shouted.

Unfazed, Li'l Bit kept swaying and snapping, his entire body getting into the movement.

At the exact instant a wailing guitar and growling singer crescendoed, Li'l Bit whipped off his robe, and began swirling his hips, slowly, purposefully, his arms stretched out as though ready to hold and swirl with each and every one of them.

Hands started waving money. A pair of red-and-black panties flew through the air onto the stage.

"Damn," murmured Braxton, "swirling really does drive women crazy."

As a guitar wailed and jungle drums hit a pounding frenzy, Li'l Bit suddenly stopped, his eyes wide open, his arms reaching, as though frozen in time and space.

Then he fell back like a mighty redwood, crashing onto the stage floor.

## *CHAPTER THIRTEEN*

BRAXTON AND FRANCES stood in a corner of the stage, watching the paramedics carefully lift Li'l Bit onto a gurney. As one adjusted the IV bag, the other quietly spoke to Li'l Bit, who lay with a strap over his forehead that kept his head immobile.

As Li'l Bit's lips moved, the paramedic leaned closer, listening attentively.

"I can't hear him," Braxton murmured.

Frances squeezed his hand. "Your grandmother's here," she said quietly.

He looked out at the audience of women, some of whom were holding up lights and saw his grandmother drive up to the edge of the stage in her wheelchair, his mom walking alongside.

"Be right back," he said quietly.

He headed to the edge of the stage and crouched down to talk to them.

"How is he?" his grandmother asked, tears welling in her eyes.

"He's able to talk to the paramedics."

He didn't want to say there was concern he might have suffered a cervical spine fracture. Li'l Bit was able to blink and talk, but the rest of his body was still, motionless.

"Do they have his insurance information?" his mom asked, her face etched with worry.

"Yes. He's alert, and was able to tell them where to find his wallet."

He heard a clattering sound, turned to see the paramedics pushing the gurney off the stage.

"Gotta go," he said, standing.

"I'm driving Grams home," Dorothy said. "It's been a long day, and she needs to rest. Richmond's out of town tonight, so I'd like to stay with her."

"I'll call when I have news."

Heading back across the stage, he spied Li'l Bit's robe where it had landed during the dance. He picked it up and gently draped the soft robe over his arm, choking back a teary laugh at its scents of popcorn and ganja, regretting all the times he hadn't been kinder.

Braxton caught up to the paramedics as they were gently lowering the gurney off the back end of the stage onto the marble lobby floor below, aided by several Manwiches who murmured words of encouragement to Li'l Bit, still lying motionless, his shiny eyes staring at the ceiling.

As the paramedics pushed the gurney, Braxton jogged alongside.

"You're gonna be okay, man," he said, forcing himself to sound a helluva lot more together than he felt.

Li'l Bit slid his eyes to look at Braxton.

"Got your robe," he said with a smile, holding it up.

Li'l Bit blinked. Twice.

Braxton flashed on a TV drama he saw years ago. A guy was paralyzed from the neck down and could only communicate through blinks.

*At least Li'l Bit can still speak.*

*Like that'll give him comfort when he has to deal with all this crap.*

Then it dawned on Braxton that Li'l Bit's life wasn't about "dealing" with things, but accepting them. And he'd find a way to live with a dude dignity other people wished they had.

What Braxton was finally learning was that it wasn't about getting, but loving.

As the clattering gurney approached the main casino doors, doormen opened them while hotel security directed crowds to step back.

One of the paramedics ran ahead to open the ambulance's back doors, while the other slowly navigated the gurney.

Walking alongside, Braxton placed his hand on Li'l Bit's, startled at how cool it felt.

"Is he going to be all right?" Braxton asked.

A general question. Nothing specific. Didn't want to scare Li'l Bit.

"I don't know much," the paramedic answered, "and I shouldn't even talk to you unless you're a family member."

As the gurney rattled to a stop, Braxton looked down into Li'l Bit's eyes.

"Yes," he said. "I'm his brother."

Li'l Bit's eyes moistened. His lips moved.

Braxton leaned over, placing his ear closer.

"Yeah, well, you know," Li'l Bit whispered hoarsely, "that's just, like, your opinion, man."

THIRTY MINUTES LATER, Braxton, who'd changed back into his jeans and sweater, and Frances sat outside the ER treatment room, drinking coffee from paper cups, waiting for news about Li'l Bit. They sat quietly, surrounded by the murmured conversations of other family members and friends waiting for news.

The air had a slight disinfectant smell, reminding Frances of the many days she and her dad had visited her mom in the hospital during those long, long months of her illness. Frances hadn't been in a hospital since.

Braxton's voice pulled her out of her reverie.

"I called him my brother."

She knew instantly what he was talking about, of course, although he didn't know. She also knew from the tone of voice, how deeply Braxton regretted hurting Li'l Bit.

"I haven't been—" a sorrowful expression settled into his face "—kind to Li'l Bit."

"Never too late to change," she said gently. "You and I probably know that better than most people."

"Last night, he told me I was his brother, and I—"

"Don't," she said, not wanting him to beat himself up all over again.

She'd been feeling guilty about her skulking about

last night, and had already decided to tell him soon what'd she'd done. Obviously soon had become now.

"I know about your conversation last night," she continued, "because I was there."

He stared at her for a beat or two, then gave his head a disbelieving shake. "What?"

"I surveilled you last night."

"You...followed me after I left your condo?"

She nodded.

"To Li'l Bit's apartment," he said, understanding filling his eyes. "Because you didn't believe my dancing lesson story." He paused. "Bulky black men's jacket. Miami Heat baseball cap."

"I feel so dumb. I'm sorry."

"I'm sorry, too. I should've trusted you enough to tell you about the auction. As it was, you were probably meant to be there, meeting up with Detective Parks and all." He paused. "We left off where you were telling me that they don't know whether Dmitri's involved. Did he ask if you'd seen anything suspicious at the office?"

"I told him I haven't, but that I'd seen Ulyana at Bally's sports book Thursday afternoon, and suggested he interview Ross. By the way, he says he hasn't told anyone that I'm an insurance investigator because he doesn't want to jeopardize my safety. I told him I'm investigating the whereabouts of some coins Vanderbilt thinks Dmitri stole, but didn't mention the heist. That's between Vanderbilt and the Palazzo." She paused. "There's something else. Remember when I said I found something? It was a GPS device attached to my car."

His face clouded over. "Dmitri."

"That was my first thought, too. But who knows. Maybe it was Oleg, although I'm not sure why he would want to track me."

"Or maybe it was Detective Parks."

"The thought crossed my mind. I asked him if he knew about the device, but he said no. He seemed genuinely concerned. He offered to trace the registration number on the device, but there isn't one. I asked if Dmitri had mentioned tracking me, but Parks said they're not tight and that he knows very little about the day-to-day operations. Apparently, his main 'dirty cop' job is to provide Dmitri with information about how many off-duty officers work special events. Altered, of course."

Braxton frowned slightly, thinking. "Let's get you another rental tonight that you can drive without worrying about being identified. You can keep driving the Benz to work and back so whoever's tracking you doesn't get suspicious."

"Has to be Dmitri. A scary thought, but could be Ulyana, too."

"And then there's Yuri. I think it's time I pay my old friend a visit." Braxton straightened. "Here comes the nurse," he murmured, standing.

A plump Hispanic woman wearing a smock decorated with frolicking cats strode purposefully toward them. She'd introduced herself earlier as Rosa, asked Braxton some questions about his brother, and promised a report as soon as she knew anything.

Frances stood next to Braxton, her arm tight around his back, his wrapped around her shoulder, each giving the other strength.

"Nathan's condition has stabilized," Rosa said. "We've not yet pinpointed what's wrong, but the good news is that there's no cervical fracture and he has feeling in his extremities."

"No paralysis, right?" Braxton asked cautiously.

"That's right." Rose smiled, her teeth white in her brown face.

With a whoop of joy, Braxton grabbed Frances in a fierce embrace and crushed her to him. She held on to him, fighting the lump in her throat, not wanting to make a scene in public, but when she heard Brax's choked sob, she gave up the fight and let her own tears flow.

After a few moments, they pulled apart, silently falling back into their side-by-side position, arms wrapped around each other, as naturally as if they'd done it for years.

"Nathan also shows positive neurological signs," Rosa continued, "as well as appropriate orientation to time and place."

Hugging Frances close to him, Braxton laughed. "'Appropriate orientation to time and place?' How'd my brother pull that off?"

THE NEXT MORNING, Braxton knocked on the front door of a stylish stucco row house in a Las Vegas suburb. After a minute or two, a dark-haired, heavily made-up woman in her twenties answered the door.

"How may I help you?" she asked in a thick Russian accent.

"I'd like to talk to Yuri."

"Your name?"

"Braxton."

"Wait here." She shut the door.

Moments later, the door opened. Yuri, his face thinner, but with that same funky Nero hair-cut, stood there. He wore a blue jogging suit and gold chains around his neck.

"Look who's here," Yuri said, "Mr. Star Witness for prosecution! Maybe you drop by to see if I have bags packed to go to prison?"

"I have something of mutual interest to discuss with you," Braxton answered calmly.

"Oh, something of interest! Perhaps the knife you stuck in my back?"

"You want to fight like a couple of old women? Or talk like two men who might be able to help each other. Let me put it another way, Yuri. Yes, I'm the star witness. That means I'm the gatekeeper at the garden of all information in that courtroom. Now, want to invite me inside for a gentlemanly chat?"

A few minutes later, they sat in the living room filled with antique furniture. On a side table sat a copper samovar and old black-and-white family photos, which Braxton guessed to be Russian ancestors. A large flat-screen TV filled one wall. Yuri's cologne nearly overpowered the smell of boiling cabbage wafting in from the kitchen.

Braxton sat on a faux leather couch.

"Mr. Star Witness Gatekeeper," Yuri said, sitting in a high-backed chair opposite him, "let me hear about *mutual interest*."

"A friend of mine found a GPS device attached to her car. Know anything about this?"

"Oh, sure," Yuri said sarcastically. He pulled up the cuff on his jogging pant, revealing a heavy black ankle monitor. "As you see, I leave house often to do fun things."

"Your friends don't have ankle monitors."

Yuri barked a laugh. "Not smart for defendant in big government federal case to ask friends to hang GPS on cars." He frowned. "Why you think I have problem with this friend?"

"This friend is close to Dmitri."

"Dmitri." Yuri muttered something in Russian. "He steal gold from dead people's teeth! I feel sorry for your friend."

"Dmitri doesn't seem to like you much, either."

"How you know? He your new friend?"

Same old Yuri. Baiting, testing. Braxton used to find it irritating, but now it was almost amusing. To his surprise, he felt sorry for Yuri, too. Maybe because he knew how it felt to live so high, then fall so far.

But pity was all Yuri would ever get from him.

"Rumor is he's keeping an eye on you," Braxton said.

"On me?" Yuri snorted his disgust. "I should keep an eye on *him*. GPS his..." He smiled, then turned serious. "I tell you why Dmitri not like me. When I go to prison, he wants my businesses on the street."

That was news to Braxton. He figured Dmitri would be leaving Vegas soon, not staying to take over petty street crime, loan sharking, and protection rackets. On the other hand, those would provide a steady, tax-free income stream.

A thought hit him. Yuri had ears on every street in the Russian community. Maybe somebody knew something about those coins Frances was looking for.

"Have you heard of anyone holding old coins for Dmitri?"

Yuri looked interested. "Why you want to know?"

"Let's just say...if I had that information, I'd get Dmitri out of the country and away from your turf." Not that he had any idea how he'd do it...yet.

"Ah, Braxton," Yuri said with a sly smile, "I have something you want. You have something I want. Let's talk."

## *CHAPTER FOURTEEN*

SHORTLY BEFORE 7:00 a.m. on Saturday, March 1, Braxton quietly let himself into the Morgan LeRoy office, heading past his desk to the hallway leading to Val and Drake's apartment. Halfway down the hall sat their metal equipment cabinet—not the most convenient place for it, but there hadn't been room elsewhere in the offices.

After unlocking the cabinet doors, he began carefully sifting through the items on the middle shelf, trying to remember where he'd stashed the miniature wireless camera.

"What's up, bro?"

Startled, Braxton dropped a pack of batteries onto the wood floor.

"Damn it, Drake," he whispered, picking it up. "Don't sneak up on me like that."

After setting the batteries back on the shelf, he turned to his brother, dressed in a plaid flannel robe, holding a bag of ground coffee, his face crumpled and sleepy.

"We ran out of coffee, had to get some from the office kitchen," Drake said groggily. "That's the denim jacket Dad gave you, right?"

"Yeah. Found it in the back of the closet. Feels good wearing it again—makes me think of him."

"Sometimes hard to believe...."

"That he's gone," Braxton finished.

They were quiet for a moment.

"So," Drake said, "whatcha looking for?"

"That miniature wireless camera. The one shaped like an eyeball."

"Third shelf. Left side." He yawned. "I know because I put it there a few days ago. Batteries should be good—probably wanna check, though."

"Thanks."

"No prob."

Over the past few weeks he and Drake had been getting along better, helped by Braxton never mentioning Frances, of course. After Val and Grams had clued Dorothy in on Drake's objection to Frances, no one else in the family had mentioned her either.

It also helped that Frances and Braxton had been keeping a low profile since the night of the auction, never meeting outside of their walks to her car and a few projects he'd worked with her for Vanderbilt. One being their research of court records on Ulyana and Dmitri that produced nothing. Another their visit one afternoon with Yuri, where she provided the Russian photos of the missing Greek coins.

Today everything was coming to a head with the heist—a *mock* heist, of course, as Vanderbilt had swapped the real Helena necklace with a replica, known only to Palazzo security who would conveniently not see Frances steal it.

Afterward Frances would meet Dmitri in a room at the Mandalay Bay Hotel. On camera, she was going to speak with, and coax, Dmitri to admit his role in the heist, while handing off the replica in exchange for the brooch and cash he'd promised. In the next room a tech would be taking video of the exchange along with two Vanderbilt investigators trained in protection.

Braxton wanted to be nearby in case she needed help, but Frances had refused. If one of the investigators reported seeing him, Charlie would be furious that he'd worked solo after all the warnings. But Braxton persisted, promising he'd stay at a distance, and insisting that he'd never be able to live with himself if something happened to her because he hadn't been there to protect her.

Accusing him of guilt-tripping her, which he agreed he'd done and quite well, too, Frances finally agreed.

"Found it." He retrieved the small round camera and transmitter.

"Started work on that monster Scrabble board yet?" Drake asked.

"Not yet."

"If you need help, let me know." With a yawn, he ambled down the hall to the back apartment.

As Braxton put new batteries into the eyeball camera, he heard the adjoining door shut.

A few minutes later, he sat at his desk in the front

office, double-checking the camera's wireless connection when his cell rang.

"Braxton Morgan," he answered.

"Yuri. I find slugs. It was Kodak moment. Exactly like Kodak."

Slugs. *Coins*.

Kodak. Had to be the digital pictures of the coins Frances showed him that day.

Yuri had always spoken cryptically in phone calls, a precaution in case the line was tapped, which challenged Braxton to figure about odd acronyms and strange references.

"Are you sure?" he asked.

"Braxton..." He pronounced the name as if it had twenty r's. "When Yuri say he sure, he *sure!* You know that."

Actually, he did. Yuri could be a sleazy, lying, backstabbing thug, but when he said he was sure of something, he was really sure.

"Listen, I tell friend to take Kodak and send to me," Yuri continued, "then I send to you. Then *you* sure, too."

"Okay. When're you sending this pic—Kodak, Yuri?"

"When I get proof candy man leave U.S., I give directions to slugs."

Candy man. Russian Confections. *Dmitri*.

He'd been mulling over an idea that might scare Candy Man into leaving the country, but Braxton needed to find the right time and place. But first, he needed photographic proof the coins were in Vegas.

"Send me those Kodaks, Yuri, and I'll do the rest." He paused. "Does Dmitri—" *shit* "—Candy Man have family here?"

"Have never heard of such person name. Goodbye."

Yuri ended the call.

Braxton realized he'd slipped, but he'd never excelled at these cryptic conversations.

As Braxton slipped his phone back into his pocket, Drake walked into the waiting room, holding a steaming mug, his gaze blacker than the coffee it held.

"What the hell are you doing talking to Yuri?" Drake growled. "Just can't stay away from the criminal element, can you?"

"Drake, chill. This has to do with a case."

"Asking Yuri to send you photos…and you'll *do the rest?* What kind of case is that? It makes me *sick* that you're in with him again."

"Give me some credit, man."

"I give you credit for every dark moment of your past with him. Want to destroy my agency? Bring Yuri into the picture. What photos is he sending you?" He took a hit of coffee.

"Some coins. Has to do with the Vanderbilt case. There's a link between Dmitri and Yuri and some antique coins, and Yuri's helping me follow the thread, and that's the truth, so help me God."

Drake frowned. "You're risking our agency working with Frances—because of her, you're getting thick with Yuri again. I warned you she's gonna drag you down, and she is."

"I'm not getting thick with—"

"You're too ga-ga to save yourself," Drake interrupted, "so I'll help you. Do you want your family... or Frances? 'Cause you can't have both. If you choose her, I'll be the first one to close the door. And I'll make sure Uncle Felon Groupie *never* has contact with my son, either."

"Drake, for God's sake—"

"You can take that threat to the bank, Brax."

When Drake drew the line, it didn't budge. Hell, Braxton could be hardheaded, too. After a few uncomfortably silent moments, Braxton said quietly, "Drake, you're my brother. Of all the family we have left..." That thought got to him. He swallowed, hard. "I probably love you the most. But sometimes, you can't see beyond the surface. You're forgetting that Mom, Grams, and even Val *like* Frances. Mom, especially."

Drake shook his head, a steely look in his eyes. "I've gone down this road with you before, Brax. Remember how you insisted Yuri wasn't a bad influence? And look how far down he took you. Get real—Frances is still serving out a criminal sentence. She's still honing her jewel thief craft, too, in that job as an insurance investigator. I only see what's on the surface? Well, bro, I see *bad news* written all over this. As your life topples, you'll lose all of us, one by one, just as you did before. Your choice."

Drake walked out of the room, his footsteps heavy

as he headed down the hallway. The door shut with a slam.

For a few moments, Braxton sat there, stunned, wanting to shake off the insanity of that exchange, even while knowing how real it was. Years ago, when he'd first hooked up with Yuri, Drake had tried to talk sense to Braxton, convince him he was making a mistake. But Braxton wouldn't listen, and for that he eventually lost his family.

*I love Frances.* He'd felt it, but now he actually put it into words.

But the thought of losing his family again was almost more than he could bear.

He gritted his teeth and shoved the wireless camera into his pocket.

AT ONE O'CLOCK on Saturday afternoon, Frances, wearing a new cream-colored Marc Jacobs pants outfit with taupe Gucci pumps, walked across the tiled entranceway toward the ornate glass doors of the Palazzo, one of the most luxurious casino-resorts in the world. Potted palms swayed in the breeze. Small clusters of well-dressed people stood around, chattering.

She hadn't detected Braxton at any time during her drive over, or on this walk inside. He was keeping his word to stay out of sight, but she knew he was out there, watching her, protecting her. She still felt those familiar preshow jitters, but for the first time, she didn't feel as alone.

She'd finished her homework days ago, told Dmitri

it would take her exactly 268 seconds, or 4.46 minutes, to walk through the entrance of the Palazzo, turn immediately right into the Luminary Lounge, which housed the Legendary Gems exhibit, steal the Helena Diamond necklace, and leave by a side door and climb into the Audi that would be waiting for her. She'd practiced this walk several times, and run the number past Oleg who thought 252 was more accurate.

Although precision was critical in a jewelry heist, it didn't matter today. She could take 4.46 minutes or ten. Palazzo security would ensure she stole the replica necklace without a hitch.

A red-coated doorman smiled as he opened a door for her.

Two hundred and sixty-eight seconds and counting.

MOMENTS LATER, SHE pulled her invitation to the Legendary Gems exhibit from her pocket and handed it to a fiftyish man wearing a purple shirt buttoned high with a bolo tie. Behind him stood a much younger man with a buzz cut, his massive shoulders evident beneath his Palazzo security guard blazer. His eyes met hers for a flickering second before he continued scanning the area.

The strategically placed lights and shiny acrylic cases filled with jewels gave the room a shimmering, otherworldly quality. She caught a whiff of vanilla. Like other high-end hotels on the Strip, the Palazzo infused the air with subliminal scents that supposedly influenced people's moods.

She'd studied the layout of this exhibit in such detail, she could be blindfolded and know exactly where to go. As she strolled casually toward the case containing the Helena Diamond necklace, two beefy Palazzo security guards focused their attention elsewhere.

She paused at the case and looked down at the Helena necklace, momentarily awestruck by its glittering beauty, reminding her how dazzling costume jewelry could be. Leaning forward, she angled her shoulder, her right hand lifting the lock as her left plucked the necklace.

A few moments later, Frances strolled out of the exhibit, across the marble floor, and out through a side door. As she stepped outside, a breeze swept past, carrying scents of the Mojave desert. The beige Audi sat at the curb, its motor running.

The day had been sweet and perfect.

She willed it to remain that way as she faced her toughest challenge, just minutes away.

BRAXTON WAS SITTING in a chair in the Mandalay Bay hotel-casino lobby, his baseball cap pulled low, pretending to read a newspaper, when he saw Frances, a vision in her sandy-colored outfit and blond hair, stroll into the room. He took a deep breath, imagining he could smell the citrusy scent of her shampoo, taste the salty sweetness of her skin, hear that husky voice.

He felt his heart twist. *I don't want to lose you.*

Couldn't think about any of that now.

He stood and checked the screen of his smartphone

before slipping it into his shirt pocket. After leaving Morgan-LeRoy this morning, he'd changed into some clothes he'd picked up at at a discount store the other night—brown cargo pants, dark blue hoodie, lace-up sneakers. Boring, badly matched clothes to look as un-Braxton-like as possible.

As Frances crossed the lobby, he jogged to the elevators.

Minutes later he stepped out onto the tenth floor, and headed down the hall to a fake ficus tree, bushy with green plastic leaves, and retrieved the wireless camera he'd hidden earlier, its lens pointed at three room doors—the middle one being Dmitri's.

Frances had texted him the room number earlier this morning with the understanding that he wasn't to come up to the floor. He'd agreed because there were supposed to be two Vanderbilt investigators and a video tech in the adjacent room. He'd placed the camera up here, with a feed to his smartphone, to see if Dmitri allowed anyone other than Oleg or Ulyana inside. Oleg had arrived a few minutes ago, and Frances was on her way. As a safety precaution, they'd spaced their arrivals to not be seen together.

A twentysomething couple was staying in one of the neighboring rooms. A ponytailed, nerdy-looking kid, carrying two equipment bags, had entered the room on the other side at nine-thirty. That had to be the video tech.

The reason Braxton had come up to the tenth floor was because the two Vanderbilt investigators, who were supposed to join the nerdy tech kid, hadn't showed. Which meant Frances was up here on her own.

Maybe Vanderbilt could abandon her, but he never could.

If the investigators showed up, he'd tell the truth—that he knew she was up here without protection, so he stepped in.

He didn't know much about the video tech except that Frances mentioned he was a film student Vanderbilt hired occasionally for surveillance jobs.

Stuffing the wireless camera into one of his cargo-pants pockets, he headed to the video-kid's room and rapped on the door.

"Who is it?" asked a voice from the other side.

He stared at the peephole. "Just got called to come in," he said confidentially.

He heard a lock click. The door opened.

"Thought there'd be two of you," the kid said, heading briskly to a camera-tripod setup. "Show's starting any minute. My name's Lou."

"Yeah, just me. I'm Braxton." He crossed to a desk where a monitor displayed a video image of the room next door. Oleg sat on a couch, thumbing his smartphone. Dmitri sat in a chair, yammering in Russian on his cell. A bottle of vodka, shot glasses and a fruit basket sat on the coffee table.

Braxton looked at the slim video wire snaking from the camera into the wall. "You...drilled a hole through the wall?"

Lou glanced at Braxton as though he'd just fallen

to Earth. "Of course." He looked back at the screen. "Did it while Dmitri was in the bathroom. The pinhole camera blends into the patterned wallpaper."

Braxton glanced at the open equipment bag on the floor, surprised at the stash of tools in it. From where he sat, he saw a small sledgehammer, hand saw, some wrenches.

Lou saw him looking, turned back to his screen. "Never know when you'll need something on one of these jobs. Used that sledgehammer once to bash down a door so I could escape...."

The kid tensed. *"She's here."*

Braxton watched the monitor as Frances entered the room, as cool and confident as the first time he'd met her. Dmitri ended his call and stood, smiled broadly as she pulled the glittering necklace from an inside jacket pocket and handed it to him.

Turning serious, Dmitri held the necklace against his chest. *"Vso khorosho, chto khorosho konchayetsya.* All's well that ends well. Oleg, my friend, pour the vodka!"

Dmitri crossed back to his chair, next to which was a small table that was clearly visible on the monitor, although hidden from view to the others in the room. With great care, he laid the necklace on the table.

After that, the three of them stood in the center of the room while Dmitri gave a toast in Russian. The men downed their shots; Frances sipped hers.

Setting down her shot glass, she gestured to the necklace and announced, "Dmitri, your long months of planning to steal the Helena Diamond necklace from the Legendary Gems exhibit has paid off. I'm honored to have worked with such an accomplished jewel thief as yourself."

Braxton watched Dmitri puff up, basking in the praise. *Agree with her. Give Vanderbilt the evidence it needs to put you behind bars.*

But instead Dmitri waved off the compliment like a coy schoolgirl. "More vodka, my friends?"

As Oleg refilled the shot glasses, Frances turned to Dmitri.

"Tell me," she said, "is it your genius, ability to build a team of experts or superior knowledge of gems that makes you the James Bond of jewel thieves?"

*Do it, Dmitri. Confess.*

"Ah, Frances," he said, admiring the necklace, "it is *you* who are a genius. You completed the task in *exactly* 268 seconds, just as you calculated."

Braxton thought he saw something within the replica. "Zoom in on the diamond."

"Gotta keep the Russian in the frame—"

"*Do it.* I'm ordering you."

As the camera closed in, Braxton saw two perfectly symmetrical hearts etched within the diamond. *It's not a myth. The image really exists.*

The realization slammed through him. Frances had handed off the real Helena Diamond necklace, worth twenty million dollars, to Dmitri. If he walked out of that room with it, the necklace would probably never be seen again.

Vanderbilt would blame Frances. Suspect her of knowing it was the real necklace and double-crossing Vanderbilt. And a sting meant to put Dmitri behind bars would snare Frances instead.

Braxton surged to his feet. "I have to stop this."

"Stop what?" The kid asked.

Adrenaline coursed through him. Couldn't waste time calling security—by the time they got here, it'd be too late.

"I need to get into that room," he said, "but the door's locked."

"What're you talking about?"

*The sledgehammer.* He yanked it out of the bag, and headed to the door with it.

"Are you crazy?" the kid yelled.

"Probably," he muttered.

Within seconds he was standing outside Dmitri's door, holding the sledgehammer like a bat, focusing on the spot next to the door handle he needed to hit.

He swung with all his strength.

Crack!

Yelling. A scream.

His hit had ripped the lock from the door. Tossing the sledgehammer aside, Braxton slammed his shoulder against the door, which flew open and crashed against the wall.

FRANCES SCREAMED AGAIN as the door smashed open and a guy wearing a baggy hoodie and cargo pants stormed into the room. His baseball cap was pulled low, shielding his eyes.

Oleg raced past the intruder and out the door.

Shaking, her pulse thundering in her ears, she wanted desperately to follow Oleg, escape this madman, but she was frozen, couldn't move.

But Dmitri wasn't. As he started toward the small table, the intruder grabbed one of his arms and flipped it behind him. Dmitri yelled out in pain as he fell to his knees, immobilized.

Panting for breath, Frances looked up.

Still holding Dmitri's arm, the guy flipped up the bill of his cap with his free hand.

*Braxton.*

"What the hell are you doing?" she rasped.

He nudged his chin toward the necklace on the table. "It's the real one, Frances. That kid zoomed the camera in on the diamond, and I saw those etched hearts."

She stared at him with horror. "Are you *crazy?*"

"Probably," he muttered, "but I know for a fact that the image has been cut deep inside the diamond—which proves its authenticity. I had to stop Dmitri from leaving with that necklace." With his free hand, he pulled out his cell, thumbed the pad, held the phone to his ear.

She couldn't believe this was happening. "It's a replica, Braxton. I told you that."

"What?" Dmitri shrieked.

"Detective Parks, this is Braxton Morgan. I'm

here at the Mandalay Bay, holding our friend Dmitri Romanov. We're in room..."

Frances couldn't believe what she was hearing. "Don't involve the police, Brax!"

He ignored her, continued talking to Parks, told him that there was a sting being conducted by Vanderbilt, that Oleg was on the run. Dmitri, hearing the word "sting," muttered darkly in Russian.

Frances tuned both of them out, couldn't stand to hear more. Deeply angered, she cursed herself for letting Braxton talk her into letting him *protect* her today.

As he slipped his phone back into his pocket, she said, "You've ruined my life."

His eyes widened with surprise. "No, I saved it."

"How? By barging into the middle of the sting and blowing it?" She shook her head in disbelief. "I told you what would happen if you slipped up—and you just did. Big time. But *I'm* the one who will pay."

An overwhelming sense of despair rose like a tsunami wave, hovering, dark and ominous.

Pressing the tips of her fingers on her lips for a moment, she tried to pull herself together...eased in a shallow breath, slowly let it out, easing in another....

After weeks of struggle, and hope, and opening her heart to the point where it ached with joy, to the point where she finally let go and dared to chase dreams of a life that could be...perfect.

And this was where she chased them to, where her folly had reached its conclusion.

"Frances, if I hadn't come in here—"

"I wouldn't be going to prison. Vanderbilt is holding me responsible for your actions, remember? That night in the Jeep at the airstrip, I told you that if you messed up this case, Vanderbilt would fire me, which means the court will revoke my suspended sentence, which means..."

Her heart hammered in her chest and her breaths seared her throat. The one thing she feared most—going to prison—Braxton had made happen.

Her phone beeped with a text message. It was from Charlie.

Parks called. My car's out front.

What a mess. The singing detective had contacted her boss, no doubt giving him the stunning news. Now Charlie would need to scramble, work damage control over this catastrophe, every second of it captured on video, and he'd need to debrief her ASAP.

"I have to go." She crossed to the table, picked up the replica necklace and slipped it into her jacket pocket.

"Frances," Braxton said, "I love you."

She looked at him, her heart turning inside out. Despite her anger and hurt, she longed for him even now.

Memories of their almost-kisses—pressed against the warehouse doors, holding each other that night at his house, cuddling in the Jeep on surveillance—hurtled across her mind. The time he'd buttoned her in his trench coat, ensuring she was safe and warm.

The times they'd been silly, teasing each other, making each other laugh.

The night Captain Brax Morgan stood on the stage, promising to be there for her.

She'd remember everything. Always.

"I love you, too," she whispered, tears slipping down her cheeks as she walked quickly out of the room.

## *CHAPTER FIFTEEN*

SECONDS AFTER SHE LEFT, Lou ran in, breathing hard, an equipment bag in each hand. "Hotel security...probably here...any minute." He frowned. "What's that smell?"

"His cologne," Braxton said, tightening his grip on Dmitri's arm. "You got a close-up of the diamond on video, right?"

He nodded. "Didn't see...any hearts, though.... Gotta go."

Braxton listened to the thumpity thump of the kid's hasty retreat down the hall, wondering how he could've missed them. *Must've been too busy working that camera, didn't look closely.*

"Tough-guy Braxton saw hearts in the *replica* diamond?" Dmitri barked a mean laugh. "Love *is* blind."

"Shut up."

But the worry took hold. Within the lights and dark planes of the complex-cut diamond, had his eyes played tricks? Imagined the hearts? Because if the necklace had really been the replica...

A chilling tremor crawled up his neck.

Then the one person whose life he wanted to protect

above all else, he had instead destroyed. Frances would pay dearly for his blunder with her freedom.

And to think that Drake had said she'd bring Braxton down. His brother had been so wrong about her... wrong to give Braxton an ultimatum, too, because there could never be a choice. He loved Frances, and whatever it took to unravel this disaster, to clear her name, to save her, he'd do it.

"Impressive how you single-handedly destroyed a sting," Dmitri continued. "Seems love is blind *and* stupid."

"And you're so smart? You lost the Helena Diamond necklace."

"But I was *brilliant* planning that heist," Dmitri snapped, "and after I'm free, which will be soon because the authorities can't hold me without proof, I'll plan another one."

Braxton heard the rumble of footsteps down the hall. "Speaking of plans," he said between this teeth, "I'm turning over our investigation notes to the U.S. Immigration authorities, which will result in your immediate, permanent expulsion from the U.S. But I have an offer for you, Dima. Immigration will never see those notes if you leave Nevada and never return."

Dmitri snorted a laugh. "I'll tell my lawyers those notes are lies."

"You can also tell them my phone recorder app's been running this entire time, and I have your confession you planned this heist."

He snarled a curse in Russian.

"Braxton Morgan," a voice called out from the shattered doorway, "it's Detective Parks. Are you all right?"

"I'm fine, come on in," he yelled back.

"I accept your offer," Dima said quickly under his breath.

"Thought you would," Braxton murmured, smiling at the detective and several officers as they entered the room.

FRANCES LEANED HER head back on the headrest and closed her eyes as Charlie drove his car down East Warm Springs Road. The outside temp had dropped to the fifties, so he'd cranked up the heat inside the Porsche, sharpening its scents of leather and wood. Since she'd left the Palazzo nearly an hour ago, gray clouds had rolled in, masking the sun.

And to think she'd hoped this would be a perfectly sweet day.

"I'm sorry," she said again, feeling sick to her stomach at the mess she'd created, at what her future held.

As soon as she'd gotten into Charlie's car, she'd admitted to telling Braxton the room number at the Mandalay, explained she'd mistakenly thought he'd keep his distance as a backup, and took full responsibility for the disaster. Her boss had asked a few questions, said they'd go over details later.

"Maybe there's hope," Charlie said, loosening the knot of his purple silk tie that matched the pocket square in his cashmere sport coat.

Tears welled up, blurring her vision. "Hope for what?" she asked, her voice breaking. "That maybe the five years in prison will fly by, instead of crawling along, second-by-regretful second?"

"Damn," he muttered, staring ahead at the road. "I just remembered the battery's dead on my phone, and I need to make a call. Got yours handy?"

She tugged it out of her pants pocket and gave it to him.

He lowered his window, tossed the phone outside.

"Why'd you do that?"

"Here's your hope," he said as the window rolled back up. "Instead of going to prison, come live a life of luxury with me."

Was he cracking under the pressure? Thinking he'd hide her in that posh Tuscan-style home of his?

"Charlie, it's been a bad day...." As though *bad* could even begin to describe what had happened. *Catastrophic* was more like it.

"That necklace is the real one, Frances. I didn't do the swap this morning."

For a moment she just stared ahead at the dotted lines in the road, unable to breathe. With trembling fingers she touched the outside of her jacket, felt the bulge of the necklace.

"I stole...the real Helena Diamond?"

"Yes! And the security staff helped you! Now we're driving to that airstrip you told me about—thank you for that—where a private plane will whisk us away to Dallas. From there, we'll hop a flight to Brussels where a fence will give me twelve million for the necklace. Within a week, the gold will be melted, the diamond cut into stones, each with its own diamond certificate, and they'll be distributed to diamond merchants in Tokyo, New York and Paris."

"You're willing to destroy the Helena Diamond?" She wished she'd believed Braxton, but everything had been happening so fast, and his claim of seeing the hearts sounded so ridiculous.

"Destroy? It'll live on dozens of ring fingers for years to come, as will we on that twelve million, sipping champagne on the Riviera...or wherever else we choose to live."

"We?"

"I've always found you attractive, Frances."

He was so egocentric, it probably hadn't crossed his mind she might not feel the same way.

Charlie's financial problems had to be much worse than she'd realized. From years working at Vanderbilt, he'd have the means to locate a fence, and he'd likely promised a substantial I.O.U. to some pilot with a private plane to help him make a great escape.

The Porsche turned onto the same side road she and Braxton had traveled the night they conducted the surveillance at the airstrip.

"You cancelled those two Vanderbilt investigators who were supposed to be in the next room," she murmured.

"We didn't need any cowboys wearing white hats around."

But one had been there anyway. "You didn't know Braxton would charge in like that, though. I might have given the necklace to Dmitri."

"I wasn't worried about that. Had a backup plan called Smith & Wesson." He patted his cashmere jacket. "I knew where Dmitri's limo was parked at the hotel, planned to meet him there for a chat."

Probably knew where it was parked because he'd attached a GPS device to it, the way he'd done to her Benz.

At first she'd wanted to think that this was all a bad dream, that she'd wake up and it would all be over.

Now she knew this nightmare was for real.

A COLD BREEZE skittered past as Braxton and Detective Parks walked out the front doors of the Mandalay Bay.

"Storm's coming in," Parks said.

Two police units were parked at the curb. Several officers were putting Dmitri, his hands cuffed behind his back, into the back seat of one unit.

"He's already lawyered up," Parks said. "Big surprise there. By the way, we're closing in on Ulyana's afternoon visits to casinos. All signs point to her working alone. Now *that* surprised me."

Braxton's phone rang. He checked the caller ID. Drake.

"One moment," he said, taking the call.

"We've got a problem," Drake said. "Just checked those motion detectors out at the airstrip…blue skies, no clouds. Impossible. Somebody's playing a game."

Drake looked up at the heavy, dark clouds rolling in. "Like put images of the same landscape in front of the lenses?"

"Exactly. Where's Dmitri?"

"Handcuffed in the backseat of a cop car. The sting fell apart, though, and the necklace is…"

An uneasiness rocked his gut. "We need to get to that airstrip."

SCREAMING SIRENS PUNCTURED the quiet. Frances pulled down the visor and looked in the mirror. A police car, its red lights spinning, barreled down the dirt road toward the airstrip. How had they known to come here?

Her eyes shifted to her reflection, saw the mottled red scar making its appearance. She felt the familiar anxiety at the thought of being exposed, but tamped it down as best she could. Her scar was a small matter compared to the shit storm that was about to take place.

"We're not doing anything illegal," Charlie said evenly, "just sitting in a car. We'll say you lost your phone, thought maybe you'd dropped it at the airstrip."

Always the lawyer, he was already piecing together his argument.

She watched the police car, dust billowing in its wake, screech to a stop on Charlie's side of the Porsche. Detective Parks got out, his hand on his holster as he strode toward them. A surge of wind pummeled the windows.

"Put your hands on the dashboard," Charlie said evenly as he put his on the steering wheel.

As she did, a crack of lightning split the sky. In the flash, she caught a face starting grimly at her from inside the police car.

*Braxton.*

Her heart froze.

More sirens in the distance. Parks kept walking toward Charlie's door. "Get out of the car *slowly*," he said loudly.

Just as Charlie pressed a button and the door locks clicked open, Frances heard the muffled drone of an engine. A small white plane flew low toward them from the north.

Watching it, Charlie slowly opened his door with one hand, his other slipping inside his jacket.

Surreally aware of every ticking second, and seeing how easy it would be for Charlie to pull his gun, Frances eyed the path of his hand disappearing into his coat. With a surge of energy she fell against him, her right hand reaching inside his jacket, touching cold metal.

Yells. Sirens.

Time sped up as Frances and Charlie tumbled out the open car door, their bodies tangled, the two of them grappling for the gun. The instant she met his fevered, intense eyes, she heard a door slam and the crack of a pistol shot.

Hands grabbed Charlie's cashmere jacket, jerked him to his feet. Braxton, his jaw clenched with fury, slammed his fist into Charlie's face. Charlie toppled backward, the gun flying through the air.

Several police officers ran over, and one of them handcuffed Charlie. Braxton gently lifted her to her feet.

"Frances," he rasped, looking deeply into her eyes, "are you all right?"

"I'm okay," she said shakily, glancing at Charlie being led away by two officers, then back into Braxton's worried eyes. She was vaguely aware of an old pickup truck lurching to a stop next to one of the police cars.

Braxton shook his head in disbelief. "Can't believe you tried to get his gun...."

"I thought he might shoot you." She glanced around. "I heard the gun go off...."

"The bullet missed all of us—blew out the detective's tire, though."

Thunder growled in the distance as Frances looked into Braxton's shiny gray eyes, overwhelmed with gratitude they were both standing here, safe, alive. But when his gaze shifted to her cheek, she tensed, started to raise her hand to cover it, but then paused.

"It happened when I was fourteen," she whispered. "I was practicing a magic trick with fire—"

"That's the past," he said, cutting her off, his eyes boring into hers. "Frances, you're a beautiful woman, inside and out."

He pressed a kiss against her cheek, her deepest secret, before moving his lips to her ear.

She closed her eyes, letting the illusion fall away, finally freeing the woman inside—the one who yearned to live and love without pretense—rise to the surface.

Opening her eyes, she smiled at him. "Thank you."

"I've got something else nice to say. You'll be bringing those fifth-century Greek coins back to Vanderbilt in a few days."

There was a story behind this, one they'd share later. She smiled up at him, her heart brimming with love.

"Kiss me," she whispered in a throaty whisper.

"Any time," he murmured, leaning forward.

"Sorry to interrupt," a male voice broke in.

Drake, hunched inside his corduroy jacket, stood nearby, looking sheepish.

"Nice timing, bro," Braxton muttered.

"Yeah, sorry about that," Drake said, looking around before his eyes wandered back to Frances's. "Just, uh, wanted to say that Parks told me what you did...trying to get the gun.... You could've died saving my brother's life." He blinked, hard. "Frances, I'm sorry for how I've..."

"It's all right," she said gently.

He nodded solemnly, then turned to his brother. "Sorry, Brax, for saying..."

"Water under the bridge," he said. "As long as there's never an ultimatum between us again."

"Deal," Drake agreed. "One more thing. They finalized the money raised at the auction and Li'l Bit won the Shelby. He wants to give it to his brother...meaning you, Brax."

Brax shook his head. "Let's give it to Grams as a

wedding gift. I don't think I'm a Mustang guy anymore. My fast-living days are behind me."

"Grams said you'd try that," Drake continued, "and to tell you...let me get this right...*owning a dream is different than living an old lifestyle.* And that if you give it to her, she'll just give it right back. Okay, I'm done playing messenger. See you at the house? Mom's making her famous meat loaf for dinner. Invited the family over."

Braxton glanced at Frances. "We, uh, had a date for March second that's pushed up a day...."

She nodded her agreement.

Drake gave a salute to Frances. "See you next family dinner, then."

As he walked away, Detective Parks walked up. "Frances, you okay?"

"I'm fine."

"Still have that necklace, right?"

"Yes." She pulled it out of her inside jacket pocket. Even in the hazy gray light, the diamond sparkled. And something else...

She held it closer, caught the shimmering outline of two identical hearts.

"Amazing," she murmured.

"Yes," Braxton said, looking at it. "The hearts are outlined in red, notice that?"

She nodded. "Each one is so perfectly shaped."

"What hearts?" The detective squinted hard at the diamond.

Frances and Braxton looked at each other and shared a smile.

"Excuse me, Detective," Braxton murmured, handing him the necklace.

He pulled Frances into his arms, and she closed her eyes, savoring their first kiss.

The first of many they were destined to share.

\* \* \* \* \*

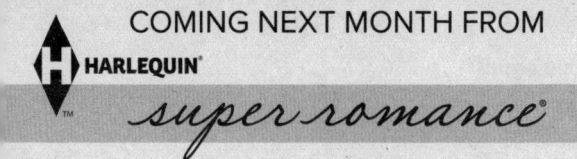

# COMING NEXT MONTH FROM
## HARLEQUIN
### super romance

Available August 5, 2014

## #1938 THE SWEETEST SEPTEMBER
### *Home in Magnolia Bend* • by Liz Talley
Of all the wrong men Shelby Mackey has fallen for, this one's a doozy. John Beauchamp is still grieving his late wife, and now Shelby's pregnant with his child. They weren't looking for this, but could that one night be the start of something much sweeter?

## #1939 THE REASONS TO STAY
### by Laura Drake
Priscilla Hart's mother leaves her an unexpected inheritance—a half brother! What does Priscilla know about raising kids? How can she set down roots and give him a home? Then she meets sexy but buttoned-down Adam Preston. Here's one man who might convince her to stay in Widow's Grove.

## #1940 THIS JUST IN...
### by Jennifer McKenzie
Sabrina Ryan never wanted to go home. But, suspended from her big-city newspaper job, that's exactly where she is. Things improve when sparks fly between her and Noah Barnes, the superhot mayor. Doing a story on him, she discovers home isn't such a bad place, after all....

## #1941 RODEO DREAMS
### by Sarah M. Anderson
Bull riding is a man's world, but June Spotted Elk won't let anyone tell her not to ride—not even sexy rodeo pro Travis Younkin. He only wants her safe, with him—but what happens when her success hurts his comeback?

## #1942 TO BE A DAD
### by Kate Kelly
Dusty Carson has a good life—no responsibilities and no expectations. But after one night with Teressa Wilder, life changes in a hurry. Teressa's pregnant and suddenly, she and her two kids have moved into his house. Now Dusty's learning what it really means to be a dad.

## #1943 THE FIREFIGHTER'S APPEAL
### by Elizabeth Otto
To most people, firefighters are heroes—but not to Lily Ashden. She blames them for a family tragedy and is in no hurry to forgive. But Garrett Mateo challenges all of her beliefs. This sexy firefighter wants to win her over and won't take no for an answer!

---

**YOU CAN FIND MORE INFORMATION ON UPCOMING HARLEQUIN® TITLES, FREE EXCERPTS AND MORE AT WWW.HARLEQUIN.COM.**

HSRLPCNM0714

**SPECIAL EXCERPT FROM HARLEQUIN**

*super romance*

# The Sweetest September

## By Liz Talley

Shelby Mackey would have been happy to *never* revisit the night she met John Beauchamp. Well, that's not entirely true. It was a good night...until the end. But now avoiding him is no longer an option!

Read on for an exciting excerpt of the upcoming book **THE SWEETEST SEPTEMBER** by Liz Talley...

Shelby took a moment to take stock of the man she hadn't seen since he'd slipped out that fateful night. John's boots were streaked with mud and his dusty jeans had a hole in the thigh. A kerchief hung from his back pocket. He looked like a farmer.

She'd never thought a farmer could look, well, sexy. But John Beauchamp had that going for him...not that she was interested.

Been there. Done him. Got pregnant.

He looked down at her with cautious green eyes...like she was a ticking bomb he had to disarm. "What are you doing here?"

Shelby tried to calm the bats flapping in her stomach, but there was nothing to quiet them with. "Uh, it's complicated. We should talk privately."

He slid into the cart beside her, his thigh brushing hers. She scooted away. He noticed, but didn't say anything.

She glanced at him and then back at the workers still casting inquisitive looks their way.

John got the message and stepped on the accelerator.

Shelby yelped and grabbed the edge of the seat, nearly sliding across the cracked pleather seat and pitching onto the ground. John reached over and clasped her arm, saving her from that fate.

"You good?" he asked.

"Yeah," she said, finding her balance, her stomach pitching more at the thought of revealing why she sat beside him than at the actual bumpy ride.

So how did one do this?

Probably should just say it. Rip the bandage off. Pull the knife out. He probably already suspected why she'd come.

As they turned onto the adjacent path, Shelby took a deep breath and said, "I'm pregnant."

**How will John react to the news? Find out what's in store for these two—and the baby—in THE SWEETEST SEPTEMBER by Liz Talley, available August 2014 from Harlequin® Superromance®.**

Copyright © 2014 by Amy R. Talley

# LARGER-PRINT BOOKS!
## GET 2 FREE LARGER-PRINT NOVELS PLUS
## 2 FREE GIFTS!

**HARLEQUIN**

*superromance*

### More Story...More Romance

**YES!** Please send me 2 FREE LARGER-PRINT Harlequin® Superromance® novels and my 2 FREE gifts (gifts are worth about $10). After receiving them, if I don't wish to receive any more books, I can return the shipping statement marked "cancel." If I don't cancel, I will receive 6 brand-new novels every month and be billed just $5.69 per book in the U.S. or $5.99 per book in Canada. That's a savings of at least 16% off the cover price! It's quite a bargain! Shipping and handling is just 50¢ per book in the U.S. or 75¢ per book in Canada.* I understand that accepting the 2 free books and gifts places me under no obligation to buy anything. I can always return a shipment and cancel at any time. Even if I never buy another book, the two free books and gifts are mine to keep forever.

139/339 HDN F46Y

| Name | (PLEASE PRINT) | |
|---|---|---|
| Address | | Apt. # |
| City | State/Prov. | Zip/Postal Code |

Signature (if under 18, a parent or guardian must sign)

**Mail to the Harlequin® Reader Service:**
**IN U.S.A.:** P.O. Box 1867, Buffalo, NY 14240-1867
**IN CANADA:** P.O. Box 609, Fort Erie, Ontario L2A 5X3
**Are you a current subscriber to Harlequin Superromance books**
**and want to receive the larger-print edition?**
**Call 1-800-873-8635 today or visit www.ReaderService.com.**

\* Terms and prices subject to change without notice. Prices do not include applicable taxes. Sales tax applicable in N.Y. Canadian residents will be charged applicable taxes. Offer not valid in Quebec. This offer is limited to one order per household. Not valid for current subscribers to Harlequin Superromance Larger-Print books. All orders subject to credit approval. Credit or debit balances in a customer's account(s) may be offset by any other outstanding balance owed by or to the customer. Please allow 4 to 6 weeks for delivery. Offer available while quantities last.

**Your Privacy**—The Harlequin® Reader Service is committed to protecting your privacy. Our Privacy Policy is available online at www.ReaderService.com or upon request from the Harlequin Reader Service.

We make a portion of our mailing list available to reputable third parties that offer products we believe may interest you. If you prefer that we not exchange your name with third parties, or if you wish to clarify or modify your communication preferences, please visit us at www.ReaderService.com/consumerchoice or write to us at Harlequin Reader Service Preference Service, P.O. Box 9062, Buffalo, NY 14269. Include your complete name and address.

HSRLP13R